SLIMY UNDERBELLY

Dan Shamble, Zombie P.I.

KEVIN J. ANDERSON

KENSINGTON BOOKS
www.kensingtonbooks.com

KENSINGTON BOOKS are published by

Kensington Publishing Corp.
119 West 40th Street
New York, NY 10018

All Kensington titles, imprints, and distributed lines are available at special quantity discounts for bulk purchases for sales promotion, premiums, fund-raising, educational, or institutional use.

Special book excerpts or customized printings can also be created to fit specific needs. For details, write or phone the office of the Kensington Special Sales Manager: Attn. Special Sales Department. Kensington Publishing Corp., 119 West 40th Street, New York, NY 10018. Phone: 1-800-221-2647.

Kensington and the K logo Reg. U.S. Pat. & TM Off.

eISBN-13: 978-1-61773-115-0
eISBN-10: 1-61773-115-3
First Kensington Electronic Edition: September 2014

ISBN-13: 978-1-61773-114-3
ISBN-10: 1-61773-114-5
First Kensington Trade Paperback Printing: September 2014

10 9 8 7 6 5 4 3 2 1

Printed in the United States of America

UNNATURAL PRAISE FOR DAN SHAMBLE, ZOMBIE P.I.

"Down these mean streets a man must lurch. . . . With his Big Sleep interrupted, Chambeaux the zombie private eye goes back to sleuthing, in *Death Warmed Over,* Kevin J. Anderson's wry and inventive take on the Noir paradigm. The bad guys are werewolves, the clients are already deceased, and the readers are in for a funny, action-packed adventure, following that dead man walking . . ."
—Sharyn McCrumb

"A zombie sleuth prowls the mean streets as he works a half-dozen seriously weird cases . . . Like Alexander McCall Smith's Mma Precious Ramotswe, the sleuths really do settle most of their cases, and they provide a lot of laughs along the way."
—*Kirkus Reviews* on *Death Warmed Over*

"Anderson's world-building skills shine through in his latest series, Dan Shamble, P.I. Readers looking for a mix of humor, romance, and good old-fashioned detective work will be delighted by this offering."
—*RT Book Reviews* (4 stars)

"A good detective doesn't let a little thing like getting murdered slow him down, and I got a kick out of Shamble trying to solve a series of oddball cases, including his own. He's the kind of zombie you want to root for, and his cases are good, lighthearted fun."
—Larry Correia

"Kevin J. Anderson's *Death Warmed Over* and his Dan Shamble, Zombie P.I. novels are truly pure reading enjoyment—funny, intriguing—and written in a voice that charms the reader from the first page and onward. Smart, savvy—fresh, incredibly clever! I love these books."
—Heather Graham

Also by Kevin J. Anderson

*Hair Raising**
*Death Warmed Over**
*Stakeout at the Vampire Circus**
*Unnatural Acts**
*Road Kill**
*Naughty & Nice**
Clockwork Angels
The Dragon Business
Blood Lite anthology series (editor)
The new *Dune* novels (with Brian Herbert)
Hellhole series (with Brian Herbert)
The *Terra Incognita* trilogy
The *Saga of Seven Suns* series
The *Saga of Shadows* series
Captain Nemo
The Martian War
Enemies and Allies
The Last Days of Krypton
Resurrection, Inc.
The *Gamearth* trilogy
Blindfold
Climbing Olympus
Hopscotch
Ill Wind (with Doug Beason)
Assemblers of Infinity (with Doug Beason)
The Trinity Paradox (with Doug Beason)
The Craig Kreident Mysteries (with Doug Beason)
Numerous *Star Wars, X-Files, Star Trek, StarCraft* novels,
movie novelizations, and collaborations

*starring Dan Shamble, Zombie P.I.

CHAPTER 1

It was a cold and snowy afternoon in the Unnatural Quarter. The blizzard struck with howling winds and whiteout conditions; temperatures dropped to well below freezing. And we still hadn't recovered from that morning's dust storm and blistering heat.

People say that if you don't like the weather in the Quarter, just wait an hour—especially when the weather wizards are feuding.

I trudged along the sidewalk, braced against the pelting snow and sleet, heading back to the offices of Chambeaux & Deyer Investigations. My sport jacket was not made for the weather, and the biting wind probed like a proctologist's cold finger through the crudely stitched bullet holes in the fabric. My dead skin couldn't much feel the chill, but even embalming fluid will freeze if it gets cold enough.

I stepped in a thick puddle of slush, which soaked my shoes and socks. Sure, I should have worn galoshes. But edgy private investigators don't wear galoshes—not even zombie private investigators. The howling wind nearly tore the fedora off my head, but I used one hand to hold it in place, ducking down as I grumbled about the weather wizards' campaign season, when the two candidates felt the need to show off their skills, although I doubted they impressed anybody.

I'd gone out to the Ghoul's Diner for a cup of coffee on a slow afternoon. Before leaving, doing my due diligence, I checked three different, and competing, weather stations. While the giggly brunette and the sculpted Ken-doll-wannabe prognosticators had predicted a range of meteorological phenomena, none of them mentioned anything about a blizzard in the next hour. I should have known not to rely on a weather forecast.

A black-furred werewolf scuttled across the street in front of me, his entire body matted with snow. He huddled under a porch overhang while he fumbled to unlock the door of his walkup, but his clawed fingers were so numb that he dropped the keys in the snow. He growled as he fished around, and when he found them, they were too ice-encrusted to fit in the lock.

No, the weather wizards were not winning any votes here. With Alastair Cumulus III and Thunder Dick campaigning to prove who was the better weathermancer, this unpredictability would go on until Election Day. . . .

The Chambeaux & Deyer offices were only a block away. I can't help my stiff-legged gait, but at least I don't slouch and shuffle like some of those poorly preserved zombies. A guy has to have some measure of pride. I keep myself as fit and limber as possible—considering my condition. There's only so much you can do with a dead body, and rigor mortis has lasting effects. With joint supplements, however, as well as a once-a-month maintenance spell performed by a pair of witches (former clients of mine), I do all right. Some people even consider me handsome in certain light . . . preferably dim light. My girlfriend, Sheyenne, certainly thinks so. Admittedly, she's a ghost, but her vision is unimpaired.

A sharp gust blew so hard I could feel snow slipping through the bullet hole in my forehead and into my skull. I had thought about adding more putty before I set out for my cup of coffee, but the day had been deceptively bright and sunny. Now, when I got back indoors and the snow melted inside my head, it was going to slosh around in there and make an annoying sound in my inner ear.

When I reached the door to our building, the whiteout parted in a backlash of wind, and I was surprised to see a figure sitting on the steps, not even trying to get out of the freezing storm. He wore rags and fingerless gloves. His bony knees, visible through holes in his trousers, were drawn up to his chest. A floppy fabric hat was tugged down on ropy clumps of gray hair that looked like dreadlocks but were actually just tangles. His skin was a blotchy assortment of grays, tans, and putrid greens.

"Hello, Mr. Renfeld," I said. "I don't often see you outside of your office." It's always good to stay on cordial terms with your building super.

Despite the blinding snow, Renfeld seemed relaxed and comfortable, and his grin showed a reasonable, though not optimal, number of teeth. He said in a wet, mucousy voice, "Just came out to enjoy the weather."

"This is the type of weather you enjoy?"

He adjusted his knees and let the white wind blast him. "It'll change."

"It'll change," I agreed.

Mr. Renfeld is a ghoul with a bad skin condition and a taste for putrid flesh, but he's nice enough in his own way. I've got nothing against ghouls . . . or zombies, ghosts, vampires, werewolves, mummies, demons, witches, or any of the other creatures that haunt (or just inhabit) the Unnatural Quarter.

Renfeld manages the building, which has office space for our agency as well as ten other tenants, most of whom keep their doors barred and windows shuttered—possibly illicit operations or storefronts for sham corporations, or the tenants might just be recluses. I don't do much snooping unless somebody pays me. On the other hand, business had been awfully slow for the past week; maybe I'd satisfy my curiosity after all. . . .

"Finally rented those basement tenements," Renfeld said. "They've been on the market for a while."

"I didn't know you had basement tenements for rent." I didn't know we had basement tenements at all . . . and I'd never even been in the building's basement.

"Couldn't afford to advertise. I just spread word on the street and under it," Renfeld said. "When I finally added a new building entrance, that did the trick. Best investment I ever made."

Snow swirled around me as I stood on the front step. If I were sensible, I'd get inside out of the wind, but I was having a good conversation. "There's a new entrance? I heard all the banging and construction. As the cliché goes, it was enough to wake the dead."

"Sorry about the noise," Renfeld said.

"Don't worry about it. These days it doesn't take much to wake the dead. They're mostly light sleepers." As a detective, though, I might need to have an alternate entrance so that I could sneak in or out of our offices without being seen; I wanted to know my options. "Where is the new door?"

Renfeld pointed a gray finger toward his feet. "Down below, direct access to the sewer system—lots of demand for that. Your regular key should work."

"Good to know. I could have taken an underground short-cut and stayed out of the snowstorm." In a hurry to get inside now, I tipped my fedora to Mr. Renfeld, dumping the accumu-lated white slush on the step. "Enjoy the weather."

Renfeld continued to grin, looking up at the sky. "I'm anx-ious to see what's next. I hope it gets blustery. Nothing beats a blustery day."

As I entered the building, a gust of wind slammed the door

shut behind me. I stomped the residual snow from my feet, once again ruing the fashion considerations that precluded edgy detectives from wearing sensible protective footgear. But, alas, style trumps sense every time. I reached our offices on the second floor, CHAMBEAUX & DEYER INVESTIGATIONS painted right on the door. It would have made my mother proud, if my mother had ever cared. I was content to be proud for myself. Maybe this wasn't the glamorous career I'd once dreamed of, but detective work paid the bills. And I wasn't getting any younger—or any more alive.

Sheyenne hovered at her desk to greet me with a sparkling smile on her luminous, half-substantial visage. She's a gorgeous blonde with big blue eyes and a great figure, and she's even smarter than she is beautiful. We no longer have a physical relationship, since she no longer has a physical body, but we satisfy ourselves with an ectoplasmic one, and sometimes that's pretty damn good.

She frowned at my blizzard-modified state. "Beaux, you shouldn't be out in weather like that—you'll catch your death."

"Already caught it." I removed my fedora and shook the snow from my sport jacket before hanging it on the rack next to the door. "I'll dry out."

"Nothing wrong with being moist and dank, ayup—that's what I always say." The burbling voice came from our conference room just off the main reception area.

Seated at the long table was a frog demon the size of a small man. He had glistening green skin with black leopard spots. His golden eyes were the size of softballs, and twitchy nictitating membranes flickered up and down over them. He wore a frock coat with a high collar to show he was a respectable businessman.

Across the conference table, my partner, Robin Deyer, stacked manila folders and removed the last few sheets of paper. Robin's a lawyer, but not a typical one. She has a heart and a compassionate streak a mile wide. "We've almost wrapped up Mr. Lurrm's file, Dan—all the i's dotted and t's crossed, signed in slime and duly notarized."

When the amphibious creature chuckled, his lower throat ballooned out. "Please just call me Lurrm, Ms. Deyer—no need to use Mister. We're all friends here, and besides, I'm in my androgynous phase. Ayup." His throat billowed out and back. "I'm so excited about this I can barely restrain myself from exuding ooze."

I think the frog demon was smiling, but with a mouth that wide it was hard to tell. "Open for business: the improved, refurbished, and totally legitimate Zombie Bathhouse. Ayup! The sign with our new name got installed yesterday. *Recompose Spa.*" He rubbed his soft hands together. "We did our VIP sneak preview last week as a shakedown for new customers, and today we're open to the public."

"If any customers can make it through this weather," Robin said. "The weather networks can't agree on when the blizzard will end."

"The weather anchors can't agree on what temperature water freezes," Sheyenne said.

Lurrm puffed his throat again. "The blizzard might help business. If you're frozen and crusted with ice, there's nothing like a good soak in a hot-springs pool. Ayup."

The Zombie Bathhouse had once been a front for the evil body-parts smuggler, Tony Cralo, an obscenely fat zombie gangster. After Cralo's downfall, the Zombie Bathhouse shut down and fell into rapid and dank disrepair, until Lurrm and his investors refurbished it.

The frog demon hopped from his chair and stood on powerful legs, adjusting his frock coat. "I know the place had a bad reputation, but I plan to change that." He was a bouncy sort. His long tongue flicked in and out of his mouth in excitement. "The Recompose Spa will be a family place, absolutely no underworld connections, everything aboveboard." When Lurrm shuddered, the leopard spots danced on his slick skin. "And everything disinfected regularly. Nobody's going to get warts from my bathhouse!"

"I thought frogs and warts went hand in hand," I said.

Lurrm blinked his nictitating membranes. "That's just an old wives' tale, Mr. Chambeaux. *Toads* cause warts, and don't let any of them tell you otherwise. They're rather sensitive about it."

Robin searched through several manila folders and brought out a certificate for Lurrm. "Recompose is one hundred percent legitimate. Your business license, sales tax forms, health certificate, OSHA clearances, immersion waiver forms—everything you need."

"I'm very grateful for your assistance, Ms. Deyer." Delighted, the amphibious creature turned to me, jittering up and down. "We even have an employee manual! I insist that you all come and take a look tomorrow. I promise a tour and special discounts. Ayup."

Robin handed over all the forms, licenses, and certificates he needed, including a leather-bound corporate manual and a hand-press seal (which might be a challenge for the frog demon with his squishy fingers). "We're very supportive of our clients. We'll be there."

"Weather permitting," I added.

The frog demon bundled up in his frock coat and left our offices prepared to face the cold and snow, but by now the clouds had vanished and been replaced by dense fog.

When the offices were quiet again, I realized I didn't have anything to do. "Slow day," I said.

Sheyenne said with the flirtatious lilt that she used just for me, "If you're that bored, we could spend more time together."

"We always spend time together. Almost all day, every day."

"Quality time."

"Every second with you is quality, Spooky."

"Good save." She picked up a set of folders and drifted off to the file cabinet.

I was eager for another exciting mystery. Solving cases is what makes me tick—in fact, I don't do much else with my life, or afterlife. I *define* myself by being a detective, zombie or otherwise. But I needed something more glamorous than preparing business licenses and health department forms.

Robin wrapped up the paperwork for the Recompose Spa and put all the folders on Sheyenne's desk. "This may not be exciting, Dan, but cases like this are our bread and butter. Our workload is just like the weather—wait a few minutes and it'll change."

And it did.

CHAPTER 2

When a huge, hulking ogre steps through the office doorway, you take notice. I was just glad he decided to turn the knob and enter the traditional way instead of smashing through, as ogres often do.

He was huge (I know I already said that, but it bears repeating), with burly shoulders, pebbled gray skin, muscles the size of backpacks, shaggy hair like a dried kelp forest, and a mouth as big as a garage. He wore a brown tunic tied at the waist with a jaunty yellow sash. The bags under his eyes were so large they wouldn't have qualified as carry-ons. He was covered with melting snow from the recent blizzard.

I greeted him with my professional smile. "New client?" I asked.

The ogre moved his mouth and puffed his chest. "I am Stentor." I expected a deafening roar, but the voice that came out was a ridiculously tiny, high-pitched squeak. "The opera singer. You may have heard of me?"

Such a clumsy voice would never have graced even a Sunday-school stage for fourth graders. "Sorry, sir, my knowledge of opera doesn't go much further than 'Kill da Wabbit!' "

Sheyenne drifted forward, letting out an exaggerated sigh. "Beaux, I am going to get you more cultured if it kills you. Again. Stentor has been performing to sold-out audiences in the Phantom's opera house for the past two months. He caused quite a stir in the cultural scene."

"The most fabulous performance by an ogre opera singer in weeks!" Stentor squeaked. "That's according to the *National Midnight Star.*"

"Know your client" is a good catchphrase, and I was sure I would have to research opera and the ogre's career. Sheyenne wanted to make me a better man, a better zombie, and I liked being with her. She had already dragged me to performances of Shakespeare in the Dark, and since I cared about her, I would even endure an opera. If I was with my beautiful ghost girl-friend, it couldn't be all that bad . . . could it?

With fist clenched and arm raised, Stentor tilted his enor-mous head back and belted out a succession of meepy atonal noises that contained neither sturm nor drang. After the abortive performance, the ogre hung his head, sniffled with the sound of a malfunctioning vacuum cleaner, and began blubber-ing. He sobbed with such palpable dismay that I felt sorry for him without even knowing the problem. Tears flowed down his seamed face in rivulets, like a potential flash flood. "It's *gone.* I've lost it."

"Lost what?" I was pretty sure I knew, but never having at-tended an ogre opera, I wanted confirmation.

Stentor blinked his huge bloodshot eyes at me. "Are you deaf? My voice is gone!" I had to lean forward to hear him. "Someone stole it, *kidnapped* it—you've got to help me. I'll do anything to get it back."

Now this was more like it, a case I could sink my teeth into (if I were the sort of creature who sinks his teeth into uncooperative flesh). I preferred to use brains, not eat them. "You've come to the right place, Mr. Stentor."

I started to direct the ogre toward my office, but realized the office wasn't large enough unless I moved the desk to accommodate him. So we went into the much larger conference room to talk. The ogre shook himself off like a shaggy, waterlogged dog, sending sprays of snowmelt everywhere.

Robin emerged from her office to join the intake meeting, where we could decide whether Stentor would need her legal expertise, my detective skills, or both. She held a yellow pad, ready to take notes—a special legal pad, given to her by Santa Claus himself after we helped him out on a case. The paper never, ever ran out, and a magically connected pencil took notes for her exactly as she thought them, which left Robin's hands free to do other incomprehensible lawyerly things.

"That isn't your normal voice, I take it?" she asked. She set the legal pad down, and the pencil dutifully jotted down the basic information.

"I'm a baritone," Stentor said in a shrill peep. He continued with greater fervor, gesticulating to demonstrate an intensity that his vocal cords couldn't convey. "My voice is my livelihood, my very soul—and now it's gone."

Before he grew too emotional, I calmed him with a no-nonsense voice. "Just start at the beginning and tell us what happened, Mr. Stentor."

"I did my nightly performance of *Don Giovanni* at the opera house—and it was a great one. An artist can feel it when everything clicks." He pounded a boulder-sized fist against his chest as if to pummel the voice out of his throat. "It was my first three-window performance."

I looked over at Sheyenne for an explanation. She said, "He means he shattered three windows with his singing."

"Is that a good thing?"

"In some circles," Stentor said. "The Phantom has an insurance rider just for that."

Robin's legal pad made notes. She said, "So your voice was fine *during* the performance."

"Yes, and afterward, I went back to my dressing room, as always. Gargled with lye, as always, then went to bed. I woke up with a frog in my throat—and my voice was gone."

I pursed my lips. This was indeed a strange case, so I asked the obvious question. "Do you still have the frog?"

"Yes," the ogre answered. "Yes, I do." He shifted his brown tunic and struggled with a small cloth sack tied to the sash, but his fingers were the size of kielbasas and too unwieldy to undo the delicate knot.

My zombie fingers weren't very nimble either, but they were sufficient. I retrieved the bag, loosened the string, and dumped a shivering frog onto Sheyenne's desk. The creature looked dazed and confused; it didn't even have the ambition to hop away.

"He's very cute." Sheyenne reached her ghostly hands down to cup the frog, but they passed right through. As a ghost, she can't touch living, or formerly living, things—including me—but she likes to go through the motions.

As Stentor gazed at the frog, his face was a billboard-sized canvas of emotions that rippled from dismay to affection. "At first, I thought I might have gotten a case of warts on my vocal cords, considering that it's a frog and all."

I corrected him with my newfound knowledge. "That's just an old wives' tale. Warts are caused by toads. Frogs get a bad rap."

"I know, I did my scientific research," the ogre said. "That's why I suspect some dark magic instead, and that led me to you, Mr. Shamble. Only you can help me—I've read your novels."

I grimaced with embarrassment. "Those stories are highly fictionalized, written by a ghostwriter. Don't put too much stock in them. Some of the adventures are . . . exaggerated."

Ever since I'd allowed Howard Phillips Publishing to use my life and cases as the inspiration for a series of "Dan Shamble, Zombie P.I." novels, I had been embarrassed by the attention—and even more so as the books continued to sell well.

"But you're the best in the business," Stentor said.

I shrugged. "Thank you. Honestly, though, I just do my best to take care of folks. If you wouldn't mind leaving the frog with us," I said, "I'll see what I can find out. Let me talk with a couple of witches who act as my special advisers in cases like this. We'll get your voice back. You'll be singing the blues again soon enough."

"Opera," Stentor corrected.

I clapped a reassuring hand on his backpack-sized bicep. "After I find your voice, you can do whatever you like with it."

CHAPTER 3

The next morning began as a nice outing with Robin, Sheyenne, and me going out to do our social duties at the refurbished and reopened Recompose Spa.

Though I promised myself I'd check out the new direct connection to the sewers soon, we left the Chambeaux & Deyer offices by the street-level entrance—and stepped into a mist so thick it felt as if we were already in the sauna. The feuding weather wizards had created some sort of inversion layer that burbled up from the manhole covers, clotted in the alleys, and curled along the streets. The fog was as thick as proverbial pea soup, and actually smelled like the digestive aftermath of pea soup.

I heard a shriek overhead and saw a shadow, but could make out no details in the mist; probably a harpy flying above the clouds, I decided. A mummy was setting up his newsstand, straightening the day's papyrus edition and arranging his selection of chewing gum, cough drops, and souvenir amulets. An enterprising clothier had set up bins on wheels filled with sun hats, parkas, rain shawls, umbrellas, bikinis, and discount all-weather combos. The bins could be swapped and rearranged as fast as the weather changed.

A love-struck vampire couple strolled along hand in hand, enjoying a rare late-morning walk made possible by the opacity of the fog. Outside a Talbot & Knowles Blood Bar, a hemoglobin barista was handing out free samples to any potential blood-sucking customers who passed by, or even humans who were hemo-curious. The vampire couple frowned in disdain at the smiling young barista. "We don't patronize chains," said the woman with a sniff. "We buy only organic, locally sourced, guaranteed no additives hemoglobin."

Even after the tumultuous upheaval that changed the world more than a decade ago, life had a way of settling back into its own definition of normal. Some days I had a hard time remembering what the world was like before the Big Uneasy. I had been alive then, setting my sights on a career as a private investigator because I couldn't make it as a cop.

A strange and unexpected sequence of events had triggered the return of all the supernatural creatures and magic to the world. The combination of a rare planetary alignment and the blood (from a paper cut) of a virgin (a fifty-eight-year-old lonely librarian) spilling on the pages of an original copy of the Necronomicon had unleashed all the unnaturals. At first it seemed like a true holocaust, the end of days, an every-kind-of-monster apocalypse, but society settled down soon enough and people, of all sorts, got back to normal. It was everyday life, but with added monsters.

Robin dedicated her career as an attorney to serving the downtrodden unnaturals, insisting that they deserved justice just as much as anyone else did. I'd come to town as a private investigator, hanging out my shingle and taking cases, no matter how unusual. Back in the outside world, I would have been stuck taking photos of cheating spouses for divorce cases. Even here, I still got hired to do the occasional sit-and-wait, but adding monsters to the equation made even simple cases a lot more interesting.

Even though Sheyenne and I were both murdered here in the Quarter, this is still the place I call home, warts and all (regardless of where those warts came from).

As the three of us strolled along, the fog cleared, then came back with a vengeance, cleared again, and came back in alternating blocks. Sheyenne flitted along as insubstantial as the mist, but a lot prettier. She said, "If this is the spa's grand opening, Beaux, then we should bring flowers." She placed a ghostly finger against her ghostly lips. "Lily pads would go with the theme, brighten the place up."

In other times, a guest might have brought a bottle of wine or champagne, but after the Big Uneasy, with so many different types of creatures drinking so many different types of beverages, flowers were a safer bet.

"I should've thought of that," Robin said. She was a thousand percent dedicated to her work, intent on her cases with a laser focus to the exclusion of etiquette.

As for me, no one had ever accused me of being socially adept. "Flowers it is," I said.

So, we stopped at a boutique florist called the Medium-Sized Shop of Horrors. The proprietor was a raspy-voiced woodwitch with thistles and moss for hair and spiderwebs for clothes; her knuckles and elbows looked like knotty hunks of driftwood. Small decorative fountains trickled in alcoves in the shop, and New Age music, complete with chimes, added to the heady atmosphere.

Sheyenne drifted down the aisles, inspecting strange mushrooms, thorny plants, flowers that talked, blossoms with inset eyeballs—and lily pads floating in a reflecting pool. After Sheyenne found what she was looking for, Robin and I carried the lily pads to the cash register so the woodwitch could ring up our purchase. Robin selected an appropriate gift card to accompany the lily pads.

Outside, we heard a buzzing engine, a squeal of tires up against the curb, then the clatter of little feet. The door to the Medium-Sized Shop of Horrors burst open, and a crowd of brightly painted lawn gnomes charged inside brandishing machine guns.

Their normally cheery expressions were angry, their painted lips curled downward, their eyes glinting with evil. The machine guns they carried were old-fashioned and miniaturized—not traditional Tommy guns, but the smaller, cuter versions known as Timmy guns.

Even in the Unnatural Quarter, with its oh-so-typical strange goings-on, a customer doesn't expect machine-gun fire inside a flower shop.

The gnomes chattered in the quaint voices that normally made gnomes so charming, but their leader, a standard-size gnome model who had painted his cap and vest an ominous black, shouted out in a surprisingly loud and commanding voice, "This is a stickup!"

The lawn gnomes pointed their Timmy guns at the flower-shop walls and opened fire with a rat-a-tat-tat of tiny-caliber bullets that sounded like popcorn popping. The gnome robbers sprayed the vases and flowers on the shelves, shattered the decorative fountains with a hail of projectiles.

Robin hurled her lily pads at the lawn gnomes, knocking one over. When they turned their Timmy guns at her, I threw myself on Robin and covered her with my body as a dozen stinging slugs pounded into my back. Even though the small-caliber slugs caused some damage, I decided it was better me than Robin. She's still young, perky, and very much alive. As for myself, a few more bullet holes wouldn't make much difference, especially tiny ones like this.

I would have protected Sheyenne, too, but she didn't need my help. She used her poltergeist powers to hurl flowerpots at the gnomes, and they ducked from side to side to dodge the projectiles.

The terrified woodwitch had the presence of mind to work a spell that turned her gentle New Age wind chimes into rattling alarms that jangled and clanged, drawing even more attention than the shouting gnomes and the machine-gun fire.

Not expecting so much resistance, the gang leader yelled, "Grab the cash register and let's get out of here."

It took four of the lawn gnomes to lift the heavy cash register, but they raced out the front door of the flower shop with it nevertheless.

I picked myself off of Robin, and she insisted she was all right. My back was perforated in a dozen places, and I knew the sport jacket would need stitching again. But not now. I drew my .38 and lurched toward the robbers.

The black-garbed leader bellowed back at us, "When the coppers come asking, you tell 'em you've been stuck up by Mr. Bignome!"

Meanwhile, the woodwitch worked druidic magic to summon an instant fecundity spell that made the plants and vines grow wildly, proliferating like spam e-mails from supposed Nigerian princes. Foliage surged upward in exuberant growth, vines covering the door and forming a barricade that would have been sufficient for landscaping around Sleeping Beauty's castle.

The leafy vines lashed across the doorway a second too late to stop the fleeing lawn gnome robbers—and just in time to prevent me from going after them. I yanked and tore at the vines, trying to get the foliage out of the way. I threw a glance over my shoulder at the woodwitch. "Timing could have been better."

She seemed embarrassed. "I forgot about the spell delay. Sorry."

As I tugged at the barricade, I watched lawn gnomes lug the cash register over to the curb and toss it in the back of a get-away jalopy the size of a go-kart. I heard police sirens in the street, squad cars rushing to the scene of the robbery.

I finally pulled the vines free from the doorway and stumbled out onto the sidewalk, nearly tripping as a persistent (or pissed-off) vine wrapped around my ankle and snagged me. "Halt!" I yelled at the gnomes, not because I expected it to work but because it was the first thing that came to mind. I hopped on one foot, disentangling the vine from my leg.

With a sneer on his painted face, one of the scuttling gnomes gave me the finger—a stubby little finger, but it qualified nevertheless.

I shot him, though I only meant to wing him. The bullet struck the rude gnome in the foot, and with a *plink* his sprightly boot turned into a puff of plaster dust. He toppled over on the street and lay writhing and wobbling, trying to get back up.

"Help!" he called in his cute gnomish voice. "Don't leave me behind."

As the other gnomes secured the cash register in the jalopy, Mr. Bignome took a step back toward his fallen comrade. With an angry glare, he swung his Timmy gun around. "Dead gnomes tell no tales!" He opened fire and shattered his comrade into broken fragments.

I shot three times at the jalopy, hoping to put out one of the tires. I chipped off the top of one of the gnomes' pointed hats, but missed the tiny vehicle.

Squad cars roared in, and a familiar florid-faced, redheaded beat cop ran up, arriving on foot just as the patrol cars screeched to a halt in front of the Medium-Sized Shop of Horrors. He was gasping for breath, angry that he hadn't arrived sooner.

Other cops piled out of their squad cars and charged into the flower shop, but the lawn gnomes had already gotten away. The beat cop bent over with his hands on his knees, heaving giant breaths. "Hey, Shamble."

"Hey, McGoo," I answered.

It was our usual exchange.

Officer Toby McGoohan is my BHF, my best human friend. We've been through life, death, and afterlife together, and we remain friends through it all. Not every relationship can survive that. We both came to the Unnatural Quarter by roundabout ways, and we both stayed here. If I had to be stuck anywhere, though, it was good to have a friend like McGoo.

"Am I too late?" He took off his cap and wiped sweat from his forehead.

"It's the thought that counts."

McGoo put his cap back on. "Well, I'm not up for a promotion anytime soon. Was it Bignome again?" When I nodded, he shook his head. "Unbelievable! This is the third floral shop they've knocked over in the last two weeks."

"Unbelievable," I agreed. "The Quarter has three floral shops?"

The woodwitch managed to shut off the jangly wind-chime alarms, returning blessed silence to the foggy streets. Robin emerged, carrying the bedraggled water lilies. Surprisingly cheery, considering the mayhem, Sheyenne said, "At least we got the flowers at a discount."

After we gave our statements to McGoo, we headed off to the Recompose Spa. After an early-morning robbery, the day was bound to get better.

CHAPTER 4

The Zombie Bathhouse did not hold a lot of fond memories for me, but if I avoided every place in the Quarter that left a bad taste in my mouth (even though I couldn't taste much), I'd end up stuck in the office all day.

And Lurrm was sincerely trying his best to make the Recompose Spa a legitimate, family-friendly place.

Both Sheyenne and Robin expressed dismay over the Timmy-gun pellets embedded in my back, so I promised I would see the Wannovich sisters for my monthly body maintenance that afternoon. I had planned to talk with them about Stentor's stolen voice anyway. But first, even a zombie detective has social obligations he can't get out of.

Recompose had a humming new neon sign with intense blue lettering. Old moss had been scrubbed off the building's brick exterior, but fresh tendrils were already working their way up the mortar. Big signs in the barred windows announced: GRAND RE-OPENING! UNDER NEW MANAGEMENT! and FAMILIES AND LARVAE WELCOME!

Lurrm met us at the check-in counter after a similar-looking frog demon tried to charge us entry. Lurrm clasped his little hands together and belled out his throat. "These are friends, Carrl. I have comp tickets for them."

Robin presented the worse-for-wear water lilies, which had a strong but pleasant scent that reminded me of the peonies that had grown in a hedge near my boyhood home.

Lurrm's enormous smile broadened further. "Oh, how thoughtful of you! Just the right touch, ayup."

He carried the flowers while Carrl the attendant gave Robin and me plastic wristbands, but he was discomfited over what to do with Sheyenne. "It'll work." She extended her insubstantial arm. "So long as it's not organic."

"Finest plastic," said Lurrm.

We passed through the turnstile and went down a level to the main pools. I noted a remarkable difference from this place's previous incarnation as the Zombie Bathhouse. The last time I'd been here, when the place was managed by a fat zombie gangster, the bathhouse had a seedy appearance with patterns of mildew creeping up the tiles as if some fungus fairy had taken up drunken finger painting. Now the tiles on the walls and floor were sparkling clean.

"It's very sanitary," Lurrm pointed out. "No risk of communicable diseases. Bathhouses have a bad reputation, but we insist that all patrons, regardless of species, take a shower before entering our pools."

I looked around. "You have quite a crowd already for your first full day."

Lurrm flicked out his long tongue and then reeled it back into his wide mouth. "We gave out a lot of coupons. I'm hoping for repeat business. Ayup."

There were three dressing rooms marked Male, Female, and Other. Four zombies sat together in a bubbling hot-springs pool, their eyes closed in ecstasy, their slack mouths open and emitting a long string of vowels. Another gray-skinned undead shuffled past with a white towel wrapped around his waist, though it didn't quite cover his wrinkled butt crack.

"We just opened a new set of pools with the proper chemical and marsh balance," Lurrm said. "Recompose is an amphibian-friendly bathhouse. We even set up an egg-laying pond, but it's currently for employees only."

We heard squeals and splashing from a separate kiddie pool. When we were drawn to the sounds of mirth, I expected to see pint-sized zombies, but instead the shallow pool was full of black torpedo-shaped creatures with slick skin and broad sucker mouths.

Lurrm explained, "Zombie kids have priority if they want to use the pool, but for now it also doubles as a tadpole pond."

Catering to all possible customers, a concession counter sold lemonade, electrolyte drinks, self-serve blood packets, and even embalming fluid, for both oral and intravenous consumption.

The mineral pools were at different temperatures, burbling up from deep aquifers with a sulfur smell. Runoff slopped onto the floor and flowed down into drains. Frog-demon attendants skimmed the floating scum from the pools.

"We plan to open up spa services, too, including manicures, claw restoration, facials—ayup, there's a demand for that." Lurrm's throat belled in and out.

I said, "I've always advocated for zombies to take care of themselves. Look at me." I touched my face, felt the firmness of the skin there. "Once you let yourself go, there's no coming back."

Robin inhaled deeply, and her forehead furrowed with questions. "The disinfectant is strong—and I'm used to the usual odor of zombies." She glanced at me with an embarrassed look on her face. "No offense, Dan."

"I'm a zombie, no denying it."

"But there's also an undertone of"—she sniffed again—"sewage?"

"Can't be helped," Lurrm said. "With the refurbishing and the expansion, we're connected to the greater sewer network. But if we bring in large enough zombie crowds, no one will notice the smell."

Lurrm placed the lily pads on the surface of one of the unoccupied pools, spreading out the fleshy green leaves as if he were laying out placemats. He stepped back to regard his work. "Charming! Ayup."

Next, he showed us a set of wooden doors. "A bathhouse and day spa would be nothing without a sauna. We imported the wood from Finland for that authentic touch. There's an automated water-dispensing system to maintain a high level of steam." He yanked open the door, and we were greeted by an unpleasant ripe stench. A skeleton sat on one of the wooden benches, lounging back, with a towel wrapped around his pelvis. On the floor at his bony feet was a pile of sloughed-off flesh.

Lurrm groaned. "They're supposed to limit their time in the sauna to fifteen minutes. I hate it when they stay in too long." He closed the door.

Sheyenne let out a startled gasp, then chuckled. A disembodied hand scuttled across the floor, running on its fingers like a spider. It crawled to a damp towel that had been discarded on the tiles, held it between thumb and forefinger, then used the other three fingers to drag the towel toward a bin. The crawling hand deposited the towel where it belonged, then scuttled away. Prowling across the floor, it picked up another towel and continued its tedious work of cleaning up.

Lurrm was delighted. "That's Crawling Hand, or C.H. for short. He's very *handy* and eager to please, ayup. Does so many errands around here, I don't know what I'd do without C.H. He's my right-hand man—except he's a leftie." He called out, "C.H., come and meet our guests."

The disembodied hand trotted over, bounced up and down on its fingers, then popped into the air. I reached out to catch it, and the hand seized my grip.

I swung my hand around, with C.H. still attached, and passed him on to Robin, who also shook the hand vigorously, while Sheyenne merely waved.

"Where did he come from?" I asked.

The frog demon shrugged. "Not quite sure. Somebody just left it here. You should see how much he helps in the massage rooms. C.H. can work stiff and sore muscles so you forget all about rigor mortis."

Robin set C.H. on the floor, and he waggled his index finger at her, wanting something. She bent down. "I don't understand. What is he asking?" She looked up at Lurrm.

"It's just one of those pull-my-finger gags. Don't fall for it. Go on, C.H., run along." The frog demon shooed away the disembodied hand, who scuttled off and picked up a candy wrapper that someone had dropped. Crumpling it in the palm of his hand—clearly annoyed with sloppy and discourteous patrons—C.H. hopped over to a trash can and tossed the balled wrapper in, making an expert rim shot.

Lurrm insisted that Robin stay for a lemonade, which she sipped while we met in Lurrm's private office. He was clearly proud to show us where he had hung the framed business license and sales tax certificate on his wall. Rubbing his soft hands together, he said, "Ms. Deyer, humans are welcome too. I know you have a stressful job—come down here for a soak. Relax a bit. I'd always be happy to have you and Mr. Shamble here."

"I'll think about it," Robin said, which was her polite way of saying, No, thank you.

For myself, I couldn't drive away the image of being forced to sit in a hot pool next to the obese crime lord with his perpetual and offensive outgassing. "Maybe another time," I said.

CHAPTER 5

It was stiflingly hot and humid when the three of us headed back to the Chambeaux & Deyer offices. The sun shone bright, and vampires and other nocturnal dwellers returned to their lairs, grumbling. Robin and Sheyenne had admin work to do, and I needed to pick up the frog that had come out of Stentor's throat before I went to see the Wannoviches.

In the hallway outside the door to our second-floor offices, we encountered a shriveled old hunchback in a lab coat pacing impatiently. He was bald, with drooping earlobes, and his face had so many wrinkles that it looked like a wadded ball of flesh-colored tissue paper. He wore enormous round black spectacles with magnifying-glass lenses that made his eyes look the size of dinner plates.

Sheyenne had taped a note to the door, promising to "Be back soon."

The shriveled old man peered at us through his telescopic glasses, swung his hunch around, and tapped a finger meaningfully on his wristwatch. "It's fifteen minutes past *soon.* I can't wait all day. I need to hire your services, and you were the only zombie private detective listed in the Yellow Pages."

"You actually looked in the Yellow Pages?" Sheyenne asked. "I guess the ad was worthwhile."

"I also ran an Internet search." The wrinkled old man rounded on me, poking his head forward like an emperor penguin I had once seen in a nature documentary, back when I had the time to watch nature documentaries. "But first, a test to see how good your detective skills are." The hunchback waggled a finger at me, aiming to stab at the center of my chest but ending up only reaching my abdomen. "I'm a lab assistant for a mad scientist who uses only Apple products. Can you figure out my name?"

I had a sense of foreboding that I was about to get hit with a McGoo-level bad joke, but I played it straight in case he was on the level. I tried to remember all the lab assistants and mad scientists I knew in the Quarter, regardless of their preference for electronic devices. "Should I have heard of you?"

"I want you to figure it out." His voice held a hint of a pout. "It's a riddle."

"I'm a detective, not a riddler. Is there a crime you'd like me to investigate?"

"Maybe not, if you're going to be a stick-in-the-mud."

Robin crossed her arms over her chest. "A mad scientist's assistant who uses only Apple products? Your name is iGor."

The shrunken man laughed aloud and pranced in the hallway. Under his lab coat the hunchback bounced up and down like a beach ball. "Yes! Get it? *iGor—*"

"I get it," I said, "but that's not your real name."

"No, but I had you going. Ha, ha! In fact, I fooled you in every way."

Sheyenne used her poltergeist skills to unlock the door without bothering to use a key. "Won't you come inside? Be careful, you look rather frail."

"Fooled you again!" He unbuttoned his lab coat and shucked it off, squirming from side to side, then unbuckled a strap across his chest. His entire hunch fell off to land in a tumble next to the discarded lab coat. He straightened with a groan. "Oh, that thing is heavy, and it makes my back stiff!"

Next, he dug fingernails into his wattled throat, pried loose a pink edge of skin, tugging and stretching flesh-colored rubber. He was too eager, though, and the mask ripped. Finally, he discarded the whole thing, peeled off a skullcap, and shook his head to reveal a freckle-faced redheaded boy with blue eyes and a sparkling grin. "Golly, that's so much better! Now I can really introduce myself. My name is Jody, Jody Caligari, junior mad scientist and master of disguise."

"And also potential client, I presume?" Sheyenne said.

I stood next to the kid. "How old are you?"

"Twelve," Jody said, "and well on my way to being somebody. You'll want to say you knew me when." He blushed and looked away. "So I'd appreciate a little help out of a tight spot. You won't regret it. When I become an evil genius, or the world's most powerful supervillain, I'll remember my friends and supporters."

"Are you here because you've read those Dan Shamble, Zombie P.I. books?" I asked, wanting to get rid of any unrealistic expectations from the beginning.

Jody looked confused. "No, have they been turned into graphic novels?"

"Not yet, but I'm sure that's in the works."

"I did my research." Jody piled his torn wrinkled mask on top of the false hunchback and his lab coat, then took a seat at Sheyenne's desk, spinning around in the office swivel chair. "And I've decided to present you with a great opportunity to do some pro bono work."

Sheyenne, the most practical member of our office team,

frowned. "Right, because opportunities to investigate cases for free so rarely present themselves?" Her tone was teasing, but Jody didn't seem to notice.

He nodded. "Especially an opportunity like this one! I need your expertise, and it'll make you feel good, I promise. There's nothing like that warm, fuzzy glow when you help somebody reach his potential."

"Assisting supervillains in training isn't necessarily the most surefire way to feel good," I said.

Jody's grin was irresistible. Even I thought he looked adorable, and I'm not a soft sell. "But what if I end up being a *good* supervillain?"

The kid was so eager and earnest I didn't want to correct his misunderstanding. I resisted the urge to tousle his hair.

"Do your parents know you're here?" Sheyenne asked. "Won't they be worried about you?"

"I'm at Junior Mad Scientist Camp, and I send them postcards. I'm here on a scholarship."

Robin said, "Well, then, they must be very proud of you."

"Not really, but they try. My dad's an insurance salesman and my mom's an accountant. They don't understand my interests. They smile and attend my science fairs, but they think this whole mad scientist thing is just a phase I'll grow out of." Jody flushed. "But, golly, I want to change the world! Ever since I got my first chemistry set when I was eight years old, I've been creating potions and experiments. I turned the neighbor's poodle into a German shepherd and then back again, just to prove the concept."

"Is there practical value in that?" I asked.

The kid shrugged. "Doesn't every poodle aspire to be a German shepherd? Anyway, I was hooked. Once, I blew up the garage and created a blob that ingested half the block before I found a way to evaporate it. My parents were worried and sent me to a counselor. Fortunately, the counselor encouraged me instead of trying to cure me."

"That's a rare kind of counselor," Sheyenne said.

"I came out here hoping to make my mark. I set up a world-class laboratory in prime mad-scientist real estate and was making unbelievable progress in the development of a supervillain—even analyzed and reproduced a bunch of the classic powers. I might have become the youngest person ever to win a Nobel Prize in superhero dynamics."

"All right, kid, you've got me interested." I hung my fedora and jacket on the rack. "What's your case? How can we help?"

"I need you to retrieve my stolen work. And, Ms. Deyer, I could use your legal expertise, too. This is a heinous, heinous miscarriage of justice."

"Describe for me how heinous it is." Robin pulled out her special yellow legal pad and set it on the table, where the magic pencil began taking notes.

"I had a lab down in the sewers, the full nine yards . . . although as a scientist I really should be using the metric system. My landlord evicted me," Jody said. "He's a corrupt slumlord, with no patience and no sense of humor. We didn't get along at all. He marched in one day with his eviction goons—gator-guys—and kicked me out, just like that! He said professional lab space was at a premium, and that he had a waiting list for the unit. Every mad scientist wants a secret lab down in the sewers, you know. So he took all my stuff and chased me out. No argument, no notice." Jody flushed. "He said I'm just a child, and the lab space should go to a more deserving mad scientist."

Robin looked angry, and I could tell Jody had pushed just the right buttons. "That's age discrimination. You can't evict a tenant on the basis of age."

"That's exactly what I said," Jody replied, "but without

sounding so legal about it. He confiscated everything: my lab notebooks, my experiments, my supervillain devices, my patent applications, my costume. It was my life's work."

I raised my eyebrows. "Life's work? How long did it take you?"

"At least six months. I started it even before I came to the Quarter."

"So he stole your work. Doesn't that make him a villain, too?"

"Villains have style, Mr. Chambeaux. He's just a bully."

Under other circumstances I might have found the whole situation amusing, but Jody looked so earnest with his puppy-dog eyes. He seemed to have been incarnated from a Norman Rockwell painting, and he exuded a nostalgic innocence that everyone missed but few people ever experienced. Again, I had to resist a strong urge to tousle his hair.

Robin wore a stormy expression, and the magic pencil furiously wrote down notes. She paced back and forth. "If what you say is true, he had no basis for evicting his tenant and absolutely no cause to seize your private possessions. Can you place a value on them?"

Jody nodded. "Yes, I can—they're priceless."

"We'll need an itemized list," I suggested.

"No, I truly mean they're *priceless.* That's all of my research. The sky is the limit, or as we used to say down in the sewers, the manhole's the limit. Gosh, don't treat me like a silly kid just like my landlord did." He sounded stung.

"We don't think you're silly," Sheyenne said. "But, remember, you're the one who came dressed up as a fake hunchback lab assistant."

Jody snickered. "Yeah, iGor—that was a good one. Wait until you see my other disguises." Then he became angry again. "I can prove I'm a serious researcher. I have five patents under review at the Mad Scientists Patent Office. You can check that out for yourself. They take me seriously. I'm a prodigy."

"And modest, too," I said.

"Hey, you don't get ahead in the mad scientist world by being shy and polite. Did Dr. Frankenstein say, 'I'd consider it a great favor if you would please throw the switch'? No, he was forceful and commanding: 'Throw the switch!' "

"All right, you convinced me," I said. "We'll look into your landlord and see what we can do about retrieving your possessions."

Robin didn't want to stop there. "And I can file a suit against him for wrongful eviction." The pencil tapped itself against her legal pad as she pondered. "On the other hand, I'm not sure how a lease signed by a minor would be valid. He must have found some kind of loophole."

Sheyenne took out a new client contract. "*We're* running a business here, however. We need to come to terms about your method of payment for our services."

Jody blinked his blue eyes at her. "Golly, I thought we agreed it was a pro bono case?"

"You *suggested* that it be pro bono. . . ." Sheyenne said.

He kept looking at her and grinning hopefully.

Robin's heart had already melted as her indignation rose, and I said, "It might be a good idea to show some generosity. You never know when it'll come in handy to have a junior mad scientist and possible future supervillain on your side."

Sheyenne, unable to maintain her stern expression, tore up the client agreement. "All right, pro bono it is."

I glanced down at the remnants of Jody's disguise on the floor. "Don't forget your hump on the way out."

CHAPTER 6

The cases don't solve themselves, and I had an ogre's voice to recover. And bullets to get out of my back. Fortunately, with the Wannovich sisters it would be one-stop shopping.

I made a call to Mavis hoping that she had some knowledge of voice-abduction sorcery, particularly the kind that used amphibians as catalysts. Since I was also due for my monthly maintenance touch-up spell, I could kill two vultures with one stone. Mavis and Alma Wannovich asked me to meet them at the publishing offices.

I stood outside the tall glass-and-metal headquarters of Howard Phillips Publishing (with their slogan "We Love Our Craft" engraved in stone tablets on the front of the building). The sisters were adorable and unusual in their way, and they had certainly come a long way since their original dispute with the publisher, when a typo in one of their spell books had turned Alma into a sow, permanently. At Chambeaux & Deyer, we had brought the matter to a satisfactory resolution.

Robin had strong-armed the publishers, Howard Phillips and Philip Phillips, into recalling all copies of the spell book, printing an erratum sheet—and hiring the sisters to work in editing and production. The Wannoviches rapidly moved up in the ranks; Mavis was now senior production editor and Alma, despite being a sow, was senior acquisitions editor. Their meteoric rise was due in no small part to the success of the "Dan Shamble, Zombie P.I." adventures they had released.

Under my arm, in a reusable (and now ventilated) plastic container that had held Robin's lunch the day before, I carried the frog that had come out of Stentor's throat. Not knowing what to do with a pet frog, Robin had added some lettuce and a few berries, but the frog didn't seem hungry, or at least not interested in what she had put on the lunch table.

When I was a young boy I'd caught frogs and kept them in cardboard cigar boxes my dad gave me. I had never known how to feed them, and those pet frogs didn't last long. That was why I needed to solve this case as quickly as possible. I wasn't about to catch gourmet flies to feed this one.

Inside the clean, cold lobby of the publishing house, a young human receptionist waited behind a high desk that was like a fortress wall. Posters showed new releases, including two more Dan Shamble adventures, memoirs of various undead celebrities, and the obscure scholarly texts that had been the original fodder for Howard Phillips Publishing.

The company had announced a forthcoming special edition, a perfect facsimile of the Necronomicon to celebrate the twelfth anniversary of the Big Uneasy. I didn't understand what was so special about a twelfth anniversary, but they seemed very excited about the book, announcing a silver edition bound in calfskin, a gold edition bound in goatskin, and a platinum numbered, limited edition bound in human skin. The caption said, "Makes a perfect Valentine's Day or Walpurgis Night gift." I wasn't sure the marketing approach would be effective, but it wasn't my business.

I signed the visitor's log at the receptionist's desk. "I'm Dan Chambeaux, here to see Mavis and Alma Wannovich."

The receptionist looked at my sport jacket with its stitched-up bullet holes, my fedora, the bullet hole in my forehead, my grayish skin. She raised her eyebrows. "Sure you are. That's what *he* said." She nodded toward a man sitting on the black-upholstered sofa in the waiting area. He was apparently a zombie, or at least a human who had applied generous makeup to his face; he also wore a fedora and a crudely stitched sport jacket.

"He doesn't look a thing like me," I said. "Do you get imposters often?"

She continued to regard me with skeptical eyes. "I've gotten two today."

I opened my billfold and showed her my PI license, as well as my driver's license, which displayed my birth date, death date, and recertification of ability to drive. "Believe me, I'm the real one. Mavis will vouch for me, and Alma will give her snort of approval. I do have an appointment."

The receptionist made a phone call, talked briefly with Mavis's office, then hung up. Without apologizing, she gave me a guest badge. "Affix this to your jacket and pass through the metal detector, then go on up."

Publishing houses had been forced to add security measures because so many aspiring authors did not take rejection well. And when most of the would-be writers submitting manuscripts in the Quarter were monsters, editors couldn't take any chances.

When I sauntered through the metal detector, alarms immediately sounded. Pale and terrified, an armed rent-a-cop guard dashed in with his pistol drawn. It was hard to find good human security guards these days, and most applicants had watched enough movies to know that security guards and monsters didn't mix well. This rabbity guy looked ready to shoot first and ask questions (or at least fill out the forms) later.

I put up my hands and stood perfectly still—I'd already been shot several times today. Then I realized what had set off the metal detector. "It's just a bunch of bullets in my back." I had left my handgun back at the office, knowing it wasn't wise to carry a loaded .38—or a loaded gun of any caliber—into a publishing headquarters.

The guard kept his gun trained on me, his hands shaking. He seemed to think the frog in the plastic container might be some kind of concealed explosive.

I said, "Let me turn around slowly. I'll show you the bullet holes in my back."

I did, and the guard easily spotted the numerous tiny perforations. He frowned. "Did you get trapped in a BB gun shooting range or something?"

"Those are from Timmy guns," I said. "Lawn gnomes."

"Ahh." The guard kept his gun ready. "I can't let you through without special dispensation."

And that involved another phone call to Mavis, who finally came down in person to escort me through security and up to her office.

Mavis Wannovich was a big-hipped witch who wore a voluminous black muumuu emblazoned with stars. She also sported a traditional pointy hat perched on top of her nest of unruly black hair. Her hips weren't the only part of her that were larger than average, just the first thing one tended to notice.

"Mr. Chambeaux, I'm so sorry for the trouble." She scolded the guard. "This man is my dear friend, and it sounds like he's had a rough day. Did you say there are bullets in your back?"

"Small ones," I said, "but quite a few of them."

"We have a spell to take care of that." She took me by the arm and led me to the elevator, finally noticing the plastic container under my arm. "Oh, you brought me a frog. How sweet!"

"It's for a case I'm working on," I said, "something I hope you can help me with."

The elevator doors closed, and she punched the button for thirteen. Mavis's eyes lit up. "A case, how wonderful! Is it something we can include in a future novel?"

"Maybe. I don't know how the case will turn out yet." Even when I didn't find my investigations particularly interesting, Mavis claimed that the stories were marketable. So far, her instincts had proved correct.

Sheyenne insisted that the "Dan Shamble" series had generated business for Chambeaux & Deyer Investigations. "Advertising is expensive," she always said. "Publicity is cheap."

The elevator doors opened on the thirteenth floor, and Mavis led the way. "Just give us the bare bones of the story, and we'll make sure it's plotted well. My sister and I will include ourselves as glamorous characters, if we provide the key pieces of information."

She guided me to Alma's office, a large corner unit where the desk had been removed to accommodate an inflatable plastic kiddie pool filled with mud. Alma liked to sink her large body into the mud as she rooted through manuscripts. The big sow was nosing through stacks of paper, using her snout to riffle pages. With a snort, she knocked over an eight-inch-thick manuscript, giving her opinion on the book.

Seeing me, Alma rose from the mud with a squeal of delight. Mavis draped a bath towel over her sister's back, and Alma stepped out of the bath, daintily placing her trotters in a rinse tub.

"Mr. Chambeaux is here for his monthly maintenance. He's had a little wear and tear today." Mavis's eyes sparkled. "He also needs our help with *a case*. He brought a frog!" Alma added more sounds of delight.

I bent over to set the frog container down on a credenza, and Mavis studied my back, poking her fingers into bullet holes in the jacket. "These holes will require stitches. We can find a magical refabrication spell and run it in tandem with your maintenance."

"Only if it's not too much trouble," I said. "I do like the jacket."

"Of course you do. It's part of your image."

Alma gave an affirmative snort.

"Let's take care of your patch-up first," Mavis said. "Please take off your jacket."

I hung it on the doorknob.

"And your shirt, too, please."

"Is that really necessary?"

"Absolutely. You want to get rid of all the pellets, don't you? Otherwise you'll keep setting off metal detectors whenever you come to visit us."

I dutifully unbuttoned my shirt. I'm not a particularly glamorous specimen, and you'll never find me bare chested in *Zombie Vogue*. I function well enough, and all the patches have taken hold, but there's only so much you can do with multiple bullet holes. Fortunately, the small-caliber Timmy gun bullets could be smoothed over.

Mavis went to Alma's bookshelves and studied the spines. I didn't know how the sow managed to pull down volumes from high shelves, but the two witches worked closely together. Mavis opened a particular tome to a particular page. Her brow furrowed. She looked in the index, tried several other pages, and grinned. "Ah, a fabric repair spell! Yes, we can do them both at the same time."

She lit candles and set the book down on a low shelf, where Alma could see it as well. Then Mavis began chanting my usual monthly rejuvenation spell. The witches did it as a favor to me, in exchange for me granting them access to my case records, so long as the names were changed before any adventures saw print.

Mavis was chatty as her spell work continued. "By the way, I wanted to tell you the wonderful news. We just learned that our first Dan Shamble volume, *Death Warmed Over*, was nominated for the Shamus Award!" She grinned, no doubt waiting for me to express my awe and excitement.

"What's the Shamus Award?" I asked.

"Given by the Private Eye Writers of America. It's very prestigious, but I doubt we'll win because it's a very nontraditional novel."

"I'm a nontraditional detective," I said.

"It's an honor just to be nominated," Mavis pointed out. "And we can put it on the cover of the book. We've contracted with Penny Dreadful to continue the series, and she's doing a few online short stories, too."

Alma grunted a reminder, and Mavis snapped her fingers. "Oh, yes, I forgot to tell you! We're expanding our Undead Detectives line. We'll be introducing a whole new set of characters: vampire detectives, werewolf detectives, even a skeleton detective."

"And people will want to read those?"

"Most definitely. Those were the characters that tested highest on our marketing surveys. We also proposed a ghoul crime fighter, but apparently there's not much interest in heroic ghouls."

"I can understand why," I said.

When the two finished their spell, I felt a sudden staccato relief as numerous BB-sized projectiles popped out of my back and pattered on the floor like little ball bearings. "Thanks. I'm glad to have those gone."

Mavis removed my sport jacket from the doorknob and handed it to me with a flourish. "See, all the little marks in the fabric are gone. We left the original bullet holes in front, though. It's part of your debonair flair."

"It does remind me of getting gunned down," I said.

Now, to the case. I picked up the frog in its container and opened the lid to show the spotted creature looking up at us. I explained how Stentor's voice had been stolen, and that the frog had something to do with it.

"Like a catalyst. Hmm, I've heard of this," Mavis said.

That surprised me. "Really? Someone using a frog to steal the voice from an opera-singing ogre?"

"Not precisely that, but in general terms." Mavis pulled down other books from Alma's shelf and flipped through them. "This will be so much easier once we get all of our backlist digitized."

Alma rooted around the manuscripts on the floor, let out a satisfied squeal, and nudged a pile of paper toward us. It was a previously published and badly formatted book called *Esoteric Uses for Frogs and Toads.* I picked it up. "This could be what we're looking for."

Mavis also discovered an obscure reference in one of her other volumes, and when we compared it to the self-published book, we discovered that the enthusiastic amateur author had plagiarized entire sections. Regardless, the summary was the same.

"It appears that someone used the frog as a vehicle to steal Stentor's voice. It's something called the 'amphibious transference protocol.' "

"Does that mean you can find where his voice went? That voice is Stentor's livelihood."

Mavis nodded slowly. "We can confirm that the voice wasn't just lost. It *was* stolen, as you suspected."

"Is it gone, then?" I asked.

"No, someone else is using it, and this cute little frog is the key. Would you mind leaving the frog here for further study?

We can try to run a tracer spell, divine the future from the patterns in its spots, and see if we might find any sort of magical linkage with the fiend who stole Stentor's voice. Alma and I will take care of it, I promise."

The sow snuffled and lifted her head to inspect the frog in its plastic container. Mavis agreed with her sister. "Yes, it's intriguing—and absolutely adorable."

CHAPTER 7

Clients like to have updates, and I wanted to tell Stentor the ogre what I had learned, even though there wasn't much to report. I might have half a dozen cases going at any one time, and to each client *their* problem is the most urgent matter. Sure, finding an ogre's lost voice isn't like curing some terrible disease, or running an orphanage, or ending world hunger, but solving cases is what I do. Does everybody need a *world-shaking* purpose for existence?

I made my way to the Phantom's opera house, where I would find Stentor. Even without a voice, he would be practicing his singing, trying to convince his boss not to let an understudy take over the role of Don Giovanni, although I doubted anyone could fill the ogre's shoes (it would probably require six or seven feet inside each one).

Out on the streets, people were pointing up at the sky. Though the afternoon remained blessedly clear and blue, clouds gathered in ropy strands like vapor trails from high-flying jets. As I watched, the white smears bent around like finger painting in the sky. The vapor trails formed giant words, using the air above the Unnatural Quarter as a wide-open billboard:

VOTE ALASTAIR CUMULUS III
FOR CLIMATE CHANGE YOU CAN BELIEVE IN

Suddenly, a wild wind gust nearly blew the fedora off my head, but I grabbed it in time. I'd had a lot of practice recently. As the breeze strengthened, I could hear a thin whistling sound through the bullet hole in my forehead; I really did need to patch that up with mortician's putty.

Pedestrians shouted and ran, and the vengeful wind became so strong that two ghosts flitting along the boulevard were scattered apart, fighting to make their way. Outside an apothecary shop on a rack marked down for quick sale, several magic amulets jangled together, until the locomotive of wind barreled down the boulevard, knocked the stand over, and swept up into the sky.

A man in his late forties with a bushy brown beard and disheveled brown hair stood in the street wearing an eyeball-offending tie-dyed wizard's robe. He clutched a handheld sundial talisman at his throat and gesticulated with his other hand, drawing imaginary letters with his middle finger. At his feet crouched a black tuxedo cat that looked extremely annoyed at having its fur ruffled by all that wind. The cat stalked off in a huff, leaving the wizard to continue his antics.

Manipulated by the gust of wind, the words in the clouds were erased, then rearranged, replacing the name of ALASTAIR CUMULUS with THUNDER DICK. The tie-dyed wizard seemed delighted with his work. "Ha! Showed you!"

Seconds later, a competing wind blast came in from the opposite direction, scrambling the skywritten letters once more. The battling breezes tangled the vaporous campaign slogans into illegibility, and the wizard in the tie-dyed robe—Thunder Dick—strode away, both frustrated and satisfied.

As storekeepers picked up the mess in the wake of the gusty commotion, I knew we would all be glad when the election was over. . . .

The opera house was a grand old building built in an ornate Gothic style, with pillars, flying buttresses, pointed eaves, and numerous shadowy alcoves. Gargoyles had once adorned the façade, but the Phantom had chased them away for squatting, calling them deadbeats.

The Phantom was a bitter, humorless old man who had dreamed of a career in the opera, but possessed no singing talent. He was also hardened because of his loveless life, unable to find a girlfriend despite his frequent patronage of unnatural singles services. He blamed his romantic misfortune on his acid-scarred face, but many women would have overlooked that, given his stylish mask. No, it was the Phantom's prickly personality that made them place a moratorium on second dates.

Posters outside the box office showed a dramatic picture of Stentor the ogre decked out in his full Don Giovanni costume. The oft-quoted quote from the *National Midnight Star* graced the bottom of the poster: "The most fabulous performance by an ogre opera singer in weeks!"

A sticker across the top of the poster announced, *On indefinite hiatus.*

I went around back to the performers' entrance, where a vampire set director and three zombie carpenters in overalls lounged against the brick wall, chain-smoking. Mounds of crushed butts around their feet implied how long they had been standing out there.

The rate of cigarette smoking had skyrocketed among unnaturals, much to the delight of tobacco companies. One brand marketed specifically toward the undead was called Coffin Nails. What did they have to lose? It wasn't as if they had health considerations.

"I'm here to see Stentor," I said. "Is he inside?"

The vampire stage director gestured with his cigarette in a long, lacquered holder. Vampires loved their affectations. "Sure, he's varming up—but it's pointless. Just follow the sqveaks. You can't miss him."

I went through the back hallways of the opera house, where understudies mumbled to themselves, practicing lines. I heard female singing coming from deep below, wafting through the grates in the floor. It was a warbling voice, heart-wrenching in an operatic sort of way.

I knew the Phantom ran an academy for would-be opera singers down in a large sewer vault, where he kept his best pipe organ that had been relocated from Paris, piece by piece. He claimed that the sound quality down in the tunnels was perfect for his purposes. He had a portable Wurlitzer for other occasions.

I wondered if he had the same landlord down there as Jody Caligari, our junior mad scientist.

From behind a closed door, I heard singing, of a sort. It sounded like the lead vocalist from a chipmunk cover band having a bad voice day. The words were delivered in bombastic Italian in a dramatic fashion, but because they sounded as if they were sung by the Munchkin boys' choir, the effect was absurd.

When I knocked, the singing stopped, mercifully. The ogre's big eyes lit up when he opened the door to let me in. He grabbed a glass, upended it into his enormous mouth, gargled, and spat the liquid into a bucket, where it smoked and steamed. He cleared his throat, but his voice remained a squeak. "Mr. Shamble! Do you have news?"

I said, "You were right: Your voice was definitely stolen. Using a spell called an amphibious transference protocol, someone kidnapped your voice for his or her own purposes."

"But who did it? Can you track them down?" Stentor asked. "I want my voice back."

"I was hoping you could suggest the names of anyone who might have a use for your voice? Do you have any enemies . . . say, operatic rivals?"

He shook his enormous shaggy head. "It's a small field, Mr. Shamble. If one of my rivals started using my voice, everyone would know right away. We don't even have an understudy for my part in *Don Giovanni*. No one can handle it. The thief can't be anyone from the opera world."

I sighed. "I'll keep digging. Don't you worry."

Stentor began singing again, to my dismay. Even worse, he seemed to want me there to listen so he could draw moral support.

A man barged into his dressing room, decked out in a black tuxedo. The white porcelain mask that covered half of his face didn't manage to conceal his sneer. "Enough, Stentor!" He clapped a hand to his forehead, almost dislodging the mask. "I can't stand it anymore. I've taught many abysmally talented students down below, but you make their worst caterwauling sound like a superstar diva. We are done—do you hear me? *Done!*"

"Maybe you could find a different part for me," Stentor squeaked.

"No! I am canceling *Don Giovanni* as of today. The show is ruined."

"But," the ogre said, his inner-tube–sized lower lip quavering, "but you can't! The opera is my life."

"And the opera is my livelihood," said the Phantom. "And until your last name is 'Of The Opera' like mine, you're expendable. Since you don't have an understudy and can't sing anymore, I'm changing the docket. As of today, I'm starting auditions for a revival of *Cats*. We've been waiting a long time for a popular show, and I think the Quarter is ready for it."

"No!" Stentor wailed. "Not *Cats*. Just give me a little more time—Mr. Shamble here is tracking down my voice. He's the best detective in the Quarter."

"Best *zombie* detective," I said, always careful to define the parameters.

The Phantom dismissed me with a quick glance. "I thought he was just a fictional character. Well, when he finds your voice, maybe you can get some work as a radio voice-over artist. But not here in my opera house!" With a flick of his tuxedo tails, the Phantom swished out of Stentor's dressing room.

The ogre started blubbering, and tears flowed in rivulets down the canyons of his face. I tried to reassure him, patting him on the shoulder. "The only way you can make this better is to find my voice, Mr. Shamble," he said.

"I'm on it. I promise." I left the dressing room, heavy-hearted. I knew how much this case mattered to the big guy.

The Phantom stalked off and entered his own office down the hall, where a sign on an easel announced, "Auditions today." A yowling and caterwauling came from the room, and I saw half a dozen feline shapes run down the hall: Siamese cats, calicos, Persians, Russian blues, orange tabbies, Maine coons, even a tuxedo cat that looked like the one I had seen next to the tie-dyed weather wizard in the street.

When the Phantom announced auditions for *Cats*, it was like setting out saucers of cream. Felines from all over the

Quarter came racing in to practice their best Webberian chorus, instead of yowling on fences and in back alleys.

I left the opera house, not wanting to hear those auditions, and headed off to another case. Robin and I had an appointment at the Mad Scientists Patent Office.

CHAPTER 8

Suffering from the usual red-tape asphyxiation, the Mad Scientists Patent Office was a typical cookie-cutter government bureaucracy, despite its unusual and provocative name.

After Sheyenne tracked down the address, Robin and I drove off in her battered, rusty old Ford Maverick, which we affectionately called the "Pro Bono Mobile." By now the deteriorating muffler was loud enough to announce our presence to all passersby, drawing attention, but not in a good way.

Robin had owned the car since her law-school days, and she viewed the Maverick as a family member. "Once you've rolled over an odometer once or twice, you're invested in a car," she had told me.

Every month or so, when we brought the car in for yet another round of repairs, we talked about buying a more professional-looking business vehicle for Chambeaux & Deyer Investigations. Somehow that never went beyond talk.

In order to get a handle on Jody Caligari's case and the real worth of his confiscated items, we wanted a clearer picture of who he was and just how important his research might be. For a boy of twelve to have filed five separate patent applications said good things about him. The kid had an endearing personality and enough confidence that he could always become a pint-sized motivational speaker if the junior supervillain gig didn't work out.

The Mad Scientists Patent Office was a squarish building on the outskirts of the Quarter, located in a nondescript business park. The companies in adjacent buildings had likewise nondescript names such as Bovar, Inc., or AlbyTech, or Smith Associates, all of which offered indefinable services or products. The patent office occupied one of the larger units. Robin parked the Pro Bono Mobile in a spot marked, VISITORS ONLY. VIOLATORS WILL BE VIOLATED AND THEN PROCESSED.

We entered the office together. One entire wall was a white project board with magnets in different columns to indicate the progress of numerous patent applications. Three secretaries sat at desks, typing forms in triplicate on actual manual typewriters. Apparently, the patent office hadn't yet approved the use of desktop computers.

Deeper in the building, I saw cubicle after cubicle after cubicle, each one occupied by a quiet civil servant, displaying a demographically appropriate mix of humans, vampires, werewolves, mummies, ghosts, ghouls, and various demons, as well as a smattering of underrepresented unnatural minorities. The Bureau of Unnatural Labor Relations had imposed strict quotas, especially for government offices inside the Quarter.

A loud explosion came from the testing labs in the far back, accompanied by the hissing jets of a fire-suppression system. The clerks in the cubicles continued their work without even flinching.

We went up to the front desk, where the human receptionist ignored us as she filed paper cards in an actual Rolodex. We waited. Robin cleared her throat. The receptionist testily pointed to a bell on the countertop, where a sign said, RING BELL FOR

SERVICE. When I rang the bell, the receptionist smiled and greeted us. "How may I help you?"

With government agencies, every step of every process had to be done in a particular approved way.

"We're here to inquire about some patents," Robin said.

"Are you scientists?" She reached toward a rack of pigeon-hole shelves next to her typewriter, ready to withdraw an appropriate form.

"I'm a detective," I said, "and a zombie."

"And I'm an attorney," Robin answered.

"A patent attorney?"

"Just an attorney seeking justice for unnaturals."

The receptionist frowned at her selection of forms, drew one out, then slid it back in. She seemed at a loss. "I don't appear to have a form for unnatural detective and natural attorney with queries regarding patent oversight and office questions."

"We're here to inquire about the status of pending patents for a client of ours," I added.

When the receptionist continued to dither, Robin suggested, "Could we speak to your supervisor?"

That did the trick, providing the receptionist with an alternative she could embrace. "Yes, I'll call the DAMP." She pressed a buzzer button on her desk, and a woman in her late fifties emerged from one of the front offices. She was solid and hefty in a matronly sort of way, gray-brown hair in a no-nonsense perm, sensible glasses, a pantsuit. She might have been a zombie, but if so she was even more well-preserved than I am. Or maybe she'd been in her job for so long she had fossilized into the part.

"I am Miz Mellivar, Deputy Assistant Manager of Patents. How may I help you?"

Robin explained, "We're researching the background on patent applications filed by a client of ours, an ambitious young mad scientist named Jody Caligari."

The woman gave a small smile, which was no doubt the extent of her cordiality as a civil servant. "Ah, Jody! That boy shows great potential." She clucked her tongue. "He's not quite there yet, more ideas than follow-through, but he does have the imagination . . . and mechanics can be learned." She gestured us into her office. "Let's have a look. We're a busy office here, as you might expect. The Unnatural Quarter being what it is, every evil half-wit and his sub-genius brother thinks he can be a mad scientist. Someone has to impose standards. These days there's just too much mad and not enough scientist to go around."

Robin and I took seats in front of Miz Mellivar's too-neat desk. She swiveled in her office chair to reach a credenza behind her and pulled a rectangular file box onto her desktop. "People don't understand that a patent can only be issued for something truly new and innovative. We had one particularly clueless man in here last week trying to patent his evil laugh."

"You can't patent a laugh," Robin said.

Miz Mellivar rolled her eyes behind her glasses. "I know! We sent him over to the Mad Scientists Trademark Office, where he might have better luck."

She took the lid off the rectangular box and ran her fingers through a long line of index cards. She couldn't seem to find what she was looking for, flipped back and forth among the cards. "Please excuse the inconvenience. This is a very outdated system, but we're undergoing an upgrade. Within six to twelve months, we'll be using uniform manila file folders."

She had an idea and looked in a different section of the box. "Ah, I thought so! I filed under 'J' for 'Jody' instead of 'C' for 'Caligari, Jody.' Since he's only twelve, I think of him on a first-name basis."

The Deputy Assistant Manager of Patents looked at the reference number stamped on the index cards, got up from her desk, went to a large metal filing cabinet, found the correct drawer, and pulled out his patent applications.

"That young man has some very interesting ideas." She held up a legal-sized form. "This is for an Evilness Sieve, and this one is a Dark Powers Magnet. And this one"—she smiled gently— "X-ray Spex specifically tuned to see through the walls of girls' locker rooms. He even built and submitted a working prototype." DAMP Mellivar shook her head. "Denied, of course—nothing original in that patent."

Oddly, the X-ray Spex made me think that Jody was more normal than I had first imagined. "He is twelve," I pointed out.

Mellivar looked at the other cards and forms. "A Glove of Destiny, and finally a cape that flutters dramatically even indoors without wind."

"What was it all for?" Robin asked.

"Jody was trying to build a complete do-it-yourself super-villain kit, but couldn't find ideas that weren't covered at least peripherally by other existing patents. Villain territory is pretty well trampled here in the Unnatural Quarter, you know."

"So you declined his patents, then?" I asked.

"I didn't want to break the kid's heart, so I filed them under Pending Further Review. Now that his ideas are safely nestled in the bureaucracy, it could be a very long time before anything makes it through the red tape."

Robin frowned in disapproval. "How does any patent ever get through the system?"

"Sheer momentum." The Deputy Assistant Manager of Patents' voice took on a scolding tone. "But if a mad scientist tries to circumvent the system and create a monster or test a super-power or immortality treatment without going through proper channels, he'll find himself in deep slime. All new discoveries must be certified with our office's Mad Scientist Seal of Approval. Don't underestimate the power of this office. You've heard about the laws of physics—even *they* have to follow the laws of patents."

Robin got back to business. "Jody hired us, ma'am, because his work was confiscated by his landlord, who evicted him from his lab in the sewers. Before we begin legal proceedings and pressure the landlord, we wanted to know the merits of the young man's work, objectively speaking."

"He is only twelve," I said again, "and it's a pro bono case."

Miz Mellivar flashed that maternal smile again. "Oh, make no mistake, there's plenty of merit. The boy shows promise. I'd keep my eye on him. Give Jody a chance, and he could be truly evil someday."

CHAPTER 9

When we returned to the offices, Robin stopped just inside the door and wrinkled her nose. "What's that smell?"

"Welcome back to you, too," Sheyenne said as she flitted around from behind her desk.

My olfactory senses are not what they used to be, but even I noticed the aroma. "It does smell like something is off—very off. Has a new client come in?"

Sheyenne was unwrapping packages of evergreen-shaped air fresheners, the kind you normally hang from the rearview mirror of a car. She had purchased an economy-sized multipack. After hanging one of the fresheners in my office, she levitated to affix one to the light fixture in the conference room, then came back out. "The smell's been getting worse for days—a fishy stench like slime and sewage mixed together, bubbling up from down below. I've been trying to mask the odor, but it's a losing battle."

Robin frowned. "An odor that strong could drive away business."

"Or, around here, it might *attract* a certain sort of clientele,"

I said. "I'll go downstairs and have a look. I've been meaning to check out the new entrance into the sewer labyrinth anyway."

Sheyenne asked, "Do you want to take a bottle of wine or some cookies to welcome the new neighbors?"

Robin suggested, "Or some nice air fresheners?"

"Let's start with a bit of recon. Since we don't even know what species they are, I'll just say hi if the new neighbors happen to be down there, and do a little investigating."

Back down on the first floor, I followed the hall to the normally closed door labeled BASEMENT ACCESS. Chambeaux & Deyer had kept offices in this building for years, but I'd never investigated down there. Unnaturals have a highly developed sense of privacy, and it's not polite to go snooping in other people's basements. You never know what you might find there.

Now, however, the door was unlocked, and Mr. Renfeld had added ACCESS FOR TENANTS ONLY PLEASE and another sign, CONSERVE MIASMA. PLEASE CLOSE THE DOOR BEHIND YOU.

I entered the stairwell, dutifully pulling the door shut behind me. Oily fumes wafted up from the lower levels, and a standard Exit sign glowed above the door. The steps creaked as I descended, an intentional add-on for atmospheric effect.

I reached the sublevel and walked along the corridor where I saw the closed doorways of the four recently renovated apartments. The doors were numbered, –1, –2, –3, –4. There were no names listed. I could hear burbling sounds from behind one, eerie snake-charmer–style music from another. The other two were quiet.

At the end of the basement corridor, I discovered the source of the stench—and it wasn't the new tenants. A door leading into the Unnatural Quarter sewer levels was propped wide open with a doorstop. The odors of the underground labyrinth swirled in, undeterred, and the stink was rising up to the second floor and beyond.

I kicked loose the doorstop and closed the door tight. Problem solved. Once the underlevels aired out, that should stop most of the stench.

From my glimpse of the sewers, it certainly didn't seem like a place where a mad scientist could concentrate on his work, but for some reason evil geniuses preferred the redolent underground tunnels. I knew I would be going back there soon to track down Jody Caligari's landlord. First, though, I wanted a little more background. And I knew exactly where to get it.

It's good to have a friend in the real-estate business, even if that friend is a troll. Even if he lives in a cemetery. Even if his main business offices are inside a crypt left untenanted when the former owner rose from the dead and surrendered the property.

I had first met Edgar Allan the troll when I retrieved a stolen painting by a ghost artist. Since then, he'd been a good resource for certain types of information, and he had used me for real-estate leads. An ambitious agent with a wide range of properties to sell, from haunted houses to no-longer-needed cemetery plots, Edgar Allan was always looking for customers. I thought he could help me out now with Jody's case.

Robin was ready to use any legal means at her disposal to get justice for the young genius, to retrieve his possessions and his security deposit, as well as restore his laboratory space— preferably with six months' rent as punitive damages. But when you dig deep in the Unnatural Quarter, you often find more than you expected, and I wanted some background about the sewer slumlord before we provoked him.

I hadn't visited the Greenlawn Cemetery for a while, and I saw that the grave plots had been neatly mowed, fresh bouquets arranged in vases, and even a playground added. Edgar Allan had been working hard to make this place a respectable post-life community, to keep the customers happy, and to increase property values.

I easily spotted the crypt that served as his home office. Streamers with colorful plastic triangular flags fluttered in the breeze. Balloons bobbed up and down, and a sign said, MODELS NOW OPEN.

Edgar Allan had turned his own crypt into a show home. As I shambled up to the front door, his business partner, Burt, an ugly troll who served as an eviction specialist when necessary, lumbered out carrying a stack of OPEN HOUSE TODAY signs. He grunted a greeting to me. Burt was a troll of few words and many teeth. He could be a rough customer, but we were on the same side. Usually.

Spotting me, Edgar Allan scurried out the front door of the crypt. "Mr. Chambeaux! How can we meet your real-estate needs?" He was a much smaller troll than his partner, with fidgety hands and simian features, grayish skin, pointed ears, pointed nose, and a pointed face. He continued to chatter, as if he feared he would lose a sale if he let me get a word in. "I have some fine new properties to show you. Lovely locations. I've been following your adventures, by the way. I see the novels on the best-seller lists."

"Those aren't exactly my adventures," I said, aware that it was a losing battle. "They're just—"

"Now that you're such a famous zombie detective, you really should upgrade your office space. Chambeaux and Deyer Investigations could be the flagship of an entire new business park. I'm an investor in several that are under construction."

Even with the smells, though, I was comfortable with our current location. "Thanks for the offer, but I'm a creature of habit. You're our guy if we ever decide to move, but that's not in the cards just yet. We still have two years left on our lease."

"Plenty of ways out of that, Mr. Chambeaux, provided the customer's motivated."

"We're not at all motivated at present," I said.

He looked saddened but accepting. "That's often said about

zombies, I'm afraid. Lack of motivation. Well, if you do find someone who's in the market to buy or sell, be sure to pass them along."

"I always do," I said.

Before I could blink, he whipped out a stack of business cards and pressed them into my hand. "If you need more, tell me."

I still had hundreds of his cards back at the office, but it was more polite to accept them than to turn them down. Edgar Allan used a fast and cheap online printing service that produced his cards by the millions.

"I need some background information for a pro bono case Robin and I picked up. We're fighting a wrongful eviction. Our client was kicked out with no warning, and all his possessions were confiscated."

Edgar Allan invited me into his headquarters crypt, so we could discuss the matter. "I've been on both sides of these sorts of conflicts, Mr. Chambeaux. Although the evicted tenant may seem to be a poor, downtrodden victim, landlords are often the oppressed ones. Renters will trash a place, move out in the middle of the night, and then complain about not getting their security deposits back when they've left the place a shambles."

I lowered myself into a chair next to his desk. "That's not the case here." The stone walls were graced with framed photos of Edgar Allan shaking hands with satisfied customers, celebrity visitors, and lots of smiling people I did not recognize. "Our client is twelve years old, and he had a mad scientist laboratory in the sewers. I was hoping you might know the landlord, give me a little background—confidentially, of course—before I start turning the thumbscrews."

The troll froze. His large yellow eyes blazed like lamps. "A landlord . . . in the sewers, you say?"

"Yes, I hear laboratory space there is at a premium, a waiting list a mile long."

Edgar Allan said cautiously, "Oh, there are units for rent, but priced out of the market. Evil crime lords and supervillains like to have their bases underground, but the only real landlord in the sewers is . . . you don't want to mess with that one, Mr. Chambeaux."

"I've been hired to do exactly that," I said, on guard. "What can you tell me about him?"

"He's taken over the underworld. His name is"—Edgar Allan paused as if afraid to say it, and then spoke quickly— "Ah'Chulhu!"

"Gesundheit," I said.

The troll nervously shuffled papers on his desk. "No, that's his name. Ah'Chulhu. A demon with a bad disposition, and he's one of the worst. A burbly, tentacle-faced type. He's been taking over the sewers, buying up property. He wants to be the real-estate agent for the whole underworld."

It could just have been professional jealousy I was hearing, but Edgar Allan seemed genuinely frightened. "Ah'Chulhu's been expanding his holdings, selling off some of his less desirable properties. You might have seen the flyers he mailed out advertising his crazy sale, the End of Days Days?"

"I never look at the sales flyers, just throw them right in the recycler. What do I have to worry about with this Ah'Chulhu?"

"Everything," Edgar Allan said.

"I mean specifically."

"*Everything*, specifically," the troll said. "I wouldn't go near him. He owns those sewers, has gator-guys for henchmen, mutated alligators that were once flushed down toilets and now they walk upright, though still with a slouch. If your client has run afoul of Ah'Chulhu, he'd better just slink away."

I frowned. "That's not how I like to solve cases."

"Maybe you should worry more about surviving this case than solving it."

I didn't point out that I was dead already, but young Jody Caligari had more to lose. "Thanks for the warning. Good thing I stopped by."

I was glad I hadn't let Robin barge right in and stir up trouble. I'd met tentacle-faced demons in passing once or twice before, and they were definitely not warm, fuzzy types. They preferred cold and slimy.

"Beware of Ah'Chulhu," Edgar Allan warned me again. "But if you see him, could you give him one of my cards and ask if he'd be interested in co-representing a property or two?"

CHAPTER 10

After I got back to my desk, I had barely started investigating various underworld laboratory subdivisions managed by Ah'Chulhu Underground Realty when a smiling McGoo entered the offices. "Just walking my beat and decided to stop by to see my favorite lawyer and zombie detective." When Sheyenne flitted in front of him, he quickly added, "And ghost. Any crimes you need to report?" He sniffed several times, looking around. "What's that smell?"

"Evergreen Fresh?" Sheyenne suggested.

McGoo sniffed again. "No, nothing with the word *fresh* in it. Have you started decomposing again, Shamble?"

He's my best friend, but never seems to get tired of the same old joke. We were very close as humans, and McGoo did his best to cope with the fact that I'm a zombie, and that often involved off-color humor. He wasn't inclined to learn from his mistakes, and he never passed up an opportunity. "Hey, Shamble—what do you call a zombie without arms or legs hanging on a wall?"

"Art," I said. I had heard that one before.

"Okay, what do you call just an arm hanging on a wall?" He waited a beat. "A piece of Art."

We all groaned as expected, but not enough to encourage him to tell another one. I tried to distract him. "Any luck catching that lawn gnome gang?"

"They're still on the Quarter's Most Wanted list," McGoo said. "We don't have any leads as to their hideout, but we know they'll strike again."

"I'll keep an eye out. I'm working several cases right now, but there's no telling what I might hear on the streets."

Our cases often intersected. I helped McGoo with my unofficial investigations, using contacts that didn't require department approval, and McGoo could pull in the resources of the UQPD when I needed a favor. We had cracked down on the golem sweatshops together and the rumble among werewolf gangs; he had rescued me from the back of a truck when I was coffin-swapped with a vampire entering the witness protection program, and he'd helped me arrest two kleptomaniac gremlins terrorizing a vampire circus. We weren't keeping score anymore, and sometimes he even managed to kick loose a consultant's fee when we did particularly good work for the department.

He wasn't usually so obvious when he came in asking for a favor—unless it was something personal. "So what's up, McGoo?"

"Oh, just wanted to check if you'd be at the Goblin Tavern tonight."

"That's a safe assumption. Got something on your mind?"

"If I do, will that make you want to eat my brains?"

"Very funny. With you, that would just be empty calories."

He groaned. "And you say *my* jokes are bad. See you at the Tavern—first round's on you."

It usually was.

"Sure, see you there." I smiled and waved, but I felt troubled as he left. Something was definitely bothering him.

I had no particular interest in the weather wizards' campaign, except for how the rapid pace of climate change affected us all. Then the campaign landed right on our doorstep when Thunder Dick entered our office.

The weather wizard entered our offices accompanied by a gusty breeze. His tie-dyed wizard robes rippled around him, and his long brown hair and beard were windblown, probably an occupational hazard. He had a small portable sundial hanging on a thin chain at his neck.

The annoyed-looking tuxedo cat walked at his feet, always on the verge of being trampled, always a half step away from tripping his master—on purpose, it seemed.

"I am Thunder Dick," the weathermancer said, as if expecting cheers at a campaign rally. "The Quarter needs my services as best weather wizard, and I have my heart set on public service." He brushed down wiry strands of his beard, which sprang back out. "Can I count on your support?"

He withdrew a campaign poster from one of his voluminous multicolored sleeves and unrolled it. He showed off his picture with the bold campaign slogan, "Be a Dick Supporter!"

Sheyenne said, "We don't endorse candidates. I'm afraid we can't let you hang your poster here."

Robin came out of her office. "It's against our policy to take sides. For legal reasons."

"And good business practices," Sheyenne added.

The weather wizard was surprised, and he fumbled with the poster, trying to roll it back up again. "Oh, that's not why I'm here! I want to hire you to investigate nefarious shenanigans that my opponent is perpetrating upon my reputation."

"Then you've come to the right place," I said, still not knowing what he meant. "We specialize in the investigation of the perpetration of nefarious shenanigans."

Relieved, Thunder Dick unrolled his colorful flyer again. "The Quarter needs a good Dick. This is one of my intact campaign posters, but malicious vandals—no doubt hired by my opponent—have been defacing them all around the Quarter, tearing off the bottom word." He was indignant. "Instead of saying, *Be a Dick Supporter,* the poster just reads, *Be a Dick,* which is much, much worse."

I said, "Well, not *much* worse." Having seen their previous skywriting duel, I assumed the vandalism was just the usual campaign rivalry. "Do you have any proof that Alastair Cumulus the Third is involved? Would you like me to go to your opponent's campaign headquarters and have a talk with him?"

"Campaign headquarters? Ha!" Thunder Dick snorted. "He's so stubborn and arrogant, no one would work for him. He's running his campaign all by himself—unlike me."

"So you have your own campaign headquarters?" Robin asked. "And staff?"

"I have my cat." He reached toward the cat at his feet and tried to scratch his head, but the animal deftly avoided his touch. "This is my familiar, Morris."

In a disdainful voice, the cat said, "It's *Maurice.*"

Embarrassed, Thunder Dick chuckled and explained to us, "That's just an affectation. He fancies himself an artist."

"I *am* an artist, whether you can see it or not," the cat said. "Just another reason why I loathe you."

The weather wizard seemed embarrassed. "We're bonded, but sometimes being in such close proximity day after day, especially with the high-pressure campaign . . . well, you can understand how he might get testy. I don't know what I'd do without Morris."

"Maurice," the cat corrected again, dodging his master's hand as the wizard tried to pet him. "And someday, Richard, you will find out what you'd do without me. Every afternoon when I nap in the sun, I dream about a life in which I'm not stuck with you!"

Thunder Dick let out his nervous chuckle again. "Morris likes to act out."

"Definitely," the cat said with a barely concealed hiss. "You don't know half the places I pee in your apartment, or the secret little gifts I leave for you when you don't clean out the litter box often enough." The cat looked up at us. "Why couldn't I have had an intelligent master? Or even an *interesting* one? Bad karma. I must have done something miserable in a previous life."

Thunder Dick's continued laughter had an edge of embarrassment. "Oh, Morris, you're so silly!"

Disturbed, Sheyenne bent down to the cat. "But if you're his familiar, why do you dislike him so much?"

The cat answered, "Because familiarity breeds contempt."

We all nodded in sudden understanding. "Aah," I said.

The weathermancer commanded our attention again. "Now, now, we don't have to worry about my personal squabbles. Morris is on my side, no matter what he says. I need you to investigate the nefarious shenanigans being perpetrated by Alastair Cumulus. It's not fair!"

With the competing snow, fog, rain, and wind—not to mention the nonstop and tedious coverage that filled all of the competing weather networks, twenty-four hours a day—I was more than a little jaded about the election so far. I had to ask, "And what about your own campaign tactics, Mr. Dick? Would your opponent make the same charges against you? Each side seems to have its share of mudslinging."

Robin added, " 'He did it, too' is not a valid defense—it's been challenged in court."

Thunder Dick lifted his chin and sniffed. "I assure you I've done nothing untoward whatsoever."

"He's done nothing *noteworthy* whatsoever," snorted the cat.

I said, "We'll look into your case, Mr. Dick. Is that what we should call you?" I couldn't imagine it was his real name.

"It's a long story."

The cat impressed us with an extravagant yawn. "And if his *name* is a long story, you can see the challenge he has getting his message across."

Robin had retrieved her special legal pad, and the magic pencil was poised to take notes. She said, "As a client, you benefit from our full nondisclosure agreement. Whatever you say to us will be kept in strictest confidence. Your identity will remain a secret."

"Oh, I didn't say it was secret. Just that it's a long story. My real name is Richard Thudner, and when I became interested in weathermancy I needed an impressive stage name. All the good ones were taken, though, like Stormin' Norman and Misty Weathers. At first I tried Lightning Dick."

The cat interrupted, "I told him that was a bad idea."

The wizard grinned. "I even had a catchphrase about the speed of my weathermancy, 'Nobody comes faster than Lightning Dick!' "

I winced. "Not a good slogan."

The weather wizard sounded defensive. "It's supposed to mean when you need a weather wizard to come to the rescue—you know, drought, tornadoes, what have you—nobody comes faster than—"

I shook my head. "Still not good."

"That's what I said," the cat repeated, "but he wouldn't listen."

"Thunder Dick is better anyway. A play on my own name. Thudner—Thunder. Get it?"

"Right away," I said.

"Would you like to sign up for my newsletter?" he asked, sounding too hopeful. "The *Dick Insider*."

Robin cleared her throat and somehow maintained her professionalism. "If we're going to work on your case, Mr. Thudner, maybe we need more general information about the entire election."

I agreed. "As in . . . what is the election all about? What are the two of you even running for? Most of us don't have a clue."

Thunder Dick looked dismayed. "People are so disinterested in politics these days. Surely you've seen the campaign? Aren't you aware of the issues?"

"We know that you and Alastair Cumulus are running against each other, but I don't think we're even allowed to vote in the election."

Thunder Dick blinked. "Of course not—it's for members only. You aren't weather wizards."

Sheyenne said, "That's why we haven't paid much attention. It's not relevant to us."

"Not relevant? But weather affects everyone's daily life."

"Especially lately," I added. "Thanks to your campaign."

Thunder Dick explained, "Every four years there's an election to pick who will be the next leader of Wuwufo."

"Sounds like a head cold," I said.

"It's a very respectable organization. The WWFO—the Weather Wizards Fraternal Order. Very influential. Meteorologists and weather forecasters all over the world look to our guidance, but only active members of Wuwufo are allowed to vote. And choosing the most powerful weather wizard is a heavy responsibility. I'm the right candidate to lead Wuwufo, obviously."

"Obviously," said the cat, then yawned.

"I suppose Alastair Cumulus the Third has a different opinion?" Robin asked.

"My opponent lies! That's why he has to resort to nefarious shenanigans. Once you prove that he's cheating, I'll have the election all sewn up."

Robin's magic pencil, apparently bored, began to doodle on

the yellow paper of the legal pad. "We agree that elections should be untainted and that a campaign should be run cleanly. Fair and square. We'll take your case, Mr. Thudner, and look into the purported shenanigans."

The client is the client, and I don't make judgments. I had surreptitiously tailed Harvey Jekyll to get evidence for his wife Miranda's divorce settlement, I had exposed a Shakespeare ghost as an arsonist, and even solved a case of accidental embezzlement in an illegal cockatrice-fighting ring.

Exposing dirty campaign tricks shouldn't be too hard.

CHAPTER 11

At the end of a long day, even zombies like to sit down, relax, and put their feet up. I particularly liked to put my feet up on the rungs of a barstool—and particularly at the Goblin Tavern. It was my favorite watering hole, a place I'd frequented even back in my human days. McGoo and I met there almost every night. It was a habit, not because we didn't have anyplace else to go, but because we genuinely enjoyed the atmosphere and the camaraderie.

At the Goblin Tavern everybody knew your name, as well as your species and your beverage of choice. McGoo and I had our regular barstools; on the rare occasions when we left them empty, Francine, the tough-as-nails human bartender, did her best to keep them available, just in case we came in.

McGoo was already there when I arrived and had settled back to contemplate the remaining half of his first tall beer. The fact that he had ordered one for me—and paid for it, despite his earlier teasing—told me he was preoccupied. We had always been able to tell each other anything. I hoped I could help him out with whatever was bothering him.

"Hey, Shamble," he said as I approached my usual stool.

I worked my stiff muscles to climb aboard. "Hey, McGoo. Thanks for the beer."

"So, Robin tells me you've got a mad scientist kid as a new client. Reminds me of a joke—what did Dr. Frankenstein get when he put his goldfish's brain in the body of his dog?"

Seeing he was troubled, I promised myself I would laugh, just to make him feel better. "I don't know, McGoo—what *did* Dr. Frankenstein get when he put his goldfish's brain in the body of his dog?"

"I don't know, but it's great at chasing submarines."

I managed a dutiful chuckle, then got down to business. "I'm concerned, McGoo—so out with it. What's eating you?"

He looked at his hands, turned them over. "No bite marks that I can tell."

I just waited. He had called me here with a problem, and now he was avoiding talking about it. No one had ever accused Officer Toby McGoohan of being too sensitive or too eager to share his feelings—not that I was prone to oversharing either.

"It's Rhonda," he finally said.

The name conjured up many feelings and memories, as well as blotted-out memories, in my mind. "Which Rhonda?"

"Mine," he said. "I mean the one I was married to."

That clarified things. I took a sip of beer to give me time to process.

Back in our younger and more foolish days, we had each married a woman named Rhonda (different women, just to be clear about it); I chose a strawberry blonde, and he chose a brunette. In those days, the future was bright, and romance was in the air. McGoo and I were ambitious, optimistic—and utterly naïve. The Rhondas made us both miserable, and we each realized we had made a terrible mistake. They say good friends do everything together, and McGoo and I both divorced our wives named Rhonda.

For a time I thought my mistake was that I had simply picked the wrong Rhonda, but after a very brief fling, I realized that McGoo's Rhonda did have precisely all the bad qualities that had driven him nuts. I half-suspected that McGoo might also have dated my Rhonda after our breakup—if I was too dense to learn my lesson, then he was just as dense.

There are some things guys avoid talking about.

When we were both single again, living the decidedly mundane and unglamorous bachelor life, we each eventually made a fresh start in the Quarter. After I got killed on a case years later, my start didn't turn out to be so fresh after all. But the two of us were still at it.

"So, what's up with Rhonda?" I didn't really want to know how she was doing, but I would be as supportive as necessary.

"How is she doing?" McGoo asked. "When people from the past turn up like that, it's not usually because they want to share their lottery winnings." He finished his beer in one long succession of swallows and set the glass down. He seemed to be bracing himself.

I signaled Francine. "I've got the next one."

The bartender came over, looking as young and fresh as a preserved meal from World War II. "Boys, you're gloomy tonight," she said as she poured McGoo a new beer. I was still nursing mine.

"Don't we always look that way?" I asked.

"It's part of your special charm," she said.

Francine was human, in her late fifties, and a lifetime of cigarette smoking and heavy drinking had added a decade to her appearance. But she was as sturdy as a statue and drew upon plentiful experiences to offer her special brand of counseling to any natural or unnatural customers who came into the Goblin Tavern. She had worked in biker bars, broken up knife fights, shouted down drunken werewolves, and memorized fifty different froufrou martini recipes. (In the Goblin Tavern, though, she had more opportunities to break up snarling fights than to mix fancy martinis.)

After she served us, Francine went back down the bar, where she was paying a great deal of attention to an old balding vampire who was missing his left fang. She seemed engrossed in his conversation and laughed too often, and I noticed that she had on more makeup than usual. I sniffed the air and realized she was wearing heavy perfume, too. Francine seemed to be actively appreciating the attentions of old One Fang. Good for her.

"Child support," McGoo said.

I was startled and turned my attention back to him.

He said, "Rhonda's asking me for child support."

Now that was a surprise. "I thought we told each other everything, McGoo? I didn't even know you had kids."

"One kid," he said, "apparently. A daughter. I didn't know about it either."

"But you've been divorced for ten years."

"Almost eleven," said McGoo. "Not that I was counting. In fact, I'd put the whole thing out of my mind. But our little girl is ten years old; apparently it happened right around the time of the breakup. How's that for a gotcha? There was a time when we actually tried to have kids but couldn't. I realize now that would have been a bad idea, but it might have changed the whole marriage picture."

I was troubled. I had set aside all my thoughts of Rhonda—both Rhondas—for a long time as well. I tried to think of how I would react if my own ex-wife showed up with a surprise like that after so many years. I think I'd have preferred almost any other kind of surprise—even a serial-killer-popping-out-of-a-closet-with-a-butcher-knife kind of surprise.

"And she didn't think to mention it before now? A daughter . . ."

Down the bar, Francine laughed very appreciatively at a

joke made by the old vampire. She laid her fingers on his arm in a casual gesture.

McGoo shook his head. "I agree. It's not like her. Maybe she didn't want me involved in the girl's life. Maybe she's embarrassed?" He shrugged. "How do I know? I could never figure out what she was thinking back when we were married."

"So what are you going to do about it?"

"I'm not going to duck my responsibility. I've gotten off scot-free for almost eleven years, but I'd at least like to meet my own kid. So I told Rhonda to come here to the Quarter, and I'd pay her in cash every month if she wanted it. She never called back."

He slurped his beer. I had to hurry to catch up with him.

"So now I wonder about everything," he continued. "What if there isn't even a daughter, and Rhonda was just after money but thought better of it? She knows I wouldn't fall for a scam."

"Rhonda wouldn't try something like that," I said. In fact, some of my memories of her, very brief ones, were sweet. But what do I know? I'm obviously not a good judge of character.

The Tavern doors opened and a mummy shuffled in, all stiff-legged, entirely wrapped in bandages, peering through a thin slit in his face wrappings. With the ponderous, determined gait that mummies often exhibit (partly due to supernatural determination and partly due to being hindered by so many bandages), the mummy lumbered past the pool tables, walked right in front of the dartboards where two zombies were playing a round, hurling projectiles with bad aim, most of which didn't even manage to hit the wall. One dart struck the mummy, but with the wrong end, so it bounced off and clattered on the floor.

Although the bar was mostly empty, the mummy shuffled directly toward us. He reached the stool next to mine, contemplated its height, then worked his way up onto the seat, adjusting his legs, then his bandages, then his arms.

Seeing the customer, Francine touched old One Fang's arm one more time, then came over to serve the mummy. In a voice muffled by bandages, he gestured clumsily toward our beers. "I'll have what they're having."

"Coming right up, hon," Francine said.

The mummy leaned closer to me. "Nothing like a good cold beer at the end of a day. I always seem to have a dry throat."

I wondered how he intended to drink the beer. Maybe let it soak the facial bandages and then slurp it through?

Francine stood at the tap and looked over at the vampire. "And how about you, hon. Can I freshen your drink?"

One Fang lifted his nearly empty glass and swirled the ice cubes with a rattle. "Absolutely, my dear. Another B positive on the rocks. And make it a double. I plan to stay here for a while."

She giggled and picked up a pint glass, ready to pour the mummy's beer, but he started laughing so hard he almost fell off the stool. "Hold that, bartender. I was just kidding!"

He began laughing harder and I thought I recognized the muffled voice. With clumsy fingers he loosened the gauze wrappings and began to unwind them until a shock of red hair poked up. "I so fooled you guys!"

As soon as I saw the freckles on the forehead I knew it was Jody.

"Told you I was a master of disguise," he said, "not just an evil genius in training. That lady was about to pour me a beer without even carding me."

Francine frowned, not knowing what to do. "Mummies are usually thousands of years old. They get offended when I ask for ID."

I lifted a hand. "It's all right, Francine. This kid is a client of mine. He's a very bright young man." I added a stern edge to my voice. "In fact, he's smart enough to know better."

"I was just testing you," Jody said as he finished unwrapping the bandages. His grin was infectious. "Have you made any progress on my case? I don't have much time left at Junior Mad Scientist Camp, and I want to get my certificate."

After I introduced Jody to McGoo, I told the young man that we had checked out his story at the patent office and that I'd gotten some information about his landlord. "Is Ah'Chulhu as bad as I've heard?"

"He'll be no match for you, Mr. Chambeaux," Jody said. "You'll wipe those tentacles right off his face."

I wasn't sure that was exactly the tactic I would use.

McGoo said, "A demon *and* a real-estate agent. Sounds nasty. Nastier than a surprise message from Rhonda, I guess."

"Let's wait and see what she does, McGoo," I said. "I'm here for you." Then I turned to the kid. "Tomorrow, I'm planning to go down into the sewers and meet your landlord face to, uh, face."

Disasters, however, can disrupt the best-laid plans.

CHAPTER 12

I don't know what I'd call the heart of the Unnatural Quarter, but the sewer tunnels were definitely its intestines. And, continuing the anatomical metaphor, the sewers occasionally exhibited symptoms of intestinal distress—possibly caused by a subterranean storm from either Thunder Dick or Alastair Cumulus III. The tunnels beneath the streets of the Quarter roiled and gurgled and resulted in citywide incontinence.

Thankfully, the Chambeaux & Deyer offices were on the second floor, but even so our plumbing went into conflict mode. Pipes thumped, gurgled, and regurgitated smelly brown effluent in runny staccato spurts.

Sheyenne was in our kitchenette preparing to brew a pot of coffee when the nasty liquid spewed out of the faucet. She drew back in disgust, looked at the sludge in the carafe. "No coffee today, Beaux."

I wrinkled my nose at the brown liquid in the pot. "I've had worse at the Ghoul's Diner."

Police sirens wailed through the streets. Outside, manhole

covers popped up like tossed coins as the underlevels flooded. A fire hydrant exploded, spraying a geyser of brownish water. Three ghoul children ran out into the streets laughing, playing, and splashing in the unexpected downpour.

With a yelp, Robin emerged from our employee bathroom, fleeing the sounds of bubbling and splashing. "The toilet's backing up." She held a plunger as if she were a knight about to go into battle. "And it's not backing down."

I relieved her of the plunger, since I'm more equipped to handle dangerous cases, and went in to tackle the situation. "Plumbing doesn't solve itself," I said. As a zombie, I could be relentless and determined, and if I needed to plunge for hours, I would. I worked and worked, but even our industrial-strength toilet plunger had no effect. The sheer sewage force was beyond me.

"We're going to need a lot more air fresheners," Sheyenne said. "Bigger air fresheners."

Sludge continued to leak out of the bathroom and into the main offices. We called the building super, but Mr. Renfeld said he was "backed up at the moment."

I said, "When you agreed to partner with me, Robin, did you ever imagine our business would be so glamorous?"

Robin wiped sweat from her forehead. "I had dreams of fighting man's inhumanity to inhumans, making a mark . . . but this is just making a *stain*." She found a container of Kleen Wipes and did her best to disinfect her hands.

The phone rang, and Sheyenne answered politely and professionally, even in the middle of an actual shit storm. "Chambeaux and Deyer Investigations?" She brightened and handed the phone to me. "It's Ramen Ho-Tep."

I took the phone, already concerned. My former client had once been the pharaoh of all Egypt (as he constantly reminded anyone within earshot), but after Robin had successfully emancipated him from bondage as a museum exhibit, Ramen Ho-

Tep remained there as a special guest speaker, giving popular presentations and dramatic lectures about daily life in ancient Egypt. The mummy became quite a celebrity, and the exhibit held many priceless sarcophagi, papyrus scrolls, and souvenirs he retained from his ancient life, including one of his mummified cats.

"Mr. Chambeaux, I need your help!" he cried, his dry voice so brittle it was about to break from the strain. "The museum is flooding, all the exhibits, and my nice, clean bandages! Please come and save me."

"On my way. Just hold on," I said. Anything for a client. I grabbed the car keys for the Pro Bono Mobile, called to Sheyenne and Robin. "You two stay here. This could get unpleasant."

"I already don't like the smell of it," said Sheyenne.

I drove through the streets, fishtailing through standing puddles and shooting up rooster tails of murky water. The old tires were bald, and water leaked in through small holes in the floorboards. I had to divert from a side street, where I could see the flow rippling across the intersection. Up the block, I watched brown water gurgle down into storm drains and manholes.

The Metropolitan Museum was a fortress of ancient architecture. It held the usual natural history exhibits that had been there since before the Big Uneasy, but the museum was famous for its archive of magical items, cursed objects, stuffed creature specimens, artists' interpretations of demonic manifestations, Civil War uniforms (oddly enough), and volunteer corpses or other undead who took turns being on display as a sort of performance art.

The museum was located in a low-lying part of the Quarter, and now all the crap drained downhill, pouring through the gutters, along the streets and intersections, directly toward the museum.

In front, a team of gargoyles and golems were working furiously like unnatural ants to stack sandbags in a barricade. Additional gargoyles flew in on their black batlike wings to deposit more sandbags for the golems to redistribute. Other golems formed a bilge-brigade of buckets, scooping and dumping water outside, although it flowed back in.

After parking the car, I splashed forward, again reconsidering my stance against wearing galoshes, and spotted McGoo on the stone steps. Other policemen were doing their best to guide the work crews and to discourage curious bystanders. Public service warnings on all the competing weather stations told everyone to stay inside.

McGoo was glad to see me. "We've deployed plumbing-response vehicles all over the Quarter, but we need every hand we can get. The museum is flooding, and they're doing everything they can to save the Necronomicon."

He accompanied me inside, and we hurried along the museum corridors. Workers were frantically mopping and shoveling sludge that oozed through the halls. The original, and collectible, copy of the Necronomicon was featured in the main gallery on a shielded pedestal. The popular exhibit brought great amounts of revenue to the historical society, but because the book was so important, and dangerous, numerous security systems had been built around it. The book couldn't just be moved and propped on a higher shelf. Right now two docents and their interns were piling towels around the pedestal, while a third official-looking man tinkered with the locks and security systems.

"Is the book safe?" McGoo asked.

The official-looking man glanced at us. "For now. We were preparing to move the volume anyway, since Howard Phillips Publishing needs access to the original for their special twelfth anniversary facsimile edition." He shook his head. "I'm glad the book didn't leave the museum, though—there's no telling how much damage it might have suffered in the publishing offices."

I thought that if the smelly flood managed to get as high as the thirteenth floor of the Howard Phillips skyscraper, we would have a lot more problems than just saving the Necronomicon. Then I remembered all the slush-pile manuscripts Alma had been reading, and I knew she had enough material to build a solid barricade around the precious volume.

"Ramen Ho-Tep called for my help," I said. "I've got business in the Egyptian wing."

"Number one or number two?" McGoo asked. I don't think he was suggesting there was more than one Egyptian wing. He jogged along beside me. "I'm at your side, buddy."

He soon regretted his decision as we began wading in sludge water, sloshing forward to the exhibit room, where I could hear a breathy and despairing series of moans.

Ramen Ho-Tep, a small-statured and shriveled old mummy, stood up to his waist in backed-up brown water. His ornate sarcophagi now bobbed on the surface of the liquid, drifting along. The vitrine cases holding the papyrus scrolls had collapsed, and hieroglyphic-covered sheets floated like discarded grocery lists. (Maybe that was what they were; I couldn't read hieroglyphics.)

In his sticklike arms, Ramen Ho-Tep held a small pet-sized sarcophagus painted with an iconic representation of a cat. When he saw me, his ember-like eyes lit up within their sockets. "Help, Mr. Chambeaux! Everything else is ruined—can't lose Fluffy, too."

Wading forward, I relieved him of his mummified cat and its case. McGoo began gathering up the floating papyrus. Canopic jars bobbed about like discarded milk bottles.

"This is even worse than the Nile floods of September 4016

BC," Ramen Ho-Tep said. "Every object here is worth a fortune, even though I got some of it in mausoleum sales."

On the wall of the Egyptian exhibit, I noticed that Ramen Ho-Tep had tacked up one of the posters for the weather wizard elections: *Be a Dick Supporter!*

McGoo helped the mummy slosh out of the main chamber toward a set of stairs that led up to the next level, so that he could stand on the relatively dry landing. His bandages were soaked, waterlogged, and stinky (like everything else around us). He was shivering. "I was made for an arid climate. Even in the worst slums of ancient Cairo, we never had sewage problems like this."

Then a loud, crisp voice rang through the hallway. "My foggy bottom! I arrived just in time—Alastair Cumulus the Third, here to save the day."

I recognized him from his campaign posters, advertisements, and the weather network coverage of the Wuwufo elections. Cumulus flounced forward in his sky-blue wizard's robe. He had golden brown hair and a thick beard that split in a wide fork, each prong of which curled up from his chin like long tongues. His hair was a mop of tight curls, as if freshly permed. He walked up to us. "Alastair Cumulus the Third, pleased to meet you. I'm running for Wuwufo president. I hope I have your vote."

"We can't vote in the elections," I pointed out. "We're not weather wizards."

"My foggy bottom! Of course you're not, but that doesn't mean I can't be a hero anyway. A good Wuwufo leader cares even for the little non-meteorological people."

"How generous," McGoo said with clear sarcasm. "But we've got this under control."

"Oh, I don't think you do, Officer." Cumulus twirled one prong of his beard. "Better leave the matter to a professional."

He glanced at the drenched and stained mummy, then peered into the flooded Egyptian exhibit. "I believe a drought is in order."

He licked his finger and held it up as if to test the direction of the wind inside the hallway. Satisfied, he stepped down the steps, waggled his fingers—and the puddles of effluent parted in front of him. He concentrated, twirled his fingers in the air again, and frowned further. "Something seems to be resisting my efforts." He looked around. "Ah, I see what it is. A worthless distraction."

With a gesture, he parted the brown sea so he could walk through the exhibit without getting damp. The sludge flowed back together behind him. He reached the wall by Ramen Ho-Tep's private sarcophagus and, with a flourish, tore down the "Be a Dick Supporter!" poster on the wall, ripped it in half with great verve, and let the pieces float on the water. "There, now I'm unencumbered."

He raised his hands, and bright light emanated from the ceiling and the walls. The air became parched, and the puddles of standing foul water receded, drying to an unpleasant film that covered everything. Roiling mists swirled around the chamber, but they, too, dissipated as Alastair Cumulus maintained his drought spell.

At last, the Egyptian wing was protected. Ramen Ho-Tep was also dried out, though still stained. "You're a hero, Mr. Cumulus the Third!"

The weather wizard fondled his beard again. "Of course I am. And while I was at it, I took care of the rest of the museum, too." He glanced at the stained mummy, then at McGoo and me. "See how much I care for the Unnatural Quarter? I hope you'll support me in the election."

"My girlfriend was a Dick supporter," said the mummy, "but after this, I wouldn't vote for anyone else."

I knew that Ramen Ho-Tep had a long, long, *long*-term relationship with Neffi, the mummy madam of the Full Moon Brothel. I hoped the relationship was strong enough to survive an in-family political disagreement.

"You are a hero," McGoo agreed, taking the weather wizard's arm. "Now let's go see what else we can rescue around town until the sewers settle down."

CHAPTER 13

Whatever had caused the intestinal distress in the sewers passed quickly. The waters receded, the manhole covers drifted back into place, and the underworld labyrinth became quiet and peaceful again.

Nevertheless, I decided to postpone my expedition to the underworld to find Jody Caligari's lab and speak with his intractable tentacle-faced landlord. I wanted to give the effluent a little time to settle.

Back in the offices, Robin was queasy as we worked to clean up the mess. The toilet had finally backed down, and the water running out of the sink faucet returned to its usual murky color. Even so, it was going to take a long time and a lot of Evergreen Fresh to get back to normal. We opened all the windows, but the rotten smell of the outside air seemed even worse, yielding a net loss in freshness.

After hours of scrubbing stains out of the carpet, and a fresh downpour washed down the streets (for once I didn't complain about the vagaries of the weather), I decided we had to go. "It's time for an expedition down where the sun don't shine."

Robin gathered some documents and placed them in a manila folder. "If we're going to confront Ah'Chulhu, I want to let him know personally that his case has no chance of winning—especially not when he's up against *me.*"

After the recent upheavals, however, I wanted to pay attention to the grim warnings Edgar Allan the troll had given me. I said, "Robin, you're an impressive attorney, and I wouldn't want you anywhere but on my side and at my side—but this is not a job for a human. The sewers are growing restless, and there's no telling what's lurking down there."

"Jody had his lab down there," she pointed out. "He's just a boy, and he commuted to work every day."

"True, but that kid is an evil genius supervillain in training. You're just a lawyer."

"Some people might say there's not much difference," Robin said, but I could tell from the tone of her voice that she was having second thoughts.

Sheyenne offered, "I'll go with Beaux. Nothing sticks to me."

That seemed the best solution. Sheyenne followed me down to the basement level. The downstairs tenants were all still closed in their apartments, but I went straight to the sewer entrance. "Did you bring the address for Jody's lab?"

"Of course." She waved a sheet of paper. "I even downloaded directions in case we get lost. We can take the main sewer thoroughfares or, if there's a clog, I have an alternate route through the subsurface streets."

Through the door and down into the tunnels. I stepped into the gently flowing water, took care to find solid footing, and waded along while Sheyenne drifted ahead of me. I had to squint in the dim greenish glow of the tunnels. My eyesight hasn't been the best since I rose from the dead; I think the bullet hole through my skull affected my vision, but I hoped I didn't need glasses.

As we passed under drainage openings from the streets

above, rivulets of water splashed down; one culvert let in a wide, gushing flow. Sheyenne proved she could find beauty in even mundane things. "Look, a waterfall!"

Nothing gets Sheyenne down. She sees the bright side of life, and afterlife, even though she's been through enormous difficulties—having to support herself after her parents died, taking care of a younger brother who turned out to be a genuine dick (and no thunder about it), trying to make it through med school, supporting herself by singing in a monster nightclub, where she'd been poisoned.

Our time together as humans had been all too brief, but it was good, a solid relationship with a lot of potential. I should have spent more time with Sheyenne, but there'd been no more time to spend. . . .

Now her ghost led the way, assessing the tunnel intersections, flitting ahead to double-check. Many of the catacombs didn't have street signs, making navigation difficult. I plodded along, refusing to ask for directions. Far off, I heard the warbling notes of a pipe organ, but distances were deceptive in the labyrinth.

We were lost for a while, but at an open sewer pipe Sheyenne found a family of mutant brown rats—a single mother and five children. The rats explained where we had gone wrong, and we set off again in search of the laboratory district.

"If the lab doors are locked, I'm willing to break them open and retrieve Jody's stuff," I said. Another reason to do this without Robin, because she sometimes has inconvenient ethical objections to straightforward solutions. "Depending on how heavy the equipment is," I added, picturing giant turbine engines, Van de Graaff generators, specimen tanks, chemical supplies, toxic waste barrels. "We'll get the kid's possessions back, one way or another."

Sheyenne had a wistful tone in her voice. "I still remember

when you went to my old apartment to box up my belongings after I died. How sweet."

"That was a hard day for me, Spooky."

She had died of toadstool poisoning. I'd remained in the hospital room with her because she had no one else. In her painful glimmers of fading life, she made me promise to find out who had murdered her—and I wanted to kill the bastard for taking away this woman who meant so much to me.

After she was gone, I went to her apartment to gather up her few things—sadly few, for she had collected very little in her life. But I wanted to keep every speck that was left of Sheyenne. Afterward, I went hunting for her killer—and ended up dead myself. Funny how things don't turn out the way you expect them to. . . .

We finally found the right address after crossing a side channel and reaching a raised section of the sewers. It had vaulted ceilings, nice stone walls, and occasional graffiti, which I couldn't read because it was written in ancient arcane languages.

We found the entrance to Jody's old lab. I could still see the large hand-painted letters of JODY CALIGARI on the door, but they had been covered over with masking tape, beneath which was a new neatly stenciled name, NEUMANN WENKMANN, M.A.D.

"Looks like Ah'Chulhu's already rented out the space," Sheyenne said.

"Never too late to be just in time," I said. "Maybe Jody's possessions were put into storage. We can worry about finding him a new lab after we get everything back."

I knocked on the door, pounded louder, but heard no answer. Buzzing, clacking sounds came from inside, along with electrical discharges and bubbling, foaming bursts. Sheyenne drifted through the door and opened it from inside. "He can't hear you knock," she said. "The experiments are too loud."

The new tenant had set up an ambitious mad scientist lab, a forest of beakers and connected glass tubing, fractionation tubes over Bunsen burners. Pumping bladders were connected to motors; crackling lightning bursts traveled up the prongs of a Jacob's ladder. Boxy computer banks displayed multicolored lights blinking in a chaotic order; oscilloscope screens plotted sine waves and double sine waves. (They might have been arctangent waves, for all I knew; I was never good at trigonometry.) The bleeping, humming equipment spat out an endless curl of punched paper tape.

The units were so new that some of the cellophane wrapping remained in place. Sales tags and price stickers were affixed to the sides, many components not even installed. Neumann Wenkmann, M.a.D., must have bought the whole modular setup like a man with too much money and a sudden passion for a new hobby. Deluxe laboratory kits like this were available from Lab Depot warehouse stores.

Wenkmann bent over one of the modules with a screwdriver, adjusting a pair of fittings, taking readings, and frowning at the screen. He slapped at the side of the unit, grumbling in frustration.

Sheyenne flitted up to him and said, "Boo!" Although it's what ghosts are expected to do, I had never seen Sheyenne play such a dirty trick before.

Wenkmann nearly jumped out of his skin. He whirled, holding the screwdriver as a weapon. He wore spectacles and a bleached white lab coat that didn't have a single fresh stain on it. His plastic pocket protector held six neatly spaced retractable pens. "Who are you? How did you get in here? Are you from the cable company?"

"We're here on behalf of the former tenant of this lab," I said. "Jody Caligari."

"Oh, he's not here anymore." He set the screwdriver down.

"I was expecting the new cable installation service—and my phone. Do you do installations?"

"Afraid not," I said.

Wenkmann looked disgusted. His thick brown hair stood up in unruly shocks, as if he had discharged his new electrical apparatus without properly grounding it first. "They said they'd be here between noon and five, but they're late. I can't wait here all day."

"How long have you occupied this lab space, sir?" I asked.

"Just moved in yesterday morning, and I've barely had time to unpack. I'm expanding from my home laboratory, since my wife says the workbench clutters up too much of the basement. This is my new secret lair."

"Secret lair with a lease." I raised my eyebrows.

"My man cave. And it's better than the garage."

"When you leased the place, did the former tenant leave any of his possessions?" I pressed. "We believe our client's research was unlawfully confiscated, and he hired us to retrieve it."

Wenkmann shook his head, looking around the laboratory. "No, it was perfectly empty, everything clean and tidy, scrubbed down with bleach. It could have been the site of a mass murder."

"Our client's not a serial killer," I said, "just a supervillain in training." I hadn't really expected to solve the case so easily. "We'll have to speak with Ah'Chulhu ourselves, then."

Wenkmann looked disturbed. "Good luck. I've only met him once, when I signed the lease. He offered me an End of Days Days special, first and last month's rent covered—but he didn't say covered *in what*—and for the term of the lease he wrote 'Imminent.' "

He went over to another box, removed the lid, and lifted out a detached hard drive and a computer monitor. "But I was happy to get it. Good sewer lab space is at a premium—and expensive." He sighed. "Still, moving is an awful lot of work. I really need to get some minions. Say, do either of you know how to hook up a computer system? I've got my stereo, too."

Sheyenne and I politely bowed out. We had other demons to face: We would have to find and confront Ah'Chulhu.

CHAPTER 14

We left Jody's former lab before Dr. Wenkmann could press us into service unpacking boxes or hooking up the office sound system. Sheyenne and I headed into the sewers in search of Ah'Chulhu's main real-estate offices.

As we moved into the dank tunnels, I said, "Told you I'd show you interesting things and exotic places, Spooky."

Sheyenne's ethereal form flitted beside me as I sloshed along. "I'm not complaining. And you're the one getting his feet wet. I should get you a pair of galoshes."

"Edgy private eyes don't wear galoshes."

"No, but people with dry feet do."

We strolled through the Laboratory District, where numerous underground tenants conducted sinister and imaginative experiments with varying degrees of success or disaster. Maniacal chemists worked on immortality formulas, super-strength serums, transformative potions, horrific nerve toxins, and even sentient ambulatory wads of phlegm. Biological specialists occasionally joined forces with their chemistry colleagues to build monsters, transplant heads, clone brains, and mutate naïve volunteers who hadn't read the fine print before signing their release forms. Engineering mad geniuses tinkered with gadgets and built killer robots, death rays, teleportation rigs, and garage spaceships. According to rumor, there were preserved alien bodies down in one of the sewer labs, but that had turned out to be a false statement used to drive up the property values.

We passed three empty labs with signs on the doors that said, FOR RENT. CONTACT AH'CHULHU UNDERGROUND REALTY, with a phone number. No price was listed. When I tried to call the number, however, I got no cell reception down in the catacombs—and no one seemed to have a landline. Sheyenne found an old pay phone, but it was submerged beneath three feet of murky water, where it could only be used by amphibious creatures. I didn't have a quarter anyway.

At one of the empty labs, Sheyenne picked up a folded brochure that described the full catalog, with photos, of available laboratory properties and a description of the wonders of the underground. The ad touted, "Phase Two coming soon. Massive expansion expected. Now you can own sewer-front property."

Creatures skittered along the catacombs. Escaped lab rats with prehensile tails and bat wings swooped low through the tunnels, squeaking. Slithery things gurgled just beneath the surface, minding their own business and paying little attention to a zombie wading past.

Shrieking and chattering, four lime-green rhesus monkeys gamboled along, grabbing pipes in the brick ceiling overhead, as another mad scientist ran out of his lab after them. "You come back here! You're not done with your tests."

I wondered how many half-finished experiments had gotten loose and run amok down in the sewers. It was a real melting pot down here... or maybe a chamber pot was the better metaphor.

A shrunken troll-like creature hunched in a tiny canoe, paddling along; he passed me by without saying a word. The back of his little boat was filled with groceries.

Perched on a platform at an intersection, four frog demons much like Lurrm wore red-and-white-striped suits and straw boater hats, and sang an eerily harmonious barbershop quartet. They had placed a hat on top of a floating lily pad to appeal for donations, but so far they had raised only a few coins. I peeled a dollar from the soggy mass in my waterlogged wallet and dropped it in the hat.

"We're looking for the offices of Ah'Chulhu Realty," I told the frogs. "Do you know where we could find them?"

The four amphibious demons sang out in rising barbershop harmony, "No, no, no, *noooo!*" Then the tenor gestured with a squishy fingertip. "But you can try over there."

We thanked the amphibious creatures and moved on. Behind us, a flying mutant lab rat swooped in front of the quartet. Just before they began to sing, one of the frog demons lashed out with a long, sticky tongue, grabbed the creature out of the air, and swallowed it in a big gulp.

We asked several other underdwellers about Ah'Chulhu, but they all seemed too frightened or too stupid to be able to answer (by my guess, the numbers were running about fifty-fifty).

Sheyenne shook her head. "It doesn't make good business sense for a real-estate agent to hide his office. How does he know we're not customers looking to rent his lab space?"

"Typical tentacle-faced demon," I said. "They believe they're omniscient and omnipotent, and they think everyone else should be, too."

"I'll bet that makes them score low on customer-satisfaction surveys," Sheyenne said.

We passed under an overhang where a misshapen ghoul played a mournful banjo; then we turned down another tunnel that seemed dimmer, more sinister, and homey. The greenish catacomb glow was augmented by flickering lights in ceiling cages.

"Ah'Chulhu!" I yelled out, and my words echoed in the damp air like a succession of diminishing sneezes.

Something stirred in the water around me, which would have been alarming even under normal circumstances—not that there was a *normal* circumstance in which I would have been wading through the sewers in the dark. Rough, scaly figures drifted close, looking like lumpy logs. They came from three different directions.

Sheyenne hovered next to me. "I don't like this, Beaux."

I braced myself, removing my pistol from its holster, where I had managed to keep it dry. "It's not my favorite thing either."

Three hideous creatures rose up, standing erect and covered with scales, dripping greenish brown water. They had muscular arms, thick claws, and long snouts that bristled with teeth. Their golden eyes had reptilian slits. I hoped they weren't muggers.

I faced them. "You look like crocodiles playing dress up."

The three creatures looked at one another, confused. "Crocodiles?" one said in a deep voice that sounded like a belch forming a word.

"Not stinkin' crocodiles!" said the second, deeply offended.

"We're *alligators*." The third tapped the extended end of his face. "Note the snout."

"How can we help you?" Sheyenne asked.

"We hear you're looking for Ah'Chulhu. We're his lieutenants."

"If he's a real-estate salesman, why does he need lieutenants?" I asked. "Why not additional sales associates?"

"Told you," muttered one of the gator-guys to his companions.

"Lieutenant sounds better," said the second one. "And we can't spell associates."

"Can you spell lieutenant?" I asked.

"L-O-O . . ." Then the creature gave up and shook his head. A second tried. "L-U-T."

"Not right either," I said.

"Damn this reptilian brain," said the first gator-guy. I started thinking of them as Moe, Larry, and Curly.

"We'd like to see Mr. Ah'Chulhu about one of his laboratory spaces," Sheyenne said in a crisp professional manner. "But we can't seem to find his office."

"We'll escort you," said one of the gator-guys.

"That's it! We're escorts. E-S-K-O-R-T-Z."

"Don't strain yourselves," I said.

The indignant gator-guy—Larry—said, "Cut us some slack. We had a hard childhood. All of us were cute little alligator pets with wonderful lives, a nice home, little boys who played with us."

Moe said, "But we got too big and too hungry, and when the families lost a few pets—"

"And a little sister, in my case," said the third gator-guy, Curly.

"They decided enough was enough and flushed us down the toilet," said Moe. "Abandoned us. We were homeless, frightened and alone in the sewers. But Ah'Chulhu took us in, raised us, gave us jobs as sales associates."

"Lieutenants," said Larry.

"Escorts," said Curly.

"He's a civic-minded demon," said the first gator-guy. "So many reptiles get flushed down into the sewers that he opened up his own orphanage, where Ah'Chulhu cares for all the innocent scaly creatures. He raises us right."

"Sounds like a real inhumanitarian," Sheyenne said. "We can't wait to meet him. Can you take us?"

"We insist," said the gator-guys.

Pressing close, they turned at an intersection of underground corridors and led us onward.

CHAPTER 15

The gator-guys were precisely as intelligent as I suspected. As thuggish lieutenants they were frightening enough, but as effective sales associates they weren't particularly warm and fuzzy. (Most reptiles aren't.)

As escorts, they totally sucked.

Larry, Moe, and Curly got lost three times trying to lead us to the headquarters of Ah'Chulhu Underground Realty. We headed down one tunnel to find a bricked-up dead end; then we passed a large effluent drainage pipe that didn't look familiar to any of them. After a long, hissing consultation, the gator-guys turned around and backtracked to the main intersection, where we finally found the barbershop quartet of frog demons again.

Moe looked down at his scaly palm, on which he had written an address with ballpoint ink. "This is in case I forget where we live." He held his hand up to the frog demons. "Do you know where I can find this street?"

"Turn left," sang the first member of the amphibious barbershop quartet.

"Then right," sang the bass.

"Then right again," sang the baritone in a rising register.

"And then LEFT!" sang the tenor.

The gator-guys were overwhelmed by the information, looking down at their submerged feet. I suspected they had *left* and *right* marked on their shoes to help them keep track, but they couldn't see through the murky sewer water.

"We'll take it from here," I said and headed off in the lead, letting the three gator-guys hurry after me. I could tell Sheyenne was growing impatient.

We finally reached a cavernous grotto, which was like a sunken cathedral—Ah'Chulhu's main office complex. Moe, Larry, and Curly led us through an arched opening into the huge chamber, where mushrooms grew on the walls, and flying bat-winged rats swooped around the ceiling like hummingbirds. Dozens of erect gator-guys kept themselves busy next to frog demons and other slithery things.

The center of the chamber held a raised and ornate stone dais carved with ancient writings, starfish-headed creatures, and hieroglyphics laid out in patterns like crossword puzzles. On top of the dais, the awe-inspiring tentacle-faced Ah'Chulhu sat upon his porcelain throne.

His smooth gray head was rounded like the abdomen of a fat spider, and it glistened with a thin coating of ultra-gloss slime. His widely set eyes blazed a baleful red, but the lower half of his face was a distraction of quivering tentacles that extended from nose level all the way down to his chest, like a beard of eels. He had human arms and legs, and wore a dapper gray business suit, sharp-creased gray dress slacks, white shirt, and a blue power tie. He primly crossed one leg over the other.

Seeing us, Ah'Chulhu half-rose from his commanding white throne. His voice echoed out with a deep resonant power, as if thrumming partly from another dimension. The oddest part of all was that he spoke with a pronounced Australian accent.

"G'day, mates! Welcome to my grotto. Here to talk about real estate?"

Ah'Chulhu's facial tentacles twitched, and I had no idea whether or not he was grinning. He gestured with a human hand toward one of the frog demons. "You there, go throw another tadpole on the barbie for our friends! Then we can get down to business."

I stood in my damp and rank sport jacket, adjusted my fedora, which I considered part of my business attire even though I had no use for a hat down in the sewers. "I'm Dan Chambeaux, zombie private investigator, and this is my associate, Sheyenne." Unable to resist, I turned to the gator-guys next to me. "Associate: A-S-S-O-C-I-A-T-E."

"I knew that was how to spell it," said Curly.

Moe snickered. "He said A-S-S!"

I turned my attention back to the tentacle-faced demon. "We're here on behalf of a client, regarding some mad scientist laboratory space."

"Ah, so you're lookin' to rent? I'll be a waltzing Matilda!"

"What's with the accent?" Sheyenne asked. "It's a little overboard."

Ah'Chulhu said, "This is my natural voice. I'm from down under."

Now it made sense. "A young man rented lab space from you so he could work on some very important research projects that would have let him conquer the world."

"Or destroy it," Sheyenne added.

Ah'Chulhu was unimpressed. "That's what they all say. Crikey! I don't want any dramas. Who is this person you're talking about?"

"Jody," I said. "Jody Caligari."

"Oh, the kiddiwink! Cute bloke," Ah'Chulhu said. "He'll never get far in this world looking like that. Much too normal."

"A person can't help how he's born looking," Sheyenne said.

The comment seemed to sting Ah'Chulhu. His face tentacles twitched, and he looked away. "I remember the ankle-biter. Talks heaps, but he's charming in a human sort of way. Never should have rented to him in the first place, though. Crikey, he's irresponsible!"

I said, "He claims you evicted him without cause and confiscated his possessions."

"I confiscated his possessions all right—just might have to sell 'em at auction to get back the money he owes me. No matter what he told you, the little bugger was not evicted without cause. There's a waiting list on those labs, you know."

"We did see several empty ones for rent."

"Offers pending."

I pressed the issue. "So Jody's possessions are intact?"

Ah'Chulhu reached over beside his porcelain throne to tap one of several rectangular lockers piled up beside him. "Everything is right here, safe and sound, but these items aren't going anywhere until he pays his back rent and late fees."

Now that was new information. "We didn't know about the late rent," I admitted. I wondered how much else Jody had neglected to tell us.

"Three months behind," Ah'Chulhu said. "Bugger, I was perfectly within my rights to evict the kiddiwink and get a new, more reliable tenant."

"I can't believe you signed a lease contract with a minor in the first place," Sheyenne said. "Jody's only twelve."

Ah'Chulhu let out a long sigh that blew his facial tentacles outward. "First you complain that I evicted your client, and now you're upset that I signed a lease in the first place? Crikey, what are you, a lawyer?"

"No," I said, "but our partner is."

The assistant frog demon came over to us holding skewers

of barbecued tadpoles, but Ah'Chulhu held up a hand. Now he seemed pissed. "Bring those to me. This isn't a social visit anymore, and these aren't potential customers."

The frog demon hopped over to the porcelain throne, and Ah'Chulhu snatched the skewers. The snakelike appendages on his face plucked the crispy tadpoles off of the skewers and drew them into his hidden mouth. After slurping noisily, he tossed the skewers to the side.

"Real estate is a bonzer cutthroat business," Ah'Chulhu said. "And property values are going up. I'm a businessman specializing in unreal estate, and I'm within my rights to hold the kid's toys until he pays." Now he pressed his hand firmly on the locker beside the throne, as if to keep the confiscated objects from escaping. He leaned forward, his facial tentacles squirming. "I might suggest you move your offices underground, just so you can be prepared."

"Prepared for what?" I asked.

"You never know." He sounded suddenly crafty. "The Big Uneasy was just a start. There's an upheaval coming, then a downheaval. Sooner or later, the whole Quarter is going to be worthless slum territory. It'll be bloody glorious!"

"We already have our own real-estate agent," I said. "I'll bring you his card next time."

Ah'Chulhu commanded the three gator-guys, "Escort our visitors back home."

"Yes, escorts!" said Curly.

I decided to play it safe. "We can find our own way." Sheyenne and I turned to leave.

CHAPTER 16

When we called him back to our offices to explain himself, Jody looked embarrassed and guilty, as only an innocent twelve-year-old kid can do. The self-proclaimed "master of disguise" showed that he understood the seriousness of the situation by arriving as himself rather than pretending to be a vampire with orthodontia and a swirling black cape, or a fuzzy werewolf with tufts of glued-on fur applied all over his face and head. He was just a kid with mussed-up red hair, mournful blue eyes, and a blush that almost, but not quite, obscured his freckles.

"I thought I'd have a little more time," he said. "Junior Mad Scientists Camp will be over in a few weeks, and my work is sheer genius. You went to the Mad Scientists Patent Office yourself."

I said with the ponderous patience that zombies are particularly skilled in, "Miz Mellivar says your work shows promise, but that's not quite the same as sheer genius."

"It's where genius starts," Jody said.

Floating close, Sheyenne said, "Creative types aren't always good in business matters."

"Maybe I just need a younger sidekick with a different set of skills," Jody said. "Someone trained as a mad accountant . . ."

Robin took a seat next to the boy, who sat on the office swivel chair, shuffling his sneakers. "The fact is you didn't pay your rent, Jody. As evil as Ah'Chulhu may be, as a landlord he has certain rights."

The kid's lower lip trembled. "I didn't pay the rent because I had already spent all my allowance. When my parents paid the registration fee, all expenses were supposed to be covered—but that just included food and a tiny dorm room. Students still have to buy our own specimens, lab materials, and pay our electric bills—that adds up to a lot! I didn't have enough allowance left over to pay rent." He flashed his bright smile. "But I was planning to make millions from my patents when they come through."

"They're in process," I said. "It could take a while."

Jody continued to fidget. "Do they expect me to wait my whole life for an answer? I might not hear back from them until I'm *thirteen*. With all those patents, I was going to change the world."

"By becoming a supervillain?" I raised my eyebrows.

"It's a goal to aspire to. An all-powerful supervillain would certainly change the world. And I wouldn't have to be an *evil* supervillain."

"That does sort of go along with the territory, kid," I explained.

Now Jody seemed indignant. "Please don't call me a kid, Mr. Chambeaux. I'm Dr. Darkness!!!—with three exclamation points. Or I will be, as soon as I finish my homework."

He brought out sketches that showed his planned costume,

his weapons, his superpowers. Jody had hand-drawn a comic strip showing a kid-sized costumed fighter, complete with a form-fitting suit and a cape.

I looked at the comic sketches with great interest. "In order to be a hero like that, you've got to keep yourself in good physical shape. You're welcome to come with me to the gym sometime. All-Day/All-Nite Fitness."

He brightened. "Golly, thanks, Mr. Chambeaux."

Sheyenne considered. "Good and evil are a matter of perspective, especially here in the Quarter. It gets confusing when monsters are the good guys—and we've dealt with humans who were decidedly the villains."

I was reminded of the intolerant "humans only" Straight Edge group who were willing to commit genocide on all unnaturals, or the grim and constipated Senator Balfour who tried to ramrod the passage of his repressive Unnatural Acts Act.

"It just sounds better if you don't call yourself a supervillain," I suggested to the kid.

Jody seemed confused. "I thought girls liked the bad boys."

Sheyenne grinned. "He's got you there, Beaux."

We told Jody that Ah'Chulhu was keeping all of his inventions and possessions safe in a locker beside his porcelain throne. The boy seemed relieved about that at least.

"Those were my prototypes," Jody said. "My Evilness Sieve, my Dark Powers Magnet—even the suit itself. I've done a lot of costuming, but the sewing and fitting is always the hardest part." He pointed down to his sketches, unable to contain his excitement. "And I added a special auto-wardrobing function. Another work of sheer genius! Didn't you ever wonder how villains and heroes get into their costumes so fast? With Dr. Darkness!!!, all I'd have to do is snap my fingers and the suit leaps onto my body. It feels a little funny, especially when it crawls up my legs, but it saves a lot of time."

"I'll bet it does," I said.

Robin added, "The patent office also said that you invented some kind of X-ray Spex, but those infringed on other patents."

Jody flushed an even brighter red. "Those were for, uh, something else."

Robin led the young man into her office to strategize. He had managed to track down a copy of his lease, which she wanted to review thoroughly. I supposed that a tentacle-faced demon from a line of Elder Gods would be able to hire the best lawyers, but if anyone could find a loophole, Robin could.

The amount of rent had been based on the property value of prime mad scientist laboratory space, and that wasn't cheap. The outstanding rent was probably more than the allowance the boy was likely to receive for the rest of his life. Even if the patent office approved every one of his evil inventions tomorrow, he was still looking at a long time for product development, test marketing, and finally, retail distribution.

Regarding the legality of the contract, Jody's parents had signed a waiver when their son attended Junior Mad Scientists Camp, and Ah'Chulhu's lawyers had somehow amended that to apply to the conditions of any lease signed during camp outings. Worse, the terms granted the landlord partial ownership of any intellectual property developed during the camp's recreational activities.

Jody might imagine himself a scientific genius, but he really needed to read his contracts better. Or maybe invent some kind of high-tech contract nullifier.

Robin went over the document with him, clause by clause, which Jody found more grueling than a hundred spelling tests or English essays. Much as my heart went out to the kid, though, I had other cases to work on. I still had to find an ogre's voice and get to the bottom of nefarious campaign shenanigans.

I took my fedora and glanced out the window to check what this hour's weather was: gray, cloudy, and drizzling slightly. I pulled on my freshly laundered sport jacket, grateful that Sheyenne had found a new one-hour post-sewer dry-cleaning service, and headed out.

CHAPTER 17

A downpour began as soon as I left the building. Naturally.

I didn't carry an umbrella, because edgy private detectives don't carry umbrellas any more than they wear galoshes. Fortunately, since I'm undead, the clammy damp doesn't bother me. I'd clawed my way through piled grave dirt and managed to get back to my career. I could handle a little rain.

I splashed along through the downpour, until I discovered that if I just walked a block over, I entered a different climate zone, where it was still cloudy, but warm and oppressively humid. I followed that street instead, but the sticky humidity caused another set of problems—especially since in the miasmic puddles left behind from the recent sewer upheaval, mosquitos had bred in a frenzy that would have made an insect pornographer giddy.

To make matters worse, some of the mosquito larvae had fallen down into the sewers, where they were contaminated by effluent from the mad scientist laboratories. The mutated creatures that flew up were large enough to shove manhole covers aside, and their buzzing sound was as loud as the deteriorating muffler on the Pro Bono Mobile. Mosquitos don't tend to bite zombies, having no taste for embalming fluid, but these were either too stupid to know the difference or just plain malicious. I didn't need the added annoyance. Preferring the rain, I ducked back over to the first street.

I found the weather wizard Alastair Cumulus III holding a pre-election rally. I wanted to confront him—or at least question him, since I had very little evidence—about the sabotage that had plagued Thunder Dick's posters, as well as the malicious rumors that were being spread about our client's "proclivities" (undefined). It was an old tactic that had been used in elections since the campaign for Mammoth Hunter of the Year, and I doubted even a zombie detective could prove anything, but if Cumulus knew I was on the case, maybe he would rein in some of his more outrageous stunts.

The snooty weather wizard chose to hold his rally in an abandoned lot, which gave him room to perform. A sign marked the property as COMING SOON, ANOTHER FINE TALBOT & KNOWLES BLOOD BAR AND BISTRO!

The rally was sparsely attended. I couldn't tell how many people were there to hear Alastair Cumulus III and how many had simply stopped to get a respite from the rain. The wizard's pale blue robes seemed to be a reflection of the sky overhead. He had used his weathermancy to create a more pleasant climate, generating warm breezes to dry the area from the recent downpour, while miserable rain continued in the surrounding streets. His forked beard was neatly moussed and his curly hair sparkled with moisture, or perhaps glitter. I couldn't tell from a distance.

As I came up, I saw Ramen Ho-Tep standing there as a campaign supporter. In his bandage-wrapped hands, he held a picket sign declaring, VOTE CUMULUS: CLIMATE CHANGE YOU

CAN BELIEVE IN! His wrappings had been laundered, although a few tan skid marks still showed where he had recently been stained.

Cumulus called out, "I am a weather wizard of proven abilities and demonstrated civic mindedness. My foggy bottom, any politician can kiss babies, but I also saved the museum and the original Necronomicon."

"The Necronomicon was fine," I muttered.

Ramen Ho-Tep jabbed his sign up in the air. "He rescued the Egyptian exhibit. So many priceless objects saved. I was once pharaoh of all Egypt—and I'm voting for Alastair Cumulus III. He's my hero."

I saw numerous television cameras filming the event. Each one sported the logo of one of the competing weather networks that serviced the Quarter. The networks reflected forecasts from dramatically different portions of the political spectrum: while one insisted on sunshine, the other declared rain, and no facts or proof would get them to change their minds. With the currently feuding climates, each weather network was able to cherry-pick their own weather to prove their point.

"After our recent climatic events, the Unnatural Quarter is an even dirtier place than usual," Cumulus continued. "And while a certain amount of dinginess and grime adds character, I vow to clean up this city." He swirled his hands in the air, calling up a mysterious incantation that sounded like gibberish. "You'll note that unlike my rival, I require neither a talisman nor a familiar."

He jabbed his fingers toward the sky, and I heard a resounding crack of thunder. Several blocks away, sheets of rain came down in well-defined areas.

"As a show of good faith, I will target rinsing rainstorms to wash away any residue left behind by the recent sewer upwelling. Clean as a whistle. I will, however, focus my efforts on those neighborhoods that show the most support for Alastair Cumulus III, according to recent polling data."

The reporters from the weather networks declared their predictions—completely contradictory—about which neighborhoods would be cleansed and which ones would remain encrusted in filth.

"You're just a show-off!" came a loud voice. The audience turned to see the tie-dyed robe and windblown hair of the other Wuwufo candidate. "Let's have a public debate right now." Thunder Dick clutched the portable sundial talisman at his throat. He reached down to scratch the annoyed-looking tuxedo cat Morris/Maurice, who again dodged his touch.

Thunder Dick shouted an incantation, and hot, dry winds snatched the sign out of Ramen Ho-Tep's gnarled hands and flung it up and away like Dorothy's house on a field trip to Oz. Tan veils of dust appeared from nowhere. Gritty pellets of sand spun through the air and pelted Cumulus's audience. As the dust storm thickened, I held on to my fedora and bent over, trying to make my way to Thunder Dick in hopes that I could get him to stop.

Because I was still wet from the recent rain showers, the blown dust caked me with mud. The bystanders grumbled and screeched, then scattered, some of them plunging into the dry-zone streets, others escaping into the downpour.

The weather networks captured all of it, though they would no doubt edit the footage to show their own chosen candidate in the best possible light.

Alastair Cumulus III fought back, lashing out with narrow columns of drenching rain, and even a thin writhing waterspout, which Thunder Dick dodged. The only real victim was the cat, who got caught in the downpour and bounded away, yowling.

Stumbling against the dry wind and dust mixed with occasional rain, I finally reached my client. "You can stop now, Mr. Thudner! The crowd has dispersed."

The weather wizard ceased waving his hands and released his talisman. As the weather calmed, he looked around to see that we were indeed alone in the vacant lot. Even Alastair Cumulus III had stormed off in a huff. The TV cameras had fled.

"I'm not your campaign adviser, just your zombie detective," I said with a frustrated sigh. "But that stunt didn't gain you any friends—it just annoyed a lot of people."

"And my cat, too," Thunder Dick said, suddenly dejected. "I have to think these things through better."

"If you want us to crack down on your rival's nefarious campaign shenanigans, you've got to stop using the same tactics he does."

I could see I hadn't gotten through to him, though. Thunder Dick said, "He did it to me, so I'm justified."

"You know Alastair Cumulus can say the same thing about you."

"But he lies!" Thunder Dick said and stalked off.

I happened upon Stentor the ogre on a street corner, looking forlorn. The skies were clear now, but he looked the worse for wear. "I've been here all through the downpour and the dust storm. Still, almost no donations."

I was disappointed to see how far the ogre had fallen after losing his employment at the opera house. The once-celebrated Stentor now sat singing arias with his hat out. His hat was large enough to cover his head, so it was the size of a suitcase, but he was having no more luck than the barbershop quartet of frog demons singing down in the sewers.

I heard Stentor finish a song that should have been compelling and dramatic, but passersby scurried past, preferring to flee rather than listen. His squeaky voice would have made even a chalkboard cringe. On a scrap of cardboard he had handwritten, *Will Stop Singing for Change.*

When I greeted the ogre, he looked with great sadness down at his nearly empty hat, and I tried to encourage him. "Nothing wrong with being a street performer. It's a very respectable profession."

"With my voice," Stentor cheeped, "maybe I should just become a mime. I'm more qualified for it."

A chill went down my spine, and I hardened my resolve. "No, not that. The witches are studying connections to trace back the amphibious transference protocol. If only we can find out who *has* your voice, then we can retrieve it." I patted him on the shoulders. "Once you become the great Stentor again, voice and all, the Phantom will hire you back. Audiences will demand it."

The ogre picked up his hat and tipped it over to let a few coins fall into his enormous palm. "I think I'll call it a day." He settled the hat like a pup tent on his head, nestling it on the shaggy mass of his hair.

At the end of the street, a corner gift shop sold cards and novelties, "that special something for unusual and unnatural occasions." I decided to get a card to cheer Stentor up. I wondered if the gift shop had a section of "Get Your Voice Back Soon" cards.

Leaving Stentor, I set off toward the shop. Soon I heard a buzzing engine and the squeal of tiny tires. A ramshackle jalopy screeched to the front of the novelty shop, bumping up onto the curb. The black-painted lawn gnome and his gang of porcelain punks were haphazardly stacked inside the car, and they tumbled out as soon as the driver brought the go-kart–sized getaway vehicle to a halt. Swinging their Timmy guns like fire hoses, Mr. Bignome and his gang peppered the front of the novelty shop and shattered the windows.

"Hurry up, boys!" yelled Bignome as they clattered and

scurried toward the front door, shooting all the while. "Before the coppers get here!"

Determined and, yes, I admit it, downright annoyed at the gnomes, I didn't intend to let the gang get away after what they had done to us in the Medium-Sized Shop of Horrors. Screaming pedestrians of all species ran from the robbery site, from which a shrill school-bell alarm rang out. I drew my gun from its holster and bounded down the street. The police would be coming, but probably too late; the gang of lawn gnomes knew how to be fast. I wasn't going to let them get away this time.

I normally move at a sedate pace, but in emergencies when adrenaline mixes with the embalming fluid, I can become one of those fast zombies that are infinitely more scary. I hurried down the block yelling, "Stop!" I didn't care about being stung with small-caliber projectiles again; I was going to end this threat to my town.

As I ran past a narrow alley, however, in a completely unexpected—and completely clichéd—moment, Thunder Dick's black-and-white cat yowled and sprang out in front of me, startling me and everyone else on the street. Morris/Maurice ran right under my feet, got caught on my shoes, and tangled in my ankles. I tripped and went sprawling into the gutter, my pistol flying out of my hands. The cat bounded away, turned to look at me, nonchalantly licked his shoulder to pretend that nothing whatsoever had gone wrong, then sauntered off.

By the time I picked myself up, some gnome gang members were scurrying out of the gift-card shop carrying the cash register, which they dumped into the back of the jalopy. The driver revved the puttering engine.

A big hand on my shoulder helped me lurch to my feet—Stentor. "You took quite a spill there, Mr. Chambeaux. Cats have a way of getting underfoot."

Mr. Bignome emerged from the gift shop, sprayed the lintel and the open sky with tiny bullets, then yelled in his improbably loud and domineering voice, "You'll never catch me! Now, let's get outta here!" He swung himself into the back of the jalopy, where the other gnomes caught him. "Bye-bye, suckers!" The jalopy squealed away.

I heard police sirens and saw McGoo puffing up again, service revolver drawn. He grimaced in dismay. "Late again, Shamble?"

"Miss Congeniality for the second time in a row." I turned to the ogre. "Thanks for helping, Stentor."

But he was standing there in astonishment, his eyes wide, his inner-tube–sized lip trembling. His mouth was open, as if waiting to receive an air drop.

"That was *my voice*," he squeaked. "That lawn gnome is the one who stole my voice!"

CHAPTER 18

The getaway jalopy raced off, dodging through streets in the Quarter before it vanished into a convenient fog bank that one of the feuding weather wizards had stored there.

All the while, Stentor kept pointing after Mr. Bignome, squeaking in anger. "That's him! He stole my voice."

Although McGoo had seen enough unusual things in the Quarter that he took it all in stride, he was disgusted that the gang had gotten away again. As squad cars rushed up, he went into the novelty shop to talk with the manager and retrieve the security camera footage.

McGoo might have lost his suspects, but I had gotten a major lead on my case. I turned to Stentor. "Now that we know who has your voice, let's go to the Wannoviches to see if they can help us reunite you with your vocal abilities."

He brightened as we headed off to the headquarters of Howard Phillips Publishing. "I'm willing to try anything, Mr. Chambeaux. My legacy to the arts is at stake."

Inside the lobby, we again encountered problems with security. Even though the receptionist recognized me from the last time, she had seen so many "Dan Shamble" impersonators that she remained suspicious. Even worse, Stentor couldn't find his ID, so he fumbled through his pockets, crevices, and other embarrassing hiding places, hoping he had just tucked it away somewhere. Meanwhile, the human security guard stood in the corner, trembling as he watched us.

So, once again, I had to wait in the lobby for Mavis Wannovich to come to the rescue. This time I didn't see any would-be zombie detectives loitering in the waiting area. The only other person was a tan-furred werewolf meticulously and nervously combing his face and the backs of his hands. He wore a dark pinstriped suit and polished wingtip shoes. A fresh and sprightly sprig of lavender flowers poked up from his lapel. At first I thought they were lilacs, but then I realized they were lupines.

The werewolf sized me up and down and stepped forward, thrusting out a paw. "You must be auditioning for that Dan Shamble character. Have you talked to marketing yet?"

I took his grip automatically. "I *am* Dan Chambeaux. The real one."

"That's the spirit—stay in character, no matter what!" said the werewolf, adding a classy-sounding growl to his voice. "I'm up for Lou Lupine, Werewolf P.I. It's the launch of their new Unnatural Detectives line."

"A werewolf detective?" said Stentor. "Oh, I'd read that!"

"You don't think it's just a little derivative?" I asked.

The actor playing Lou Lupine snuffled through his dark snout. "Sounds better to me than Francis, ghoul bounty hunter. I'm pretty sure they've canceled that one already."

The elevator doors opened, and Mavis Wannovich emerged. She brightened when she saw me, waving her hands. "Yoo-hoo, Mr. Chambeaux!"

The werewolf adjusted his pin-striped suit, straightened the lupine on his lapel, and waved after me. "Good luck with the audition, bro."

When I introduced Stentor the ogre, Mavis was cheerful. "Yes, we have your delightful frog. This is a very interesting case—it'll make the backbone for a great new novel in the Dan Shamble series."

Stentor blinked incredulously. "I'll be a character in a book?"

"Well, somewhat," said the witch. "Our stories are inspired by actual events, but our ghostwriter has a certified poetic license."

Stentor's case sounded like no more than a B storyline to me, but then I'm neither a writer nor a publisher.

After the ogre signed a waiver, promising to cause no mayhem in the publishing offices, Mavis got each of us a visitor's pass, led us through security, and again up to the thirteenth floor. We went straight to her office, where Alma sat white and clean, with no sign of her editorial mud bath.

Robin's plastic lunch container sat on the desk between two copyedited manuscripts. The lid was ajar, and the speckled frog seemed content. Stentor brightened and used his ham-sized hands to slide the lid aside. "There he is! I missed him." He looked at the Wannovich sisters. "You took care of my frog?"

"The best of care," Mavis said, and Alma snuffled.

Stentor touched the frog with a frog-sized finger and looked at me. "He and I were very close."

"Frogs don't pick just any throat," I said.

"It was a happy circumstance," the ogre answered, "despite the way it turned out."

I explained to the Wannovich sisters that we now knew who had stolen Stentor's voice, and the ogre asserted that his distinctive baritone voice was much better suited to opera singing than to yelling commands during a robbery.

Mavis had already set out the books about vocal displacement spells and their uses, using a sticky note to mark the section on amphibious transfer protocols. "Lawn gnomes aren't generally loud," said Mavis. "They keep quiet so as not to scare fairies that might visit the gardens. But this Mr. Bignome sounds like he has compensation issues." She adjusted her pointy hat. "I believe he stole the ogre's famous voice so he could command his gang."

"Now that we know who took the voice, can we get it transferred back?" I asked.

Mavis wasn't as enthusiastic as I would have liked. "Alma and I studied the spell books, and yes, we think we have a way to reconnect Stentor with his voice."

The ogre leaped to his feet with such excitement that he jostled the desk, scattering manuscripts. The frog sprang out of the plastic container and landed on the floor, hopping around in confusion. The ogre backed away, afraid he might hurt it. Alma scurried after the creature, trying to corner the poor frog with her snout. I fumbled after it, but Mavis finally removed her pointy hat, scooped up the frog, and deposited it back in the plastic container.

"From what we can tell, it's a simple enough spell," she said, putting the lid over the top of the plastic container so the frog couldn't escape again. "We can reestablish the connection between you and your distant voice, but there's one catch. In order to implement the spell, we'll have to use the same catalyst that was used to steal your voice in the first place."

"A catalyst?" Stentor asked.

"Yes," Mavis said. "You'll have to swallow the frog."

Inside the plastic container, the spotted creature hopped and thumped against the lid, as if it had heard and understood its fate.

Although determined to get his voice back, Stentor was also

concerned about his amphibious friend. He stroked the plastic lid. "It's all right. This won't hurt," he said in his squeaky and not-quite-soothing voice. "There's plenty of room in there, and I promise not to swallow all the way."

Alma trotted around the desk, which I realized was part of the spell preparations. I assisted in setting out the candles, copying designs for specific runes from the spell book. As he waited, the ogre clutched the plastic container to his enormous chest, obviously nervous.

When we finished setting up, Mavis drew a deep breath and prepared for her incantation. "It's time for the frog to go back in the throat," she said.

I gave Stentor a reassuring pat on his sofa-sized arm. He closed his eyes as if to be brave, popped open the plastic lid of the container, and upended it into his mouth. The frog tumbled down his throat, and the ogre closed his lips tight.

Mavis quickly read her spell after reassuring us that she had proofed the words herself to make sure there were no typos. Stentor squirmed. I could see his throat convulsing, his Adam's apple bobbing up and down as he struggled not to swallow.

As the witches continued their work, I could sense magic flying through the air as the spell's crackling energy swirled around the ogre. His clumps of hair began to stand out straight from static electricity.

Suddenly, Alma blew out the candles, ending the spell. Mavis let out a sigh and leaned back in relief. "There, it was a complete success!" she said. "Stentor, you are now reconnected with your voice."

The ogre tried to talk, but even less sound came out now—just a breathy few words, like a ghost of a voice. "This doesn't seem like a success to me."

I realized the problem. "Of course not. You've still got a frog in your throat."

I pounded him on the back, and Stentor opened his mouth and coughed. The panic-stunned frog flew out like amphibious sputum to land among the manuscripts on the editor's desk. The ogre's shoulders bounced up and down as he chuckled and said, "There, that's better."

But his voice was still a nearly inaudible breath.

His expression fell like a curtain at the end of a performance. "What's wrong? Where's my voice?" He clutched his throat.

The dizzy frog kept hopping in circles around the desk.

Mavis studied the spell book with concern, and Alma grunted a few suggestions, but her sister shook her head. "Wait a second, I'm checking something."

Trying to be useful, I scooped up the frog and returned it to the plastic container, where it huddled in the corner, traumatized.

"Let me revise my opinion," Mavis said. "This spell was a complete *partial* success. You are indeed reconnected with your voice, Stentor, but the voice hasn't been put back into your larynx yet."

"What does that mean?" Stentor breathed.

"It means that your voice is yours again, but the words you speak are coming out of Mr. Bignome's mouth."

The ogre groaned in dismay.

Not what either of us had hoped, but I pondered the problem. "Hmm, that might still be useful. If you talk, but your words come out of the lawn gnome's mouth, then he has no control over what he says. We could use that to our advantage—like a game of long-distance Marco Polo across the Quarter."

Stentor understood. "I see." He drew in a deep breath and began to bellow, though he produced almost no sound. "Stop! Thief! Somebody call 911. This lawn gnome has kidnapped my voice."

Even though we couldn't hear anything, if Mavis was right, his displaced shout would be coming out of Bignome's mouth, somewhere across town.

Smiling, I handed Stentor the plastic container with his frog. "Let me talk to my policeman friend. We may be able to wrap up two cases at the same time."

CHAPTER 19

Since the lawn gnomes were armed and dangerous, I wanted to bring McGoo the new development about Stentor's displaced voice as soon as possible. I headed to the main precinct station of the UQPD.

McGoo is not a desk cop. He walked the beat every day, claiming that he enjoyed the fresh air more than a stuffy office job. I knew he was kidding himself, because no one had ever accused the Unnatural Quarter of having an abundance of fresh air . . . especially after the recent sewer uprising.

"A desk job just gives you hemorrhoids and a big gut," McGoo had once told me after he was passed over for a promotion.

"And you prefer sore feet," I said.

"Damn straight, Shamble." With the dramatically changing weather due to the Wuwufo campaign, he couldn't have enjoyed being outside very much.

At this time of day, I knew he would be back at the station. I arrived at the dingy building whose façade had come from a large crypt that was dismantled stone by stone and then moved across town. Perpetrators and victims were a motley mix of species and levels of scruffiness. A mummy sat on a bench smoking a cigarette, careful not to set his bandages on fire. A vampire was hauled into the rear holding cells by two uniformed cops as the vampire yelled, "It wasn't me. It wasn't me! That was somebody else's coffin."

Two poltergeists had been brought in for causing a domestic disturbance, rattling the neighbors with their ectoplasmic argument. A group of teenaged zombie slackers looked sullen as they waited for their parents to bail them out; they had been picked up for vandalism, using spray paint to tag the side of a building, and were apprehended because they moved so slowly that they couldn't finish writing their statement.

A small bald man in a plaid sport jacket handed me one of his cards. "You in trouble? I can get you out of it." I glanced at the card, recognizing him as another slimy cop-car–chasing bail bondsman. "Been Busted? Call Ghost *Fixers!*"

"Sorry, no," I said. "Zombie detective. Here on business."

"I should have noted the lack of handcuffs." He scurried into the station, handing out cards to anyone who might need his services.

Behind a high desk, the watch chief lorded it over anyone coming and going in the station. A poster on the back wall showed a muscular werewolf with a torn cop uniform holding a gigantic magnum in his furry hand. It was the rogue vigilante cop, Hairy Harry, a hero to policemen everywhere. The poster was even autographed.

I knew my way around the station well enough. After asking a couple of the cops on duty where I could find Officer McGoohan, I was directed back to the lunchroom. I bumped into him in the hall, where he was just clocking out. He looked tired, wrung out. I wondered if it was due to frustration from the lawn gnome robbery, or—worse—if Rhonda had called him back with more surprises (twins, this time?), but I didn't ask. Sometimes it's best not to disturb junkyard dogs. Or ex-wives.

"Man, what a day, Shamble—I'm ready for the Tavern," he said. "Those lawn gnomes are really giving me a bad opinion about landscaping fixtures. Four violent robberies so far. No one's been hurt yet, despite all the firepower in those Timmy guns, but sooner or later they're going to poke somebody's eye out with those things."

I hid my smile. "Cheer up, maybe you'll catch them tomorrow—all it takes is some good detective work."

He was too distracted to pick up on the hint. "Around here, the detectives have desk jobs."

"I meant some *zombie* detective work, McGoo. I've got a connection to Mr. Bignome." His eyes lit up as I explained how the Wannovich sisters had established a linkage with Stentor's voice, so that whenever the ogre talked, the loud words would come out of Mr. Bignome's mouth. "I told him to keep shouting. The neighbors are bound to hear it and call in a report."

"Like somebody with a stolen cell phone calling their own number to harangue the thief." He raised his eyebrows. "Interesting—but if Bignome is holed up in an isolated hideout, we might not hear it."

"Stentor is very motivated," I said. "We can get him to yell for quite some time—and that ogre's got a three-window-pane voice. If he yells enough, *somebody's* going to report a disturbance."

McGoo chuckled as the possibilities occurred to him. "If he's clever, Stentor could cause Bignome lots of trouble. Say, by making the gnome shout, 'I'm overcompensating. I need a big voice because I have a very tiny penis.' Good work, Shamble. I'll tell the report desk to pay close attention. I'd like nothing better than to shut down those gnomes."

Next to the front desk of the precinct house, business cards covered a corkboard, tacked one on top of the other. I saw the Ghost Fixers bail bonds, various attorneys, and estate-planning services. Even Lurrm had put up a flyer offering a special rate to anyone recently arrested: *Feeling stressed? Come relax in the Recompose hot springs. Get a massage from our expert masseuse C.H. (Convicted felons excluded).* The frog demon was an ambitious marketer, but if he wanted to establish a new, clean reputation for the former Zombie Bathhouse, I thought he should go after a different class of clientele.

As we walked out the front door, I finally had to ask, "Any more word from Rhonda?"

"Not a peep. Maybe she reconsidered . . . or maybe she's got something else up her sleeve."

I felt sorry for him. "Rhonda's not the type to reconsider."

"Nope," he said. "I'll just wait for the other combat boot to drop."

CHAPTER 20

On my way back to the office, I got sidetracked by the brothel. Although I had no interest in their services (honest), the Full Moon still managed to get my attention. The twenty-four-hour ladies of the night had a way of doing that.

As night fell, a cold snap slammed on the Quarter, making sparkles of frost creep up the walls of buildings like a spreading plague. Shivering mummies tightened their bandages, wrapped their arms across their chests, and hurried inside to shelter. Werewolves blew out frosty breaths and rubbed their paws together as they huddled on street corners.

Always enterprising, Neffi—the madam who ran the Full Moon Brothel—sent a couple of her girls out with flyers that said, *Need someone to keep you warm tonight? Our fine women can drive away the chill of the grave. (Succubus service no longer offered.)* Cinnamon, the sexy werewolf call girl, pushed one of the flyers into my hands with a flirtatious lick of her tongue along her muzzle.

"Haven't seen you in a long time, Dan," she said. "Stop by and visit. At least show your support for the rally."

I had no idea what sort of rally the vixen werewolf was talking about, but I had my suspicions . . . and my dread. "Haven't heard about it."

"Come on over, then. Be a Dick supporter. It'll be a lot of fun—I promise." She licked her muzzle again.

Neffi was not much of a political activist, but she was a businesswoman. Chambeaux & Deyer had helped her out in a conflict against the corrupt Smile Syndicate, and she had offered me some of the Full Moon's services in payment, but we preferred cash or credit card. With Sheyenne as our business manager, what did Neffi expect?

Because Thunder Dick was a client, I detoured to the standalone row house that, through a quirk of architecture, seemed to have discreet back doors on every side of the building. Maybe it had been designed by Escher's ghost.

In the unseasonable cold snap caused by the weather wizards, the Full Moon Brothel looked like a magical winter wonderland from a classic Currier & Ives Christmas card. A white blanket of snow had fallen on the roof and eaves, piled up in a perfect coating along the bannisters and the shrubs. Thick, puffy flakes continued to fall through the air like glitter.

Thunder Dick was there in person to create his own microclimate, a cheery, snowy scene that invited hot chocolate and caroling (if that was the sort of thing that intrigued unnaturals). Because the weather wizard limited his cheery snowfall to such a discrete (and discreet) area, it looked as if the brothel were enclosed in a snow globe.

Outside, Neffi and her girls were holding a political rally that seemed more like a party. Thunder Dick wore his tie-dyed weather robes, clutching his portable sundial talisman, finger painting incantations in the air as he waved at passersby. "I hope I can count on your vote."

Campaign signs had been pounded into the lawn in front of the brothel announcing, WE ARE PROUD DICK SUPPORTERS.

Of course they were.

I doubted that the old mummy madam had read either candidate's platform statement; she simply chose which of the two she wanted to support based on their names. Seeing me, the weather wizard waved vigorously to get my attention, thereby causing an inadvertent swirl in the wind pattern, which picked up some of the clean white snow and splattered it on a group of werewolves who had come by to observe.

Thunder Dick's cat familiar huddled near his feet, shivering in the cold. Cats rarely find anything charming about snow.

"Look, Mr. Chambeaux!" the wizard called. "I took your advice to heart! See my clean and honest rally? I'm a nice guy, everybody's favorite uncle. You were right: Being fair and aboveboard is the best way to get support. I want Wuwufo voters to choose me because of my ability and integrity, and because they like me—not because of some childish spat with an arrogant jerk."

"You've matured a great deal," I said.

"I wouldn't say 'a great deal,' " said the cat. "Can we go now?"

"Soon." Thunder Dick smiled and kept waving at the attendees. "I thought you'd enjoy being at a cathouse."

Neffi came over to me, walking with stiff and jerky movements, as if she had been produced in a bargain-basement special-effects shop. "There's my favorite zombie private investigator. It's been far too long since you darkened our door and brightened our lives."

"Business elsewhere," I said.

"Oh, we can definitely take care of business," she said with a seductive lilt in her voice, a habit she had developed after thousands of years of practice. She was the oldest madam in the world working the oldest profession.

I noted the Dick Supporter signs around in the brothel yard. "Since when did you get into politics, Neffi?"

"Oh, it's not politics—we just like the slogan. It attracts attention, brings customers over for our Happy Hour, and then we can give them special coupons for our Happy Endings Hour."

Listening in, Morris/Maurice glared up at the weather wizard. "You can have my coupon. I've been neutered. *He* did it to me."

Thunder Dick dismissed the cat's concerns. "Don't be silly—I had a professional vet do the snipping. After I read the instructions, I decided it would be too complicated to perform myself. I only did it because I care for you so much, Morris. Everyone says that neutered cats are happier cats."

"Who says that?" asked Morris/Maurice, then sneezed, still miserable from the snow. "Not any cats, I guarantee you."

Slender vampire seductresses, gray-skinned but well-preserved zombie ladies, two werewolf hookers including Cinnamon, and even a slippery-looking shape-shifting creature who was a new acquisition (offering "endless possibilities" according to the Full Moon's advertisements) handed out campaign buttons, even though some of the spectators didn't have garments to which they could attach them. The ladies called out, "Join us. Be a Dick supporter!"

The weathermancer was delighted and proud, as well as oblivious to the snickers. Even Neffi could barely cover her grin, but because the skin of her lips was so dried and leathery, she never managed much of a smile anyway.

"I thought Ramen Ho-Tep changed his support to Alastair Cumulus the Third," I said. "Aren't you two still an item?"

Neffi stiffened even more than she already was. "We've been on again, off again for millennia. Politics and relationships don't mix. I had him wrapped around my gnarled finger, even put up a Thunder Dick poster in the museum—but now he supports that prissy fop just because he dried out a few damp bandages. He should have more of a backbone than that. Ramen Ho-Tep *was* the pharaoh of all Egypt, after all."

"I know," I muttered, "he reminds us often enough."

"But pharaohs are too focused on the upper class, the one percent. Thunder Dick, though, speaks for the common people."

The cat snorted. "He is exceedingly common."

Several of the ladies called for Thunder Dick to make a speech (because Neffi had encouraged them to do so). The weather wizard chuckled in embarrassment, brushed down his perpetually windblown hair and beard. "As president of Wuwufo, I promise only the best weather across the Unnatural Quarter throughout my administration. That will be my number one priority."

"Best weather for which species?" called a reptilian person in a hooded cloak.

"And that is where I promise to achieve a consensus," said Thunder Dick. The werewolves began to howl, and he turned to them. "For werewolves I promise a full moon every night."

Two of the younger werewolves looked excited, their tongues lolling out of their mouths, but their pack leaders responded with active scorn and cuffed their younger furry brothers. "Don't ever believe campaign promises," one snarled. "Besides, a full moon is astronomical, not meteorological. You don't control the movement of celestial bodies. Wuwufo doesn't have that much power."

"But I could make sure the moon isn't covered with clouds," said Thunder Dick.

"Either way, we still transform," answered one of the werewolves.

The cat hissed at the wolves. When they raised their hackles and growled back at Morris/Maurice, the tuxedo cat bounded back to hide behind the tie-dyed robes.

"And for vampires," Thunder Dick continued, raising his voice, "I promise no bright sunlight. Always a protective haze and—"

"My foggy bottom, what nonsense!" yelled a thunderous voice, which was conveniently accompanied by a peal of thunder. Alastair Cumulus III appeared, suddenly illuminated by flashes of lightning. His arrival seemed staged, even operatic, as if he had taken inspiration from *Don Giovanni.*

"Don't make promises you can't deliver, Richard. And with your level of incompetence, you couldn't cause rain during monsoon season. The Unnatural Quarter deserves consistency in their weather, not climate change that plays favorites." He bowed to the gathered audience. "Ignore this amateur. Vote for me—for climate change you can believe in!"

Listening to this, I was confused, because I had thought Cumulus was the elitist candidate. I could barely tell the two apart from their positions.

By now, cameras from the competing weather networks had showed up and their staff meteorologists made bold predictions about the outcome of the Wuwufo elections, accompanied by contradictory weather forecasts.

Thunder Dick was so outraged at his rival's arrival that he conjured a wind that blew straight at Alastair Cumulus, flapping the curled prongs of his forked beard, and the other weather wizard countered with an equal and opposing wind. The campaign signs rattled on their wooden sticks. Coupons and flyers for the Full Moon fluttered in the air. When the ladies ran for shelter, each grabbed a potential customer and rushed into the brothel, where it was safe and warm and dark.

Unsuccessful with his weathermancy, Thunder Dick scooped up a big handful of snow and smacked Alastair Cumulus in the face with a snowball.

The other weather wizard's eyes flared, and he summoned a powerful spell that brought down a crackling heat wave that instantly melted all the fresh white snow and removed any nostalgic Currier & Ives trappings. Runnels of water streamed off of the eaves and left the surrounding area a soggy mess.

"Oh, that's not fighting fair!" yelled Thunder Dick.

Cumulus snorted, "Says the man who threw a snowball in my face."

Thunder Dick turned to me. "You see why I hired you, Mr. Chambeaux? You see what slimy tricks he uses?"

"Yes, I saw it all," I said, my voice carefully neutral. "For all our sakes, I'll be glad when this election is over."

CHAPTER 21

While I was busy at the brothel, Sheyenne had done her homework about Jody Caligari's landlord. Officially, I'm the detective, but my ghost girlfriend has connections and resources. She knows who to call, and she can track down information that eludes other detectives—whether humans, zombies, or even werewolves in pin-striped suits.

She levitated from her desk to greet me. "I dug up everything I could find about Ah'Chulhu, Beaux—and it's a sordid story."

"Hmm, I never expected that." I hung my fedora on the hat rack. "He seemed like such a normal person."

Sheyenne looked determined as she reviewed files and printouts, calling up more scraps of detail from online records. "Ah'Chulhu had a twisted life. It's no wonder he's at war with the world."

"I thought he was a real-estate agent and a slumlord."

"It's all interconnected. He has great power and great potential, which comes from his parentage, even though his mother and father are no longer in this universe. They retired to another dimension, but in their day they were quite notable Senior Citizen Gods."

I had never heard the term before. "Don't you mean Elder Gods?"

"Not quite the same. Senior Citizen Gods get discounts, and they tend to cause most of their mayhem between four and six P.M. But you don't have to worry about those two, Beaux—they're long gone. Ah'Chulhu hasn't had any connection with them since his childhood. In fact, he's probably bitter."

"Plenty of us have parental issues," I said.

"This guy has it worse than most. He was discarded as a baby, dumped into a manhole, and left to die or fend for himself. Apparently, since so many alligators had been flushed down toilets, the parents assumed their infant half demon would be devoured in the sewers."

"They couldn't just put baby Ah'Chulhu up for adoption? With all those wriggly tentacles on his face he must have been a cute little tyke."

"This is the sordid part." Sheyenne pointed to pictures. I was surprised she had been able to find the old photos and obscure reports, until I remembered that people have a tendency to share even the most intimate and uninteresting details of their lives on social media. "When Ah'Chulhu was born, his parents were horrified—a tentacle head like they expected, but a *human* body. It caused quite a scandal. The mother was forced to admit that she'd had a torrid affair with a human and gotten pregnant, which resulted in the half-breed child. The mother attempted to keep her infidelity secret, but she couldn't deny it once the baby was born."

I glanced at the blurry image of the horrific, slimy, and tentacle-faced female that was Ah'Chulhu's mother. I tried to imagine any human man entangled in a passionate embrace with that squid demon from another dimension. And then I couldn't get the image out of my mind. "Ewww," I said.

"Some people have a foot fetish, some people get turned on by tentacles," Sheyenne said. "The two Senior Citizen Gods had such a titanic domestic dispute that it nearly ripped the cosmos apart."

"I think I remember that," I said.

"They initiated divorce proceedings, but finally committed to do their best to patch up the marriage. Since baby Ah'Chulhu was a painful reminder of the mother demon's indiscretion, however, they discarded the half-breed creature, and the two Senior Citizen Gods disappeared into the Netherworld, where they vowed to go through couples' counseling and attend a relationship-building retreat."

I nodded. "Ah'Chulhu must have been a tough little creature if he survived and thrived in the sewers."

"Yes, even as a toddler he befriended the gator-guys who were supposed to have eaten him, trained them to walk erect and be his henchmen, then built up a successful business selling sewer laboratory space for mad scientists, before expanding to other real-estate investments in low-lying areas. In fact, he's made quite a name for himself."

"*Ah'Chulhu* is, indeed, quite a name," I said.

Robin emerged from her office. It was late, and I thought she might have gone home by now, but she often worked all night on one case or another. "Sorry about his troubled childhood, but that doesn't excuse what he did to Jody. Unless Ah'Chulhu stacks the benches with enough demons, no jury will buy that sob story. Even the illegitimate half-breed son of a human and a Senior Citizen God still has to follow the law."

"Ah'Chulhu's background shows that he's a fighter, though," I pointed out. "This might end up being a rough and tumble battle."

"I'm ready to get down and dirty," Sheyenne said.

"So am I," Robin added.

Considering where the battle would likely take place, that was exactly how it would have to be.

CHAPTER 22

These days when revenge extends far beyond the grave, you want to keep your former clients happy.

Next morning, we received good news for a change. Although it wasn't the solution to one of our pending cases, Sheyenne was positively glowing as she waved a slip from her phone message pad. "Just got a call from the Unnatural Quarter Beautification Committee. Because of his renovations to the old Zombie Bathhouse, Lurrm has been named Amphibian of the Year. He's getting an award and a certificate of appreciation."

"That's wonderful." Robin brightened. "And he deserves it."

I was happy for him, but also confused. "Why would the committee call here?"

"We're the contact point on his business licenses and permits," Robin explained. "Lurrm doesn't like to talk on the phone, says his tympanic membranes aren't what they used to be. And he thinks it makes Recompose a classier establishment if it has an unlisted phone number."

"Isn't that part of doing business?" I asked. "How do people make reservations?"

Robin shrugged. "I tried to convince him otherwise, but that ship has already sailed—and sunk. He can call out, but we can't call in."

I didn't get it, but I wasn't a crack businessman either; I just liked solving cases: that was what kept me ambulatory.

"Then how do we tell him about the award?" Sheyenne said.

Robin looked at me, and I could see the answer in her eyes even before she said, "Dan and I are going to deliver the news in person."

When Robin and I entered, the spa attendant Carrl was flipping through the pages of a fishing magazine. "Need towels? Change for the lockers?"

"We're here to see Lurrm," I said.

He let the two of us through the turnstiles, and we descended the dank stairs into the steamy lower levels. Our noses were assaulted by the smell of sulfurous vapors, a hint of rotting flesh, and a strong undertone of sewage so thick it actually left an aftertaste.

In one of the large family pools, several zombies were playing water polo with a detached eyeball, which disoriented the owner of the body part with the conflicting views as his eyeball shot back and forth, even though he squeezed his other eyelid shut.

Something oozed out from under the wooden door of the sauna, and I heard deep satisfied moans coming from the massage rooms. Just another day at Recompose.

Two gaunt older zombies sat in one of the steaming hot pools along with a sticklike, completely unwrapped Aztec mummy who was softening up and rehydrating. In one of the private VIP spawning pools, two giggling amphibious creatures were flirting and making extremely large eyes at each other.

A skittering movement on the floor caught my attention. C.H. hurried toward us on light fingertips. He waggled his fingers in greeting.

Robin said, "Talk to the hand."

I bent down. "Can you take us to Lurrm? We've got good news for him."

C.H. extended his index finger to point toward one of the offices, then scurried ahead of us as we followed. Inside his management office, Lurrm sat at his desk, still wearing his frock coat and tapping out answers to e-mail on his computer screen. C.H. got a running start and sprang up onto the desk, where he tapped his fingers impatiently.

Lurrm puffed out his rounded throat, obviously pleased to see us. "You came back for a soak? Ayup, we're happy to have you!"

I let Robin do the honors. Smiling, she said, "We're pleased to inform you that the UQ Beautification Committee has named you Amphibian of the Year. There'll be a plaque, a ceremony, and you'll get the recognition of your peers."

"You've done a good thing with Recompose," I said. "I'm glad to see that your efforts are being recognized."

At first Lurrm was delighted, and he spun around in his chair like a kid on a playground. C.H. leaned to one side on his pinky so he could give an approving thumbs-up.

Then Lurrm began to dither. "Well, I really don't deserve it. Perhaps the attention should go to someone else. I, um . . ." His tongue flicked in and out of his wide mouth. "I don't really like the attention. I prefer to keep a low profile. Ayup."

"With success comes exposure," I said. "Don't you want to expose yourself?"

His eyes flicked from side to side, as if to follow a zigzagging fly. "I, um, hadn't thought it through. Can I send someone else to accept the award?"

Robin tried to sound reassuring. "No need to be shy. Dan and I would be happy to accept for you if you insist . . . but think about it."

We were interrupted when the attendant bounded down the stairs to Lurrm's office. Carrl sprang forward in great leaps, still clutching the fishing magazine in one soft hand. In a terrified voice, he belched out the name over and over again. "Lurrm! Lurrm! Lurrm! Lurrm! Lurrm! Lurrm! Lurrm!" He sounded like an annoying digital clock with a broken snooze button.

I put my hand on the holster of my .38. Lurrm sprang out of his desk chair. C.H. scuttled to hide behind a stack of papers.

"We've got company, Lurrm," Carrl cried. "Gator-guys!"

We emerged from the office, ready to face the threatening alligator lieutenants/associates/escorts, but I didn't see them. "Where are they?" I asked.

The attendant swiveled his round head to look at me. "Still trying to figure out the turnstile upstairs. We don't have much time!"

I wondered how long the turnstile would confound the dim reptilian brains. Soon enough we heard a loud crashing sound, and three gator-guys lumbered down the stairs. They stood in the steamy expanse of the bathhouse, either looking around for their intended victim or just taking in the sights.

Lurrm clutched his moist fingers together. "Bad news, ayup."

I couldn't understand what Ah'Chulhu would have to do with the former Zombie Bathhouse. "Have these guys been bothering you?"

"No, but they're going to. I knew they'd come after me, apply pressure." His throat bellowed out, then shrank back in. "But this is my battle." He licked his wide lips, then extended his tongue to lick his nose, his forehead, and the top of his head. It was an odd nervous habit, but I couldn't blame him.

"We can be of assistance," Robin said. "You're still our client."

In the spawning pool, the two flirting amphibious creatures

plunged under the surface to hide. The older zombies and the Aztec mummy were in such ecstasy soaking in the hot tub that they didn't move a single stiff muscle.

Spotting Lurrm, the gator-guys stalked forward. All reptilians look alike to me, but I was pretty sure the three gator-guys were Larry, Moe, and Curly.

"Lurrm, Lurrm, Lurrm," said the one I thought was Moe. "We're disappointed in you."

The frog demon was nervous. His nictitating membranes flickered shut, then open. "I don't want any trouble."

"Too bad, because we do want trouble," said Curly.

Larry said, "No, we don't. That's not what the boss told us. We want a . . . a . . . satisfactory resolution to the matter."

I had to step in. "You memorized that, did you?"

"Yeah, that's what the boss told us to say."

"But can you spell it?" I asked.

The gator-guys looked confused. "Why would we have to spell it?"

"Because nothing's legal unless it's written down," I said, glancing at Robin.

She picked up on my idea. "Indeed, a legally binding contract has to be written down, notarized, and ratified. Can you boys even sign your names?"

"My name is . . . X," said Moe.

"So is mine," echoed the other two.

"If Lurrm doesn't wish to engage your services, then he is not required to do so," Robin said.

"Our boss says that he's required to accept," said Curly. "We have to offer him protection."

"Protection against what?" I asked. "I'm Lurrm's detective. I can offer better protection." I tried to loom as tall as I could, and zombies are generally good at looming. I kept my hand meaningfully on the butt of the pistol in its holster. "We don't need you around here."

Now Lurrm grew more bold. "You guys don't frighten me. I'm free of all those underworld dealings, ayup. I've gone straight. *Legitimate!*"

"That's not what the boss says," Moe said.

"We've got you cornered," I said to the gator-guys, taking a step closer to them. "You'd better get out while you still can."

"Cornered." The gator-guys looked at one another. "How do you have us cornered?"

"Can you find your way back to the front door by yourselves?" I was betting that their sense of direction was as good as it had been in the tunnels, and that I could count on the reduced intellectual capacity of their brains. "Or are you trapped and lost down here?"

More confused than before, Moe, Larry, and Curly looked panicked, and they drew together. "It's a trap," Larry said.

Curly clutched at his scaly throat. "Gotta get out of here. Can't breathe. Claustrophobic."

"Can you spell claustrophobic?" I asked.

This panicked them even more.

"You won't get away with this!" Moe hissed.

"Carrl will show you out." Lurrm nudged the frightened attendant closer to the gator-guys. "And tell Ah'Chulhu I've already got my security, ayup. I don't need to pay for protection."

Clutching his fishing magazine, Carrl bounded across the floor as the gator-guys hurried after him. They looked around in confusion, totally lost.

When the threatening reptiles were gone, Lurrm let out a long, shaky sigh and huddled on the damp bathhouse floor. C.H. scurried up, sprang onto Lurrm's shoulder, and patted him consolingly.

"I was so scared I almost milted myself!" Lurrm shook his head from side to side. "See why I didn't want to draw attention? I'm aboveboard now and aboveground. I want nothing to do with that life."

"Ah'Chulhu seems to have his tentacles in a lot of different businesses," I said.

"If Ah'Chulhu is harassing our clients, we're going to take him down, Dan." The anger was clear in Robin's voice. "If we can prove he did anything illegal."

"Nothing you can prove," Lurrm said. "Believe me, you don't want to go up against him, ayup."

"We're already on his radar," I said. "I know about Ah'Chulhu's past, but I don't know about all of his present dealings. I'm inclined to do more digging."

Despite C.H.'s consoling, Lurrm still trembled. "I've got to protect myself. I'm going to install a turnstile at every door—for extra security."

CHAPTER 23

The lawn gnome gang struck again—as we knew they would. But this time, we had a secret weapon.

The waiting, though, was maddening.

Stentor the ogre was as anxious to help as he was eager to get his voice back. He had asked to stay at the opera house, on a provisional basis, even if only to sweep out the hall, but the Phantom had sneered at the idea. He claimed he couldn't tolerate having such a failure around, because it would sour the notes of his other singers, particularly the promising young women he taught in his underground grotto.

So, while Stentor waited for a call to come in about Mr. Bignome, he hovered in the Chambeaux & Deyer offices. For hours. We like to welcome our clients, but we're not a recreational center, especially not for enormous, hulking, clumsy, and depressed ogres. He had nothing else to do.

Sheyenne worked at her desk, waiting for the phone to ring. The clock ticked. I tried to concentrate on other cases inside my office, which was a refuge because Stentor couldn't easily fit through the door.

The ogre paced in the main lobby. He bumped into our potted artificial plants. He jostled Sheyenne's desk. He lumbered into and through her ghostly form, which he found more unsettling than Sheyenne did. He apologized profusely. He even offered to help do the dishes in our kitchenette, but his large hands had a tendency to crush the coffee cups. Sheyenne barely managed to rescue my sentimental mug that said, "World's Greatest Detective."

It was a relief when the lawn gnome gang robbed another store.

When McGoo called, Sheyenne thrust the phone toward me, and I had to dodge Stentor, who turned around, bumped the wall with his big shoulder, and knocked my fedora off the hat rack. I caught it as it fell, knowing I was going to need it.

McGoo said, "Showtime, Shamble! Alarm just went off at the Wilted Blossom. Squad cars are on their way, but it's only blocks from your offices."

"We'll beat you there." I tossed the phone back to Sheyenne, who caught it in her ectoplasmic hands as I beat Stentor to the door. Racing out, the ogre crashed into the jamb, damaged the frame, and hurried after me.

The Wilted Blossom was an ecologically conscious specialty shop that had made a business out of recycling and refurbishing used floral arrangements from funerals, sprucing up bouquets to be repurposed "for all occasions."

Since Mr. Bignome and his gang targeted only specific categories of businesses, McGoo and I had put an alert on all likely shops. Living in fear, every one of the business owners had the police station on speed dial.

As we ran down the sidewalk, I knew that today Mr. Bignome's reign of terror would end.

Distant wailing sirens grew louder, howling like frustrated werewolves on the day before a full moon. Ahead, I heard the rat-a-tat-tat of small-caliber machine-gun fire. Stentor bounded ahead of me on his long, muscular legs, yelling in his incongruous mousy voice, "Stop, thief! Stop!"

Farther down the block, I heard a much louder echo of the same words coming from the Wilted Blossom. The getaway jalopy was parked halfway up on the curb, and a lawn gnome sat gripping the steering wheel, racing the engine, ready to zoom away. The black-painted gnome leader and his fellow gang members backed out of the shop carrying bags of cash, firing their Timmy guns in the air.

Stentor whispered at the top of his lungs, "Stop—surrender!"

Unable to help himself, Bignome bellowed, "Stop—surrender!"

His gang members were confused. "What do you mean, boss?" asked a gnome in a jaunty red cap and red vest. "Why should we surrender?"

"Drop the loot!" Stentor cried in a little squeak.

Again, Bignome couldn't help himself. "Drop the loot!"

The lawn gnomes dropped their bags. "I don't like this new plan, boss," said a grinning gnome in emerald green with a special St. Patrick's Day shamrock on his lapel.

Struggling to control his voice, Bignome yelled, "I didn't mean that—pick up the cash. Let's get out of here."

Stentor yelled, "No, we should surrender."

Bignome repeated in a thunderous operatic voice, "No, we should surrender."

As the squad cars came closer, the lawn gnomes were frightened of their leader's peculiar behavior, but they knew what to do. They all piled into the jalopy as Bignome hopped up and down, gesticulating.

"We gotta escape, boss," cried the shamrock gnome.

The getaway driver revved the puttering engine. Bignome tried to grab a sack of the stolen cash discarded on the sidewalk, but the jalopy had already started moving. Finally, the leader tottered forward to hop headfirst into the back of the jalopy. "Go, go! The cops are coming."

Stentor squeaked, and Bignome echoed, "No, change of plans—shut off the engine. Put it in park. We have to wait to be arrested."

"Boss, you're scaring me," said the driver, and accelerated out into the street, heading toward us.

Even with all the excitement, I noticed dark clouds gathering overhead like gray water balloons pregnant with a downpour. Several streets up, rain began streaming down.

The ogre shouted, and Bignome was mortified when his mouth yelled for all to hear, "I like to wear pink underwear! Especially lacy underwear."

Stentor bounded in front of the getaway jalopy, but the panicked gnome driver swerved around him, just as I was trying to stop the car. The jalopy slammed into me, right at knee level, and knocked me flat before it squealed away.

Finally, two squad cars arrived at the Wilted Blossom and raced down the street in hot pursuit.

As the lawn gnomes fled down the block, Stentor yelled in his displaced ventriloquist-like voice, "Turn left. No, turn right! Stop right here. Look out for that pedestrian! We really should surrender. Turn around."

The gnomes' jalopy wheeled and spun away on a wild course, ricocheting from one direction to another. They accelerated toward the heavy rainstorm a few blocks away. As Bignome flailed and tried to reassert control of his voice, he yelled, "I pick my nose and eat my boogers!"

The squad cars tore past as I picked myself up from the street, and I saw McGoo in the front seat of the first one. He waved at me but didn't stop. They were in hot pursuit.

The gnomes' jalopy screeched through an intersection and careened forward into the rain, slipping down an alley, despite the contradictory directions being shouted from their leader in the backseat. The squad cars were half a block away and closing.

Then I heard a rumble and a hiss, a rushing sound . . . and displeased yelps and shouts from many unnaturals on the cross street as they scrambled up front steps to get out of the way.

The sudden torrential rain had created a roiling gray flash flood, far too much for the gutters to handle. The stampede of water scoured the street, surged through the intersection, and swamped the squad cars, picking them up like little toys. The sirens wailed and warbled, then died, sounding like a banshee with a sudden-onset head cold.

The flood continued to stream down the street, carrying debris, trash cans, sodden teddy bears with appliqued fangs, a special discounted shoe display of models designed for cloven feet. A forlorn mummy—who was naturally lightweight because of his extreme dehydration, hollow bones, and fluffy bandages—rode cross-legged on an upside-down trash-can lid, as if it were a lifeboat.

Furious that the lawn gnomes had gotten away, Stentor balled his toaster-sized fists and growled, although the sound that emerged was more like a "meep."

As the sudden flood waters subsided, McGoo and the pursuing cops fought their way out of the scattered squad cars and stood soggy and disgusted. The storm front rolled through the Quarter, and the police resigned themselves to the fact that the evil gang had gotten away again.

A grinning weather wizard strolled along the sidewalks, unbothered by the fresh puddles he sloshed through. Thunder Dick's drenched tie-dyed robes clung alarmingly close to his body, revealing more about his undergarments, or lack of undergarments, than he intended to show. His hair and beard were plastered to his skin, but he seemed to be in an extremely chipper mood.

"How did you like that? Just another example of my services to the Quarter," he said. "I can outdo my opponent's puny attempts at rain showers. Look how much grime and dirty residue I just rinsed away."

Behind him, the tuxedo cat tiptoed along, looking for dry patches on the sidewalk but finding few of them. The floating mummy climbed off of his garbage-can lid, gingerly touching a bandaged toe to a solid curb.

Bedraggled people of all species emerged from doorways, everyone annoyed, some actively growling.

Oblivious to the mood, Thunder Dick cheerfully waved. "If you vote for me, I'll keep all the streets clean."

Sputtering and angry, McGoo came up to him. "You just let a bunch of criminals escape! I should arrest you for obstruction of justice."

Thunder Dick was puzzled. "But I have my permit, which specifically explains that I am not responsible for delays caused by the weather."

The other monsters were closing in. Since I could do nothing for Stentor at the moment, I went to save my other client before he got lynched.

CHAPTER 24

It was time to get serious about lawn gnomes.

Since conventional, and first-order unconventional, means hadn't resulted in the capture of Bignome's gang, Robin tried a different tactic.

Now that we knew we had to find that evil specimen of kitsch landscaping before we could return Stentor's voice, she worked at tracking down Mr. Bignome's real identity. She pored through public records, business reports, licenses and certification numbers, birth dates, and manufacturing dates.

Her eyes were flashing as she came to me with an address written on a yellow sheet of legal paper torn from her self-replenishing pad. "Take this to Officer McGoohan—it's a lead you both need to check out."

"And what is this?" I saw that the address was in the Garden District, an old residential section of the Quarter.

"It's where Mr. Bignome's mother lives."

Bignome's father had been killed in an unfortunate landscaping incident. His mother had remarried, changed her name, then gotten a divorce. Now she lived alone in a house paid off with a combination of alimony and life-insurance money.

When I showed him the address, McGoo's eyes went wide. "We've been trying to track down anything about Bignome! How did you get this?"

"Robin found it."

That was all the answer McGoo needed. "All right, then. Let's go find out if Mama Bignome knows where her son's hideout is."

Mama Bignome lived in a quaint miniature Victorian. When she answered the bell, the stout matronly lawn gnome was wearing a housedress, accessorized with an apron, gardening gloves, and a blue pointed hat.

She didn't seem to mind seeing a zombie at her front door, but McGoo's uniform gave her sudden pause. "Oh, my! You're here about my boy, aren't you?"

He bent down so he could meet her at eye level. "Yes, ma'am. I'm afraid he's in a lot of trouble. If you know his whereabouts, it would be best if you convinced him to give himself up."

I crouched down beside McGoo. "Is he here?"

She shook her head. "I haven't seen my poor boy in months." Remembering her manners, for lawn gnomes are invariably polite, she invited us inside. The door was so small that McGoo and I ducked to enter the house, and the ceilings were low enough that we had to hunch on the diminutive sofa. She offered us tea, but we politely declined. Seeing our discomfort in the cramped domicile, she led us outside. "Come into my garden. We'll have more elbow room there."

"Thank you, ma'am," I said. "Both of us seem to have big elbows."

Mama Bignome's lavish garden was well tended. She took off her gardening gloves and set them next to a small trowel. She had birdbaths, gazing globes, sundials, statues of satyrs and fauns. Wind chimes dangled from a rowan tree. Toadstools

three feet high were propped at decorative angles. All the flow-
ers were in bloom: marigolds, gladiolas, snapdragons. A large
Venus flytrap whimpered "Feed me!" over and over again, but
Mama Bignome paid no attention to it.

"Lovely garden, ma'am," McGoo said. It was late afternoon,
and the shadows were growing long.

"It's just a hobby. An old woman needs something to occupy her time, especially now that the house is empty. I have no
grandchildren, not even a son who visits his lonely old
mother." She wiped a tear from her painted eye.

"You may not be aware of this, ma'am, but your son has
fallen in with a bad gang. He's been involved in numerous robberies," McGoo said. "We're hoping you can give us some clues
about where his hideout might be."

"He was such a good boy. You have to believe me." She
wandered among the shrubs, plucking out weeds, straightening
gravel on the walking paths. "I'm a failure as a mother. I tried to
raise him right, but since he didn't have a father, no role model
to look up to . . ." She sniffled again.

I heard a thrumming sound like a spinning fan, and three
creatures darted into the garden, hovering over the bright flowers. At first I thought they were large hummingbirds, but when
they alighted on a bush I could see the slender, shapely feminine
bodies, the pastel green clothes, the long, multifaceted wings.

"Fairies," I said. "You don't see them often here in the
Quarter—too urban."

Mama Bignome's ceramic face crinkled in a twinge of disgust. The fairies chirped and hummed, bouncing up and down
as they flitted around her, but the matronly lawn gnome swat-
ted at them. She picked up her hand trowel and slashed the air
like a ghetto knife fighter.

The fairies dodged and danced, blinking large, soulful eyes
at her. They sang, they tinkled, they cooed, exuding heartwarming sympathy, but Mama Bignome was having none of it.

"Out, out!" She swiped with the trowel. "I've had enough of you pests."

"Lawn gnomes and fairies have a longstanding relationship," I explained to McGoo in a low voice.

"I thought they were friends and partners," he said.

"Pests!" yelled Mama Bignome. "Just pests. They trample my flowers. They eat my berries. They think a sparkling song and a glitter of fairy dust is all they need to make up for that. But fairy dust makes crappy fertilizer. Shoo!"

She finally succeeded in driving the fairies away. They fluttered up and vanished into the sky in search of more welcoming gardens. Mama Bignome was rattled. "I can't leave this place unattended for an hour." She took a seat beneath one of the large umbrella-like toadstools. "I ordered a scare-fairy from the Toscano catalog, but it hasn't arrived yet."

"Now, ma'am—about your son?" I prodded. "It's very important that we find him before he hurts someone else. Apprehending him and his gang is the department's top priority. It would be best if he turned himself in without any trouble."

"I fear he's too far gone. There's nothing even a mother can do," Mama Bignome moaned. "If I knew where he was, I would tell you, officers. Honest."

"I'm an officer," said McGoo. "He's just a private detective."

"A zombie private detective," I added, although I wasn't sure whether that raised or lowered my cachet.

"He used to be such a good boy," Mama Bignome repeated, "but something turned him bad. I can remember that day. I wanted to be a good mother, show him the finer things, give him culture and the arts like every good lawn gnome should have. We went to the opera, and it was quite a performance! Loud and powerful singing . . . especially that ogre, a baritone I think."

"Stentor," I said.

"That's the one. We saw him at the beginning of his career, but now I believe he's the most famous ogre baritone that ever lived. Even my boy was impressed. But there was a particular high note in one song and"—she paused to sniffle again—"and something broke inside of him. My boy hasn't been the same since." She shook her head, deeply forlorn. "That was the day I lost him. My poor, sweet little boy." She began to sob uncontrollably. "I'm afraid . . . I'm afraid he's hollow inside."

CHAPTER 25

All work and no play makes for a dull, grim zombie ... and the world is tired of those. Sheyenne thinks I spend too much time on the job—but all I have is time, an eternity's worth ... or as long as the flesh lasts.

After the Big Uneasy, when I became one of the "lucky" percentage of dead bodies who reawakened and emerged from the grave, I kept going like an old Timex watch—but my zombie body doesn't have an extended warranty. We've all seen too many falling-apart shamblers who don't bother to think about the future.

For zombies, once your muscles atrophy, your limbs collapse, your skin sloughs off, and your organs rearrange themselves in a heap, you're in for a mighty dull existence, just sitting there as a bag of bones and watching the world go by. If worse came to worst, I supposed I could still think about cases, come up with ingenious solutions without lifting a finger bone, like that classic fat detective Nero Wolfe.

That's not my style. I put in the extra effort, since I plan to remain an ambulatory detective for as long as possible. Stay in the lurch, as it were.

In addition to my interesting caseload, however, I had a relationship to maintain. While ghosts linger for as long as zombies—and Sheyenne looked just as sparkling and beautiful now as the day her luminous form first manifested itself in our offices—she didn't have to stick with me, unless I gave her good reason to.

So this was a date, a spontaneous one (although I had surreptitiously planned it, setting aside the time). Sheyenne liked it when I was spontaneous.

I took her to Basilisk, the nightclub where I first met her, back when I was alive and she was alive, and we were both young, and the future looked bright. Basilisk was an upscale nightclub that catered to unnaturals and a few brave humans. The bar served all manner of beverages for all manner of creatures. Tonight, she manifested a very skimpy, very sexy, and very red dress for the occasion; she was going to turn so many heads that somebody might be inclined to call an exorcist.

Not only had Sheyenne worked here as a cocktail waitress, she had also sung onstage with a voice so supernaturally beautiful that she ruffled the feathers of other torch singers who felt she was stealing their limelight.

Basilisk was managed by Fletcher Knowles, co-owner of the expanding Talbot & Knowles chain of blood bars, but Fletcher kept the club because it was his dream. His pride of ownership exceeded the headaches of management.

As we approached the place, Sheyenne slipped her ghostly arm through mine in a symbolic gesture. She wore a wistful expression. "This place holds a lot of memories, Beaux."

I held the door open for her. "I like to reinforce the good ones. This is where we met." She drifted inside. "And it's where I first heard you sing." I smiled at the memory.

Basilisk was also where she had been poisoned, and I'd been killed in an alley not far from here. Such memories might have put a damper on a romantic evening, but Sheyenne and I were past all that . . . water under the bridge and down the gutter, into the sewer.

Basilisk's walls, stools, and booths were appointed in lavish red upholstery and wallpaper. There was no mirror behind the bar. Even the fittings and brushed-nickel fixtures were dull so as to avoid reflections. Crimson lighting gave the interior a warm abattoir/boudoir glow. On the stage, a lounge lizard plinked out tuneless jazz melodies on the piano to a crowd of unnaturals who didn't seem to be listening.

A mummy tore off a scrap of bandage and wrote down his phone number, slipping it to a haughty vampire cocktail wait-ress, who snubbed him but glanced at the numbers nevertheless and discreetly tucked the scrap inside the pocket of her skimpy apron.

At one table, a group of necromancers huddled around the black cocktail candle, discussing business. At the far corner of the bar, a balding ghoul with very little dermal integrity was hitting on a prim zombie woman who allowed him to buy her drinks but rebuffed any further romantic progress.

I led Sheyenne to a quiet corner of the bar, and we each took a stool. The bartender came over, a tall, gaunt man with sunken cheeks and a vacant stare; he looked like either a mortician or a greeter at Walmart. I ordered my usual beer, and Sheyenne asked for a scotch on the rocks; I offered to buy her the good stuff, but she insisted on nothing more than the cheap well brand. She couldn't actually drink it, but liked to swirl the ice cubes in the amber-colored liquid.

"Is Ivory singing tonight?" I asked with a nod toward the stage and the vacant microphone. The big-breasted vamp singer always belted out her songs in startling contrast to Sheyenne's angelic voice.

"Not tonight," said the bartender in a voice like a dirge. "Lost her voice."

I perked up, wondering if this had anything to do with Stentor and the lawn gnome gang.

Sheyenne loathed the petulant vampire singer. "Too bad. Laryngitis?"

"No, just a case of the divas." The bartender swiveled around and shuffled down to freshen the drink of the prim zombie woman as her would-be suitor waved a flabby gray hand toward the bartender, urgently trying to get her intoxicated.

Sheyenne lifted her drink to me in a toast. I raised my beer glass to clink against hers. "It's good to be with you, Spooky."

"You're always with me," she said with a teasing smile.

"And it's always good to be with you," I repeated. I wasn't just being flirtatious or buttering her up; I really meant it.

She peered into her drink. "I've been watching those weather wizards, seeing how passionate they are about their campaign, if a bit clueless. And they're making me think."

"They're making me annoyed," I said, but I realized she wasn't joking.

She gazed at me with those haunting (literally) blue eyes. "Just look at the two of them, all the energy each one pours into his campaign, the sheer determination. Both Thunder Dick and Alastair Cumulus *live* to win this election—just to become president of a minor organization that no one's ever heard of. But it's the most important thing in their lives."

I tried to figure out where she was going with this. "Are you saying that it's sad?"

"Objectively speaking, maybe—but I'm trying to remember the last time *I* was so fired up about something."

"I remember seeing the look on your face when you were on

stage, microphone in hand, and singing. That was your passion."

She flushed. "Yeah, and whenever you were in the audience I was doing that for you."

"And I definitely noticed."

Sheyenne continued to muse. "Look at Robin: When she latches on to a cause, a pack of pit bulls couldn't tear her away from it. What's your passion, Beaux? What makes you tick?"

I had never really thought about it. "Solving cases, I suppose." Too late, I wondered if she was fishing for a compliment, wanting me to say that *she* was my passion, my reason for existence. I fumbled and tried to save the conversation, but that wasn't what Sheyenne was looking for.

She asked again. "You don't sound sure. I know you were fully committed to solving my murder. You had that spark in your eyes then. Angry demons couldn't have kept you from it. But that case is over. What drives you? Really?"

I tapped my fingers on the bar, took another sip of beer, and kept considering the question. "I do exist to solve cases. That's what gets me through the day and night. It might not seem as earth-shattering to help an ogre opera singer get his voice back, or to reclaim the possessions from a junior mad scientist's laboratory, but it's a big deal to *them*. It's *their* case, *their* life. And I like the feeling of helping people solve problems that mean so much to them."

Now she had me thinking. In fact, some of my cases did indeed save the world, or at least the unnaturals—such as the genocidal plot from Jekyll Lifestyle Products and Necroceuticals, or the ectoplasmic defibrillator massacre that would have wiped out thousands of ghosts. "There's great satisfaction in just doing my job. I'm a working stiff."

"Is that enough for you?" Sheyenne asked.

I pondered, took another drink of my beer. "When you think

about it, some zombies spend their whole day just trying to find brains. At least my work benefits society, in its own way."

Fletcher Knowles came in from the back office carrying a ledger book and a laptop and took a seat at the corner of the bar. He was in his late thirties and wore round John Lennon eyeglasses; he also sported a full goatee that he bleached very blond. Taking advantage of a relatively quiet night in the club, he was ready to tackle his business paperwork as if it were a criminal sentence. Seeing us, he grinned and came over. "Sheyenne! Did you come in to sing again? We'd love to have you."

"That's flattering," she said with a slight spectral blush, "but my boyfriend and I are on a date."

I leaned closer to Sheyenne as I looked over at the empty stage, the lonely microphone. With Ivory being her usual diva self, Sheyenne would have the limelight to herself and certainly my complete attention. "Go on, Spooky—why not?"

She was reticent. "But I'm not prepared. I haven't practiced in a while." I could tell she was tempted, though.

I did my best imitation of Jody Caligari's puppy-dog expression. "You have a gift. Take pity on us mere mortals and immortals." Besides, every now and then I didn't mind showing off that I was with the smartest, most beautiful, talented ghost in the Quarter.

Her eyes twinkled, and she saw right through me as if I were the ghost. "All right, Beaux. For you." She bent close to give me an air-kiss and drifted over to the stage.

Even the intent necromancers looked up from their discussion at their little round table. Fletcher grinned and said to me, "It just hasn't been the same without her singing. And it'll be good for Ivory."

"How so?" I asked.

"It doesn't hurt to remind her that she's not the only set of sultry vocal cords in town. Maybe it'll make her less cantankerous."

Sheyenne hovered in front of the microphone in her very skimpy, very sexy, and very red cocktail dress. The lounge lizard tickled the ivories with his sharp claws. Sheyenne looked right at me, ignoring everyone else in Basilisk. She held the microphone, made that pouty look with her lips that made my heart go all aflutter (if it had been beating). "This is for a very special friend of mine."

And she began to sing a slow torch version of "Spooky." Our song. She took my breath away and resuscitated me at the same time. Everyone was transfixed, but I didn't care because the performance was all for me.

When she finished, the audience cheered, applauded, howled, whistled, and made various species-appropriate enthusiastic noises. Drifting back to the barstool, Sheyenne glowed, energized. Although she pretended to be embarrassed, she couldn't hide how completely pleased she was. I wanted to hold her and kiss her.

Fletcher was ecstatic. "You are welcome here anytime, young lady—anytime at all."

Despite his euphoria, though, the manager seemed troubled. When we had settled down again, he turned to me. "Come to think of it, Mr. Chambeaux, I've been having some troubles here. Maybe you can help me out."

"Are you looking for a free consultation?" Sheyenne asked.

"I'll listen," I said, "but the last time I got involved here at Basilisk, it didn't turn out well for Sheyenne, or for me." Self-consciously, I fingered the bullet hole in the center of my forehead.

"I understand," Fletcher said. "Although on the bright side, it's what got me and Harry Talbot together to launch our line of blood bars."

"Glad it worked out for you." *But not for me.* "What's going on?"

"A new property owner is trying to strong-arm me, and I don't understand it," said Fletcher.

"I thought you owned Basilisk outright," Sheyenne said.

"I do, free and clear—the whole nightclub and the ground it sits on. But some slimy developer bought the land *underneath* Basilisk. In fact, I hear he's purchasing property throughout the sewer system, as if he wants to buy the Unnatural Quarter right out from underneath our feet."

"Let me guess," I said. "Ah'Chulhu?"

"Yes, that was his name—ugly guy with an Australian accent, wormy little appendages all over his face. Nice business suits, though. I don't know how he keeps his power ties clean down in the sewers."

"Dark magic, I'm sure," I said.

Fletcher scratched his head. "I thought he intended to tear down Basilisk, but he's being all nice and burbly, promised me he wouldn't alter a thing about my business, swore that I wouldn't notice any difference in the change of administration." He paused.

I said, "I'm sensing an 'if' or a 'but' there at the end of the sentence."

"That's the part I don't get." Fletcher shook his head. "He told me I'd never be bothered again if I gave him fifteen gallons of pure virgin's blood."

I hadn't seen that one coming. Sheyenne sat up on the barstool. "That's a weird request."

"In many ways," Fletcher said, "not the least of which is that we sell our blood in liters, not gallons."

I started to do the metric conversion in my head, but couldn't remember the exact ratio. "And why would he come to you for that?" I asked.

"Our blood bars are starting to carry virgin's blood. It's an upscale product featured only in our boutique locations. We charge a premium for it, and most customers are just paying for the novelty. I haven't found one yet who could tell the difference in a blind taste test."

Sheyenne suggested, "So why not just give Ah'Chulhu a shipment of regular blood, then?"

"The straight vanilla stuff? Somehow I think he'd know, and Ah'Chulhu looks like a pissy sort of guy." He slipped his round glasses up on his nose. "To me the big question is, what does a tentacle-faced demon want with so much virgin's blood in the first place?"

"So are you going to give it to him?" Sheyenne asked.

Fletcher frowned and scratched his head again. "I turned him down. Flat. I know enough about slimy underworld figures that 'one-time things' are usually just a setup for the next time, and the next. No, thank you. Besides, gourmet virgin's blood is expensive stuff. We sell it in single-serve packets, and Ah'Chulhu wanted *gallons.* Harry Talbot would kill me.

"Our blood bars are turning a decent profit, and Basilisk is doing just fine, even when Ivory comes down with a bad case of the I-don't-feel-like-singing-tonight flu. It's no surprise that some shady small-time thug wants to work his way into my business."

The sewer real-estate mogul had not struck me as a small-time thug, and I couldn't figure out why he would be buying up all that property under the Quarter, confiscating Jody's lab experiments, and now wanting virgin's blood. Some kind of ritual, or underground housewarming?

Fletcher made a disgusted sound. "I'm heading out back for a cigarette before I start on the bookkeeping."

"Those things will kill you," I said. "You should take better care of yourself."

Sheyenne added, "You never smoked before."

Fletcher looked at us both in surprise. "I'm getting health advice from two dead customers? Thanks for the concern." He took out a pack of Coffin Nails and headed toward the back door behind the bar. "I'll quit tomorrow."

The gaunt bartender lurched over to ask if I needed another beer. I shook my head, since Sheyenne was still toying with the ice cubes melting in her scotch.

Romantic flirtatious moments always seem to be interrupted by some disaster. A terrified, blood-curdling shriek came from the back alley. Everyone in the club froze, but I was already off the barstool and racing toward the rear door, adrenaline racing through my embalming fluid.

With Sheyenne right beside me, I bolted into the alley just in time to see Fletcher Knowles suspended in the air, ensnared by a long, sucker-studded tentacle that sprouted like a beanstalk out of a displaced manhole cover in the street. Two other tentacles rose from the hole, questing in the air. The central tentacle squeezed tighter, crushing Fletcher's rib cage, and he stopped screaming. The tentacle swung from side to side, bashing him against the brick walls of the alley. He flopped about like a rag doll, broken and dead.

I pulled out my .38 and started firing at the tentacle, which twitched and uncoiled from Fletcher's body, letting him drop to the street. Like spaghetti being slurped into a kid's mouth, the tentacles withdrew into the manhole and vanished down into the sewers.

Fletcher lay dead, facedown in the clutter next to the Dumpster behind Basilisk. Sheyenne hovered over him, shocked, calling his name, but he didn't respond. She started sobbing. She turned paler, more translucent than before, and I wished I could hug her. Fletcher Knowles had been her boss when she worked at Basilisk, and I knew the man was a decent sort, even if he'd been selling black-market blood supplies on the side. He didn't deserve to be broken, squished, and discarded.

"I'm so sorry, Spooky," I said.

I peered (unwisely) down the displaced manhole cover but could see nothing. I just knew I was going to have to go down there.

CHAPTER 26

The gaunt bartender and a group of terrified customers rushed outside and crowded around the body, and someone had the sense to call the police. By the time McGoo arrived, I had already done as much investigating as I could. He stared at the body and shook his head. "Anybody want to tell me what happened?"

I said, "All I know is that it came from beneath the street."

Sheyenne tried to give a statement to McGoo, but was so shaken that I encouraged her to go back to the offices to tell Robin what had happened. With the police on the scene, she knew I would be caught up in the crime scene investigation. "Be safe, Beaux," she said. She was an ectoplasmic wreck.

"I will," I said. "I promise."

We knew damn well where the slimy sucker appendages had gone—plus whatever monstrous body they were connected to. And I personally had no doubt that Ah'Chulhu was in some way responsible.

After Sheyenne flitted away, McGoo hitched up his belt as

we stood at the manhole opening. "We'd better go down there after it—you and me, Shamble."

I was alarmed, with good reason. "*That's* the first solution you can think of?"

He pulled out the long flashlight at his hip. "Those tentacles murdered a man. I'll call for backup here, and it's not like you have to worry about dying again. Come on, it'll be brave."

I might have chosen a different word, but I knew he was right. As a private investigator with a strong moral backbone (sort of) and a beat cop dedicated to preserve and protect, we could not let a slimy tentacle killer go unpursued.

So, McGoo and I climbed down into the sewers. Holding the flashlight, he politely motioned for me to go first.

We made our way down the rungs and into the urine-warm and smelly waters that flowed through the passageways beneath the Quarter. The raised walkways along the tunnels were too narrow for a person to use, at least in this neighborhood, although rats commuted back and forth to work. At this time of the season, the water levels in the catacombs were less than knee-deep, despite the recent shit storm that had surged across the Quarter; even so, McGoo did not look happy about sloshing along.

He shone his bright white beam in front of us, but the ceiling lights were bright enough for us to see our way, so he switched off the flashlight. "You know the real disadvantage of following an aquatic tentacle creature, Shamble? It doesn't leave any footprints."

"We don't need footprints. I have a good idea where we should start looking." I explained what Fletcher had told us about Ah'Chulhu twisting the thumbscrews. "Follow me."

I set off in the lead, striking a confident pose like any good male, determined to convince everyone that I knew where I was going, although I mostly fumbled along and hoped. The gator-guys, not to mention Sheyenne and I, had been so lost during our last visit that I was not at all certain I could find Ah'Chulhu's main grotto. When we were in hot pursuit of a horrific tentacled monster, though, I didn't want to stop and ask directions.

"Hey, Shamble, did you hear about the girl monster with five legs? Her panties fit her like a glove!"

I peered down a dark side tunnel, but it didn't look familiar. "If the tentacles attack us, maybe you can sucker punch them with bad jokes."

As we sloshed along, I briefed McGoo on what I knew about Ah'Chulhu, his disadvantaged childhood, his parental issues, and his business suits. I think it was the latter that convinced McGoo he was a sinister criminal mastermind.

Through small speakers in the ceiling, we could hear the faint melodies of pipe-organ music, ominous, bombastic. As part of his improvements to the underworld, Ah'Chulhu had installed a sewer-wide sound system to provide pleasant background music. It seemed to be everywhere.

Now we heard the classic pipe-organ melody that I always thought of as the *"Phantom of the Opera* song," but Sheyenne (in her constant efforts to make me more culturally literate) had informed me that it was Bach's "Toccata and Fugue in D Minor." It's not my place to be a music critic, but that Bach guy really needed to pick catchier titles.

McGoo was also listening to the organ notes, frowning. "What *is* that?"

"Organ music," I answered, helpfully.

"I can hear that."

"Ah, but do you know the title of the piece?" I'm not a know-it-all, but I do like to prove that I know more than my BHF.

"Everybody knows the title," he said. "It's the *Phantom of the Opera* song."

I sighed. "Nailed it first time, McGoo."

As we followed the music, the scenery in the tunnels began to look familiar, and now I was certain we were going in the right direction. The tunnels began to converge, and the organ music grew louder up ahead—not just through the speakers of the sound system, but echoing throughout the sewers.

We reached the entrance to the large subterranean chamber where I'd first met Ah'Chulhu. Now the vault was crowded with frog demons and gator-guys, as well as numerous parents, some of them unnaturals, although many were human moms and dads.

Alarmed by the size of the crowd, McGoo asked, "Do you think Ah'Chulhu is building an army to take over the Quarter?"

"This seems more like a recital," I said.

Inside the grotto, on a temporary stage, the masked Phantom of the Opera wore his best tuxedo and sat on a bench in front of his small portable Wurlitzer organ, which had been brought in for the occasion. With his shoulders hunched and stiff, he attacked the small keys, his fingers bouncing up and down. His fingers flew along, eliciting notes with all the verve of a ragtime piano player.

A group of waifish young girls stood in their Sunday best dresses, waiting for the Phantom to finish his performance. The organ notes reached a finale, then fell off, and the Phantom turned to his audience. He doffed his white porcelain mask as he bowed, exposing his hideous features. But the audience applauded, slapping palms together, or paws, talons, or tentacles, some of them damp and squishy, others furred, others scaled.

McGoo grudgingly admitted, "That was a decent performance."

"Thus ends our interlude." The Phantom nestled his mask back into place. "Now, back to my charming students—angels who can sing like the devil."

The young girls shuffled into place, arranging themselves in a choir grouping. The Phantom directed the performance, waving his fingers back and forth. One after another, each girl performed a solo as the Phantom yelled, "Sing! Sing!" He pounded his chest. "Music must come from the heart!" Then he punched himself in the stomach. "And also from the diaphragm!"

McGoo and I worked our way through the crowd. Numerous parents were holding up camcorders or phone cameras to record the recital.

When the girls were finished, the audience applauded and cheered; proud parents called out their daughters' names. After a thorough inspection, however, I could spot no giant tentacles in the audience. To be completely honest, I was glad we hadn't encountered them while McGoo and I were alone in the tunnels.

Ah'Chulhu sat high on his porcelain throne, admiring the show. Seeing him, McGoo whispered to me, "You're right for once, Shamble—that guy really is ugly."

The half demon noticed us and rose up from his smooth white throne. "Crikey, gents, this is a private pageant! You got sprogs here among the singers?"

McGoo said in his best tough cop voice, "We're here investigating a murder. There's a monster on the loose."

I was afraid that would spark a panic, but the parents were so giddy at seeing their daughters perform that there was barely a murmur. One of the human parents said, "Lots of monsters around here."

Ah'Chulhu raised his voice. "A murder, you say? Bugger that." The mass of small, wormlike appendages around his mouth flickered and twitched. "Has anyone here been murdered?"

The muttering became an overlapping patchwork of "No," "Not me," "Nobody dead here," and "I was murdered, but not tonight."

"It didn't take place down here," I said, "but up in the alley behind the Basilisk nightclub. The owner and manager was slain by giant tentacles, and the tentacles escaped down into the sewers."

McGoo stood in a puddle that had dripped from his soaked trousers. "We're in hot pursuit."

"Good on ya," said Ah'Chulhu. "But what's that to do with us? You suspect me just because I have tentacles? That's bloody *profiling*, and I won't stand for it. Can you identify these murderous tentacles?"

"Long, rubbery, greenish brown . . . studded with suckers."

"That could be any giant tentacle creature," said Ah'Chulhu.

I knew that the ugly guy could rile up his audience and get us in even deeper poop than we had waded through in order to get here. I tried to defuse the situation. "We were just wondering if those tentacles might be friends of yours. You could help us solve a murder."

"Sorry, gents. I'm not acquainted with any murderous tentacles. I swear to you blokes that I've been here all night long listening to this wonderful recital by the Phantom's students."

The Phantom played an ominous series of notes on the little Wurlitzer, then stood up. "I can vouch for that."

All the parents lifted their camcorders and their phone cameras. Dozens of them would have time-stamped footage to prove Ah'Chulhu's whereabouts. He had an airtight alibi, although it seemed too convenient to me.

The Phantom continued, "Ah'Chulhu is a benevolent developer here in the underworld. He's going to grant music scholarships for the young singers I train."

"That's right," said Ah'Chulhu. "And I'm even piping some of the Phantom's easy-listening compositions throughout the catacombs. None of that insipid elevator music—sewer music."

"Yes, we noticed the new sound system on our way in." I tried to nudge McGoo out, knowing we could do nothing more here. "Very nice."

"Just bringing a little more joy to everyone's day," said the

Phantom in a flippant voice. "Now, the show must go on." He turned back to his Wurlitzer and played "Take Me Out to the Ball Game."

The UQPD spent the next two days running a dragnet through the entire sewer system in search of the gigantic tentacles. McGoo found himself in command of the operation, and because some of the other uniformed cops had even lower marks in their personnel files than he did, he put them on point, trudging through the labyrinth, tunnel after tunnel after tunnel.

They dredged up a lot of garbage, some of it interesting, most of it not. They uncovered numerous secrets, ruffled plenty of fins and scales, but ultimately found no gigantic tentacle creature. It had vanished.

The precinct chief announced that further efforts were not worth the cost in uniform cleaning, and the cops were put back on their usual beats.

CHAPTER 27

When the Mad Scientists Patent Office sends a courtesy notice, there isn't much courtesy involved.

The letter was delivered by a special civil-servant courier who worked for the low-bid delivery service the patent office was required to use, based on minority monster considerations, safety records, cost per delivery, plus a special government surcharge—with all the efficiency and speed *that* implied.

The courier was a gray-faced, dull-eyed zombie who seemed utterly uninterested in his job. He wore a delivery uniform that matched his skin tone, a cap that sat askew on his matted hair. His eyes had the sleepy apathy of an employee who never had to worry about being fired, and he moved with the speed of a greased glacier. When he arrived at our doorstep, he insisted it was time for a coffee and cigarette break, which he enjoyed at great length in the hallway, before he handed over the letter to an impatient Sheyenne.

Still shaken by Fletcher's murder, she had been throwing herself into work around the office to keep her mind occupied. Now she signed the receipt, handed back the courier's clipboard, and tore open the envelope. The zombie courier shuffled off to the end of the hall, where he felt he needed to take another break before descending the one flight of stairs.

From my desk, I watched Sheyenne's expression as she scanned the letter. "It's from the patent office," she called, then scowled at the date. "This was dispatched two days ago! What took the courier so long?"

Having seen him move, there wasn't much mystery about it. Even so, a zombie moving at his most lethargic, stiff-limbed shuffle should have been able to make it across the Quarter and back at least twice in that amount of time.

Robin took the letter from Sheyenne's ghostly hand and scanned it. "It reads like a summons, but not in proper legal terms."

It was an invitation, called a courtesy notice, from Deputy Assistant Manager of Patents Mellivar. "I request your immediate presence at my office regarding a matter of some concern. Come immediately, with all due dispatch, and quickly. I hope to see you very soon regarding the matter of the young man Jody Caligari."

At the bottom of the letter was a long paragraph of fine print containing disclaimers, legal notices, and CYA language that neither bound nor obligated the Mad Scientists Patent Office to any of the statements, claims, or promises made by any of their employees.

"We should have known about this two days ago," Sheyenne grumbled. "Miz Mellivar could have picked up a phone."

"That probably would have required her to fill out more forms." I realized that for a government office, responding within a leisurely couple of days did equate to "immediately."

Robin and I took the puttering Pro Bono Mobile to the patent offices in the nondescript business park. When we rang the service bell and showed the courtesy notice to the receptionist, apologizing for the delay, she blinked dully at her calendar. "Oh, the DAMP wasn't expecting you until tomorrow. If you fill out this early arrival intake form, I'll see if she's available."

She picked up an interoffice phone, paged Miz Mellivar's office, but got no answer. She finally located the Deputy Assistant Manager of Patents out in the testing laboratories. "She requests that you join her on the floor." The receptionist pointed toward the warehouse area at the back of the offices. "But before I allow you back there, you'll have to sign a waiver."

She shuffled her papers and handed us a form, which Robin perused, line by line, crossing out a few clauses, then signed before handing it over for my countersignature.

"Are the testing labs that dangerous?" I asked.

"It's a standard liability waiver," Robin said. "Probably unenforceable in the case of extreme circumstances. Primarily, they're afraid you might trip on the floor and break an arm, or bump into a desk and bruise yourself."

"Don't I have to worry about that every morning when I wake up?" I asked. "Or each time I cross a street?"

"Yes, but government facilities are prone to lawsuits," Robin said. "When you add pain and suffering, emotional distress, loss of work time and earning potential, it adds up."

I signed the form. All I needed to know was that Robin thought it was necessary, and she's my partner. And my lawyer.

The receptionist reached into a drawer beneath her desk and pulled out thick gloves and bulky safety goggles, which we were required to don. From a rack on the wall, she removed two plastic hard hats and gave us clean lab coats sealed in sanitary plastic bags "for health purposes."

"These are also mandatory," said the receptionist.

The back rooms of the Mad Scientist testing labs were full of chrome and tile, stainless-steel tables, laboratory benches, Bunsen burners, bubbling flasks, and a rack of vending machines in

the corner that sold soft drinks, snacks, and packets of preserved blood. Ventilation hoods sucked wafting toxic fumes
and released them to the outside air.

Teams of mad scientists in lab coats, thick horn-rimmed
glasses, and safety goggles meticulously worked through check-
lists. Every fifteen seconds or so explosions occurred with a
loud *pop!* that caused the testing scientists to scatter before they
returned to the area, taking notes. From the calm demeanor of
their coworkers, though, the explosions must have been planned,
or at least routine, events.

From the far end of the room came shouts, then panicked
screams. One team of scientists fled in absolute terror, flailing
their hands, eyes wide, mouths agape as they bolted for the
door. I tensed and prepared to defend Robin, just in case some
horrific monster had been unleashed, but none of the other
testing groups even glanced up from their work.

We found Miz Mellivar at a workstation against one wall,
where a straight-laced middle-aged man in a lab coat pushed his
glasses up on his nose and discussed the testing protocol. Beside him stood a drop-dead-gorgeous female lab assistant, listening eagerly as he explained even the simplest things.

Miz Mellivar turned when she saw us arrive. Her face soft-
ened just a fraction of a degree, which, for her, was apparently
the equivalent of a broad, welcoming grin. "Ms. Deyer, Mr.
Chambeaux, I'm glad you could come. I see by your rapid arrival that you understood the urgency of my letter."

"We must not delay the test, ma'am," said the scientist.
"There's been too much preparation."

DAMP Mellivar turned back to him. "Very well, I'm here to
observe. Proceed."

The scientist flipped on his equipment, studied readings,
gazed intently at the sine wave on an oscilloscope. His lab assistant stood there looking so beautiful I could tell she was a pro-

fessional. A lead-lined cubicle box faced a wire cage containing a white lab rat that squeaked and snuffled in search of treats, completely unaware of its impending doom.

Miz Mellivar explained, "We're verifying a new patent application. An entrepreneur has invented artificial Medusa heads, claiming they're just as potent as the original. He wants to manufacture them and release them on the open market."

Robin asked, "What possible use could anyone have for an artificial Medusa head?"

"Home security," said Miz Mellivar, without further explanation.

The scientist placed opaque goggles over his eyes and told us all to avert our gazes, while the lab assistant looked adoringly at him. Using black rubber gloves, he slid up a metal plate that covered a transparent window in the box. I was careful not to look at what the box contained, but out of the corner of my eye I did watch the rat. The rodent curiously looked toward the box, perhaps hoping for fresh kibble.

A pale electric-green glow pulsed out of the box. The rat reared up, its pink eyes going wide, its cute little front paws trembling in terror. Then it crackled, turned even whiter than it already was, and fell over as a petrified statue.

The scientist nodded and made a notation in his notebook, while the female lab assistant said, "Oh!" Then the petrified rat quivered and disintegrated into a pile of white powder. The scientist made another note as his beautiful lab assistant threw herself against his chest, sobbing.

"It seems to have a design flaw," I said. "Aren't Medusa heads supposed to turn things to stone?"

"Yes, but this is a kinder, gentler one," said DAMP Mellivar, "with built-in safety features designed to turn victims into powdered sugar rather than stone. The prototype appears to perform exactly as it was designed to do."

I couldn't see that turning a victim into a pile of powdered sugar was any safer than turning a victim into stone, but this wasn't my area of expertise.

Miz Mellivar complimented the scientist and his work, and he said with an appreciative glance at his beautiful lab assistant, "I couldn't have done a thing without Marilyn here." She fawned over him.

When Mellivar led us back to her office, she seemed sterner, more disturbed. "I called you here as a private matter, Mr. Chambeaux and Ms. Deyer. This is unofficial, and I would normally require approval even to consult with you, but, as you might have guessed, I have something of a soft spot for our junior mad scientist, Jody Caligari—as I think you do."

"We do," Robin admitted. "And we think his landlord may be involved in things much more questionable than wrongful eviction and illegal seizure of a tenant's property."

"Extortion and murder, for example," I added.

Miz Mellivar went behind her desk, looked down at several notes she had taken. "Yes, a Mr. . . . Ah'Chulhu. There's definitely something fishy going on. Ah'Chulhu has been in contact with the patent office, looking to secure the rights to Jody's prototype inventions. The young man submitted certain sketches, schematics, blueprints, and design specifications, and, of course, the actual working prototype of his X-ray Spex."

"I thought you said Jody's patents were denied?" I asked.

"*Pending* and under review," corrected Miz Mellivar. "Not quite the same thing. Ah'Chulhu wanted to buy them all outright. He became very aggressive about it. At the same time, he purchased the rights to numerous other patents, obscure ones like protective spells and anti-evil equipment. Those are all a matter of public record, available for sublicense or direct rip-off. He wanted to secure rip-off approval for Jody's devices, too, but I denied it. That's my job. Patents are sacred and important. This office is powerful, and I will not let it be abused."

She tapped her fingertips on her desk. "He got pretty nasty about it, said some very offensive things—at least I think they were offensive. I don't actually speak Australian."

I found this disturbing indeed. "Sounds like Ah'Chulhu wants more than just back rent."

CHAPTER 28

With a tentacle monster on the loose in the sewers after the murder of Fletcher Knowles, the gator-guy intimidation against Lurrm at the Recompose Spa, the dangerous gang of thieving lawn gnomes, an ogre whose operatic voice had been stolen, and an adorable junior mad scientist who needed his evil inventions back, I found it difficult to devote all my energy to the alleged nefarious shenanigans in the Wuwufo campaign.

But, as I had told Sheyenne at Basilisk, each client's case was the most important thing in the client's life. As Thunder Dick's numbers dipped in the polls for the upcoming election, he felt as if the entire universe were collapsing around him. And when a weather wizard was upset, an emotional tempest—even one in a teapot—could get out of hand.

Thunder Dick stood in our offices wringing his hands, distraught and infuriated. His beard and hair looked wild and disheveled, as if combed by hurricane winds. The rainbow colors of his wizard robe seemed faded, an indication of the extreme stress he had been under, not to mention the frequent rough washings by storms he himself had conjured. At his feet, Morris/Maurice licked a paw, the picture of nonchalance.

The wizard threw a folded newspaper down on Sheyenne's desk. "This goes below the belt and above the knee! These photos were never supposed to be released."

I saw the printed picture of Thunder Dick grinning, unaware of a dark and embarrassing clump of spinach caught between his teeth. Another photo showed a close-up of his face with a crusty dried booger hanging out of one nostril.

"Alastair Cumulus the Third is *evil*," he cried with such vehemence that spittle sprayed from between his lips. "And in this case, evil isn't a good thing! These photos have nothing to do with my policies or my qualifications. They are irrelevant to the campaign. They serve only to embarrass me—and to hurt my feelings."

Sheyenne looked over at the newspaper and agreed. "Those are some bad pictures."

The cat started licking his other paw.

Thunder Dick could barely control his outrage as he unfolded the newspaper to show us the full spread below the fold. "This one's the worst."

The image showed Thunder Dick asleep, his head tilted back, mouth gaping as he snored. A thin rivulet of drool dribbled from the corner of his mouth and down his chin to become lost in the saturated tangle of his beard. The caption read, *If elected Wuwufo president, Thunder Dick promises to work hard for the Unnatural Quarter.*

"And where does my rival get them? You have to stop that evil man, Mr. Chambeaux. Alastair Cumulus the Third is a pustule on our profession."

"Do you have any embarrassing photos of him?" Sheyenne asked. "We could counter with that."

I was surprised. "Don't encourage him. We don't stoop to that level."

I expected Robin to argue as well, but she said, "As an attorney, I do need to know what leverage I have, even if we don't use it. Besides, in politics I'm not sure there is such a thing as above-the-belt advertising."

Thunder Dick was dejected. "As far as I can tell, my rival never takes bad photos." He shook his head. "I even paid bribes to get a copy of his driver's license photo—only to find out that it looks like a studio portrait!"

"Uncanny," I said. "Nobody takes a good driver's license photo."

On the floor, Morris/Maurice began the strange acrobatic bathing move that only cats can perform, rolling half on his back with his tail twitching, sticking one hind leg up in the air and grasping it with the front paw so that he could reach his nether regions in what amounted to a feline Cirque du Soleil performance.

"Time for a face-to-face meeting with Mr. Cumulus," I said. "I'll try to convince him to bring a higher level of decorum to this campaign."

Thunder Dick snorted, "Ha, good luck with that. That fatassed turd face doesn't know the first thing about decorum."

"Unlike you," I said.

"Unlike me," the weather wizard agreed and stalked off with his cat.

Alastair Cumulus III lived in a fine residence in a quiet section of town where the homes were crowded close together. It was obvious that a weather wizard lived there. Instead of banners and flags for decoration, Cumulus had orange windsocks. Rain gauges adorned the shrubbery. A weather vane spun haphazardly on the top of the roof; another one with a dragon pointing north stood on a metal rod next to the driveway. A serrated copper stake allowed the measurement of snowfall or flood waters. Anemometers spun like eggbeaters as competing breezes held a battle around the small house.

I didn't see any lawn gnomes, nor did I expect to.

A swift gust almost blew my fedora away, but I caught it in time. I was getting good at that. I rang the bell at the front door, which sounded like a loud foghorn. It seemed a corny gimmick, but immediately thereafter rafts of dense mist wafted up from a sprinkler system.

The erudite and prissy weathermancer opened the door and regarded me as if I were a proselytizer selling newspaper subscriptions or religions. He stroked his forked beard with two fingers and regarded me with a frown. "How may I help you? Can I brighten a gloomy day? You look like you could use a sunny disposition—my services are for hire."

"I'd like to speak with you about the Wuwufo campaign, Mr. Cumulus the Third," I said.

He looked at me with narrowed eyes. "I've seen you before. You were in the museum when I rescued the Egyptian exhibit."

"And other places." I retrieved one of my business cards and handed it to him. "Dan Chambeaux, Private Investigator, from Chambeaux and Deyer Investigations."

Alastair Cumulus regarded the card, then pocketed it. "The walking dead certainly get around. I'll keep this in case I need a zombie detective. Would you like to contribute to my campaign? You've seen what I can do."

"I've seen. Your opponent hired me to investigate certain nefarious campaign shenanigans, such as vandalism of his campaign signs and posters, and the release of embarrassing photos to the media. Could I come inside, please?"

A storm crossed the weather wizard's face. "My opponent claims *I've* used unacceptable tactics? A pot shouldn't call a kettle black."

"No more than reasonable men should use clichés," I replied. "In any case, you may not want to have this discussion out in the open."

Grudgingly, Cumulus let me inside. The weathermancer's main sitting room had Victorian furniture, a loud ticking grandfather clock, a glass decanter of sherry and two snifters on a tray (which I had never seen except in movies). Oil paintings of storm-whipped landscapes hung on his wall. Though he had electric lighting fixtures on the ceiling, he lit the room with hurricane lamps. Four large TVs were on one wall, each tuned to a different weather channel.

"Let me explain something, Mr. Chambeaux." Cumulus took a seat in an overstuffed leather chair decorated with brass studs. "I am running for president of the Weather Wizards Fraternal Order, and I intend to win. To that end, I'll do whatever is necessary to show the voters I am the best candidate. However, I have done nothing illegal, or even nefarious. Why would I need to resort to dirty tricks? My opponent's embarrassing incompetence and social ineptitude is self-evident."

"He seems a nice enough guy," I said.

"Maybe, but would you want him running anything more complicated than a coffeemaker?"

Not wanting to give my opinion on the matter, I brought out the folded newspaper, although I was sure Cumulus had seen it. "And what about these shocking photos?"

He snorted. "I had nothing to do with those pictures. I can't even say that they're a bad likeness. Have you seen Richard in person? He actually looks like that half the time."

I was surprised he would deny his involvement so plainly, since politicians rarely give straight answers. "Are you suggesting Thunder Dick released these images himself so he could appear to be a victim, while making you the bad guy?"

Cumulus chuckled. "My foggy bottom! That level of intellectual complexity is far beyond poor Richard Thudner. I'm merely stating that *I* had nothing to do with it."

He poured himself a glass of sherry, but didn't offer me one, so I had no opportunity to refuse his hospitality. He hadn't invited me to sit down either.

"To tell you the truth, Mr. Chambeaux, I have nothing to gain by becoming the Wuwufo president. As a professional organization, it spends more time in flame wars and debating the style of the organizational tie tack than actually accomplishing anything. But I could not in good conscience allow an oaf like Richard Thudner to run unopposed. I am obviously the superior candidate, and the voters will see it as well. I don't need to release embarrassing photos to make my case. It's obvious."

"Obvious in what way?" I asked.

He leaned back in his overstuffed chair and ticked off the reasons on his fingers. "In the first place, I have no need for a familiar. I'm in charge of my own powers, and I don't require some furry animal for moral support. And I don't need a talisman either. Thunder Dick always wears that sundial thing around his neck, but it's a crutch. Without it, he couldn't create a sunny day in June, and that's a sign of weakness if you ask me. And finally, well, I'm *me.*"

As he spoke, a white cottony cloud materialized above the overstuffed leather chair. The cloud grew thicker, grayer, and then black, and a rumbling sound came from inside. Cumulus raised his left hand in a languid gesture. "Please step a bit to your left."

I lurched to the side just before a lightning bolt seared out like a spear hurled by Zeus himself. (Or maybe Thor was the one who threw lightning bolts. Sometimes I get my mythologies mixed up.) The bolt blasted the corner of the room, sending up a shower of sparks.

I staggered, grabbing a shelf to steady myself.

"A spider," Cumulus explained. "I can't abide spiders. Now, if you don't mind, I'm rather busy. I have tomorrow's weather to plan."

He didn't offer to show me out, and I didn't ask. When I left through the front door, the fog was still so thick I could barely see the sidewalk, and I had to fumble my way out to the street.

CHAPTER 29

Despite being a lawyer, Robin is normally a trusting sort of person. Now, however, she sounded suspicious. "It's a very secretive organization, the Weather Wizards Fraternal Order."

"Wuwufo is easier to pronounce," I said, then reconsidered. "Well, I guess not."

"Lawyers like to be accurate in every detail," Robin said. "On behalf of our client, I tried to get more background on the organization itself, so I requested a copy of their membership directory. I wanted to look at the other members to get a feel for the politics involved in this election. But I was flatly refused. Dead end."

"We could look at Thunder Dick's personal copy," I suggested. "I'm sure he'd let us."

Robin shook her head. "Release of private information in the directory to non-members is grounds for expulsion."

"If he's expelled, Thunder Dick couldn't very well be the president of the organization," I said. Stripped of weather-mancer membership, he would also likely have to change his name back to Richard Thudner.

Robin shuffled papers. "I researched what I could. Wuwufo has some public activities. They sponsor a nonprofit scholarship for a rainy day, and recently they financed new protective nets under the eaves of City Hall to prevent citizen impalement by falling icicles, but nobody really knows what the organization does behind closed doors or how influential the members are."

"Typical professional organization," I said.

There was also a Private Investigators Club that discussed matters of professional interest to other detectives. I had been active in it when I started out as a human PI. I even bought a lifetime membership, although many of the club's concerns didn't relate to my work in the Unnatural Quarter.

To make matters worse, after I was killed and came back from the dead, I received a notice in the mail that my lifetime membership had been terminated because I was no longer alive. They told me I could write an appeal letter to the club membership committee, but I hadn't gotten around to it, and I found that my life was just as fulfilling without their monthly newsletter.

Robin continued to skim down the list that the magic pencil had written neatly on her legal pad. "I've filed several information requests under transparency laws, hoping for a list of Alastair Cumulus the Third's public campaign donors. So far, though, all the requests have been turned down. Wuwufo is a private organization and not bound by campaign finance laws. I can't even figure out who's paying for Thunder Dick's campaign, and he's our own client. He's very tight-lipped about it."

Sheyenne flitted in. "Oh, I know a way around that—I'll get you the information."

Even Robin looked surprised. "How?"

"I'll just file a similar request to the same office. And another one this afternoon. And another one tomorrow morning."

Robin and I looked at each other, then back at Sheyenne. I said, "But if we've already been turned down, what good will that do?"

She flashed a quirk of a smile. "We can always count on red tape and incompetence. If we try enough times, we'll get lucky. Someone is bound to slip up."

At the Goblin Tavern, Stentor the ogre tried to drown his sorrows, but the metaphorical water wasn't deep enough to do the job.

I took the big guy along with me to the Tavern, because it was time to visit my designated stool with McGoo, but primarily because the impatient ogre had come back to our offices, hoping for a report. When I had no progress to tell him, the ogre paced around the waiting area, nervously blundering and bumping into the furniture. Neither Robin nor Sheyenne could get work done, and for the safety of our furniture, and walls, and ceiling, I decided I had better take him elsewhere.

Francine the bartender was good at understanding the problems of her customers, and I let Stentor squeak out his tale of woe for her. It made him feel better to unload, even though an echo of his words was probably also coming out of the distant lawn gnome's mouth. Who knows, maybe it would make Mr. Bignome feel a little guilt.

Even though she knew why the baritone ogre sounded like a chipmunk, Francine suggested a special hot toddy concoction that would surely help. Stentor's gloom brightened just a little, and I told Francine to conjure her concoction. I even offered to pay. "What have you got to lose, Stentor?"

She whipped up a batter that had the color and consistency of tar, to which she added smoking spirits from a dusty bottle beneath the bar. She sniffed, winced, and declared it perfect. "I used to make these at a biker bar where I worked. Sometimes the boys would get too loud and rowdy, and this pacified them."

Stentor took the mug in his beefy hands and slurped. "Tastes awful," he said, and took a bigger gulp.

"Better make another one, Francine," I suggested.

When Stentor finished his drink, he tilted his head back and tried to shout, but only a weak, high-pitched noise came out. I could see his clear disappointment. "Give it a little time to work," I said.

The ogre rested his elbows on the bar. "I've been shouting myself hoarse. That's what Officer McGoohan told me to do. I've been practicing my scales, singing arias—and not just to make that thieving lawn gnome crazy. I have to keep my vocal cords conditioned, just in case. Great voice talent doesn't come easy."

McGoo burst through the Tavern door, his face flushed, his cap askew. I usually expected him at this time of the evening, but he didn't normally arrive with such an uproar. I raised my hand and caught the bartender's attention. "Francine, looks like McGoo's in a hurry for a beer."

"Shamble," he said, panting. "I knew I'd find you here!"

"That doesn't take much detective work." I turned to the ogre. "Stentor, you're in his seat."

"No time for a beer tonight—we've had a breakthrough!" He grinned at the ogre. "And I'm glad *he's* here."

"What kind of breakthrough?" I asked.

"Did you find my voice?" Stentor turned around on the barstool so quickly that one of the legs groaned. I was afraid it would break.

"The station just received a very interesting complaint, a neighbor calling in to report a disturbance. A troll living near a large abandoned building complained about constant noisy opera singing."

"That can't be a coincidence," I said. "How many opera singers are there in the Quarter."

"More than you might think," said Stentor. "But what did he mean by 'noisy'?" He sounded offended.

"According to the report, the troll called it 'worse than wet bagpipes played by a Scottish ghost with a tin ear.' "

Stentor's shoulders drooped, and he hunched over the second mug of the steaming tarry concoction Francine had delivered. "Then it can't be my voice."

I patted him on the huge shoulder. "I'm afraid it might be. Not everyone has a taste for opera."

Stentor vacillated between being hopeful and insulted. "Once I get my voice back, I'd like to have a few words with this troll."

"Where are Mr. Bignome and his gang holed up, McGoo?" I asked, then turned to the ogre, raising a warning finger. "But be careful what you say out loud, Stentor. Remember, Bignome can hear every word that comes out of your mouth."

The ogre's eyes widened, and he made a zipping-his-lips-shut gesture.

McGoo nodded. "They're in the Lawn and Garden section of an abandoned department store." His eyes sparkled with excitement. "This is the break we needed. They're putting together a task force at the precinct right now, heading out within an hour. Want to go along on the raid, Shamble? Bignome is part of your case, too."

"Wouldn't miss it, McGoo." I touched my hip, making sure the .38 was there. "So long as my friend Stentor can join us."

McGoo sized up the enormous ogre. "Sure thing. We can use the extra muscle."

Stentor swung down from the barstool, which toppled and crashed to the floor in his eagerness to get going. He jabbered with all the enthusiasm and tonality of a hyperactive squirrel. "When I get my job back at the opera, I'll send you and the entire police force free tickets to my first performance."

CHAPTER 30

At the precinct station the squad cars were prepped, and the incident commander gave a quick briefing. I could take care of myself in a crisis, but I felt like a fifth wheel at the moment. Stentor tried his best to stay out of the way, and failed completely.

"Remember, be careful not to say anything," I cautioned the ogre. "You could give away the raid, ruin the element of surprise."

The big ogre nodded vigorously, again putting a finger to his lips to shush himself.

Before heading out, officers donned bulletproof vests and safety goggles for protection against Timmy gun slugs. McGoo gave me one, since my body had had enough close encounters with bullets of various calibers, thank you. The officers were flustered when they couldn't find a vest that was even remotely ogre sized. Stentor was impatient with the delay. He struggled with himself, wanting to blurt out an argument, and he finally went over to a whiteboard on the station wall and picked up one of the markers in his zucchini-sized fingers to write, *Don't need a vest. I'm bulletproof.* He picked up a stapler from a nearby desk and bashed it against his bicep, where it shattered into pieces of plastic and metal. "See."

"That only proves you're stapler proof," said one of the uniformed cops.

"They're just Timmy guns," I said. "Not much stronger than staplers."

McGoo finally said, "No more delays. That gang could be on the move." Stentor danced from foot to foot as if he'd had too much coffee and too little time in the bathroom.

Next came a debate about whether all the squad cars should roar in and surround the Lawn and Garden department with sirens blaring and ultimatums shouted through bullhorns—which would be dramatic, but not conducive to surprise.

"If you did that, you'd be asking for a shoot-out," I said.

McGoo agreed. "We haven't had a good shoot-out in months, but our objective is to arrest the lawn gnomes, not kill them all. I want to see those pint-sized creeps sentenced to twenty years of hard labor on a chain gang, chipping away at ornamental landscaping rock."

Six squad cars rolled out in the middle of the night, carrying a dozen uniformed officers loaded for bear (or lawn gnome), a zombie detective, and a vocally challenged ogre. I rode with McGoo in the front seat while Stentor occupied the entire back. The vehicles headed across town in a silent caravan.

With a minimum of roaring engines and squealing tires, the cars pulled up in the empty retail parking lot beneath darkened streetlights. As the black-and-whites parked in a haphazard cluster in front of the Lawn and Garden department entrance (carefully avoiding the faded paint of a handicapped spot), Stentor struggled to climb out of the squad car, leaning on the door so heavily that one of the hinges bent.

In front of the door, dead and dry plants—petunias, I think—filled terracotta pots with an old sign indicating that they were marked down for quick sale. Some of the letters on the store sign had fallen askew.

The building was dark and sinister, but we could see a few moving lights inside, shielded camping lanterns the gnomes must have stolen from the sporting department.

Haunted houses may seem scary, but there's nothing more sinister than an abandoned department store. It's a building of broken dreams and disappointed shoppers, promises of discounts that would never be fulfilled, holiday sales that would never meet their potential. Fortunately, I don't enjoy shopping much, so I didn't get too wistful.

McGoo put a finger to his lips, reminding everyone to be quiet. The uniformed officers spread out, creeping up to the glass entrance doors. Before anyone drew close, the automatic door whisked open, surprising us all. The cops froze. I had my pistol drawn. Stentor followed me, as if trying to take shelter behind my gaunt form.

Our officers hadn't triggered the door, though. One of the lawn gnomes sauntered out—the green one with the shamrock on his lapel. Preoccupied, he didn't notice any of us as he hunched over; a flare of light brightened the dark entryway as he lit his pipe and stood puffing.

The raiding squad stood motionless for two full seconds, not sure what to do—until the lawn gnome spotted us. His eyes sprang open so wide that he looked like one of Snow White's animated dwarves, and he yelled out in a voice that would have been the envy of any ogre opera singer. "Cops! Boss, the cops is here!"

"The cops *are* here," McGoo corrected, then raised his voice. "You're under arrest. Surrender and come out quietly."

Instead, the shamrock lawn gnome threw down his smoldering pipe and bolted back into the dark department store. Now that the surprise was blown, two cops raced back to their squad cars and flipped on the sirens, unleashing an explosion of noise. Strobe blue-and-red lights lit up the parking lot, as if the store had reopened and was announcing a big sale.

McGoo ducked into the front of his car, grabbed a bullhorn, and yelled, "Bignome, we know you're in there. Come out with your hands up."

In response, one of the plate-glass windows shattered. The skinny barrel of a Timmy gun extended and began to spit gunfire like popping popcorn. As the cops yelled and dove for cover, small-caliber bullets pinged and bounced off the squad cars, the darkened light poles, and even a few bulletproof vests. Two more store windows broke out, and additional Timmy-gun fire peppered the night.

The police shot back in a barrage of much-larger-caliber fire, and I joined in, firing my .38 because it seemed like the thing to do. We were very thorough, making sure that all the store windows were completely shattered.

During a brief lull in the gunfire, a loud voice—which properly belonged inside the throat of an ogre—bellowed, "You'll never take me alive, coppers!"

To which Stentor yelled back (and a louder echo of his voice came from the darkened Lawn and Garden department), "You'd better not damage my voice."

The lawn gnome took control of the voice again. "Stop that—it's disorienting."

Stentor pushed past me, squeaking, "Let me take care of this." He bounded toward the door, attracting more Timmy-gun fire, which simply bounced off his pebbly skin as if the bullets were no more than staples.

"Lay down some covering fire," McGoo shouted through the bullhorn, which made him sound very Stentorious himself. The cops opened fire, driving the cornered lawn gnomes farther back in the store, away from the windows.

The ogre bounded ahead faster than the automatic doors could respond; he smashed right through, knocking them off the tracks and leaving the abandoned Lawn and Garden department wide open. The machine-gun fire ceased as the lawn gnomes retreated into the darkness.

"Everyone, move out," McGoo yelled. "They've got no place to go. Let's round them up—alive if possible."

One of the other cops muttered, "Nobody's going to notice a few chips or paint scuffs if we rough them up a little."

The uniformed officers surged into the Lawn and Garden department, holding flashlights in one hand, firearms in the other. I was already chasing after Stentor. There was no stopping the ogre.

As we ran through the door together, McGoo flashed me a broad grin. "Now this is the kind of shoot-out I've been looking forward to, Shamble." Then he split off to follow the sounds of gunshots that rang out in the shadows.

The shamrock lawn gnome was trying to hide inside a stack of rolled green garden hoses, but he had underestimated his height, and the pointed top of his cap protruded above the coils. He surrendered when two cops drew down on him. Their standard-issue handcuffs proved to be too large for the lawn gnome's wrists, but the policemen used duct tape, and escorted the captive green gnome out to their squad car.

Two other lawn gnomes barricaded themselves behind a stack of plant food bags. They popped up, opened fire with their Timmy guns, and ducked back down. The cops launched return fire, bursting the sacks and sending up clouds of powdered plant food.

McGoo signaled, pointing to larger bags on shelves above the barricaded lawn gnomes—forty-pound sacks of manure, marked "highest quality." In response, the cops shot out the sacks and split them open so that their contents buried the besieged gnomes. McGoo and his companions raced forward to make the arrest. Other officers called out success as they collared two more lawn gnomes.

I made my way toward the back of the store, where Stentor had charged into the dimness, shoving aside folding plastic lawn chairs, knocking over barbecue grills. He was after Mr. Bignome himself.

"Be careful, Stentor," I shouted. "There's nothing more dangerous than a cornered rat."

"*I'm* more dangerous than any rodent," the ogre squeaked back, "cornered or otherwise." The same words echoed in a louder voice from the potted plant section ahead.

"Bignome, there's no way out!" I yelled. "You can't hide from us."

"I'll never surrender," the loud voice came back. "I'll never do time in the prison yard—or *any* yard!"

Stentor seized his stolen voice again. "Oh, yes, you will." We could hear the words emanating from the lawn gnome's hiding place.

I caught up with him. "That's it, Stentor! Keep yelling, and we'll pinpoint his location by the voice."

The ogre kept shouting, and his displaced words echoed out, "Over here. I'm over here. Helloooo! Oh, I think I just wet my pants." The last was followed by an angry mutter from the lawn gnome.

The gunfire had petered out in other parts of the store, and McGoo caught up with us. "We've got them all except the ringleader, Shamble." Then he raised his voice, yelling into the gloom. "Bignome, I'll give you one last chance—come out with your hands up."

The gnome's voice came back from the clutter of shadows and potted plants. "We've already been over this."

A rattle of Timmy-gun fire shattered the dimness. McGoo and I instinctively took cover behind large terracotta planters, but the ogre didn't bother. He blundered ahead, knocking aside anything that was in his way.

Mr. Bignome chose to make his last stand by climbing to the top of a set of rickety metal shelves, nearly five feet high. On his body I saw several white chips where the black paint on his jaunty vest and pointed cap had been damaged. Broken clay pots and upended watering cans lay all around.

In a blaze of glory, Bignome swiveled his Timmy gun from side to side, spitting out a succession of pipping and popping gunfire. "You want a piece of this?" He shot more pots, which shattered around us. His painted eyes blazed. "You'll never get me!"

McGoo started shooting, and bullets ricocheted off the metal shelves. Bignome dodged and ducked. The framework of the shelf unit wobbled, but the lawn gnome kept his balance. "You'll never take me alive, coppers!"

As Stentor charged forward, he stubbed his toe on a large overturned planter. He stumbled, reached out to catch his balance, and grabbed the edge of the metal rack, jostling the shelf unit.

The evil gang leader teetered and wobbled on the top shelf. He barely had enough time to wail, "Nooooo!" before he toppled off the shelf. He fell several feet to the concrete floor, where he shattered into a hundred jagged plaster pieces.

McGoo and I rushed forward, guns still drawn, but it was too late. Bignome was irreparably broken, and no amount of epoxy or touch-up paint could put him back together again.

We stood together, looking down at the sad debris. "Case closed," McGoo said. "He really was hollow inside."

"Case closed," I agreed. I turned to the stunned-looking ogre, who stared with round tear-filled eyes and a quivering lower lip. "Right, Stentor?"

"I sure hope so," the ogre replied.

But all that came out of his throat was a minuscule squeak.

CHAPTER 31

It took almost until dawn for McGoo and his squad to wrap up the scene of the shoot-out at the Lawn and Garden department. Two police officers had to receive Band-Aids for injuries caused by the Timmy-gun pellets, but Mr. Bignome was the only fatality of the raid; all the other lawn gnomes had been arrested, duct-taped, and sent for processing back at the station.

The coroner came in to inspect the broken Mr. Bignome and pronounced him shattered on arrival, after which a police janitorial squad swept up the pieces. While McGoo was grateful that the lawn gnomes' crime spree was finally over, he would have a tough job delivering the news to poor Mama Bignome.

I had my own client to take care of, though, and Stentor looked more anguished than I had ever seen him. Not only did he feel guilty that his clumsiness had toppled the lawn gnome from a five-foot-high shelf, but now he despaired of ever recovering his voice. Hearing the potentially operatic tones emerging from Bignome's throat had given him hope. But now . . .

I consoled Stentor as he sat hunched at a picnic table that had been marked down, unsuccessfully, for final sale before the store was abandoned. His shoulders shook like an earthquake, tears streamed down his face, and his fat lips trembled in dismay. He snuffled so loudly that his snot sounded like a garden slug being sucked down a vacuum hose.

"Now what am I going to do, Mr. Chambeaux?"

"I think your voice might be getting a little better," I lied. "Maybe the process takes a while."

"Or maybe my voice disappeared into the air when Bignome shattered. What if it's gone forever?"

"Let's talk to some real experts before we draw any conclusions. Maybe we skipped a step. It could be a simple spell, and everything will be fixed."

"Or it could be a hard spell," the ogre moaned.

"Mavis and Alma are good at hard spells, too," I said. "Come with me. It's too early to go to the publishing offices, but this deserves a house call."

I often visited the Wannovich sisters at their apartment. I had been their guest for a monthly meeting of the Pointy Hat Society, a loquacious group of women who gossiped about spells, coven matters, recipes, the best price for eye of newt, and other women's issues. I also went there for my monthly maintenance spell.

Stentor followed me along the streets of the Quarter just as dawn was breaking. I recognized the Wannoviches' apartment by its distinctive welcome mat: *Abandon Hope Ye Who Enter Here.*

I rang the bell while the ogre stood forlorn and shuffling his feet. I heard a snorting and a scrape of trotters from the other side of the door. When the door opened, the large sow filled most of the space, snuffling with delight to see me.

Behind her, Mavis wore a housecoat, and her hair was done up in sharp metal combs to continue the distressed look. "Why, Dan Chambeaux, what a surprise! I'm afraid I'm a mess."

I stepped inside. "It's not a social call, Mavis. This is an urgent matter."

Stentor worked his way through the doorway, careful not to break anything. He squeaked, "Good morning, ma'am."

Mavis's expression fell. "So you haven't found your voice yet, Mr. Stentor? Sorry to hear that."

"Oh, we found it, but something went wrong," I said, then explained how Bignome had been killed in the shoot-out.

"Completely shattered," Stentor added.

"But as you can hear, his voice still isn't back," I said. "Is there any way you can help? What did we do wrong?"

"Oh, dear. This will require some thought." Mavis bustled around. "It's breakfast time—would you like me to make you some eggs? I could scramble a whole cauldron. And don't worry, I keep the lizard eggs and the chicken eggs separated now to avoid confusion. There won't be any more embarrassing mishaps. I can promise you that."

I was glad I hadn't been there for the last mishap, whatever it was. "No, thanks. I usually just have coffee in the mornings."

Stentor said, "I could use a dozen eggs—scrambled please. And bacon, too, if you have it. I like bacon."

Alma responded with a huff and a rude snort. Mavis said, "We don't serve bacon around here, Mr. Stentor."

"Oh," he said, mortally embarrassed. "You're Jewish?"

"Just eggs will be fine, Mavis," I said. "We're more interested in the vocal-transference spell. Was there a glitch? Why didn't Stentor's voice come back when the lawn gnome shattered?"

Alma dutifully went to a low bookshelf, knocked over one of the spell books, and begun ruffling through the pages. "My sister will find what you need to know in a jiffy," Mavis said as she pulled out a full carton of eggs from the refrigerator. She sniffed them, then put them back and took a different package from a lower shelf. "Yes, these are the ones."

She cracked the eggs into a large bowl while she heated a black pot over the raging fire that formed a single broad burner on her stove. She poured the eggs into the cauldron and popped down slices of bread for toast.

In the living room, Alma selected another book and used her snout to turn the pages.

Mavis scooped the scrambled eggs onto an enormous platter for the ogre with five slices of toast. She gave a much smaller serving to me, though I had asked for none. She nudged the toast toward me. "I put some special marmalade on there for you."

Stentor tucked into the meal, but before I could take a bite, Alma let out a happy squeal. Mavis hurried over, picked up the book, and skimmed the lines of runes and strange incantations. "Ah, I think we found the trouble. Here, let me run a spell check." She muttered a set of confusing words, snapped her fingers, and looked down at an arcane symbol that had appeared in a blank spot on the page. "Exactly correct. Mr. Stentor, I'm happy to inform you that your voice *is* back—but only halfway. This spell is not complete, yet. You skipped a step.

"When Mr. Bignome was shattered, your voice left his body . . . but went back into the frog, which was the catalyst for the vocal transfer in the first place. We'll need to use the original frog to connect your voice back to you." She looked up, pleased and relieved. "There, your problem is solved! How are the eggs, by the way?"

Stentor set down his fork with a clatter, and his lower lip began bouncing again like a trampoline.

"Now what's wrong?" I asked. "That's the answer we were looking for."

He hung his huge shaggy head. "But I let the frog go! I felt bad about keeping it in that little plastic container. It seemed hungry and lonely, so I turned it loose back into the wild, where it belongs, where it can roam free."

Mavis clucked her tongue. "You'll have to get it back before you can retrieve your voice."

The ogre started sobbing. This was all starting to sound like a tragic opera in its own right. "But how will I ever find it now?"

I patted him on the big solid shoulders. "Don't give up hope. I've had harder cases."

He didn't seem to know where to start, so I made a suggestion. "We'll try the same trick you used to help find the lawn gnome gang—if you call out, the words should emerge from the frog's mouth. Keep shouting as often as possible, 'Help! Someone has stolen my voice. If found, please call the police.' A Good Samaritan is bound to call it in."

I wrote down the phrase for him so he could remember.

Stentor looked slightly less miserable now that we had a plan. "I'll try it, as soon as I finish my eggs," he said. "I'll shout it all day long."

CHAPTER 32

I hadn't been in the office much for the past day. When I got back late the next morning, I found that I had lost the use of my desk.

Jody Caligari had commandeered my office. The kid had brought in fabric, scissors, a sewing kit, modeling clay, and a fishing tackle box filled with costuming doodads and paraphernalia. When he looked up at me with his innocent expression, his red hair was masterfully tousled. His freckles looked as if they'd been stolen from an ancient *Howdy Doody* rerun, and his grin was infectious. "Hi, Mr. Chambeaux! I hope you don't mind. Sheyenne told me I could use your desk."

I wasn't sure how to respond. "That desk is where I solve cases, Jody."

The young man looked crestfallen. "Sheyenne says you mostly solve cases by wandering around and bumping into clues."

I glanced across the lobby to where Sheyenne sat at her own desk, giving me a mischievous smile. I turned back to the kid.

"It's a little more involved than that. A detective has to know *where* to wander around. There's an art to it. You get a certain feel for who or what you might bump into. It's called investigating, kid."

I glanced at the costume strewn across my desktop. Something about it looked familiar, but it wasn't a mummy disguise or the hunchback lab assistant iGor. "Where did all my notes and files go?" The disorganized arrangement had made a certain sense to me.

"I stacked them all in perfect piles," Jody said, as if expecting a pat on the head. "Everything careful, neat, and even alphabetized."

Now I'd never be able to find anything, but I didn't want to crush the kid after he thought he'd done a good deed. "Sheyenne will help me sort it all out. She's good at that." From her desk she teasingly stuck out her tongue at me. "But I have to ask, why are you using my office?"

"Because it was available," the kid said in a bright voice.

"Shouldn't you be at Junior Mad Scientist Camp? If you can't motivate yourself, how will you motivate a minion army?"

He shook his head. "This part is a directed-study program, and we're expected to have our own resources." His voice hitched, and tears suddenly filled his sparkling blue eyes. "And I have no place else to go."

I said in a rush, "It's all right. We've got temporary space. Stay here as long as you like. No big deal."

Robin stopped outside my office. "He's just keeping busy while he waits."

The boy bobbed his head up and down. "The patent office has got to approve my inventions soon."

"I wouldn't set your heart on that," I said, though I didn't have any objection to him working on his costume in the meantime. He might as well occupy himself with something innocuous. I reached out to touch the dark fabric, some kind of robe. "Is this part of your Dr. Darkness outfit?"

"This is something else, and nobody can see it until it's finished." Jody snatched away the costume, pulling it protectively toward himself. "Dr. Darkness!!!—and don't forget the three exclamation points—is going to be the world's best supervillain. Here, look, I've sketched out a modified costume. It operates on the same physical principles as the prototype that Ah'Chulhu stole, but it looks cooler. More Silver Age."

He showed me his sketch of a muscular, grinning villain. There was a hood and a mask, flashy gloves, an elegant cape that drifted about whether or not there was a breeze. In the center of his chest, where most costumed characters sported a logo of some kind, were three yellow exclamation points.

"It's mostly black," said Jody, "a fashion statement because he is Dr. Darkness!!! after all. The fabric has special absorbent properties, so that it drains dark energy from the evil all around him, which strengthens Dr. Darkness!!! while weakening his enemies." He was excited to show off his work. "And I've got an idea for a special tar-glob power that's unique among supervillains. I've read all the comics, so I know what I'm talking about."

Amused, Robin looked at me. "Isn't he cute?"

I had no practice at being paternal, and didn't have much of a role model from my own childhood, but I could try. "Why do you want to be a supervillain, Jody? Sounds like a bad thing to aspire to."

"Maybe it is in the outside world, where everything's black and white, but if you're a supervillain in the Unnatural Quarter, people don't necessarily hold it against you." I could tell he'd put a lot of thought into this. "Not *all* monsters are bad, are they? Who would ever think of a zombie as the good guy?"

I had to concede the point.

Jody looked at his sketches again. "That's why I like it here. I'll be sad when summer camp is over. I can do my work in the Quarter and not be judged or teased or bullied."

It's bad when a supervillain in training gets bullied. I could see why Miz Mellivar wanted to encourage this young man. He had a lot of energy and imagination, but it needed to be channeled properly. Being cheated and evicted by a tentacle-faced half demon was a lousy way to kick off a supervillainous career.

"I wish I had my prototype suit back," he said, and closed his sketchbook. "What do you think Ah'Chulhu's going to do with it?"

I glanced at Robin, then back to the young man. "We think Ah'Chulhu has more schemes afoot—or a-tentacle—than just trying to get you to pay your back rent."

"If I was a supervillain, I could protect everyone," Jody said, crossing his arms over his admittedly scrawny chest.

"I'm not entirely sure you understand what a supervillain is," I said.

Sheyenne drifted over. "Sometimes we can change the way people think—make new definitions of old ideas and turn the world on its head. Right, Beaux?"

Robin didn't make promises lightly, but she said, "We'll get your suit back for you, Jody. You're a very talented costumer, as well as a great mad scientist-to-be. You sure you won't tell us what that is?"

Jody covered his work. "I'll move to the conference room if you want, but I need to have my privacy. Golly!"

I couldn't keep myself from smiling. "You know those eccentric creative types, Robin."

"Especially eccentric mad scientists in training," Jody added. "And masters of disguise."

I left my office. "All right, you can use the desk as long as you like. I've got cases to solve."

"By wandering around?" Jody asked.

"That's *part* of it. It's a process."

CHAPTER 33

After an unsuccessful day trying to track down Stentor's frog, find proof of nefarious campaign shenanigans, or get any dirt on the underground slumlord to help solve Fletcher's murder or at least retrieve Jody's possessions, I headed back to the office that evening. My desk was unoccupied, and Sheyenne explained that Jody had left in the middle of the afternoon to turn in a homework assignment at camp.

As I briefed her on my lack of progress on various cases, I realized that I had forgotten to make a stop. "I think you and I should check up on Recompose and see if there's been any further harassment. The police still haven't found that tentacle creature, but I want to pin *something* on Ah'Chulhu. Want to come along?"

Of course she did, but Sheyenne was curious as we walked away from the Chambeaux & Deyer offices. "Do you really think Lurrm is in trouble?"

"Probably not at the moment, but it's after dark, and I want to spend some time with you."

"What does that have to do with anything?"

"It gives me a chance to have a pleasant nighttime stroll with my girlfriend. I need to take care of my relationship." I might have blushed, but the embalming fluid didn't let it show.

We made our way toward the seedier section of town, and in the Quarter that's saying a lot. The exterior of the former Zombie Bathhouse looked almost inviting. A new marquee sign with moveable plastic letters announced, FAMILY SPECIALS! and SIGN UP NOW FOR OUR TADPOLE SWIMMING CLASSES. But with the narrow alleys and clinging shadows, as well as the persistent mildew and grunge, Lurrm still had a lot of work to do before this became an upscale neighborhood.

When we walked into the front lobby, Lurrm was surprised to see us. "You're always welcome here, Mr. Chambeaux!" He rubbed his squishy fingertips together. "Ayup!"

"Just keeping an eye out. Have the gator-guys bothered you again?" I asked.

Lurrm's long tongue flickered in and out of his wide mouth. "I haven't seen them since you were last here, but I won't let my guard down: Could be that they just can't find the place again and they're still searching." He showed us that he had installed three more turnstiles just like the original that had confounded the alligator lieutenants/associates/escorts.

I spun one of the turnstiles, which gleamed under the bright lights. Carrl, the attendant, sat behind his window, ready to sell tickets, rent towels, and provide change for the lockers. He was still reading the same fishing magazine.

C.H. scuttled up the stairs, hopping from one step to the next, to the next, and ran on his fingers across the floor, obviously excited to see us. He flexed his fingers and hopped up and down, silent but insistent until I reached down and shook his hand, which in C.H.'s case was shaking his entire body. Sheyenne just waved, and C.H. waved back with such enthusiasm that he lost his balance and fell over.

"Let us know if you're threatened again, Lurrm, but I think Ah'Chulhu has bigger tadpoles to fry on the barbie."

As Sheyenne and I left the Recompose Spa, I stuck out my elbow so she could slide her arm through mine (even though I couldn't feel it). Despite her lack of a corporeal existence, I always feel warm and tingly when Sheyenne is that close. She says it's just my imagination, but I'm not so sure. "Care to join me in the cemetery, my dear?"

Sheyenne laughed. "Are you being romantic again, Beaux?"

"Trying to be."

"Keep trying."

The Greenlawn Cemetery was a quiet, dark, and private place where unnatural lovers went for secret trysts. Greenlawn was a city of tombstones, crypts, and memorial markers. Sightseers came looking for the grave markers of particularly well-known unnaturals. One company had even begun weekly celebrity tours, taking wide-eyed fans around to see the homes, crypts, and graves of the rich and famous.

It seemed a perfect place for a leisurely walk with my spiritual lady.

We passed tombstones and stone angels and paused to appreciate a performance-artist gargoyle who had taken up residence there, standing motionless, until he jerked out with a sudden movement to startle passersby.

Overhead, clouds gathered and obscured the moon. I heard the rumble of thunder, saw the crack of lightning, and then the clouds dissipated to show the starry night again. A few minutes later, clouds closed in with a repeat occurrence of thunderheads. The weather wizards must be doing their meteorological arm wrestling again, and it added a little drama to our peaceful pre-midnight stroll.

As part of our poignant trek we stopped by the site of my former grave. My death and burial had caused a great deal of grief to Robin, McGoo, and even Sheyenne, who had already been through death herself. After I climbed back out and rejoined my life as usual, Robin arranged for a refund from Greenlawn, since my cemetery plot was no longer being used. My tombstone was recycled, and the plot of dirt was put up for rent once more. Some of the undead retained ownership of their plots, just in case they ever needed them again, but I wasn't that fatalistic. At present, the plot remained unoccupied.

Sheyenne and I stood looking at it. "I'm glad you came back, Beaux."

"I feel the same about you."

We like to stay focused on what we have, rather than wallowing in what might have been. I didn't want Sheyenne to turn into one of those moaning, hand-wringing specters who were all about gloom and regret. We'd had our budding romance after we met at Basilisk, and I wouldn't have traded our beautiful night together for anything—except maybe a lot more nights together. But if wishes were horses, then who would need a car? She and I were lucky, in a way, because we were still together. The whole concept of a love that lasted for eternity had a different meaning now.

Sheyenne could read my moods even if she couldn't read my thoughts. "What's got you so introspective?"

I had wondered that myself. "My cases always make me think. When McGoo and I visited Mr. Bignome's mother, I realized that he must have been a cute little lawn gnome, even though his life went wrong. I had quite a few setbacks of my own."

"But you didn't turn into an armed robber," Sheyenne said.

"I didn't start out as a landscaping decoration either." I scuffed at the dirt and grass with my shoe. "And then there's Jody. I got to thinking about how he's going to handle this—no matter what Ah'Chulhu really has in mind down there in the sewers."

"You like him, don't you? Is it because he reminds you of yourself?"

I let out a hollow laugh. "No, it's because he's completely different from who I was."

She had a dreamy look on her face. "I like Jody, too. Makes you wonder. . . ."

"Wonder what?"

"Did you ever want kids of your own?"

This was a question my instincts told me to avoid. As alarms sounded in my mind, I said, "Never really thought much about it."

Her brow furrowed. "Yes, you did. It must have crossed your mind at some point. Didn't you ever maybe think about *us* having kids of *our* own?"

Of course I had, at least for a brief moment, but I'd had such little actual time with Sheyenne that I hadn't progressed beyond the warm and fuzzy wonder of realizing that I'd found a girl I liked. Really liked.

Leaving my grave, we walked along in silence for a few minutes. She waited, and I knew I had to answer her. "We're past that point in our relationship, Spooky—both of us being dead and all. There's not much point in family planning."

"We could always adopt," she said.

Somehow I couldn't picture myself as a father. I could devote myself to my cases, yes, and solve the most bizarre mysteries, but helping out with homework, taking a kid to band practice, watching Little League games—that seemed beyond my capabilities.

Sheyenne saw my consternation and let me off the hook. "I just daydream sometimes, Beaux. There's no harm in it."

"I'm glad to have you," I said.

Overhead the thunderclouds parted again, and the moon shone brighter than ever.

CHAPTER 34

After our romantic cemetery stroll, Sheyenne used the all-night drive-up window at the city offices to access court real-estate records, title deeds, and property filings. Inspired by Jody's diligence at his costuming work in my office the day before, Robin had been busy digging into the kid's case, and Sheyenne delivered the mountain of paperwork to her.

All night, while her magic pencil and yellow pad took notes, Robin pored over the incomprehensible legal details, the filing numbers, pages and pages of results from title searches. All of it was more arcane to me than the bizarre writing in the Wannoviches' spell books.

Robin brought her report to me in my office. Since Jody was meeting with a camp counselor that day, I had my desk back. "It's all clear as swamp water now, Dan. Ah'Chulhu is a very ambitious half demon. He's got his tentacles running everywhere beneath the Quarter."

"He was abandoned as a child," I said. "He probably has issues, wants to prove himself, measure up to some kind of imagined standard."

"That's one explanation. Personally, I think it's megalomania," Robin said. "But I'm not a psychiatrist."

She spread out documents and unrolled street maps, real-estate plats, and subterranean subdivision diagrams. Many were marked with flags to indicate recent sales, deed transfers; all had the fine print of Ah'Chulhu Underground Realty.

"Does that mean what I think it means?" I asked.

Sheyenne flitted close, joining the discussion. "What do you think it means?"

I'd hoped she wouldn't ask that. "It means that he's doing something too big for me to understand."

Robin explained, "Ah'Chulhu has been purchasing so much real estate throughout and beneath the Quarter that by now he owns the sewers. He's buying the city out from under our feet."

"Okay," I said, "but what can he do with it? Is he going to charge a toll for anyone who wants to go sightseeing underground?"

Robin's face turned grave. "The evil possibilities are endless." She took her papers and left me alone to get back to work on the Wuwufo shenanigans case.

Still trying to track down who was financing the two weathermancer campaigns, I called printing shops around the Quarter, hoping to discover who had produced the "Alastair Cumulus III: For Climate Change You Can Believe In" lawn signs, as well as the "Be a Dick Supporter" posters.

On my fifth call, I got lucky and found the right shop. I was surprised to discover that both candidates used the same print shop and—even more surprising—the orders were paid for by the *same person*. That was very interesting and downright disturbing.

I brought my findings to Robin, who already wore a grim expression—now it only got grimmer. She scanned the paper and looked up at me. "Just what I expected."

"How did you expect that?"

She moved the real-estate paperwork aside to show me a document fresh off the printer. "Sheyenne kept filing those campaign-finance transparency requests, as she promised—and one of them accidentally slipped through." She leaned back in her desk chair and crossed her arms over her chest. "I know who's been funding *both* campaigns."

In the reception area, the phone rang, and Sheyenne answered it. "Hello, Lurrm, you're calling early! Do your children's swim classes start today?"

Wincing at the loud response, she pulled the telephone receiver away from her ear. Even from Robin's office I could hear the amphibious creature's alarm as he belched out his words.

I came out to take the phone. As if he were hyperventilating, Lurrm blurted and gasped. "I'm in danger, Mr. Chambeaux. Everything's falling apart. It's the end of days, ayup. You have to help me—I need protection!"

"Calm down," I said. "Start from the beginning."

The frog demon panted so hard that he sounded like a tuba. He finally managed to say, "It's Ah'Chulhu—and words can't express the horror."

I didn't hesitate. "Is it the gator-guys again? I'll come right over."

"Yes, come! I need you now, but it's not just the gator-guys. It's . . . it's the end of the world."

"It can't be all that bad. We'll sort it out—I'll be right there."

"You don't understand! I learned what Ah'Chulhu is up to. I know his plans and . . . oh, I didn't want any part of them!"

He gasped, and I heard smashing sounds in the background, explosions and growls, screams, burbles. The telephone on the other end thunked to the floor, and I could hear a skittering of wet, slimy feet.

"Lurrm!" I yelled, but all that came through the phone was thrashing, a roar of bubbles, a wet, leathery slap.

I heard the frog demon wail, "Noooo, not the tadpoles! Not the innocent tadpoles!"

The violent splashing and screams reached a crescendo; then the connection ended. I imagined something large and wet smashing down on the phone.

I was already moving. My .38 was in its holster, my fedora on my head. I had everything I needed.

"Call McGoo and tell him I'm going to the old Zombie Bathhouse!" I yelled to Sheyenne as I flung open the door. "Have him send backup—all of it."

I dashed out into the street, which was socked in with thick, cottony fog. I hoped that the weather wouldn't slow the police response. I could barely see where I was going as I ran as fast as a zombie could.

CHAPTER 35

I got there too late. The Recompose Spa was a slimy disaster.

After hearing the noises and panic on the phone, I feared I would find a horrific situation, but this was far worse than I had imagined. Apparently, I needed a better imagination.

McGoo arrived before I did. He had been out on his beat, disoriented by the thick fog, and hadn't even realized how close he was to Recompose when Sheyenne called him. He had heard the screams and turmoil and blundered through the dense mist.

He stood outside the front door, crouched over, hands on his knees. I had never seen him look so sickened. "It's bad, Shamble," he said. "Really bad. Carnage. Slaughter. Evisceration. Ghastly gore."

But zombies don't get queasy so easily. "Let's have a look."

Lurrm had cried out that this was the end of the world, and it was certainly the end for him, his entire staff, all his customers, and the former Zombie Bathhouse. It was a spa Armageddon.

But the mayhem and destruction were all over by the time we entered Recompose, and the monstrous attackers were gone.

Inside the front door, the shiny new security turnstiles had been uprooted, bent so that they looked like floppy metal starfish, and hurled across the reception area. The little window where the amphibious attendant sat was demolished, and the pages of a well-read fishing magazine were scattered about. An unrecognizable spotted mess was all that remained of poor Carrl.

"You're right, McGoo. This is bad."

He turned a pale face toward me. "It gets worse as you go downstairs."

In the steaming pools, the bodies of spa patron zombies lay torn apart, many floating facedown in the pools and showing no sign of reanimation. Green slime dripped from the walls, and it didn't appear to be an intentional decoration that Lurrm had applied.

The tadpole ponds had been emptied. The whole catalog of biological debris splattered the walls. Towel racks were smashed; towels and terry-cloth robes had been tossed in all directions. The wooden sauna door lay in splinters. Crumpled on the floor near one of the clotted hot pools lay a shredded bloody frock coat—apparently all that remained of poor Lurrm.

"So what did this, Shamble?" McGoo asked. "And why?"

"Lurrm called me to sound the alarm, but he didn't have a chance to tell me any details. I said I'd come over to protect him." I looked up at McGoo. "He told me he had discovered Ah'Chulhu's plot—and that he was very afraid."

McGoo shook his head in disbelief. "You're saying a *real-estate agent* did all this?"

"Not just any real-estate agent: the half-breed son of a Senior Citizen God from another dimension."

McGoo gave a slow nod. "But still a real-estate agent."

With the monster attackers gone and everyone else dead, Recompose was eerily quiet, and our whispers echoed back at us. I still heard dripping water and oozing slime, a few bubbles as steam worked its way out of the pools, but nothing else: no groans of the injured, no moans of disoriented zombies. Body parts lay strewn all over the place. Fortunately, the heads were turned away from me, as if embarrassed at their disassembled condition.

I nudged a severed hand that lay palm up, its fingers curled like a dead spider, and it suddenly twitched, startling me. The fingers waved, and the hand rocked from side to side like a turtle trying to right itself.

"It's C.H.," I said, tipping him over.

"You know this hand?" McGoo asked. "Where's the rest of it?"

"He's a standalone crawling hand, works here at Recompose."

Agitated, the hand bounced on his fingertips.

I bent low, raising my voice, as if the hand were hard of hearing, although hands don't have ears at all. "Can you tell us what happened?" I looked down at the slime and blood puddled on the tile floor. "Can you write out what you saw? What did this?"

The hand scuttled over to the nearest red stain, dipped an index finger into the puddled blood, and then, keeping the dripping finger extended, C.H. moved to a clean tile and started to draw letters on the floor. It was a cumbersome process, though, and unfortunately C.H. was left-handed. As he tried to write letters in the thickening half-clotted slime, the side of his palm dragged over the fresh bloody ink and smeared the letters into unreadability.

McGoo and I both tried to decipher what C.H. wrote, but neither of us had any idea. We would have to think of some other way to communicate. C.H. grew more and more agitated, which made his penmanship even sloppier.

"Wait, maybe a keyboard will work better," I said. "Lurrm had a computer in his office."

I picked up the disembodied hand and carried him into the frog demon's office. Papers and folders on the desk were scattered in random piles, but that was just the normal chaos of Lurrm's office. The attackers had not ransacked here.

His computer was still on, its screen showing the Recompose Facebook fan page with a half-completed post announcing a couples' midnight special—a special that now would never be posted.

I placed C.H. on the keyboard. "What happened, C.H.? Type out what you saw."

McGoo looked at me. "Technically, he didn't *see* anything, since he's just a hand."

C.H. responded by pointing a stern index finger at him. Then laboriously, with the clumsiness of a one-fingered, one-handed typist, C.H. pecked out his answer: LET ME SHOW YOU.

The crawling hand tried to use the mouse and keyboard, and I had to help him with the pull-down menus. We managed to find the security-camera footage from the bathhouse, and McGoo and I took over rewinding the images and replaying the massacre, while C.H. crouched on the desktop and watched (or however a crawling hand received sensory input).

On the screen, gigantic tentacles rose from the hot pools, snakelike appendages composed of equal parts slime and muscle. Patrons ran toward the exits, screaming, their relaxing spa experience ruined for the day. More tentacles exploded from the kiddie pool and the spawning ponds, writhing and lashing out. They seized helpless patrons and unnatural staff, crushing them in a relentless grip, tossing bodies about.

"Same thing that killed Fletcher in the alley behind Basilisk," I said. "Only there's more of them."

McGoo stared at the horrific images. "How many more can there be? We did a full sweep of the sewers—something that gigantic couldn't hide."

The tentacles created utter mayhem, capturing and killing anyone who tried to escape, and anyone who didn't. I was appalled, but the heaviness in my chest grew worse as we watched the end of poor Lurrm.

Wearing his distinctive frock coat, the frog demon ran about, flailing, trying to flee—but one of the slimy tentacles snagged his body and drew him toward a hot and sloppy mineral pool. Lurrm shrugged out of his frock coat and dropped loose, landing on the floor. He tried to hop away, but the tentacles grabbed him again, pulled him back toward the pool. He struggled, squirmed, thrashed, and somehow managed to slide out of the tentacular grip a second time.

Before he could get to safety, the tentacle seized him and dragged him screaming toward the pool for a third time. He wailed his last words as the tentacle pulled him into the water, "Every time I try to get out, they *pull me back in!*"

Then poor Lurrm plunged beneath the surface, and a splurt of greenish red blood bubbled to the top. A glob of slime splattered the security camera lens, obscuring our view of the rest of the massacre. . . .

Police backup arrived fifteen minutes later. I had expected them sooner, given the state of the emergency, but they'd gotten lost in the fog.

Unable to stay away after receiving that fateful phone call, Robin and Sheyenne also rushed to Recompose. Robin was even more furious and disgusted when we showed her the security camera footage. Sheyenne sobbed ghostly tears and drifted up against me in need of a reassuring hug. An air embrace was better than none at all.

"Ah'Chulhu is behind this," Robin said in a voice like broken glass. "We know that."

"But we can't prove it," McGoo said.

"We'll get to the bottom of this," I vowed. "No matter how deep we have to dig."

CHAPTER 36

It was well past lunch by the time McGoo wrapped up at the crime scene. I had stayed to give him moral support, as well as detective support.

He shook his head. "I was feeling pretty good about arresting the lawn gnome gang yesterday, but this . . ."

"There's never such a good day that it can't get worse, McGoo."

"Oh, it started out bad enough," he said, looking hard at me.

"What's wrong?" I felt a chill. "Is it Rhonda?"

"She wrote again, said she's reconsidering, not sure she wants me to meet my daughter. Says the girl has 'issues'—but with Rhonda as her mother, what girl *wouldn't* have issues? I've never known Rhonda to be particularly decisive . . . or rational, for that matter." He seemed hurt, confused, flustered. "Oh, and she even asked how you were doing."

I felt another chill on top of the first one. "What did you say?"

"That you were dead. But doing okay otherwise."

Robin and I ducked under the yellow crime scene tape on

our way out, while Sheyenne just walked through it. Although the security camera footage left little room for doubt, Robin pondered the legal ramifications of whether C.H. could be used as a witness at trial, or whether the hand's testimony would be merely hearsay, given that the disembodied hand had no discernible eyes. Or ears. Or voice.

The fog had completely cleared, leaving the day bright and sunny, the sky a crystal blue of the sort that offends nocturnal creatures. To my dismay, Alastair Cumulus III was campaigning again, standing on a street corner with many leaflets but few supporters. He shouted, "This bright and sunny day brought to you by your next Wuwufo president. Enjoy!"

"If you like that sort of thing," muttered a vampire shopkeeper who scuttled along in the shadow of an awning. He ducked into a shop where he pulled down the shades for the comfort of his undead customers.

The erudite weather wizard sighed. "One cannot please all constituents." He raised his voice and rolled right into his campaign speech. "I promise to meet the needs of every citizen of the Quarter. Moist rain for the amphibians, dry heat for the mummies, regular periods of darkness for the vampires. I promise a night for every day, a black cloud for every silver lining." Cumulus stroked his curled beard, and the strands sprang back into place, as if he had used a great deal of elastic mousse.

At the moment, I saw no evidence of nefarious campaign shenanigans, but when Alastair Cumulus recognized me, I made a point of touching my eye and extending a finger toward him. *I'll be watching you.* Frowning, he turned to address other members of the nonexistent crowd of supporters.

Suddenly, the weathermancer's face lit up with alarm as a loud rumble came down the street. I heard disgusted shouts from other unnaturals scrambling out of the way. Before the weather wizard could turn and flee for higher ground, a curling wave of runny brown sludge gushed down a side street and aimed directly at him. Cumulus flung up his hands and tried to work a spell, but it was too late.

Like a battering ram, the soupy mudslide rolled over him, engulfed him, and spattered the nearby buildings. The wall of mud rolled to a halt on top of the weather wizard, leaving him flailing, coughing, and trying to extricate himself from the wet pile.

Robin and I ran to help him. Alastair Cumulus III was insulted and filth encrusted. He smeared the brown residue from his eyes and beard, shook his sleeves so that more gobbets dripped on the street. "This . . . this . . . ewww!"

It wasn't the most eloquent campaign speech I had ever heard, but it was heartfelt.

As the mud settled, a cheerful Thunder Dick sauntered up, whistling, as Robin and I hauled his rival out of the oozing mud. Beside him, his tuxedo cat gingerly minced around the wet mud. Morris/Maurice seemed unimpressed with the demonstration and annoyed by the mess.

"That'll teach you to go digging up dirt on me," said Thunder Dick. He glowered at Alastair Cumulus III. "Maybe that'll make you think twice before you try any more mudslinging."

"Mudslinging!" cried the foppish weather wizard. "I have done nothing but make my case to the voters. You're an idiot and a buffoon!"

"You've been releasing embarrassing details of my private life! You arranged to have those bad photos printed of me."

"You always take bad photos," commented the cat, then licked an imagined speck of mud from his front paw.

"I'm not responsible for that," Cumulus insisted as he struggled out of the mud, then waved his hands to summon a sudden downpour. Warm rain drenched him and us, and it did manage to wash away much of the mud. "I have held back from using what my opposition research uncovered about your deviant sexual appetites, but now the gloves are off! It's disgusting, and I think the electorate will find it just as disgusting as I do."

Thunder Dick was apoplectic. "You wouldn't dare! I've always promised to win fair and square, and I'm not the only one who'll cheat to do it. I've got dirt on you, too, Cumulus—I plan to release everything."

Robin, dripping and stained with mud, had finally reached the end of her patience. She wore a professional gray blazer and business skirt that would have looked frumpy on anyone else, but looked great on her. Now, though, her clothes were soaked with sewage and she had a smear of mud below her right eye.

She put her hands on her hips, and her nostrils flared. "I'm fed up with both of you and tired of this childish, corrupt campaign—we all are. I don't even know the size of the Wuwufo membership, but most of us can't vote. Why should we care? This election is irrelevant to us."

Thunder Dick blinked, offended by his own attorney. "But weather is relevant to everyone."

Cumulus added, "It's important to have fair and accurate weather forecasts."

"No one actually believes weather forecasts," I pointed out.

Robin didn't often lose her temper, but now she was on a tear. "Thunder Dick hired us to look into the campaign shenanigans, and we did find plenty of corruption—from *both* of you!" She looked at me.

I said, "We dug into your campaign finances, and we know about your backers. You're both dirty."

"I'm not dirty." Cumulus wrung out his freshly rinsed wizard robe.

"He did it first," said Thunder Dick.

"He did it back."

"And so we witness the dignity of democracy," I said.

Robin's anger had not diminished. "The voters will see that there's no difference between the candidates. You've both caused too much pain, suffering, and climate change here in the Quarter. We know your secrets."

"What secrets?" asked the cat, looking worried.

Robin looked from Thunder Dick to Alastair Cumulus III. "You've both been taking money under the table from the same source. Your campaigns are entirely funded by the weather forecasting networks."

CHAPTER 37

The Unnatural Quarter has many seedy dens, festering neighborhoods, houses of worse-than-ill repute, neighborhoods where even monsters wouldn't let their children play. But they all pale in comparison with the central headquarters of the weather networks.

Oddly enough, despite the blood feuds and the rancor displayed among the rival meteorologists, all four networks were housed in the same building, a cubical cinder-block structure with the name of a different network painted on each face, as well as—although we couldn't see it from street level—the call sign of a weather radio station painted on the roof, where helicopters and broom-flying witches could land.

Even during normal weather, Sheyenne often tuned to the different stations to compare prognostications, listening to the announcers claim ridiculously unrealistic accuracy percentages for their forecasts. (Such claims of success seemed no more accurate than their weather predictions.)

After the constant inconvenience, turmoil, and disruptions caused by the Wuwufo campaign, Robin had had enough of the two rival weathermancers, enough of the turmoil, enough of the irrelevant election itself, and enough of the weather networks trying to buy the results.

Her dark eyes were flashing and her jaw was set as we left the remnants of the mudslide, as well as the flustered and embarrassed Thunder Dick and Alastair Cumulus III.

"We're going to get to the root of this problem, Dan—and yank it out like a rotten tooth," Robin said.

I tried to think of a more meteorologically apt metaphor, but I experienced a severe imaginative drought. "Isn't this a conflict of interest?" I asked as we approached the network building. "Thunder Dick is our client."

"He hired us to stop the nefarious campaign shenanigans. We've discovered the primary cause—and we're going to make the shenanigans stop." When Robin was on a crusade, I didn't want to get in her way.

Each side of the cinder-block building had an identical-looking entrance. I chose the door of the most extreme network, the one I least preferred to watch. If there was going to be a confrontation, I would rather do it with someone I didn't like.

As we entered the building, I wondered how the network offices would be segregated inside, and I was surprised to see that the interior was large and open like an airplane hangar. All four of the network doors opened into the same large common studio.

Teams of weather prognosticators sat at long lunchroom tables, and a large map of the Quarter covered one wall. Two other forecasters—a vapid brunette who giggled too much and a blond-haired Ken-doll–wannabe—threw darts at the board and carefully noted their results. Others used shaker cups and poured dice on the table before rushing off to write their predictions. A roulette wheel clicked and clattered in the corner; the sections of the wheel were not painted red or black, but rather showed clouds, rain, snow, wind, sunshine, and even a total solar eclipse.

"Exactly how I thought they made their predictions," I said.

On the other side of the studio, the rival meteorologists took turns filming their forecasts in front of a green screen, smiling and cheerful as they warned of stormy doom and gloom.

Robin strode ahead of me, looking around. The brunette meteorologist saw us, which spoiled her aim, and the dart thunked on the bottom of the map. "Looks like temperatures are unexpectedly falling," she said, then giggled at her joke. "Look, everybody! We have visitors."

Ken Doll flashed a radiant smile and waved at us. I remembered that I particularly loathed his show. Grinning in unison, he and the brunette came over to welcome us. "These are exciting times," said the brunette. "Nothing more thrilling in a meteorologist's life than the Wuwufo elections."

Robin frowned. "We're investigating corruption and campaign finance irregularities. We can prove that the weather networks are in collusion, trying to influence the candidates. You're attempting to benefit from the chaos."

"Of course we are," said Ken Doll with a warm smile. "When the weather wizards are feuding, our forecast accuracy goes up to nearly one hundred percent."

"We're always right," said the brunette with yet another giggle, "so long as we stay vague on the timing and location of any particular weather event."

The hubbub in the room grew louder. A stoop-shouldered old man wearing purple latex dishwashing gloves hunched over a basin where he fondled and inspected entrails. A second meteorological soothsayer pulled up ropey intestines and compared them to the organs in his rival's basin. "Oh, what tangled entrails we must cast, when we practice to forecast."

Seeing this, I said, "I've heard that meteorology and astrology are sister pseudosciences."

"And well-respected ones, too," said Ken Doll with a vigorous nod.

The old soothsayer stripped off his purple gloves, tossed them into the bucket, and came over to join the conversation. "That's my forecast for today. Cloudy with a chance of clear, and a likelihood of additional weather events. We'll see if I'm correct, or if I just have to *say* I'm correct. Nobody ever seems to go back and check."

"Most people can tell the difference between a blizzard and a dry spell," I countered.

The soothsayer gave a dismissive wave. "During Wuwufo campaigns, the difference is often no more than half an hour. It'll settle down after the elections are over." He sounded disappointed.

All of the forecasters in the room sighed, as if we had just taken all the fun out of a party.

"Campaign turbulence is good for ratings," said the giggly brunette. "But accuracy is good, too. That's why the forecasters chipped in to support both Thunder Dick and Alastair Cumulus III. We'll have influence and lobbying privileges, no matter who wins."

"Wait, I thought we decided that Cumulus was going to win," said Ken Doll.

"Oh." The brunette blinked, then giggled. "I forgot. Did we agree on that?"

One of the prognosticators spun the predictive roulette wheel. "It was at the company barbecue, don't you remember? The one that got rained out. We decided to put our muscle into sabotaging Thunder Dick's campaign and bring him down in the polls."

Ken Doll looked at us with an apologetic smile. "Our campaign shenanigans aren't really all that nefarious. Just standard procedure."

Though Robin was angry at both candidates, I felt I had to

defend our client. "But why choose to destroy Thunder Dick? He's likable enough, and it's his dream to become Wuwufo president. What did he ever do to you?"

"He does seem a decent fellow in small doses," said the soothsayer. "Nothing against him personally, but he's just not subtle enough, and a bit too dim to be easily manipulated. Alastair Cumulus the Third is already in our pockets. After he's elected, we'll submit pre-forecasts to him. As long as we keep up our support payments, he'll create whichever weather front we desire."

"That'll make our job easier," said Ken Doll.

"And more accurate," giggled the brunette.

"But the real reason that Thunder Dick has to lose is that we have an inside man on his campaign," said the man at the roulette wheel, giving it another clattering spin. "We have tons more embarrassing stuff to release and a deep, dark secret from his past that hasn't come out yet, but I doubt we'll need it."

"Meteorologists do have some standards, you know," said the soothsayer, who went over to help his rival pack away the fresh entrails in another bucket.

Robin's interest flared. "What inside man on Thunder Dick's campaign staff?"

I amended, "He doesn't even have a campaign staff." I felt a growing dread as the answer came to me, and I knew the poor weathermancer wasn't going to like it. "It's the cat, isn't it?"

With a giggle, the brunette confirmed my suspicions. "Of course. Maurice is doing everything he can to destroy Thunder Dick's career."

CHAPTER 38

As the sun set and the skies grew dark, crowds began heading out for nightlife in the Quarter. Robin and I left the cinderblock headquarters of the rival but identical weather networks, and I felt the weight of a gravestone on my chest, knowing we would have to tell Thunder Dick about the betrayal of his cat. He had hired us to investigate the campaign shenanigans, little knowing that his own familiar was responsible.

I doubt he would be thrilled that we had solved the case, but you don't always get to give the client good news.

Robin and I reached the commercial district with cafes, a dance club called the Monster Mash (just another meat market), convenience stores, hookah dens, and an old-school gaming parlor where motionless videogame zombies stared slack-jawed at an ancient hypnotic game of Pong.

On a corner stood a new Talbot & Knowles Blood Bar, one of the upscale boutique stores that had begun opening up around the Quarter. The interior had bright chrome fittings, sparkling black-and-white tile floors, and smiling hemoglobin baristas. Vampires sat around at outdoor tables; two were playing chess, others worked on their laptops. A chalkboard out front advertised a *"Demise of co-owner special—B positive lattes, only $2.99 after 5 P.M."*

I wondered how long it would be before Harry Talbot removed poor Fletcher's name from the marquee and officially took over the company. Business had to go on, and the blood bars were certainly doing good trade, especially—from the looks of it—this boutique store.

But it was a day for disasters, and Robin and I hadn't gone far before the ground started trembling beneath our feet. The street rumbled, the buildings shook.

People began screaming as cracks shattered the pavement, and the entire boutique blood bar began to collapse and sink below street level as the ground slumped into a crater. Vampire customers spilled their specialty blood drinks as they scrambled to evacuate. Hemoglobin baristas dove out the front as the large plate-glass windows shattered. Incongruously mellow jazz music wafted out from the store's sound system.

The upper floor of the two-story building slumped, and part of the wall broke and slid to one side, scattering bricks. I pulled Robin back to safety on the opposite sidewalk as the whole street opened up.

"It's a sinkhole!" I said. The crater yawned even wider. "We don't know how big it's going to grow."

The blood bar dropped into an ever-widening pit. The crashing, groaning sounds were deafening.

Robin was more angry than frightened. "We've had floods and blizzards and mudslides—now *sinkholes?* We have to end this weather-wizard feud. The Quarter won't survive another election like this."

I didn't think sinkholes were necessarily a meteorological phenomenon, but that's not my area of expertise.

By now, the crater had sucked up half the street, pulling down peripheral buildings and swallowing the entire blood bar. Vampire customers managed to crawl out of the wreckage, dusty and battered.

"I need to talk to Thunder Dick—*after* we help out here. These people need us," I said to Robin.

She didn't hesitate. "Let's get started, then."

"This area's still dangerous," I pointed out. "We'll have to be careful."

Two werewolves assisted an old woman whose fangs were dulled with age as she hobbled to a bus stop bench where she could rest and recover. Robin and I guided a disoriented necromancer as he hauled himself out of the rubble. "I wasn't even there as a customer," he muttered. "I just came in to buy a gift card. You shouldn't have to worry about falling into a sinkhole if you're just buying a gift card. What kind of world is this?"

Sirens blaring, an arterial red fire engine rolled up with a full crew of rescue workers and firefighters—all golems, whose clay bodies were entirely flame resistant. They swung down their ladders and tossed ropes into the sinkhole.

McGoo arrived in a flurry, accompanied by Sheyenne, and both of them looked determined and overwhelmed as they viewed the disaster. "I need a less interesting job, Shamble," he said. "First killer tentacles in the bathhouse, and now this."

Sheyenne joined other helpful ghosts who flitted into the unstable rubble in an ectoplasmic search and rescue. They focused their poltergeist skills to move fallen bricks out of the way, but had to take turns as they exhausted themselves. I knew how much effort Sheyenne expended just to keep herself firm inside a glove when the two of us wanted to hold hands. Looking decidedly paler and more insubstantial, she drifted back to the top of the sinkhole and had to take a rest.

"It's those damn weather wizards, I know it," McGoo grumbled as he did his best to direct the rescue efforts. "We've never had a sinkhole in the Quarter before."

Some much-needed muscle arrived when Stentor the ogre joined the rescue efforts. He had been out on the streets, walking for block after block as he cried out in his tiny tone, "Help! Someone has stolen my voice. If found, please call the police," then listening for an operatic echo from the lost catalyst frog.

Stentor peered down from the edge of the crater, alarmed and dismayed. He proved even stronger than the golem firefighters, wrestling large chunks of broken walls, hauling up sections of collapsed countertops, even tossing an espresso machine out onto the street.

In the midst of the activity, seeing a crowd of possible undecided voters, Alastair Cumulus III arrived in freshly washed wizard robes to show his bright and sunny disposition, and handed out campaign posters. But when the crowd noticed him, they began grumbling and turned ugly (or uglier).

"Blizzards were bad enough," yelped one werewolf. "Now sinkholes. How many more sinkholes will there be?"

Undaunted, Cumulus said with an arrogant sniff, "How many more would you like? I shall see what I can do."

When the crowd snarled, howled, and flashed their fangs, the weather wizard finally picked up on the mood and beat a hasty retreat.

Over the next hour it was heartwarming, at least for those with warm blood, to watch the people of the Quarter pull together. As rescuers, we gave priority to the most vulnerable humans first, for there are plenty of human workers, tourists, and commuters in the Quarter. Two vampires were entirely buried under the rubble, but although it was an inconvenience, vampires are accustomed to being buried; some even find it nostalgic. Sheyenne recovered enough of her ghostly strength to dive down into the rubble again. By now most of the blood-bar customers had been accounted for.

The hemoglobin boutique had sunk deep, and when Sheyenne's intangible searches uncovered a vampire barista trapped in the collapsed basement, Stentor secured a rope around his own chest to help with the rescue. He lowered himself down, with three of the golems holding the rope steady. Stentor called out at the top of his lungs to reassure the trapped barista, though his voice was so small that if the victim had more than a thin layer of brick dust in his ears, he could not have heard him.

The ogre might not be much of an opera singer anymore, but he was certainly being a hero today. He went down deep, hurled rubble aside to free the disheveled vampire barista, tied a second rope around the victim, and sent him back up into the gloom of day. While the ogre was down at the bottom of the sinkhole, we heard him calling out in his minuscule voice, hoping to get an answer from his frog.

When Stentor signaled he was ready to come back up, he tugged the rope so hard that the sturdy golems were nearly pulled down into the crater. They strained to haul the ogre up again. He stood swaying on the street. "At least I helped someone today, even if I didn't find my voice."

Robin's cell phone went off with the ubiquitous "Marimba" ring tone, proving that phones tend to ring at inopportune times. She finished giving a hand to a curious mummy who had fallen into the crater, and still managed to answer her phone before it went to voice mail. Sheyenne was next to her, ready to take a message if necessary.

Robin was all business. "Good to hear from you, Miz Mellivar. Do you have anything to report?" She put her phone on speaker so I could listen in.

"Something for you and Mr. Chambeaux," said the Deputy Assistant Manager of Patents. "We've had a robbery here after hours."

"Shouldn't you call the police?"

"I thought I'd get a faster response from you, and I believe you'll want to look into this yourselves," Miz Mellivar said. "Besides, the police are busy responding to some sinkhole emergency."

"We're here, too, but the hard part is over," Robin said. "How does this robbery pertain to us?"

I was worried that some terrorist had stolen the prototype artificial Medusa head, or some of the other bizarre inventions.

"They didn't break into the testing labs, just into my offices," said Miz Mellivar. "The thief took only the blueprints, proposals, and prototypes filed by Jody Caligari, including his X-ray Spex. It was clearly a targeted robbery."

Robin and I glanced at each other. She said, "We'll be right there to have a look."

McGoo put his hands on his hips. "What a mess! Just what the Quarter needed—now people have to worry about their favorite drinking establishments falling into holes under the street." He removed his cap, wiped his forehead, and turned back to the sinkhole. "Look, Shamble, I'd go to the patent office to check up on the break-in, but that'll have to wait. Right now, even if everybody's rescued, this is still a disaster—I have to set up barriers at the perimeter to keep more people from falling in, have teams make sure the sinkhole won't keep expanding, find out if the ground is unstable, write up damage reports. It's going to be a long night."

"I think I can stop any more drama from the weather wizards," I said, knowing that I had to confront Thunder Dick and tell him that it wasn't Alastair Cumulus sabotaging his campaign, but his own traitorous cat. I glanced at Sheyenne and Robin. "Can you two handle the patent office? You know what to do, check out the crime scene and gather the information we need. Meanwhile, I'm going to stop this feud and prevent further weather events. I have to go see a man about a cat."

CHAPTER 39

It had been one of those days.

I'm not saying that tentacular attacks on bathhouses, meteorological conspiracies, and unexpected sinkholes swallowing blood bars were *everyday* occurrences, even in the Unnatural Quarter, but sometimes it felt as if all the stars, planets, and asteroids had lined up to make everything go wrong at once. The sinkhole was the low point of the day, but more raw sewage was sure to hit the fan sooner or later.

And now I had to tell Thunder Dick that his feline best friend was his worst enemy. The weather wizard would never be the same, and I wasn't particularly eager to let the cat out of the bag.

I felt a heaviness in my unbeating heart as I went to his home, a low-rent rooms-by-the-week tenement that, according to our case paperwork, Richard Thudner had listed as his address for the past two years. If he did win the Wuwufo election, I wondered if he'd move to some sort of presidential mansion where every room had a different and interesting microclimate. On the other hand, if the Weather Wizards Fraternal Order was just a small professional organization, maybe the presidency paid nothing whatsoever. Since the membership directory was held under such tight secrecy, I had no idea what size the roster was, but I couldn't imagine it was a particularly large group.

When I knocked on the door, a sound of thunder rumbled through his apartment. "Coming!" Thunder Dick called.

I steeled myself for what I had to do. He was our client, and he had to know the truth about his conniving pet, no matter how difficult it might be for him to accept. Politics was often painful, and the rigors of a hard-fought campaign tore apart relationships. I wondered if the cat would make excuses for what he had done.

When the weather wizard saw me looming in his doorway, he flashed an awkward smile and let me in. He was still embarrassed by the post-mudslide scolding Robin had given him, but even that mess was nothing compared with the damage and injury the sinkhole had caused.

"Thank you for seeing me." I removed my fedora because it seemed polite. "There have been some developments in your case. It's bad news, I'm afraid."

"Oh, no." Thunder Dick swallowed hard. "You're not going to tell me that Alastair Cumulus the Third is my long-lost brother, separated at birth?"

"Um, no. Not that at all."

The weathermancer seemed relieved. "Good, because that would have been a ridiculous plot twist."

In the main room, the tuxedo cat strolled past an elaborate and expensive scratching post and instead raked his claws on the side of the sofa.

I tried to sound businesslike to prepare the wizard for the even worse news. "Ms. Deyer and I went to the weather network central offices. We already knew the meteorologists were contributing to both of your campaigns in order to buy access to—and exert influence over—the winner."

"The networks were my only contributors," Thunder Dick admitted, "but I thought they supported me wholeheartedly. Two-timers!"

"In the end, they decided it was easier to keep Alastair Cumulus in their pockets. The meteorologists had a meeting—a company picnic, actually—and decided to pool their resources to make sure that you lose the Wuwufo presidential campaign."

"Those bastards! Even the perky ones. How did they do it? Where did they find all that embarrassing information?"

I hesitated. The cat seemed completely aloof, though I knew he was eavesdropping. On the floor, Thunder Dick had left one of the newspapers with the embarrassing and unflattering photograph of him. Morris/Maurice went over and sat in the middle of it.

"The networks had an infiltrator, someone close to you who got the photos, exposed your finances, and tore off the word *Supporter* from your 'Be a Dick Supporter' campaign posters."

Thunder Dick flushed, and his wild and unruly hair and beard stuck out in all directions. His voice cracked. "Who? Who would do that to me?"

"Your cat," I said. "Morris."

"*Maurice,*" the cat said, then licked a front paw, pretending that nothing was the matter.

Thunder Dick whirled to stare at him. "That's outrageous. Morris is my familiar. We're a team."

"You're living in a fantasy world." The cat licked his other paw. "Has anyone seen my catnip?"

Thunder Dick's mouth hung open. "Aren't you even going to deny what he said?"

The cat sneezed. "Why? Have you looked at my food dish? I can see the bottom of it, and you know how nervous I get when I can see the bottom. You're a terrible master."

The weather wizard was appalled and deeply hurt, as I had

known he would be. "You . . . you're working for the other candidate?"

"No," the cat said. "I just can't stand you anymore."

"But . . . after all I've done for you!" Thunder Dick clenched his fists and raised them toward the sky, or rather toward the ceiling of his small apartment. "I'll conjure up a thunderstorm. I'll pour rain down on you all day long. A black cloud will follow you everywhere you go." Nothing happened. He frantically grabbed at the front of his robe, patted his chest with both hands, then cried, "Where's my talisman? I can't do anything without my talisman."

The cat sniffed and stretched. "I flushed it down the toilet."

Thunder Dick was as amazed as he was horrified. "Since when do you know how to work a toilet?"

"Cats have always known how to use toilets. We just choose not to." He walked toward me as if he could charm me into petting him. He turned back to his master. "Oh, and I left you something in the corner behind the sofa."

Thunder Dick was confused. "You caught me a mouse?"

"That's not what I mean."

When I refused to pet him, the cat strolled to the door, which remained open from when I had entered. "This is goodbye, Dick. My feline friends and I are going to make our fame and fortune on the legitimate stage. We've all been cast for the Phantom's new revival of *Cats*. We've been practicing every night."

"Oh, is that what that sound was?" Thunder Dick said.

Morris trotted out into the hall. "And don't eat my cat food. I might be back when I get hungry."

The weather wizard looked at me helplessly. "What am I going to do, Mr. Chambeaux?" He sank to the floor in despair, then crawled on his knees over to wrap his arms around the pristine scratching post. "My life has fallen apart. My familiar abandoned me, and I lost my special talisman." He clutched at his robes as if to make sure he hadn't just misplaced his portable sundial, but had no luck finding it. "I'm completely impotent without the talisman."

"Let's not go around advertising that you're impotent. People will think you're confusing election with erection."

"But how do I salvage this debacle?" He shook his head from side to side. "The Wuwufo members vote in a week."

I had to put the client's needs above my own. With Robin and Sheyenne off investigating the break-in at the Mad Scientists Patent Office, and McGoo still working on the sinkhole disaster, I knew what I had to do.

"Just because the election's gone down the toilet, so to speak, doesn't mean your talisman is gone forever." I made up my mind. "I'm heading down into the sewers anyway to wrap up a case. You can come along with me and have a look."

CHAPTER 40

Before leaving his apartment, the weather wizard took a Y-shaped flexible willow rod. "Are we going fishing?" I asked, sure we wouldn't catch anything edible down in the sludge of the catacombs.

"It's a dowsing rod. Classic model. I can use it to find my talisman."

"I'll take whatever help we can get." In the confusing labyrinth down there, I might need Thunder Dick's help with the dowsing rod, or maybe an underground GPS unit, to track down Ah'Chulhu's main grotto again.

The weathermancer walked along with me as if a gloomy cloud hung over him. He didn't know what he was going to do without his cat, but I promised him that after this night was over, he could find plenty of kittens at the UQ animal shelter. "It won't be the same as Morris, but it'll help ease your pain."

I chose the direct route into the main business district of the sewers—straight through the basement doorway in the Chambeaux & Deyer building.

When we entered the front door and made our way to the

lower levels, our building superintendent Renfeld shuffled down the hall from his dim and squalid lair. He looked at me through the tangles of hair under his floppy hat and gave me an apologetic wave. "Don't worry, Mr. Chambeaux. It's already taken care of."

"What's taken care of?" I asked.

"The loud noise from the new underdwellers, a stereo playing humpback-whale mating music. Not exactly something you can dance to." He regarded Thunder Dick. "Is that a friend of yours? Remember, no after-hours parties."

"He's a client, Mr. Renfeld," I said. "We won't make any noise."

The weather wizard and I slipped down the basement stairs and found all the new tenants' doors still closed. From behind one, I heard mournful whale song, like someone belching into a PVC pipe. One of these days I was going to have to take a plate of cookies to meet our neighbors . . . but I could do that after we took care of the other cosmically important complications.

When I opened the door leading into the sewers, Thunder Dick wrinkled his nose. "Smells ripe tonight."

"Smells overripe to me—and I don't have a very good sense of smell." Nevertheless, I led the way, easing along the ever-narrowing walkway and then sloshing into the wider canals.

Uneasy, Thunder Dick braced himself and stepped into the sewage after me, soaking his tie-dyed robes. "Nothing to worry about," he muttered, convincing himself. "This is completely natural, one hundred percent runoff from the rains."

"With a few other ingredients mixed in," I said, then motioned him forward. "You've got the dowsing rod—lead the way."

He extended his flexible rod in front of him, letting it droop, then perking it up again, drooping, tilting it from side to side, as if he were engaged in some sort of an aerobic Ouija board exercise. He splashed forward. "This way."

It seemed the most obvious direction to go, with or without

the pointing dowsing rod. Thunder Dick trudged along as the sewer water rose up to our waists. Several mutated flying rats buzzed overhead, swooping down to gulp mosquitos out of the air. As he felt his wand grow stiff and full of power, the weather wizard became enthused.

He wasn't watching where he was going, though, and I had to grab the collar of his rainbow-colored robe to make him stop. I pointed to a sign at an intersection of sewer corridors. "Careful!"

Caution piranha crossing.

One of the flying rats swooped overhead, and a large fish leaped out of the murky water, chomped down on the squeaking rodent, and pulled it into the channel, which became a froth of churning fish and pink water, then nothing.

We waited for the piranhas to pass, then glided across the intersection.

Thunder Dick got even more excited as the willow wand bounced and bobbed in his hands. We passed drainage pipes that dripped and glopped effluent into the sewers. Finally, after the weather wizard swirled around in circles and got his bearings, the wand pointed straight down into the water.

"We found it! The talisman is here."

Despite the thick, discolored water, Thunder Dick dunked his head beneath the surface and fumbled and pawed the bottom of the channel. At last he came up dripping, gasping but triumphant, as he held his small, portable sundial. "Just what I needed! I'm powerful again."

I indicated his face, and he self-consciously wiped a runny smear of green slime off his cheek, then ran his fingers through his beard to straighten it. "Thanks! I guess we're a team now. So, how can I help you wrap up your case? Would you like some snow? A little sleet, maybe? How about a big wind?"

"Maybe in a few minutes—I'll use you as my secret weapon. The headquarters offices of Ah'Chulhu Underground Realty are down here somewhere, and I need to confront him. I think I know the way." Actually, I knew nothing of the sort, but I was being optimistic.

"If you want to sneak up on him, let me give us some cover," suggested the weather wizard. Using his precious talisman, Thunder Dick conjured a roiling mist that accompanied us like a smokescreen.

My uneasiness grew as we made our way toward the half-demon's grotto, trying to figure out what he was up to—something so evil and despicable that Lurrm and everyone at the Recompose Spa had paid with their lives. Ah'Chulhu had been trying to buy up the patents of evil protective gadgets, and had confiscated Jody Caligari's prototypes when he repossessed the kid's lab; I had no doubt that the tentacle-faced slumlord was also behind the recent break-in at the patent office. Even though the UQPD had been unable to find and capture the giant tentacle creature, I knew Ah'Chulhu was responsible for the bathhouse massacre, as well as the murder of Fletcher Knowles. And I was armed with only a flaccid weather wizard who needed help keeping his spells up.

Ahead, sonorous voices echoed through the enclosed catacombs: the barbershop quartet of frog demons. Ah, so we were heading in the right direction. "It's this way." I sloshed off toward the sound of music, but it turned out to be a ghost echo bouncing around corners, so it led us nowhere.

The catacombs looked less and less familiar. After an hour, Thunder Dick's enthusiasm began to wane. "Are you sure you know where you're going, Mr. Chambeaux?"

"Absolutely certain." We reached a set of metal rungs that ran up a shaft to a manhole and the street. I decided to climb up, have a look around, get my bearings, at least figure out the cross street.

Hand over hand, I worked my way up the rungs while Thunder Dick waited for me below. I was feeling stiff and soggy, and I didn't smell like flowers either. When Howard Phillips Publishing adapted this particular adventure, the vampire ghostwriter would no doubt find some way of making it glamorous.

Standing in the brown water beneath me, the weather wizard was barely visible through the mist he had conjured. Suddenly, he yelped and splashed around. "There's something down here, Mr. Chambeaux."

"Probably just an alligator," I called back to him. "A lot of people flush them down the toilet when they outgrow being cute."

"No, not an alligator. It's long and rubbery and—ack!" He began to flail and thrash.

I doubted the piranhas would have passed out of their normal sanctuary zone, so I dropped two rungs down on the ladder to try to rescue him.

That's when a large, wet tentacle wrapped around Thunder Dick's waist, lifted him out of the water, and squeezed. Hard. He grabbed at his sundial talisman, even though I couldn't guess what sort of meteorological effect he intended to conjure to drive off a tentacle monster.

With one arm locked around a metal rung, I pulled my pistol, but I couldn't see much in the mist. I tried my best to aim.

Before I could shoot, however, two more tentacles rose out of the water, probing in the air. I scrambled back up toward the manhole to get out of their reach, but one tentacle looped around my ankle and tugged hard enough to make me lose my grip (though fortunately, not hard enough to detach my leg).

I tried to hold on to the rung, but the tentacle tore me free. I was suspended in the air, wrapped in its slimy embrace. The tentacles dragged us out of the mist and around a corner, where I recognized the arched brick entrance to Ah'Chulhu's headquarters grotto, which was crowded with far more attendees than had been present at the Phantom's recital.

"Oh, we were close after all," I said.

The tentacles held us prisoner as three of Ah'Chulhu's gator-guys marched out to meet us, accompanied by a pair of spotted frog demons. Then the hideous half demon himself emerged to regard us with impatience and annoyance. He still wore his gray business suit and power tie.

The gator-guys were pleased with themselves. "Look what we found, boss."

"Crikey, you didn't find them—my tentacle watch dogs were doing their bloody jobs." The half demon looked up at me. "Mr. Chambeaux, what are you doing down here?"

"Slumming," I said. "Don't mind me."

Thunder Dick finally managed to grasp his portable sundial. "I am a weather wizard. You may have heard of me—Thunder Dick? I'm running for Wuwufo president. I just dropped into the sewer to retrieve my talisman. My cat accidentally flushed it down the toilet."

Angry, Ah'Chulhu gestured to one of the frog demons. "Take the talisman. No dramas, no disruptions. Bonzer big ceremony tonight, and we need to have good weather."

The frog demon hopped forward and grabbed the sundial pendant from Thunder Dick's hands. The creature opened his mouth wide, tossed the sundial in, chain and all, and swallowed.

Thunder Dick wailed. "Aww, that was the key to all my powers."

The frog demon said, "No worries. You'll get it back whenever the boss says it's okay."

"Get it back? How am I going to get that back? You swallowed it."

"I can think of one or two ways it could come back out," I said.

Ah'Chulhu directed the gator-guys. "See that these two

blokes are locked up in our finest dank holding cell. I'm going to need my tentacles back now. About ready for the big show."

The squirming appendages writhed and twisted, then released us. Thunder Dick and I plopped into the sewage. The weather wizard clutched his sore ribs, gasping, barely able to breathe. I was probably damaged as well, but nothing that couldn't be repaired—provided I remained intact enough to get out of this.

The huge tentacles twitched, swayed, and returned to the brownish water. I watched them shrink and deflate, growing smaller until they were no larger than struggling snakes. The disembodied tentacles squirmed, dwindling to the size of garden slugs. As they swam back to Ah'Chulhu, he bent down, careful not to get his gray slacks dirty. He reached into the water, and the now-shrunken tentacles crawled into his palms. He lifted them up, rearranged the similarly sized tentacles around his face, and applied them like leeches. The sucker ends of the miniature tentacles attached themselves, clinging like lampreys among his other squirming chin appendages.

Now I knew why the police hadn't found any gigantic tentacle creatures when they did their dragnet through the sewers. "So that's how you had an alibi when Fletcher Knowles was killed," I said.

"I'm an important bloke, Mr. Chambeaux," said Ah'Chulhu. "Had to learn how to delegate responsibility. Fletcher Knowles refused to provide what I needed. I can't abide inconvenience—it's so . . . bloody inconvenient. I'm the son of a powerful Senior Citizen God. Crikey, I deserve a little respect!" He stroked the now even-more-crowded mess of tentacles on his chin. "Besides, when you have so many of these things around your gob, who notices a tentacle or two missing?"

The gator-guys seized me and Thunder Dick. In vain, the weather wizard reached out toward the retreating frog demon who had swallowed his talisman, but the gator-guys wouldn't

SLIMY UNDERBELLY / 255

let him go. "Come on. The boss says you have to be locked in a dank holding cell."

On the bright side, that was better than being crushed or torn apart by gigantic tentacles.

As we were hauled away, Ah'Chulhu straightened his gray business suit and turned to look at us. "I'll be back with you gents soon. I have to destroy and remake the world first. G'day!" He cracked his knuckles and drew a deep breath that made the tentacles quiver around his mouth. He marched back into the grotto where his minions and followers had gathered for some kind of ceremony or inspirational talk.

In his voice I detected a hint of nervousness and uncertainty. "Tonight . . . I'll finally make my parents proud of me."

CHAPTER 41

I found myself behind bars—rusty, slimy bars that even a barnacle would have found repulsive.

The gator-guys threw us into the cell with extreme prejudice—which meant they hurled politically incorrect insults about me not being a real zombie, or suggesting that the weather wizard was probably gay. Sticks and stones—Thunder Dick and I had suffered much worse.

The gator-guys slammed the prison door and slid the lock bar into place, which was out of our reach. The chamber had scabby walls and scum-covered stagnant water that came to our knees. Moaning, Thunder Dick sat on the single narrow bench and pulled his knees up to his chest. "I have to use the toilet. Do you think they'll let me out for that?"

I gestured toward the sewage flowing around us and leaking out into the slimy catacombs. "Pick a spot."

In his frantic phone call just before the massacre at Recompose, Lurrm had insisted that Ah'Chulhu was going to end the world. Since he was not a frog demon prone to unfounded panic, and considering the slaughter at the spa, I decided to take that warning seriously.

"I miss my cat," the weather wizard sighed, shaking his head. He continued in a low voice, "I'm so pathetic. Always placing my affections where they don't belong, looking for love in all the wrong places. My relationships always go sour."

"Sorry, I can't help you with those sorts of problems. I'm a detective, not a relationship counselor." I squared my shoulders. "No use feeling sorry for ourselves, though—we have to get out of here in time to stop Ah'Chulhu and save the world."

Thunder Dick summoned courage from deep within himself. He straightened and put on a brave face. "Yes, and the Wuwufo election will be held soon. I don't want to miss that."

I rattled the sludge-encrusted cell door, hoping that the corrosion had damaged the bars enough that I could break them. But, like myself, the bars were well-preserved. I thrust my arm through the gap, straining to reach the locking bolt, but it was too far away.

We were stuck.

I ran through the clues in my mind, trying to guess what the half demon's sinister plot might be. Being dumped down a manhole as a helpless infant would mess with a person's self-esteem, no question about it. Now Ah'Chulhu wanted to impress his parents, the Senior Citizen Gods who had vanished long ago into the Netherworld for marriage counseling. I didn't know how anyone would attempt to impress a pair of titanic gods from another dimension.

Flying rats swooped by, leathery wings fluttering, naked pink tails twitching. As I peered through the bars, I realized there was a lot of traffic in the sewers. Gator-guys, frog demons, and various amphibians continued streaming toward the great chamber where the half-demon real-estate agent sat on his towering porcelain throne.

Thunder Dick stood next to me at the cell gate. "Ah'Chulhu seems to be attracting a crowd. Maybe it's a buffet dinner."

I rattled the cage bars again. If I used all my strength, I wondered which one would break first, the bars or my limbs. "Are you sure you can't perform any weathermancy without your talisman?"

"I wouldn't know how," said Thunder Dick. "Are you needing more sunshine?"

"A cold snap might help to break these bars. Or a lightning strike to blast the lock. Maybe a conveniently placed tornado?"

He hung his head. "Not without my talisman." As if to prove it, he squeezed his eyes shut and strained, pushing hard as if battling constipation. The humidity level might have increased by a little bit due to his efforts, but nothing significant.

I could hear distant chanting, drumming, even pipe-organ sounds coming from the main grotto. It sounded like a warm-up act to the big show; the dire ceremony would begin soon.

Now would have been a good time for Sheyenne to come flitting through the catacombs in search of me, or McGoo leading an entire police squad, or even Stentor the ogre practicing his squeaky voice.

I tried to find some other way out of the cell, but came up with nothing. Thunder Dick and I would have to rely on ourselves.

Then I heard a faint scuttling sound, a stealthy, fleshy pattering. The sewers had grown quiet with all the flying rats gone and all of Ah'Chulhu's minions already inside the chamber.

I pressed my face against the bars, peering out into the main tunnels, studying the rusty pipes and electrical conduits through which the half demon had piped his sound system. Then I saw a shape moving along like a giant tarantula, flesh colored . . . a hand. A crawling hand!

"C.H.!" I yelled, and the hand paused as it scuttled along the pipes. He raised his pinky in a query. I stuck my arm through the bars and waved frantically. "We need your help, C.H."

The severed hand backtracked on the pipes, found a cross support, and hurried over to the moss-encrusted bricks of the sewer wall. Gingerly, C.H. worked his way down the wall, fingerhold by fingerhold, until he reached our barred door.

Seeing C.H., Thunder Dick grinned with relief. He couldn't keep himself from asking, "Can you lend us a hand?"

C.H. cringed, then gave a brisk thumbs-down signal.

I turned to the weather wizard. "That was a little obvious, don't you think?"

"We're desperate," Thunder Dick said.

I leaned closer to the hand. "We need to get out of here, C.H. Ah'Chulhu is about to launch some kind of horrific plot, and it's bound to be even worse than what he and his slimy minions did at Recompose."

With heroic finger acrobatics, C.H. grabbed the slippery bars of the cell door, swung his way over like a graceful lemur on the monkey bars, and finally reached the metal latch that held the cell's locking bar in place. Straining, wrapping his two forefingers around the crossbar, C.H. tugged and hooked his thumb around another bar for support. Gaining traction, he tugged again. Finally with a scraping sound, the latch lifted. The cell door opened a crack, and I pushed. With a howling shriek of unattended hinges, the door swung open.

"Thanks, C.H.!" I said.

He raised his fingers in an open palm gesture, so I gave him a high five—which, unfortunately, knocked him sideways and into the water. Embarrassed, I fished him back out and set him up on one of the pipes. C.H. raised a thumb to give me the all clear, and I grabbed Thunder Dick by the sleeve.

Ahead in the great chamber, I could hear the chanting of the crowd and the ominous pipe-organ music growing louder. "We don't have much time. We have to stop this."

Thunder Dick wiped down his beard and his matted hair. "Good plan, Mr. Chambeaux—but what are we going to do?"

I was already moving toward the grotto. "A zombie detective and an impotent weather wizard to save the world—who could ask for more?"

"I'm not impotent," Thunder Dick said, and he splashed after me.

CHAPTER 42

Crackling with power and prominence, the great Ah'Chulhu rested on his porcelain throne. Below, the Phantom sat on a bench decked out in his formal wear in front of his enormous pipe organ, a forest of brass and chrome above so many keyboards that it looked like a waterfall of ebony and ivory. He played lilting melodies on the mammoth setup, which had supposedly been relocated from Paris. Apparently, for such an important occasion, the portable Wurlitzer just wouldn't do.

Several gator-guys stood in important-seeming positions on the new stage that surrounded the main dais. They all wore scarlet ceremonial robes that made them look awkward and uncomfortable. By the porcelain throne, numerous trunks, lockers, and equipment boxes were piled up, as if visitors had brought birthday gifts and stacked them beside Ah'Chulhu.

The center of the tableau was a large stone basin, like a birdbath for a pterodactyl, which was mounted next to a rune-etched concrete altar. Arcane symbols were carved around the perimeter of the stone, like festive decorations.

When Thunder Dick and I hurried into the chamber, we ran

into shoulder-to-shoulder crowds as if it were a Black Friday sale of that year's hottest toys. The amphibious groupies stared forward, trying to get a better view of the main stage. I stood on my tiptoes, jostling two frog demons who flicked long tongues at me in annoyance. One creature said to her husband, "I hate festival seating. Next time, we pay for tickets up front."

Feeling the urgency, Thunder Dick and I worked our way toward the dais and the altar stone. This was harder than getting through the Refunds and Exchanges line on the day after Christmas. The weather wizard kept muttering, "Excuse us, please . . . excuse us." The underdwellers elbowed him back.

When I finally got close enough to the concrete basin, I could see it was half-full of a thick red liquid. Frog demons were busy filling the sacrificial bath with—I suddenly realized it—virgin's blood! That was what Ah'Chulhu had demanded of Fletcher Knowles, who had refused him. That was why the gripping tentacles had killed Fletcher. Ah'Chulhu needed virgin's blood for his ceremony.

I turned to Thunder Dick as I understood something else. "You didn't create that sinkhole under the blood bar, did you? And neither did Alastair Cumulus."

He blinked at me. "Of course not. Weather wizards don't do sinkholes. Our magic isn't grounded."

Ah'Chulhu must have undermined the structures beneath the new Talbot & Knowles boutique blood bar to drop the building down into the catacombs. It hadn't been an accident or a natural tragedy. It was a robbery. The half-demon real-estate agent had found a way to steal all the virgin's blood he needed for his dramatic End of Days ceremony.

Unfortunately, virgin's blood was a new specialty item at the blood bars—very expensive and not sold in bulk. It was packaged in small, single-serve pouches, no more than a shot each, barely larger than a to-go packet of ketchup.

Frog-demon henchmen surrounded the stone basin, tearing open the tiny pouches and squeezing bright red blood into the basin, an ounce at a time. They discarded the empty wrappers and took up more packets. They spilled as much on their ceremonial robes as they poured into the basin. I got the impression they had been at it for some time, and they were showing signs of impatience. The crowd was also getting restless.

Ah'Chulhu distracted his minions, bellowing out in his heavy Australian accent, "All right, mates! No dramas. We'll get this bonzer show on the road." He scolded two rambunctious front-row reptiles who hopped about in extreme impatience. "Crikey, keep it down in front."

In his well-tailored business suit, Ah'Chulhu stood on the edge of the stage and shouted, "You're all here for the big show, and you'll get it! Tonight, the sewers will rise again—with your kind support. What goes down must come up. We will create a dimensional doorway and open the floodgates, unleash all the sewage of the Netherworld into the Unnatural Quarter." He paused, and the audience began to applaud on cue. "We will pour forth enough fertilizer to transform the entire world." His facial tentacles quivered with glee. "Oh, my parents will be so proud!"

"He is kind of cute, don't you think?" Thunder Dick said in an oddly wistful tone.

I shot him a glare, still trying to plumb the depths of this plan. It was far more nefarious than any shenanigans in the Wuwufo campaign.

Ah'Chulhu glanced at the stone basin and the waiting altar. "Are we ready yet?"

The busy frog demons continued draining tiny packets of blood, one at a time. "Not yet, boss. We've got about another inch to go."

With a sigh, Ah'Chulhu turned back to his audience.

"Thank you all for your patience. The show will begin momentarily. And now . . . the Phantom has more music to entertain you." He gestured over to the gigantic pipe organ.

The Phantom adjusted his mask. "Here's something from the revival of *Cats* that'll be opening at the opera house in a few weeks. You all know this one." He began to play "Memory."

Thunder Dick hung his head. "*Cats.*" He sighed. "If this really is the End of Days, I wish Morris could be here."

Around the grotto, I heard sizzling, crackling sounds, electrical arcs skittering around upthrust wires, like some of the off-the-shelf equipment that Dr. Neumann Wenkmann, M.a.D., had installed in Jody's lab. Tall, metallic devices generated glowing fields that pulsed into nebulous chemical mists charged with static electricity.

While the Phantom continued to play his musical interlude, Ah'Chulhu directed the final preparations. "Are all the shields and wards operating effectively? Those are prototype devices, but I want to be sure we're protected. We don't want anything unexpected to come through."

Now I understood. Ah'Chulhu had been buying up the patents of magical-enhancement devices and protective equipment. He wanted to be reunited with his monstrous parents, but maybe he was afraid his spell could backfire. In case the Senior Citizen Gods weren't exactly thrilled to see their long-lost offspring, it probably was a good idea for Ah'Chulhu to be cautious. I could imagine a lot of things that might go wrong when trying to back up all the sewage of the Netherworld.

The basin was nearly filled with virgin's blood; the exhausted and frustrated henchmen had almost finished emptying their boxes of single-serve packets. Soon, it would be too late, and the crowd was so packed I could barely move forward. I had to do something to flush out this evil half demon.

I needed to be extremely bold and completely unexpected.

Maybe it would only buy us a few minutes of time, but I removed my fedora and waved it high in the air, shouting, "Stop! All of you stop! This is an emergency order from the fire marshal." I whipped out my wallet and flashed my private investigator's license. "This chamber has exceeded its capacity. You are required to evacuate immediately. This is a fire hazard."

Considering how stupid the gator-guys were with their reptilian brains, I thought the fire marshal ploy might be convincing enough. After all, in a place like these enclosed sewer tunnels, judging from the smell, *methane* would be a serious hazard. I remembered that McGoo had once convinced me to light our farts when we were stupid college-age kids. A fire down here would be much worse.

Several robed gator-guys hurried dutifully toward the exits, as instructed. The Phantom stopped playing, the chanting ceased, and the crowd looked over at me. We had their full attention now, but if Ah'Chulhu's followers broke into a chaotic panic, then Thunder Dick and I might be trampled underfoot, under tentacle, and under flipper.

"Do you have a Plan B?" Thunder Dick asked as we backed away. The crowd churned, not knowing what to do.

"I hadn't actually assigned letters to the plans," I said.

Ah'Chulhu was outraged by the interruption. "It's just a trick, you idiots—there is no bloody fire hazard." He waved his human hands toward us and shouted (as all decent villains do at one point or another), "Seize them!"

The gator-guys followed their master's command. Hissing, opening their fang-filled jaws in very threatening yawns, they stalked toward us like bargain-basement dragons. The red-robed special ceremonial assistant gator-guys stood around the dais, looking confused.

As the crowd churned and the reptilian lieutenants/ associates/escorts pressed closer to us, I pulled out my .38 and fired a shot into the air (thereby demonstrating the lack of a methane fire hazard). The loud boom echoed around the grotto, and several of the amphibious spectators ducked out of the way. The ricocheting bullet pinged into one of the Phantom's organ pipes, sounding a dissonant note.

Thinking of the fate of the world before we were all buried under an outpouring of Netherworld effluent, I shot twice more, trying to strike the poured-stone basin full of virgin's blood. White starbursts of chipped concrete spattered off, but the basin remained intact.

Ah'Chulhu rose from his porcelain throne. "Crikey, you morons didn't take away his gun when you captured him and put him in the cell?"

The gator-guy henchmen paused, looked at one another, then turned back to the business-suited half demon. Their fanged jaws hung open. "You didn't tell us to do that," said one.

Ah'Chulhu muttered, "Destroying and re-creating the world isn't supposed to be a solo job."

I told Thunder Dick, "Now would be a good time to call down some lightning strikes. Or summon a tornado. A big one."

"Sorry." He clutched at his chest where the talisman should be. "I could maybe manage a sprinkle, if I have a chance to concentrate."

The Phantom blatted a few dramatic notes on his organ, but couldn't find the melody.

Impatient with his reptilian henchmen, Ah'Chulhu grabbed at his face, yanked off two chin tentacles, and tossed the squirming appendages down from the dais. They were already swelling, growing, and grasping as they struck the puddled water.

Thunder Dick and I tried to run, but the restless crowd was too dense, although they did make way for the ever-enlarging independent tentacles.

I fired two more shots, aiming carefully to hit the tentacles instead of innocent bystanders (although anyone attending a ceremony to end the world had to be at least tangentially evil).

The fat tentacles twitched as the bullets struck, and I saw Ah'Chulhu on his high dais wince as if someone had poked him with a needle.

The squirming appendages were undeterred by bullets, however. One of them whipped out and encircled Thunder Dick, lifting him in the air and squeezing. Trying to rescue him, I hammered at the tentacle with my fist, but it didn't do any good.

A second tentacle wrapped around me in a crushing grip, lifting me above the crowds. Thunder Dick gasped out, "I have nothing against tentacles—in fact, I've always found them rather attractive—but this is not how I wanted to spend my evening."

As the swaying tentacle waved me back and forth, I could see the basin of virgin's blood and the adjacent altar with its carved magical symbols. Ah'Chulhu stood at the edge of the wide stage, looking powerful and impressive as he commanded his minions.

Oddly, though, as I thrashed and hammered at the tentacle around my waist, I saw one of the red-robed ceremonial assistants leave the others and move to the side of the porcelain throne. He fished in the pocket of his robe and withdrew a set of black horn-rimmed glasses. He fumbled to place them over his eyes. While Ah'Chulhu's attention was diverted, the robed gator-guy bent closer to the boxes and lockers stacked next to the throne, peering through the spectacles as if searching for something. He stared with such intensity that he seemed to be looking right through the solid strongboxes.

"Do you have a Plan C?" Thunder Dick asked me in a hoarse voice.

"I told you I haven't assigned letters," I said.

Concentrating hard, Ah'Chulhu scrunched his face tight, looking like a half demon who had been struggling with intestinal difficulties for a week, and the tentacles tightened around me like a vise. Embalming fluid rushed in my ears as the slimy appendage continued to squeeze. Any second now, I was going to pop like an overripe zit.

Our night had definitely gone into the toilet.

CHAPTER 43

Suddenly, the background noise in the ceremonial chamber was shattered by a loud baritone voice. "Help! Someone has stolen my voice. If found, please call the police."

The crowd whirled, and a frog hopped into the chamber, splashing in the puddles. He seemed right at home in the sewers. Stentor's loud voice bellowed out from its mouth, "Help! Someone has stolen my voice. If found, please call the police."

There's nothing better than an irrelevant distraction at a pivotal point in a crisis. The tentacle twitched as Ah'Chulhu's concentration flickered, and he lost control of his remote appendage. With marginally more elbow room, I managed to squirm out of my sport jacket, thus slipping out of the slimy embrace and dropping to the floor.

As Stentor's frog hopped among the audience, calling out in the ogre's voice and demanding assistance, I wasn't the only one using the distraction. The mysterious red-robed gator-guy adjusted his black-rimmed glasses as he studied the stacked containers beside the porcelain throne, then he tossed the spectacles away in triumph.

I suddenly realized what they were—X-ray Spex!

The gator-guy fumbled with scaly hands to tear at his head and neck. With a loud, sucking sound, he peeled off a bulky alligator mask to reveal a freckle-faced, red-headed kid with sparkling blue eyes and an impish smile.

Jody Caligari in disguise!

Now that my arms were free, I could fire my pistol again. I'm a good shot, and I had to make it count. I had to shatter that basin, spill the virgin's blood, and end that End of Days spell.

But when I pulled the trigger, the gun made only the disappointing hollow *click* of an empty chamber. I considered throwing the empty gun at Ah'Chulhu, but I knew from enough old *Superman* episodes that such a show of defiance would be completely ineffective, and I would also lose an otherwise-reliable firearm for later cases (provided I survived this one).

I turned to help Thunder Dick and hammered, pounded, and poked at the tentacle with the gun, then used my hands to grip the slimy appendage, trying to free the weather wizard. I had to do something.

Ah'Chulhu noticed Jody and whirled. His remaining facial tentacles thrashed in annoyance. "G'day, mate! What are you doing here? Hey, and where's my rent?"

Seeing that Ah'Chulhu was distracted, I redoubled my efforts and managed to loosen the tentacle, finally freeing Thunder Dick from its crushing grip. I pulled him out of the muck, and the weather wizard sprawled on his face, gasping for breath.

With the heavy reptilian mask tossed to one side, Jody hurriedly fumbled with the locker he had identified before anyone could catch him. I realized that the box must contain everything Ah'Chulhu had stolen from the kid's junior mad scientist lab—all of Jody's confiscated prototypes. He tore off the cumbersome gator gloves and finally managed to open the latch.

In the midst of all the drama, the Phantom played an ominous three notes on his organ, then adjusted several of the pipes, still not satisfied with the sound.

As gator-guys rushed up the steps toward him, Jody rummaged frantically in the locker, found what he wanted, and yanked out a wad of slithery black fabric. It looked like Spandex made out of midnight shadows, and in the center was emblazoned a white circle, some kind of emblem, with three bright yellow exclamation points.

"I summon Dr. Darkness!!!" Jody yelled, as if imagining his voice would sound loud and portentous, but a prepubescent kid could accomplish only so much. When he finished his command, I half-expected him to say, "Golly gee!"

Ah'Chulhu bellowed to the red-robed gator-guys who were not, I presumed, other junior mad scientists in disguise. "Stop him! Don't let him don that evil suit."

I pulled Thunder Dick to his feet, and he groaned. "Never had a cracked rib before, but at least my spine is aligned now."

"We need to get to the altar stone before that virgin's blood gets spilled," I said, then added, "and causes the end of the world." It really wasn't an afterthought.

Fortunately, Ah'Chulhu had a potential supervillain to worry about, for the time being. Jody tossed the black fabric over his head like a bedsheet, and the Dr. Darkness!!! suit took on a life of its own, like an oil slick, twitching and probing, covering the kid's body as he struggled to shuck his red ceremonial robe. I was impressed by the special automated donning feature he had bragged about.

Then, as if there weren't enough going on already, another commotion occurred at the entrance to the grotto—shouts, splashes, footsteps. McGoo and an entire squad of uniformed policemen sloshed in with their service revolvers drawn. In front of them, C.H. bobbed up and down on his fingers, pointing the way.

"All right, everyone—put your hands up!" McGoo shouted. "Or any similar appendages."

With a wheeze of exasperation as he dealt with too many distractions at once, Ah'Chulhu's evil, otherworldly eyes blazed crimson. "How am I supposed to get anything done?" He recalled his detached facial tentacles, and they shrank down and wriggled back through the crowd. The police fanned out to impose order on all of the participants at the end-of-the-world ceremony.

I saw my chance to rush toward the altar, and Thunder Dick followed me, eager to help or maybe just afraid to be left behind.

As the police cleared a path, McGoo saw me and made his way toward the front. I shouted through the din, "McGoo! We have to stop the spell. Wreck the altar stone."

He caught up with me and the weathermancer just in time to run into three burly, hissing gator-guys—why did they always come in threes? The big reptiles tried to stop us, and we resorted to good old-fashioned fisticuffs, slugging the elongated snouts. I landed an uppercut to a scaly chin and heard rows of fangs clack together. The gator-guys snapped their jaws, but McGoo ducked, punched one in the abdomen, and nearly broke his knuckles against an armored underbelly.

That was enough time for me to duck between two of the reptiles, though, and I lunged toward the altar stone, hoping to topple, shatter, or maybe just misalign it somehow. If I could spill the virgin's blood off to the side, it would take hours and hours to refill the basin one tiny packet at a time, even if the demon had enough supplies in a back room.

But Ah'Chulhu also knew he was out of time. Ignoring Jody, he bounded to the blood-filled basin, and his hideous eyes locked on mine. "Too late, Chambeaux!" He grabbed the edge of the blood-filled container, shoving with all his strength. "Crikey, this is heavy!"

I reached the edge of the engraved altar just as Ah'Chulhu dumped the pterodactyl bath onto the ceremonial stone, with its preprinted doomsday spell. "I will not disappoint my parents!"

Blood ran in rivulets through the incised sorcerous symbols. I couldn't stop it, though I certainly made a mess trying. Ah'Chulhu just laughed at me.

Mounted near the wall, the anti-evil protective machinery crackled and sputtered as it began to overload. A dimness penetrated the air, as if the light itself were being wrung out of the chamber.

Ah'Chulhu cried out, "Open the effluent gates!"

CHAPTER 44

Blood swirled in the deeply cut designs, raced like scarlet fire along the tracks, and glowed as Ah'Chulhu's powerful spell pulled together the cosmic energy.

Panting and just a second behind me, McGoo arrived, but the blood was already spilled, much of it all over my hands and jacket. Too late. "No use crying over spilled blood," I said.

Ah'Chulhu laughed so hard that his remaining face tentacles wiggled. "You can't stop the flood!"

Around the grotto, the stolen anti-evil protective machinery throbbed and pulsed. Sparks flew everywhere as the shielding increased until automatic fail-safes kicked in. To Ah'Chulhu's alarm, the machinery short-circuited and imploded, unable to handle the sheer surging power of the unholy realms. So much for the safety systems.

As the spell accelerated, however, some of the blood on the rune-etched altar bubbled and turned black, clogging parts of the etched runes. The sizzling dark magic sputtered and stalled as blood backed up across the stone.

"Oh, bugger!" Ah'Chulhu wailed.

McGoo gave me a knowing look, and I nodded. "Talbot and Knowles might have paid a premium, but obviously not all of the donors were as virgin as they claimed to be."

"But enough of them were!" In desperation Ah'Chulhu wrenched the stone basin and poured the remaining red liquid onto the altar, flooding the arcane symbols with blood that was at least mostly pure. "I will not be scuttled in my moment of triumph!"

Stentor's frog hopped in front of us, bellowing, "Help! Someone has stolen my voice. If found, please call the police." I scooped up the spotted creature and stuffed it in the pocket of my bullet-riddled sport jacket.

While we were fighting Ah'Chulhu at the altar stone, another transformation had taken place. Shadows like inky black fumes roiled around the side of the stage next to the porcelain throne, and the supervillain suit finished applying itself to the scrawny body of Jody Caligari. As supervillain strength poured into the young man, he now rose up as Dr. Darkness!!!

The black oily Spandex uniform clung to a well-sculpted bodybuilder physique that Jody definitely had not possessed a moment ago. A black hood covered his face down to his nose, and black goggles masked his eyes. An ebony cape swirled behind his shoulders, dramatically wafting about despite the conspicuous lack of a breeze inside the grotto. He wore gloves up to his elbows like something a welder or a crab fisherman might have used. His boots were high and stylish, black rubber and waterproof—the type of galoshes that even an edgy zombie detective would have been willing to wear. His chin and lower cheeks, though, still showed tiny freckles, and when Dr. Darkness!!! smiled, he flashed incongruously white teeth.

Ah'Chulhu reeled back, astonished. He stepped away from the smoldering altar.

"We're in trouble now," McGoo said.

"We were in trouble before," I pointed out.

Then, better late than never, the gator-guys charged McGoo and me again, remembering what their master had commanded them to do. They were powerful, but slow and stupid. At the back of the grotto, the cops rushed forward to join the fray.

Dr. Darkness!!! faced the business-suited half demon, his black cape still waving.

Now Ah'Chulhu drew back for the battle, recognizing his true nemesis. "These sewers aren't big enough for both of us."

He detached all the rest of his facial tentacles and hurled them at his opponent on the other side of the dais. Enlarging dramatically, dozens of deadly appendages writhed toward Jody, as if somebody had dumped the lost-and-found box from a giant-squid convention.

The gator-guys showed support for their master by applauding and cheering. In the distraction, I was able to slug one under his long scaly chin with a full-fledged roundhouse, knocking him back into his fellows. It was an impressive blow, but nobody was paying attention to me.

On the expanded stage, Jody's chuckle came out as an impressive booming, maniacal laugh. "Ha, ha, ha! Ah'Chulhu, you aren't even a worthy opponent for Dr. Darkness!!! You're no match for my tar globs."

He thrust his black gloves forward, unleashing splurts of thick, gooey ink that closed around the approaching tentacles, staining and sticking to them. One stray tar glob sprayed onto Ah'Chulhu's new gray suit, and the frown of disgust was clear on the half demon's oddly naked face.

In annoyance, he shouted for his gator-guys to attack, which only confused them because they were trying to fight me and McGoo. The tentacles lunged forward without hesitation, though. Meanwhile, Dr. Darkness!!! fought back by hurling more globs like a rowdy vandal in a mud-ball fight. The gator-guys, who had attempted to look menacing as they charged the stage, turned around, ducked, and ran splashing back into the crowd. They decided to go back to fighting McGoo and me again, seeing us as more desirable opponents.

Even Thunder Dick confronted one of the frog demons, trying to figure out which one had swallowed his sundial talisman and vowing to get it back, whatever it took. "When I find the right one, I'm going to need a moment of privacy."

"If you could summon a tornado, that might come in handy now," I suggested.

Thunder Dick strained again, but remained unsuccessful without his talisman.

The great battle between Ah'Chulhu and the junior supervillain was so spectacular and dramatic that even the Phantom did not need to play clamorous organ music to increase the suspense. Dr. Darkness!!! drove back the minions of Ah'Chulhu, and I realized that the fate of the world now depended on an amateur supervillain with Norman Rockwell roots.

Even though the real battle was taking place on the stage, the gator-guys tried to block us from the bloody altar stone. Frog demons joined the fray as more cops charged the dais. This was turning into a full-fledged brawl as the spell continued to work its way through the runes etched in the concrete.

A pair of giant tentacles wrapped around Dr. Darkness!!!, but the supervillain flexed his bulging Spandex-enclosed muscles until he burst free. In retaliation, he unleashed a flurry of shadow webs that forced the tentacles to retreat. In the titanic battle, the combatants even toppled the impressive porcelain throne.

I fought my way back to the altar stone just in time to see the bubbling, smoking blood suddenly grow brighter as it completed the sorcerous circuits, activating a color out of space, a shadow out of time, and a smell beyond imagining.

Pausing in his battle with Dr. Darkness!!!, Ah'Chulhu pointed in triumph toward the spangles of twisted interdimensional light. "It's about bloody time!"

A great boom like thunder tore asunder the very fabric of the underworld. The shock wave rippled through the air and hurled us all backward—me, McGoo, Thunder Dick, and an assortment of henchmen. Fortunately, the frog demon minions we crushed beneath us were soft and cushiony.

The cosmic doorway opened, sparkling with baleful green fire around its rim. Foul brown sludge began to stream from the bottom of the gate.

Ah'Chulhu held up a victorious fist and turned to sneer at Dr. Darkness!!!—who threw a tar glob in his face. But their battle dwindled to insignificance as the gateway to the Netherworld swelled and blossomed. A second violent shockwave hurled Jody aside.

My eyes hurt just from looking into that other dimension, and then I saw even darker shadows moving inside—enormous, horrifying figures that appeared at the threshold.

CHAPTER 45

As a zombie, I don't tend to get creeped out easily—but those things were *ugly:* each had a slumped, rounded head boiling with tentacles, some of which sported bloodshot eyeballs on the tips, and a large, glowing cyclopean eye stared from the center of the gray-green forehead. Their mouths were jagged gashes that drooled a smoking yellowish mucus. Perky red bows tied onto a head tentacle indicated that one of the creatures might be female.

Even as the otherworldly effluent continued to flow from the cosmic gate, the two gigantic figures shuffled through the threshold. They moved with painstaking slowness that implied unspeakable age, or perhaps arthritis. These must truly be Senior Citizen Gods.

Barely able to keep his feet, Ah'Chulhu looked up in amazement. With a quavering voice and an uncertain smile, he said, "Mom? Dad?" Mustering his courage, he spread his arms and yelled out to the cowering minions in the chamber, "Behold, the titanic gods—Ma'Chulhu and Pa'Chulhu!"

The male Senior Citizen God bellowed back at him, "I am not your father!"

The female put a slimy, rubbery flipper against her husband's side. "Now, dear, we discussed this in therapy. You have to move on and be more accepting, for the sake of our marriage."

"Look at him, though," burbled the male. "He's something of a disappointment."

Ma'Chulhu scolded him again, "He's my *son*, dear." The gigantic female Senior Citizen God pushed her way through the cosmic gateway, as effluent continued to surge into our universe, although the huge forms blocked most of it.

The smell was dizzying. McGoo looked as if he might vomit (which, in my estimation, would only have sweetened the aroma). Thunder Dick squirmed to get free from where we had piled on top of him, although I was doing him a favor by not letting him see the hideous things.

Ma'Chulhu leaned forward. "What's wrong with your face, baby boy? And you've got a stain on your suit."

Ah'Chulhu made an embarrassed gesture, and his detached facial tentacles came swarming back to him. As they attached themselves, he brushed at the inky smear from the supervillain's tar glob. "It'll come off."

"No, it won't," yelled Dr. Darkness!!!, still trying to scramble to his feet. His impressive black cape now looked wilted and limp.

The two Senior Citizen Gods ignored the pint-sized supervillain and peered out at the cowering crowds. "We were surprised when you summoned us, boy," Pa'Chulhu said. "What have you been doing in this place? Causing trouble, I expect. And what's with that ridiculous accent?"

Ah'Chulhu gathered his pride. "I've made something of myself, even though the odds were stacked against me." He raised his squirming chin. "I'm an important bloke here. I even have minions, lots of them—and I really, really, *really* wanted you to see my big plan for converting the entire world, a bonzer ambitious project as a real-estate developer to open up new property, flooding the entire Unnatural Quarter to create vast acres of new sewer-front property." Nervous, he talked so fast that his Australian accent garbled some of his words, and then his voice hitched. "I just wanted to impress you."

"By stealing all of our effluent?" said Pa'Chulhu.

Again, Ma'Chulhu urged her husband to be calm. "That's charming, baby boy. You've done so well after . . . after we had to leave you behind." She hung her head in guilt, and the lamplike orb grew dimmer in the middle of her forehead. The eyeball-tipped tentacles drooped downward as she turned to the gigantic male creature. "I told you we were going to scar him for life, dear. We never should have dumped him down that manhole. We were thinking only of ourselves."

Pa'Chulhu said, "That's what saved our marriage. We had to do it. The lesser of two evils."

Dr. Darkness!!! sprang forward. "*I'm* the lesser of all evils!"

Impatient with the distraction, Ma'Chulhu flicked a tentacle and sent a blast of otherworldly cosmic energy, which tumbled Jody back behind the fallen porcelain throne. She sniffled, a loud, wet sucking sound, and turned back to the domestic problem at hand. "But think of the harm I did to my baby boy."

"You brought it on yourself with your disgusting affair," Pa'Chulhu grumbled. "Because you can't keep your tentacles to yourself."

Finally, Thunder Dick managed to crawl out from under the pile of frog demons. He stood up, his tie-dyed wizard robes dripping with fresh drainage from the Netherworld. He shook his head, dazed, and stared at the interdimensional gateway. His jaw dropped open, and he gasped. "Merde!"

Ma'Chulhu whirled at the sound. Her singular lamplike eye glowed brighter, her tentacles quivered in a frenetic mass. "Richard! Oh, dear sweet Richard!"

I turned to the weather wizard. "Merde?"

"It was my pet name for her. We adored each other, and she loves it when I talk French."

My head was already aching from trying to encompass the hideous Senior Citizen Gods from another dimension, but the idea of Thunder Dick having an affair with Ma'Chulhu ... I thought my brain was going to explode and leak out through the bullet hole in my forehead.

"You *slept* with that?" I asked him.

He shrugged helplessly. "What can I say? Beer goggles."

"That would take a lot of beer!"

Beside me, McGoo bent over and retched.

"Oh, Richard!" Ma'Chulhu's voice was longing and wistful.

From the dais, still trying to reaffix the shrunken tentacles to his face, Ah'Chulhu looked at the scruffy weather wizard in astonishment. "You? *You're* my real dad?"

"No, *I* am your father!" yelled Pa'Chulhu, completely contradicting himself.

Pale and nervous, Thunder Dick shuffled his feet in the rising levels of Nether slop that was filling the chamber. "Awkward ..." he muttered.

Ma'Chulhu wrung her tentacles. When she began sobbing, tears spewed from her numerous eyeballs.

Pa'Chulhu grew louder and sterner. "I will not let this undo all the relationship building, all the therapy. Now we're going to need more counseling." He thrashed a tentacle, pointing at Ah'Chulhu, who began to quiver in fear. "And you, boy! Stay away from that weathermancer. He's a home wrecker, a despicable philanderer."

Thunder Dick seemed to want to sink even deeper into the effluent.

"Oh, Richard . . ." Ma'Chulhu sighed again, eliciting even more ire from her husband.

The male Senior Citizen God roared at her, "Obviously, I have to take you away from him. The temptation is too great—I can see it in all of your eyes."

She sniffled that loud, unpleasant sound again and turned away. "You're right, I have to think of my family. The heart wants what . . . no, my marriage is strong! Come with me, Pa'Chulhu—let's go home and take our son with us."

The male creature snaked a long tentacle around Ah'Chulhu's waist and yanked him toward the cosmic doorway. "*Our* son."

Ma'Chulhu also enfolded her half-demon son, and the smoking mucus dripped onto his gray business suit.

Thunder Dick was thunderstruck, cringing and longing at the same time. The shadowy figures began to dissolve in the cosmic gateway, but Ma'Chulhu thrust one last tentacle out to wave a forlorn goodbye.

Then Ah'Chulhu and the two Senior Citizen Gods were gone. With a sucking roar, a cosmic vacuum slurped all the effluent back into the Netherworld, draining the grotto . . . and the rippling dimensional doorway vanished.

When all the virgin and not-so-virgin blood burned out on the altar stone, the sorcerous designs turned black. The stone shuddered, split asunder, and collapsed with a loud thud.

From the dais, Dr. Darkness!!! rose up and shouted, "At last, the world is mine!"

CHAPTER 46

After such a long and difficult day, the last thing I wanted to deal with was a megalomaniacal supervillain. I pushed aside the multiply-confused gator-guys and tried to work my way toward the kid, hoping I could make him see reason.

Now that he had the spotlight to himself again, his ebony cape flowed out, rippling in a stiff supernatural breeze. Black lightning bolts surged from his suit. Dr. Darkness!!! flexed his gloved hands, and shadow webs spun out to cover the ceiling, then slammed down as impenetrable bars to prevent any potential minions from escaping the grotto. As he grinned, Jody's white teeth were dazzling.

At his organ, the Phantom pressed down on the ivory keys and blared out an ominous note. Annoyed, Dr. Darkness!!! flashed one of his black gloves and sent out a bolt of black lightning. The Phantom dove out of the way just as a bank of pipes exploded into a shower of atonal debris.

A pair of trapped cops in the grotto swung their service revolvers and opened fire, but the three exclamation points glowed on the supervillain's chest, and he deflected each bullet with a darkness shield. Careful not to hurt anybody, Dr. Darkness!!! hurled tar globs like bowling balls, which splattered against the officers and plastered over their guns.

"I am your master!" His voice was so loud it throbbed in the chamber. "Kneel before Jody." Then he remembered the puddles of standing effluent. "Never mind, too messy. Bow your heads—that'll be good enough. Now I shall rule the world."

I reached the front of the dais and I knew what I had to do. "Now why would you want to do that, Jody? You're just a small-town kid who likes to build gadgets in his parents' garage. You came here for Junior Mad Scientist Camp, not to conquer the Earth."

"It's for extra credit," said Dr. Darkness!!!

I wasn't afraid of the black power emanating from his suit. "You're a good kid, Jody, and there's no question you have a lot of talent. A genuine master of disguise. That gator-guy costume was incredible. Even the real gator-guys couldn't tell the difference."

At first, Dr. Darkness!!! swelled with pride, then he frowned. "Well, they're not all that bright."

When some of the orphaned semi-sentient alligators hissed at the insult, Jody hurled tar globs at them, which quieted the complaints.

"Do you know how much trouble it is to rule the world?" I didn't think the kid understood all the headaches he was going to suffer from being an omnipotent evil overlord dictator of the planet. "Nobody really wants the job. You may be a scientific genius, but have you taken civics class? Do you watch the news? Do you understand the stress that goes along with politics?" I gestured toward the weather wizard in his tie-dyed robe. "Look at Thunder Dick and Alastair Cumulus the Third. One little campaign nearly ruined them, and that's for an office that nobody cares about."

"I care about it!" cried Thunder Dick. "Wuwufo is very important."

In my pocket, Stentor's squirming frog tried to bellow out its usual announcement again, but I shushed it by pressing my hand against the side of my jacket.

Crackling with power, Dr. Darkness!!! loomed over me, but he seemed unsure of himself. I continued, "Remember when you first came into our offices dressed as iGor?"

He grinned. "Yeah, that was a great disguise."

"When we took your case, you promised you would remember the friends who helped you. I'm your friend, and now I need you to take it down a notch."

Finally, Jody's cape drooped and his shoulders slumped. He reached up with a gloved hand and pulled back the clinging hood to reveal his red hair. "Golly, I didn't really think through the whole world-domination thing, Mr. Chambeaux."

"It's all right, Jody," I said. "Not many supervillains do."

The shadow webs enclosing the chamber dissipated, and I climbed the dais steps to pat the kid on the shoulder. He adjusted his black Spandex outfit, tugging at the folds. Although he'd worked hard on the automated self-donning feature, he hadn't perfected the details of how to get the suit back off again.

Outside the main entrance to the ceremonial chamber, I heard more splashing as people arrived. Sheyenne's beautiful ethereal form flitted in first. "We've been looking all over the place for you, Beaux! These sewers are confusing."

Behind my ghost girlfriend came a determined-looking Robin, as well as Miz Mellivar from the Mad Scientists Patent Office. "There is no standardized map of the sewers," grumbled the DAMP. "I'm going to file a complaint with the UQ Water and Sewer Highway Department."

Miz Mellivar seemed not to notice the broken altar stone, the crowded amphibious supplicants, the toppled porcelain throne, and the police still struggling to claw off the clinging tar globs.

The Deputy Assistant Manager of Patents pointed at Jody. "You don't fool me, young man. *You're* the one who broke into my office and stole your records, design sketches, and proto- types."

Jody pouted. "I needed those X-ray Spex to find my stuff. Besides, they're mine in the first place."

"They were submitted for patent applications," Miz Melli- var said, "and they were currently under review, pending thor- ough testing in our special labs. Your evil powers and super weapons might have been dangerous."

Jody sighed. "Sometimes I just get impatient."

"You'll have to surrender the items. Please take off your Dr. Darkness!!! suit and get back into your street clothes."

Robin said, "We'll send a note to your camp counselor ex- plaining that not only did your inventions work, you already used them to kick some serious demon butt."

"And I'll write up a letter of recommendation from Cham- beaux and Deyer," Sheyenne added. "I'm sure they'll accept you back next year."

Jody brightened. "Then I can go on to the advanced level." He struggled to peel off the dark suit, but even though his body had shrunk from its previous muscular physique, the black Spandex was ruthlessly clingy. Robin and I helped him, and soon enough he was just a brainy, sheepish kid again.

Jody handed over the wadded supervillain outfit. "I only wanted people to like me."

I tousled his hair; I couldn't help it—he was the sort of wholesome young man who seemed to demand that treatment. "Don't worry about it. I like you better as a nerdy kid anyway."

CHAPTER 47

Stentor the ogre, who had been miserable for days, was now overjoyed to be reunited with his long-lost frog and, as soon as we could arrange it, with his long-lost voice.

After I brought the frog back from the sewers, the contented spotted creature sat in one of Robin's plastic lunch containers. When I held out the frog to him, Stentor gave me an exuberant thankful embrace that was going to require an earlier-than-usual restoration spell from the Wannovich sisters. I swung the plastic container out of the way to keep it safe (otherwise the ogre's enthusiasm would have crushed the frog, resulting in an unsatisfying end to the case for all concerned, including the frog).

Stentor also gave a huge, and intangible, bear hug to Sheyenne, who giggled and didn't mind at all. When the ogre attempted to do the same to Robin, I intervened. "Our office has a strict no-damage-to-my-legal-partner policy."

"Sorry," he said, still in his embarrassing squeak. He gingerly took the plastic container in his ham-sized hands and made little cooing noises down at the contented frog. "Hello there."

The frog echoed in a much more Stentorious voice, "Hello there."

The ogre looked up at me. "So how do I get my voice back? Do I swallow the frog again?"

The frog eerily echoed the same words, although I don't believe the creature knew what it was saying.

"I suggest we leave that to the experts."

Because this was a happy occasion, we all went together to the Howard Phillips Publishing offices. In the lobby waiting area, two full-furred werewolves stood around, comparing each other's pin-striped suits and lapel flowers; I assumed the marketing department was still taking auditions for the role of Lou Lupine, Werewolf P.I.

For once, none of us caused any security problems, and we all trooped up to the thirteenth floor.

The two witch sisters were waiting in their editorial offices; Alma sat in her kiddy pool filled with mud again, relaxing with a stack of manuscript pages off to one side. Both witches were extremely eager to hear how I—"Dan Shamble, Zombie P.I."— had managed to solve another thrilling and undeath-defying case. They had even brought in Linda Bullwer, the frumpy vampire ghostwriter who wrote the series of novels "based on" my adventures, under the pen name Penny Dreadful. Bullwer had her notepad and a pointy-toothed smile ready for me when we entered the offices.

"We have the frog," I said, "as instructed."

Robin had offered to carry the plastic container, but Stentor wouldn't let go of it. Now, he set the frog down on Mavis's desk, while Linda Bullwer took notes and then embellished them with a flourish. "This is going to be very exciting! An explosive ending to another convoluted mystery."

"Explosive?" Stentor squeaked. "You're not going to blow up my frog!"

"The vocal reunification spell does not require that," Mavis reassured him. "But be aware, the spell is experimental."

"What are the possible side effects?" Robin asked, always the lawyer. "Can I see the fine print in the spell?"

Mavis handed her the dusty old book, and Robin studied the language, frowning as she concentrated. "It says the spell designer assumes no responsibility."

Mavis nodded. "You'll have to absolve Howard Phillips Publishing of any and all blame. Alma and I are all too familiar with how a misprint can make a spell go terribly wrong." Sitting in her mud-filled kiddy pool, the sow agreed. "Now that we're on the other side of the editorial desk, we have to protect our company and our jobs."

Concerned, Robin turned to the ogre. "Mr. Stentor, I advise that you not agree to this until I've had a chance to review the spell and consider all possible ramifications."

The ogre, however, was anxious and distraught. "I need my voice back, and I need it now! I can't stand this hell I've been living in." The statement would have been dramatic, except for the breathy thinness of his voice, echoed by the frog.

Robin seemed about to argue, but I put a hand on her arm. "It's his choice. We know how much this means to him."

Sitting in its plastic container, the frog didn't seem to have an opinion.

Mavis made the spell preparations while Linda Bullwer took reference photographs with her camera. Alma climbed out of her pool, dripping mud around the office, as she went to the plate-glass windows that looked out on the sprawling jumble of the Unnatural Quarter. With her snout, the sow smeared designs on the glass.

"What was that for?" I asked Mavis.

"Protective spells to reinforce the windows."

"Why do we need that?"

"Just in case."

I didn't ask what "just in case" meant.

After she had her candles lit and her spell designs drawn, Mavis bent over the printed verses, moving her lips as she silently practiced the words. She cleared her throat. "And now for the frog."

Gently, Stentor cradled the spotted creature, which looked resigned and dejected as the ogre placed him inside his mouth again. Mavis re-read the spell, then cross-referenced another passage. Stentor mouthed a garbled sound, careful not to crunch or otherwise damage the frog in his throat. I think he was saying, "Hurry up."

Mavis dutifully worked the spell.

Sheyenne, Robin, Linda Bullwer, and I stood out of the way, watching the magical pyrotechnics—which were not nearly as impressive as Ah'Chulhu's efforts to open a cosmic sewer grate and unleash the effluent hordes from the Nether regions. Nevertheless, I'm always impressed to see professionals practice something that I can't do myself.

When it was over, Stentor clutched his throat and began hacking and coughing, until the frog flew out onto the desktop. Though an amphibian should be accustomed to slime, the frog did not seem pleased by its intimate acquaintance with ogre mucus.

The frog opened its mouth, flicked out its tongue, then let out a normal-sounding croak. I took that as a very good sign.

Eyes wide with hope, the ogre tried to speak, but only a tight noise came out. He frowned, cleared his throat with great vigor, picked up the plastic container, and filled it with an ogre-size wad of phlegm. Then he spoke again in a loud and deep voice. "Ah, that's better!"

His large lips inflated with a smile. He pounded his chest and hummed a loud thrumming note; then with immense exuberance he let out a continuous caterwauling that sounded like a banshee being strangled.

The office windows shuddered during this atonal ear-piercing wail, as if trying to cringe out of their seals. The protective wards Alma had snout-smeared on the plate glass glowed bright, reinforcing the panes—and the windows held.

By the time Stentor finished his hideous sonic torture and fell silent, my ears were ringing. I groaned at the two witches. "Now what went wrong?"

"Why, nothing, Mr. Chambeaux," said Mavis. "His voice has been restored perfectly."

Stentor had a huge grin on his face. "Just the way I used to sound!"

Sheyenne drifted close, shaking her head as if it was all she could do not to give up on me. "That's opera, Beaux."

On the day of the Wuwufo election, Thunder Dick returned to our offices, tense and fidgety as he waited for the results, but he forced himself to be optimistic. His wizard robe had been freshly laundered, and the colors were bright and vibrant. It was strange to see him without the tuxedo cat at his ankles.

Sheyenne suggested, "Have you thought about getting another kitten, Mr. Thudner?"

"Right now the pain is too fresh," he said with a loud sigh. "Morris left me, and with the pressure from the campaign, I'm afraid—heck, I'm petrified—but I will survive. I can do just fine without him. In fact, I've given up on relationships. I've had my heart broken by a cat and by Ma'Chulhu. I'll be a lone wolf from now on." He happily showed us his portable sundial talisman, which now hung where it belonged at his throat. "I'm focused on my political ambitions. I can promise clear skies and a sunny day for the Wuwufo election. That'll encourage a high turnout at the polls."

"How did you get your talisman back from the frog demon who swallowed it?" I asked.

Thunder Dick self-consciously wiped the small sundial on the front of his robe and dropped his voice. "Don't ask." He prepared to leave. "Wish me luck. I still have some last-minute campaigning to do—don't forget to cast your vote."

"Only full Wuwufo members are allowed to vote," I reminded him.

"Well, I hope you'll watch the election returns tonight. It'll be on all the weather channels."

"We wouldn't miss it," Robin said.

Later that night, after the polls closed, we turned on the station to watch as the vapid brunette and the smiling Ken Doll reported the results . . . which did not, after all, take very long to tally. The weather networks made the call.

"With all precincts reporting," said the brunette, "the total vote count is one vote for Alastair Cumulus the Third." She giggled.

"And one vote for Thunder Dick," Ken Doll added. "The Wuwufo election is a draw."

We switched to the other networks, but they all announced the same results. Their reporters scrambled out to get interviews, reactions from the average creature on the street. A group of investigative meteorologists spoke with the erudite and pompous Alastair Cumulus III. "My foggy bottom! Wuwufo was never a large organization, but most members don't even bother to vote."

When they talked to Thunder Dick, he was miffed but determined. "I'm going to demand a recount!"

Alastair Cumulus vowed he would take the matter all the way to the Supreme Court, if necessary.

Outside, through no intervention whatsoever from the weather wizards, it began to rain.

With Junior Mad Scientist Camp over for the season, it was time for Jody Caligari to return to his mundane life doing small-scale experiments with a chemistry set in the garage, and going back to school, where he would have to endure gym class, cafeteria food, and talking to girls. He also promised to take a civics class, so that he could better understand world domination and megalomania, as well as the related infrastructure and logistics, should he decide to pursue that as a career path.

Robin gave the boy a big hug. "You keep up with your studies and get good grades in school. I wasn't kidding—we all see a lot of potential in you."

"I know I'm smart," Jody said, without sounding smug about it. "The other kids always tease me, call me a brain."

"What's wrong with having a brain?" I said. "Lots of zombies like brains."

"My parents want me to be a doctor—not even a *mad* doctor."

"I was a med student," Sheyenne said. "The skills are pretty useful, and you could always add the 'mad' part later."

"Or, you could become a lawyer," Robin suggested.

"We should let the kid make up his own mind," I said. "You don't have to set the entire course of your life yet, at least not until puberty."

"I'm almost to puberty," Jody said, and his voice cracked ridiculously.

I tousled the kid's hair again, because I simply couldn't resist. "I've set up a surprise for you. Come down to the street, and we'll send you home in style."

Mystified, Jody followed me down the stairs and out onto the front steps. We waved hello to Mr. Renfeld, who slouched in the hallway like a pile of rags in a folding chair.

Outside, McGoo was waiting for us in full uniform, leaning against a squad car. Seeing us, he lifted a hand and came to greet the blue-eyed, freckle-faced kid. "Hello, young man," he said in his best Officer Friendly impression. "I have an important question for you."

The boy blinked his eyes. "What's that, Officer?"

"Why did the Cyclops professor stop teaching?"

Jody was puzzled. "Why?"

"Because he had only one pupil." He, too, tousled the boy's hair.

"McGoo, don't scare the kid," I said, then turned to the young man. "How would you like a police escort out of the Quarter? It'll impress your parents."

"Oh, gee, will it ever! I've never ridden in a police car before."

McGoo gestured to the squad car at the curb. "If you do decide to become a supervillain, you'll have plenty of chances to ride in the back. Today, you can sit up front with me."

McGoo was in good spirits, since he had heard nothing more from his ex. He also felt good because he had managed to help C.H., who had been left homeless by the destruction of the Recompose Spa. Since wandering hands cause a lot of trouble, McGoo had arranged for C.H. to get a job with the UQPD working in the precinct station to help fingerprint suspects. "He's now a member of the police force," McGoo had said. "Get it, a *member*—"

"Got it right away," I had said. At least it wasn't one of his worst jokes.

Jody was beaming with anticipation for his squad car escort. The kid gave Robin another hug, tried to hug Sheyenne, and firmly shook my hand. "Thank you for everything you've done."

"Work hard at saving the world, Jody, and make us proud," I said.

He climbed into the front seat of the cruiser next to McGoo, who drove away, turning on the sirens and flashers just to thrill his passenger.

"And that," Robin said with great satisfaction, "is why we do pro bono work."

CHAPTER 48

It was opening night at the opera house, and we attended the first performance of *Cats*—because we had to, according to Sheyenne. She told me that it wasn't an actual opera by any means, but it was a start. Baby steps.

I wore my best suit, my burial suit, and Sheyenne manifested a sexy green cocktail dress, which certainly made my spirits rise. She wore special elbow-length gloves, which allowed us to hold hands. And in her glittery white dress Robin managed to appear less like a hardworking lawyer than a presently undiscovered supermodel. Those two ladies looked damned good, and with them accompanying me I felt like the luckiest zombie in the Quarter.

I didn't know much about the musical *Cats* other than the fact that it featured actors singing and dancing while dressed up in cat costumes. What could be better? The Phantom's new revival was a unique production, though, because it included a cast of actual cats as well as the costumed ones. (And many of the performers were also unnaturals.)

As part of my continuing cultural education, Sheyenne instructed me that we would have to see a true opera one of these days, something like *Don Giovanni,* which had made Stentor famous. *Cats,* though, was supposedly more of a crowd-pleaser, something more comprehensible to the layman, you know, like people in cat costumes singing and dancing. . . . Well, at least it wasn't in Italian. The Phantom insisted that art was all well and good, but he also needed to make a buck to keep the doors open, especially now that he had lost Ah'Chulhu's patronage of his private singing school for girls.

As the crowd settled for the show, I spotted Thunder Dick in one of the front-row seats. He still wore his bright multicolored robe, but he had added a bow tie for the formal occasion, because bow ties were cool. He clung to one of the program booklets, flipping through, then going back to the page that showed the supporting cast.

Robin had picked up programs for each of us, and I turned to what had caught the weather wizard's attention. I saw that "Maurice" was listed in fine print among the supporting cats.

The show turned out to be what I had thought (and feared): an incomprehensible storyline performed by full-grown vampires, werewolves, and even some human cast members prancing about in feline costumes.

Thunder Dick whistled and applauded at an entirely inappropriate time as a black tuxedo cat strolled across the stage. The cat arched his back, pretended not to notice the attention, and strolled more slowly.

When Stentor appeared, he stole the show. The big ogre was dressed in an enormous but tight-fitting cat costume. When the spotlight fell on him, he opened his cavernous mouth and with his newly restored voice belted out his song with all the gusto he could manage.

He brought down the house, almost literally. The operatic ogre was so loud that first one window shattered outward from the upper stories, then other windows smashed, but he kept up the chorus, singing louder and louder, until windows broke throughout the Quarter.

Stentor was extraordinarily pleased with himself. The audience roared—and growled and cheered and applauded. Robin, Sheyenne, and I rose to our feet, happy for our client. I gripped Sheyenne's gloved hand, and she gave me that look that I wouldn't trade for anything.

In a small, separate chair all by himself, C.H. was propped up on his stump waving madly, but all I could hear was the sound of one hand clapping.

Regardless of how the Wuwufo election had turned out, Thunder Dick needed his life back to normal—preferably better than his previous normal. "You should have a healthy relationship for a change," I told him. After a cat familiar who despised him and his never-ever-a-good-idea affair with a tentacled female Senior Citizen god, he deserved something better.

Sheyenne was beside me for moral support. "Don't underestimate the power of love."

"I don't underestimate it," he said. "It's the *availability* I have trouble with."

"Then come with us," I said. "I think we can help."

He was embarrassed. "I don't really need . . . I mean, um, I've already got coupons for the Full Moon Brothel."

"Not what I was suggesting," I said.

Sheyenne smiled. "We were thinking of something a little . . . furrier."

Now Thunder Dick looked disturbed. "The Full Moon offered furry options, too."

Instead, we took him to the Unnatural Quarter's animal shelter. FIND A FRIEND FOR LIFE . . . AND BEYOND, said the sign.

The weathermancer quailed when he saw where we were headed. "I'm not sure I'm ready."

"Just take a look," Sheyenne said. "Scratch a few ears, wag a few tails. That's all."

The barks, growls, purrs, and squeals created an indescribable cacophony. The species were divided into various wings—cats and dogs forming the bulk of the population, with a special room for the Hounds of Hell (by appointment only). There were cages of cute reptiles, slithering and multicolored scaly things that reared up, spread their hoods, and flashed fangs in their best and most adorable attempts to say "please adopt me." There were even some small alligators whose owners had chosen not to flush them down the toilet.

The arachnid section had tarantulas, black widows, brown recluses, and scorpions of various sizes. Some of them were scuffed and abused by various owners, and just needed a loving home.

The Exotic and Mythical Creatures section had blacked-out windows and a locked door.

A hunchbacked lab assistant stood at the front counter, and for a moment I thought it was Jody Caligari in his iGor disguise, but then I realized he was a real hunchbacked lab assistant. He was being scolded by one of the shelter workers. "You've adopted thirty white lab rats in the past week. Are you certain you're keeping them as cherished and adored pets?"

"Absolutely," said the lab assistant. "My master loves rats."

"And I see here that you also adopted a giant python six months ago. Are you certain there's no connection?"

The hunchback swung his head from side to side in denial. His eyes were the size of ping-pong balls as they widened in feigned astonishment. "Just a coincidence. The python was a traveling companion."

After a long moment, the animal shelter employee sighed and handed over a set of adoption papers and a cage that contained six squeaking white lab rats.

"Maybe I could have a look at the kittens," said Thunder Dick with great hesitation. "Just for a few minutes."

Inside the feline wing, an old dull-tusked saber-tooth hunched in a cage that was too small for him, though it was the largest pen in the cat section. Rows and rows of cages held domestic cats of all sizes and colors.

Thunder Dick's eyes were as wide as his grin. "Look at the kitties!" He went from cage to cage, but winced whenever he spotted a black-and-white tuxedo cat. He shook his head. "No . . . I really don't think I'm ready yet."

"How about this one?" Sheyenne said, pointing to a cage that held a fluffy tortoise-shell kitten.

The attendant arrived and stood next to us. "Would you like to hold him?"

Thunder Dick was shy. "No, I don't think . . ."

When the kitten came to the edge of the cage and rubbed his head against the mesh, the weathermancer couldn't help but waggle his fingers and scratch the kitten under the chin; the kitten responded with a very loud purr.

"Maybe just for a minute," he said.

The attendant took the kitten out of the cage, and Thunder Dick cradled it, petted it. The kitten was all tiny sharp claws as it climbed the rainbow-colored wizard robes to perch on his shoulders. Thunder Dick smiled and giggled, then said, "Sorry, not today," but with less conviction than before. He plucked the kitten from his shoulder and tried to hand it back to the obviously disappointed attendant.

Just then a rambunctious group of tusked and leathery demon children boiled into the feline room, chattering, grunting, and jostling each other while the exhausted-looking parent demons let the monstrous kids burn off energy. The young demons saw the tortoise-shell kitten in Thunder Dick's hands and started yelling, "We want that one! We want that one!"

They held out clawed hands, trying to grab the kitten, which looked up at Thunder Dick with its huge bright green eyes. The wizard protectively drew the shivering furball back to him. The kitten climbed up his robes and crouched for shelter on his shoulders, hiding against his neck.

The demon children hopped up and down.

The attendant asked Thunder Dick, "Would you like to put the kitten back, sir?"

The weather wizard regarded the demon children with alarm. They were supposedly here to shop for a pet, but to me they looked rather hungry. Thunder Dick saw it, too. "No, I don't think so," he told the attendant, then turned to the demon children. "This one's already adopted."

The little cat began to purr. Very loudly.

The weather networks all agreed that temperatures would be stable for the next few days, but unfortunately they could not agree on what the current weather actually *was.* At Robin's suggestion, we played quiet music in the background and left the news off. We were tired of being under the weather and under the gun.

Some people enjoy a little downtime, and—in theory, at least—I was glad to have the luxury to catch up on paperwork and close the files on all the recent cases we had wrapped up. That lasted about five minutes before I was itching for another mystery to solve. Forget about brains, this zombie detective wanted a *case* to sink his teeth into.

I was about to start wandering aimlessly around the Quarter, and I much preferred to wander around with a real purpose.

Fortunately, before I could get too restless, a new client came through the door. Literally, *through* the door. At Chambeaux & Deyer, we've had plenty of ghost clients before, and we serve undead clientele along with any other kind of unnatural. But this spirit was special.

Sheyenne recognized him right away, and she leaped up from her desk with such poltergeist excitement that her papers scattered in a whirlwind. "Fletcher!"

I had to admit, Fletcher Knowles looked much better as a ghost than the last time I had seen him, crushed and covered with slime from one of Ah'Chulhu's roving freelance tentacles. He manifested himself with his bleached goatee, John Lennon glasses, professional clothes. Since murder victims have a higher chance of returning as unnaturals, I should have guessed Fletcher might reappear sooner or later.

"That was very strange," he said, sounding distant. "Being killed was extremely unpleasant, but being a ghost is just . . . confusing. It takes some getting used to, just figuring out how to walk without sinking too far or floating too high."

"Doorknobs are really hard to use," Sheyenne commiserated.

"I haven't even tried that yet," Fletcher said, "but I'll have plenty of time to practice."

I automatically extended my hand to greet him, even though I knew he couldn't touch it. Fletcher tried, though, and his grip passed right through. "Sorry, I keep forgetting."

"In case you were wondering, we did solve your murder," I said. "Ah'Chulhu is off in the Nether regions, where I doubt we'll ever see him again."

Sheyenne was excited and relieved to see him. "We're so sorry about what happened."

"Don't worry about it, and you did warn me that cigarettes weren't good for my health. If I hadn't gone out for a smoke . . ." He looked at Sheyenne. "Besides, you were poisoned at my club, so I can't really be all indignant about it." When Robin came out to greet him as well, Fletcher smiled at all of us. "I'm here for a reason, not just to visit. I need to engage the services of Chambeaux and Deyer."

I liked the sound of that.

Robin already had her yellow legal pad ready, and the magic pencil poised itself to take notes.

"I may be dead, but I'm still legally co-owner of the Talbot and Knowles Blood Bars chain, a very lucrative franchise. I intend to remain in place and help manage the business, with fully as much power and influence as my partner. I need some legal advice, and maybe a little detective work. Something is *off*. I suspect there's been some embezzling, maybe supplies tainted. I don't know the extent, but I'd like you to find out for me."

Robin and I exchanged a glance, but we both knew what the answer would be. Sheyenne was already opening a case file.

"Fletcher," I said, "this makes my day. The cases don't solve themselves—you need a professional."

I realized that, yes, I did exist to help people solve their problems. I love a good mystery. I was ready to get to work.

Special bonus!
Keep reading to enjoy another delightful
Dan Shamble adventure. . . .

STAKEOUT AT THE VAMPIRE CIRCUS

First time in print!

CHAPTER 1

The circus is supposed to be fun, even a monster circus, but the experience turned sour when somebody tried to murder the vampire trapeze artist.

As a private detective, albeit a zombie, I investigate cases of all sorts in the Unnatural Quarter, applying my deductive skills and persistent determination (yes, the undead can be very persistent indeed). Some of my cases are admittedly strange; most are even stranger than that.

I'd been hired by a transvestite fortune-teller to find a stolen deck of magic cards, and he had sent me two free tickets to the circus. Gotta love the perks of the job. Not one to let an opportunity go to waste, I invited my girlfriend to accompany me; in many ways her detective skills are as good as my own.

Sheyenne is beautiful, blond, and intangible. I had started to fall in love with her when both of us were alive, and I still like having her around, despite the difficulties of an unnatural relationship—as a ghost, she can't physically touch me, and as a zombie I have my own limitations.

We showed our passes at the circus entrance gate and entered a whirlwind of colors, sounds, smells. Big tents, wild rides, popcorn and cotton candy for the humans, more exotic treats for the unnaturals. One booth sold deep-fried artichoke hearts, while another sold deep-fried human hearts. Seeing me shamble by, a persistent vendor offered me a free sample of brains on a stick, but I politely declined.

I'm a well-preserved zombie and have never acquired a taste for brains. I've got my standards of behavior, not to mention personal hygiene. Given a little bit of care and effort, a zombie doesn't have to rot and fall apart, and I take pride in looking mostly human. Some people have even called me handsome—Sheyenne certainly does, but she's biased.

As Sheyenne flitted past the line of food stalls, her eyes were bright, her smile dazzling; I could imagine what she must have looked like as a little girl. I hadn't seen her this happy since she'd been poisoned to death.

Nearby, a muscular clay golem lifted a wooden mallet at the Test Your Strength game and slammed it down with such force that he not only rang the bell at the top of the pole, he split the mallet in half. A troll barker at the game muttered and handed the golem a pink plush bunny as a prize. The golem set the stuffed animal next to a pile of fuzzy prizes, paid another few coins, and took a fresh mallet to play the game again.

Many of the attendees were humans, attracted by the low prices of the human matinee; the nocturnal monsters would come out for the evening show. More than a decade had passed since the Big Uneasy, when all the legendary monsters came back to the world, and human society was finally realizing that unnaturals were people just like everyone else. Yes, some were ferocious and bloodthirsty—but so were some humans. Most monsters just wanted to live and let live (even though the definition of "living" had blurred).

Sheyenne saw crowds streaming toward the Big Top. "The

lion tamer should be finishing, but the vampire trapeze artist is due to start. Do you think we could . . ."

I gave her my best smile. With stiff facial muscles, my "best smile" was only average, but even so, I saved it for Sheyenne. "Sure, Spooky. We've got an hour before we're supposed to meet Zelda. Let's call it 'gathering background information.'"

"Or we could just call it part of the date," Sheyenne teased.

"That, too."

We followed other humans through the tent flaps. A pudgy twelve-year-old boy was harassing his sister, poking her arm incessantly, until he glanced at me and Sheyenne. I had pulled the fedora low, but it didn't entirely conceal the bullet hole in my forehead. When the pudgy kid gawked at the sight, his sister took advantage of the distraction and began poking him until their mother hurried them into the Big Top.

Inside, Sheyenne pointed to empty bleachers not far from the entrance. The thick canvas kept out direct sunlight, protecting the vampire performers and shrouding the interior in a pleasant nighttime gloom. My eyes adjusted quickly, because gloom is a natural state for me. Always on the case, I remained alert. If I'd been more alert while I was still alive, I would be . . . well, still alive.

When I was a human private detective in the Quarter, Sheyenne's ghost had asked me to investigate her murder, which got me in trouble; I didn't even see the creep come up behind me in a dark alley, put a gun to the back of my head, and pull the trigger.

Under most circumstances, that would have put an end to my career, but you can't keep a good detective down. Thanks to the changed world, I came back from the dead, back on the case. Soon enough, I fell into my old routine, investigating mysteries wherever they might take me . . . even to the circus.

Sheyenne drifted to the nearest bleacher, and I climbed

stiffly beside her. The spotlight shone down on a side ring, where a brown-furred werewolf in a scarlet vest—Calvin—cracked his bullwhip, snarling right back at a pair of snarling lions who failed to follow his commands. The thick-maned male cat growled, while the big female opened her mouth wide to show a yawn full of fangs. The lion tamer roared a response, cracked the whip again, and urged the big cats to do tricks, but they absolutely refused.

The lions flexed their claws, and the werewolf flexed his own in a show of dominance, but the lions weren't buying it. Just when it looked as if the fur was about to fly, a loud drum-roll came from the center ring.

The spotlight swiveled away from the lion tamer to fall upon the ringmaster, a tall vampire with steel-gray hair. "Ladies and gentlemen, naturals and unnaturals of all ages—in the center ring, our main event!" He pointed upward, and the spotlight swung to the cavernous tent's rigging strung with high wires and a trapeze platform. A Baryshnikov look-alike stood on the platform, a gymnastic vampire in a silver lamé full-body leotard. He wore a medallion around his neck, a bright red ribbon with some kind of amulet, and a professional sneer.

"Bela, our vampire trapeze artist, master of the ropes—graceful, talented . . . a real swinger!" The ringmaster paused until the audience realized they were supposed to respond with polite laughter. Up on the platform, Bela lifted his chin, as if their applause was beneath him (and, technically speaking, it was, since the bleachers were far below).

"For his death-defying feat, Bela will perform without a safety net above *one hundred sharpened wooden stakes!*" The spotlight swung down to the floor of the ring, which was covered with a forest of pointy sticks, just waiting to perform impalement duties.

The suitably impressed audience gasped.

On the trapeze platform, Bela's haughty sneer was wide

enough to show his fangs; I could see them even from my seat in the bleachers. The gold medallion at his neck glinted in the spotlight. Rolling his shoulders to loosen up, the vampire grasped the trapeze handle and lunged out into the open air. He seemed not to care a whit about the sharp wooden stakes as he swung across to the other side. At the apex of his arc, he swung back again, gaining speed. On the backswing, Bela spun around the trapeze bar, doing a loop. As he reached the apex once again, he released, did a quick somersault high in the air, and caught the bar as he dropped down.

The audience applauded. Werewolves in the bleachers howled their appreciation; some ghouls and less-well-preserved zombies let out long, low moans that sounded upbeat, considering. I shot a glance at Sheyenne, and judging by her delighted expression, she seemed to be enjoying herself.

Bela swung back, hanging on with one hand as he gave a dismissive wave to the audience. Vampires usually have fluid movements. I remembered that one vamp had tried out for the Olympic gymnastics team four years ago—and was promptly disqualified, though the Olympic judges could not articulate a valid reason. The vampire sued, and the matter was tied up in the courts until long past the conclusion of the Olympics. The vampire gymnast took the long view, however, as she would be just as spry and healthy in the next four-year cycle, and the next, and the next.

A big drumroll signaled Bela's finale. He swung back and forth one more time, pumping with his legs, increasing speed, and the bar soared up to the highest point yet. The vampire released his hold, flung himself into the air for another somersault, then a second, then a third as the empty trapeze swung in its clockwork arc, gliding back toward him, all perfectly choreographed.

As he dropped, Bela reached out. His fingertips brushed the bar—and missed. He flailed his hands in the air, trying to grab the trapeze, but the bar swung past out of reach, and gravity did its work. Bela tumbled toward the hundred sharp wooden stakes below.

Someone screamed. Even with my rigor-mortis-stiff knees, I lurched to my feet.

But at the last possible moment, the vampire's plummeting form transformed in the air. Mere inches above the deadly points, Bela turned into a bat, stretching and flapping his leathery wings. He flew away, the medallion still dangling from his little furry rodent neck. He alighted on the opposite trapeze platform, then transformed back into a vampire just in time to catch the returning trapeze. He held on, showing his pointed fangs in a superior grin, and took a deep bow. On cue, the band played a loud "Ta-da!"

After a stunned moment, the audience erupted in wild applause. Sheyenne was beaming enough to make her ectoplasm glow. Even I was smiling. "That was worth the price of admission," I said.

Sheyenne looked at me. "We didn't pay anything—we got free tickets."

"Then it's worth twice as much."

With the show over, the audience rose from the bleachers and filed toward the exit. "The cases don't solve themselves," I said to Sheyenne. "Let's go find that fortune-teller."

CHAPTER 2

As Sheyenne and I walked along the midway in search of the fortune-teller's booth, we suddenly heard screams—not the joyful yelling of riders on a rickety roller coaster, but loud, terrified cries. Bona fide bloodcurdling shrieks. The screams of children.

I was moving before I even knew it, and Sheyenne flitted along beside me. Five children came running toward us, eyes wide enough to qualify the kids as anime cartoon characters. They yelled wordlessly, pelting past us.

They were running from a circus clown.

I had seen him on the circus posters: Fazio the Clown, grinning with a painted smile so wide he could have swallowed a bloody feast and not even left stains on his chin. His very appearance was supposed to be joyful and comforting, but I thought it looked diabolical—as did the kids, apparently.

Fazio implored, "Wait! I just want to make people laugh!"

Pursuing panicked children was not how *I* would have tried to make them laugh.

Panting, the clown stumbled up to us in his big floppy shoes. "I don't know what's wrong with kids today." His face was covered with white greasepaint, and he wore a bright red nose the size of a tennis ball. His bald cap was wrinkled over the top of his head, and shocks of pink hair stuck out in all directions. His teeth could have used whitening (a lot of it) and orthodontia (a lot of it). He held out a bicycle horn and honked it in my face. "Does that make you laugh?" Then he giggled, an edgy Renfeld-catching-a-whole-handful-of-flies laugh.

"Sorry, not today," I said.

Glum, Fazio hung his head and shuffled off with his floppy shoes.

We found the booth of Zelda the fortune-teller, a rickety affair made of plywood and two-by-fours painted bright blue, festooned with crepe paper and a stenciled sign that said, FORTUNES TOLD: $5. But the price had been crossed out and reduced three successive times to the bargain rate of $1.

At the booth, a customer forked over a dollar bill, so we kept our distance, watching the fortune-teller in action. Zelda had told me to be discreet.

The customer was a potbellied man in plaid shorts and black socks. (And they say unnaturals look odd?) Zelda wore a curly wig of platinum-blond hair, eye shadow and blush that must have been purchased in bulk and applied with a trowel; the five o'clock shadow had come in a few hours early on the fortune-teller's cheeks. Gold hoop earrings, gold necklaces, and gold bangles accessorized a dress with a high neckline, but still showed planetary-sized bosomic curves, which were obviously just stuffing.

Zelda shuffled a well-worn deck of regular playing cards, then laid five cards face-up on the wooden tabletop in front of the customer. "The eight of clubs is a good sign—it shows you have worthy goals and are determined to achieve them." The supposedly female voice was falsetto and unconvincing.

He laid down another card. "The king of hearts indicates that you will be happy in romance, lucky in love."

"But when?" the man asked, plaintive.

"Unfortunately, the cards have no time stamp," Zelda said. "Now, the third one . . . ah, the three of spades! A very significant card. You are destined to have great financial success, but it may take a while, so be patient."

The man took hope from that. He looked at the last card. "And the jack of diamonds?"

Zelda shook her head. "That, unfortunately, is a minor card. It merely signifies that your breakfast won't satisfy you for long and you should seek refreshment from one of our fine food booths." The fortune-teller gathered the cards and restacked them in the deck as the customer bent down to pull up his black socks, which had slid lower on his ankles, then he walked off.

Taking our cue, Sheyenne and I stepped up to the fortune-teller. Zelda shuffled the deck, gave me a skeptical look. "I charge extra to determine the fate of the undead."

"We're not here for a reading, uh, ma'am. You hired us—I'm Dan Chambeaux, private investigator, and this is my associate Sheyenne."

Her voice dropped at least two octaves, and she lit a cigarette. "Of course, Mr. Chambeaux—thanks for stopping by." Zelda eyed my gaunt form, looked at my complexion, frowned at the bullet hole in my forehead. "Your business card didn't say you weren't alive."

"Those are old cards. I need to get them reprinted."

Sheyenne joined in. "We have references available upon request."

I got down to business. "I understand your magic fortune-telling deck has been misplaced? You need us to find it?"

"Not misplaced—*stolen*. I'm sure of it this time."

Some questions beg to be asked. "*This* time?"

"It's my second deck gone in six months! I thought I must have misplaced the first one—it happens in the circus, packing up, tearing down, day after day. But real magic fortune-telling decks are hard to come by, so I kept careful watch on the replacement cards. It was the last deck the supplier had in stock, and I couldn't afford another. But it's gone, too. Somebody stole it . . . somebody who's out to get me." He lowered his voice. "I predicted that, even without the cards!"

The customer is always right, as the saying goes; and also, the customer is sometimes paranoid. "We'll look into it, Mr., uh, Ms. Zelda."

"Aldo. My real name is Aldo Firkin. Zelda's just a stage name." He dabbed at the layers of peacock-colored eye shadow. "It's all an act."

"You don't say," I said. Sheyenne pretended to jab me with her spectral elbow, though I couldn't feel her touch. She sometimes has to remind me to show a proper professional attitude in front of the clients.

The fortune-teller frowned, plucking at the absurd dress. "You think I *want* to dress up like this? I'm not a natural-born transvestite, but I can't make a living otherwise. It's a stereotype we can't shake—nobody wants male fortune-tellers. What a sham! All these decades of fighting for equal rights, and I have to do this." He adjusted the ridiculous wig. "Now, about my stolen cards? I really need them back. I've been doing my best." With a burring rattle of laminated paper, Aldo/Zelda shuffled the regular playing cards. "But there's nothing magical about these. I'm just making it up. My other deck—now, those cards were *real*, the magic just barely starting to wear off."

His brow furrowed as he looked down at the old playing cards. "Oddly enough, my fortunes seem to be just as accurate with this ordinary deck. I must be really good at this." He tapped the deck, drew a card, looked at it, and smiled. "Ah, correctly predicted that one. Maybe there's real magic here!"

"Or maybe you're just telling people what they want to hear," I suggested.

Aldo grinned. "Ah, and that's the real magic, isn't it? Give cryptic fortunes and let the customer figure out the true meaning. 'You will lose something very valuable to you, but you will gain something unexpected.' That's one I told the fat lady a few months ago."

"Sounds like a bad horoscope," I said.

"Actually, it sounds like a *good* horoscope," Sheyenne said.

The gaunt vampire ringmaster walked by, still wearing his equestrian jacket; he kept to the awnings, shading his head with his black top hat to avoid the direct sunlight. Aldo waved. "Oscar! Come here—this is the private detective I was telling you about. Dan Chambeaux, meet Oscar Kowalski, ringmaster and circus owner."

The ringmaster gave a formal nod, and we exchanged a cold grip. "Dan Shamble?"

"Chambeaux," I corrected. "People always mispronounce my name. And I wouldn't expect a vampire to be named Oscar Kowalski. I'd think something more like . . . Bela."

Kowalski let out an annoyed snort. "Bela is a drama queen and a pain in the ass, but he does draw a crowd, and that's what it's all about." He lowered his voice. "I'm glad Aldo called you to look into the thefts. We've had a rash of them over the past two weeks." He shot a narrow-eyed glare at the transvestite fortune-teller. "But we need to be discreet."

Aldo sounded indignant. "He's a *private* detective, not a public one. And I couldn't wait any longer—I need my magic cards back."

"What other thefts?" Sheyenne pressed.

"Mostly minor items, low value," Kowalski said.

"My fortune-telling cards are extremely valuable!" Aldo insisted.

The ringmaster continued, "But it causes a lot of nuisance and unease. We like to think we're family here at the circus."

"I miss the Bearded Lady," Aldo muttered. "Harriet was like a mother to us all, really kept the circus tight-knit, like a family. Things were so much nicer before she went off to lead a semi-normal life of her own."

Kowalski shook his head. "We all miss Harriet, but there's not much call for everyday freaks after the Big Uneasy. People can see weirder creatures on any walk through the Quarter."

I got back to business. "We need to know what the other items are. All the clues should lead to the same suspect."

"I can get you a list—a long one," Aldo said, then considered. "But if you're investigating all of the thefts in the circus, then Oscar should pay your bill."

The ringmaster's shoulders drooped. "I'll pay *half* . . . provided Mr. Shamble—uh, Chambeaux—can help us all out. Most of the other items aren't worth much."

"If there's a thief running loose, maybe we should report it to Officer McGoohan?" Sheyenne suggested.

I explained, "I have a good friend on the police force. He'll take your problems seriously."

Kowalski cleared his throat. "That won't be necessary. We must count on your discretion, Mr. Chambeaux. People don't trust circus folk as it is, even here in the Unnatural Quarter, and I don't want to do anything to reinforce that stereotype. You probably don't like it when people consider all zombies to be brain-eating clods with speech impediments."

"Not at all," I said. "I work hard to stay well preserved."

Kowalski tipped his hat. "I hope you can resolve this quickly and quietly. The circus is your client."

"But find my magic cards first," Aldo insisted as he jotted down the list on a scrap of paper.

"If we find the thief, we should find all of the stolen items," I said.

Sheyenne and I read the list as we walked away. In addition to the magic fortune-telling cards (two sets, but I doubted we'd find the one he'd lost six months earlier), Aldo had listed a hammer (standard hardware store issue), glass milk bottle from one of the game booths, dagger from the knife thrower's act, three costume-jewelry necklaces from Annie the fat lady (hence a rope-length of jewelry), and a cold Reuben sandwich from a refrigerator in the Flag. I figured we could discount that last item.

We had no trouble finding the fat lady, mainly because she wasn't very mobile, but also because she was so large. In her open tent, Annie reclined on—and covered most of—a queen-sized bed. Plates mounded with chocolate chip cookies, brownies, and Danishes sat within reach of one hand; by the other side of the bed sat a tray of chicken wings and ribs. She had apparently been through several plates already, but despite the aftermath of her obviously enormous appetite, her face looked saggy. I didn't think the fat lady looked healthy at all, but since I'm undead, I'm not one to point fingers.

Annie's wide throat was round and somewhat tubular, like a pelican with a particular lucky catch of fish. She had permed gray hair and wire-rim glasses that made her look like the world's kindest, and largest, grandmother. An enormous floral muumuu extended all the way down to her ankles; sleeves covered the wrists where they met the gloves. Under her gigantic tent of a dress, her mounded belly stirred and squirmed in a disturbing way, as if her intestines were rearranging themselves before our eyes.

Annie gave us a twinkling smile. "Hello, dears! Come in and stare—that's what I'm here for. Would you like a cookie? I've got plenty." She extended the tray to us.

"No thanks, ma'am," Sheyenne said. "I'm ectoplasmic."

"And I'm on a low-carb diet," I added, even though it was just an excuse. My undead taste buds were no longer very discriminating, and Annie needed a constant stream of calories just to maintain her bulk. She consumed the rest of the cookies with methodical swiftness, as if it were her mission.

"We're from Chambeaux and Deyer Investigations, and we're here on a case." I set one of our business cards on the bedside table next to the chicken wings. "We've been hired to investigate certain items that have gone missing. If there's a circus thief, we'll catch him."

"A thief? Oh, my!" Annie held her hands to her face, licked a few crumbs from her fingers. "I refuse to believe members of my dear circus family are thieves." Her mounded stomach shifted and churned, and Annie let out an embarrassed giggle, placing her hands flat on her belly. "Just a bit of indigestion—it tends to get extreme in my case."

I held up Aldo's handwritten list. "According to this, you've lost several items of jewelry?"

"Oh, dear me, I may have misplaced a few cheap necklaces— I'm always doing that. When I manage to walk around, I can't see the ground, and if something falls . . . well, I just give it up for lost. I wouldn't call them *stolen*. The circus people are my family. I'm like a mother to them since Harriet's gone. Someone has to watch out for everyone."

I tipped my fedora. "If you think of anything, please let us know, ma'am. Any clue would help."

Leaving the fat lady's tent, we strolled along the midway, and soon Fazio the Clown buttonholed us again. "I saw you two talking with that fraud fortune-teller! He's a fake—a complete fake. I doubt he could predict *yesterday* if he had a newspaper in front of him."

If you had asked me before the Big Uneasy, I would have said that all fortune-telling was fake. Now, though, I'd seen plenty of evidence of functional spells. "He's at a disadvantage if he lost his magic cards."

"Not the cards—the sham costume. Him in his stupid wig and his clumsy makeup! It's an embarrassment. Makeup is no joke. I work hard on my appearance, greasepaint over every inch of exposed skin." He tugged at his shocks of pink hair, straightened the bald cap, then tweaked the bright red nose. "It's a beautiful design, the perfect clown face—I've even got it trademarked. But Zelda, or Aldo, or whoever or whatever the name is, does it just to make a buck. It cheapens the art of face painting."

"And why do you paint your face?" Sheyenne asked.

"For a greater purpose, of course—to get a laugh."

Or a scream, I thought, remembering the terrified children.

"We're investigating a rash of burglaries, not makeup techniques," I said. "Any comments about his missing deck of fortune-telling cards?"

"I don't know anything about the first one he lost, and not the second one either." He snorted, then stormed off. "You should be investigating Aldo. His eye shadow is a crime!"

CHAPTER 3

After gathering as much information as we could, Sheyenne and I returned to the Chambeaux & Deyer offices in the seedy, run-down section of the Unnatural Quarter (I realize that's not very specific).

Sheyenne began compiling a list of circus suspects and digging up dirt on them. She's good at uncovering details, whether they be sordid details, suspicious details, or just plain bookkeeping details.

A large part of my job is time management. Real life as an undead private investigator isn't like a TV detective show, where the PI works on one mystery at a time and solves it without other clients getting in the way. In addition to investigating stolen items at the vampire circus, I had several active cases.

My partner, Robin Deyer, came out to brief me on the legal battles she had fought during the day. As a lawyer, Robin makes sure that downtrodden and underrepresented monsters get a fair shot in the legal system. She's a young African American, as pretty as she is determined—and she is extremely determined.

Her eyes had a faraway, preoccupied look because case subtleties ran through her head at all times.

I had taken her under my wing back when I was a human private detective. We shared office space, offered assistance on each other's cases, and enjoyed working together. After my murder, I think Robin was hit even harder by my death than I was. When I came back from the grave, she welcomed me with open arms (after she got over the shock and uneasiness). She made a special point to treat me just as she'd always done, and we quickly got back to our usual routine.

"Any word on the gargoyle case?" I asked.

For several weeks Robin had represented a gargoyle who was suing the Notre Dame cathedral for unauthorized use of his likeness. Comparing the gargoyle himself with photographs of several specific stone figures on the ancient cathedral, the resemblance was undeniable.

Her expression tightened. "I think we're going to lose that one. There seems to be an unbreakable statute of limitations clause in church law. Today, I'm neck-deep in that unnatural voting rights case."

Robin was tilting at a different windmill, challenging voter restrictions recently put in place for the sole purpose of denying unnaturals the right to vote. (No one seemed to remember that in some corrupt cities, dead people had done more than their share of voting over the years. . . .) Both political parties insisted that the proposed voter suppression rules against unnaturals were disenfranchising their constituents, although neither side had been able to prove that unnaturals leaned toward any particular affiliation, as a rule.

After Robin described a brief she had filed and her court appearance schedule for the week, I told her about the vampire circus and headed to my office to take care of my own work. "I think I can wrap up the Amontillado case this afternoon."

"Good," Sheyenne called from the receptionist's desk. "We need to send them a bill."

Robin cautioned, "The outcome wasn't what the client expected. Maybe we should offer a discount—"

Sheyenne cut right in. "The client is a client, and a fee is a fee." If Robin had her way, she would do all cases pro bono, and Sheyenne often had to remind her about the facts of business. Even though I was undead and Sheyenne was a ghost, *Robin* still needed to eat, and we all had to pay the rent on the office space.

I suggested a compromise. "Give the client a coupon for his next case with us. We did solve the mystery, which is what he hired us to do."

A wealthy man had asked me to track down a very rare cask of Amontillado, more than a century and a half old, and I found the cask behind a brick wall, along with an animated skeleton that had been manacled there. In the years since the Big Uneasy, the skeleton had managed to break loose from one manacle by detaching his entire bony hand. With his wrist released, he was able to reach the cask, work the bung loose, and pour the extremely expensive sherry down his throat. Of course, since he had no throat, the rare Amontillado spilled all over the vault floor and dried up. When I found the very expensive and very empty cask I'd been hired to track down, the skeleton laughed and laughed at the joke, saying in a rattling voice, "I drank it all, I drank it all!"

Now I sat at my desk and wrote up the report, reducing the total number of hours billed on the case just to make Robin happy, and to make me feel better as well; Sheyenne didn't need to know.

It was full-dark outside by the time Sheyenne flitted through my closed office door. She carried a stack of papers, which could not spectrally pass through the barrier, so they fluttered to the floor outside. With an impatient frown, she flitted back out, picked up the papers, and opened the door to enter via the normal way.

"I ran down the usual suspects at the circus. Some very interesting background material."

I took the papers. "Anything suspicious?"

She arched her eyebrows. "Naturals and unnaturals all working for a traveling circus run by a vampire—isn't that suspicious enough?"

"I was hoping for something more specific."

"So many aliases, stage names, plenty of skeletons in the closet—and not like the one you found with your cask of Amontillado." She grinned at me.

"Speaking of that. . ." I handed her the bill and final report, which pleased her very much.

She continued with her summary, "First off, Oscar Kowalski is not a very talented businessman. He's filed for bankruptcy twice since the Big Uneasy, barely scraped through, and seems to be in rocky circumstances right now."

I said, "I don't see how stealing a deck of fortune-teller cards, costume jewelry, and a cold Reuben sandwich would help his financial situation."

"Probably not." Sheyenne glanced down at her papers again. "Checking back along the circus route over the years, I found that two goblin roustabouts were arrested for petty theft, but they escaped and disappeared. Young twins. Their juvenile records should have been sealed, but Robin pried them loose because the law is still murky."

"Robin used a murky law to her own advantage?" I asked. "Good for her."

Sheyenne blew an imaginary breath through her lips. "The goblins were over eighteen years old—adults according to the letter of the law—but goblins live a long time, and those twins are still adolescents as far as *goblins* go. Still, nobody's bothered to change the law, so we got the arrest records. Not that it does us much good, if the twins are no longer with the circus."

Robin would probably decide to challenge that law, now that she'd noticed the injustice.

"What else?" I asked.

"Aldo—or should we call him Zelda?—is late on his child support, and his ex-wife is trying to track him down." She checked off items on her list. "Fazio got arrested for drunk driving in his clown car, but that was never prosecuted. Oh, and his clown license has expired."

I frowned. "I didn't know there was such a thing as a clown license. I find that very suspicious."

Sheyenne blinked her blue eyes at me. "More suspicious than all the other things?"

"He's a clown. I'm always suspicious of clowns."

CHAPTER 4

With the information Sheyenne had uncovered about the circus personnel, I went back to the midway early enough to catch the nighttime monster matinee. While unnatural crowds started to gather inside the Big Top for Bela's performance, I stopped by Oscar Kowalski's office trailer just outside the main tent. I wanted to ask him about bankruptcy filings, late child-support payments, Fazio's expired clown license, and anything else that came to mind. Instead, I stumbled into another crisis.

"I refuse, Oscar!" Bela cried with an exaggerated and obviously fake Transylvanian accent. He raised his chin with an imperious air and flared the nostrils on his beak-like nose. "You must cancel the show. I can't perform under these circumstances—it is impossible!"

"Nothing's impossible, Bela." Kowalski sounded long-suffering and annoyed. He sat at his desk with an open, and messily scribbled ledger. "Nobody's canceling the show. You *can* go on, and you *will* go on."

"But it's been stolen!" Bela clutched at his throat, where I noticed the gold medallion was missing. (The far-too-clingy silver lamé bodysuit had previously demanded most of my attention.) "It's my Air Commander medal, given to me for being a Flying Ace in World War Two—or World War One, I forget which. If I don't wear the medal, then I won't have the confidence to transform into a bat at the climax of my show."

I interrupted, startling them. "You need a magic talisman to change into a bat?"

"Have you ever tried it?" Bela snapped, then whirled on Kowalski. "Have *you?* Most vampires are incapable. It requires the utmost concentration. My Air Commander medal is the perfect focusing aid."

"So it's like Dumbo's magic feather?" I said. "Without it, you wouldn't have the self-confidence to fly?"

Bela raised himself up, looked down his nose at me, and said with withering sarcasm, "Yes, exactly like that." He sniffed.

"It's all in his head," Kowalski explained to me. "Nothing magical whatsoever. The medallion's just a piece of junk."

"It is part of my act! I feel naked without it."

Again, I had trouble tearing my attention from the excessively form-fitting lamé bodysuit.

The ringmaster looked at his watch, closed his ledger with finality. "Sorry, Bela, but the show must go on. So follow that advice—*go on!*"

In a huff, the vampire trapeze artist strutted out of the admin trailer.

With a flicker of relief on his face, Kowalski turned to me. "Every week he's got some other excuse, imagines he's been cursed whenever he passes gas, threatens to quit the circus, but I doubt any rival show would have him."

"Are there other monster circuses?" I hadn't heard of any.

"No. Hence, my point. And I admit it takes a lot of concentration to turn into a bat, especially on the fly, but he doesn't have to be such an ass about it." He brushed down his jacket, looked at the watch again. "Now, I didn't expect to see you back so soon, Mr. Chambeaux. Come up with answers yet?"

"Even better—I've got a lot more questions."

"How is that better?"

"That means I'm making progress."

Kowalski stood from his desk. He looked tired as he reached for his top hat. "I can't talk with you at the moment. The show must go on for me, too, and if there's any unreasonable delay in the performance the lions start complaining."

"Don't you mean the lion tamer?" I asked.

"No, Calvin's easy to deal with, but the lions want their treats, and they can get quite demanding." He showed me out of the trailer and locked the door behind us.

With the audience crowded in the Big Top for the monster matinee, the midway was quiet and dark. I decided to lurk and snoop, two things for which a zombie detective is eminently qualified.

Since the Air Commander medal was the latest stolen item, I made my way to Bela's darkened tent. Though he considered himself the star of the circus, the vampire's mobile domicile wasn't much more than a place to shelter his coffin when he needed some quiet time—wide open and not secure. If Bela had gone to ground to take a nap, someone could easily have snatched his medal from the nightstand and run off with it.

I walked around outside Bela's tent, senses alert and scanning the ground for any unusual clues . . . such as that playing card lying faceup on the ground not far from the tent.

It was the jack of diamonds, the same card that predicted a person would be hungry soon after breakfast. I guessed it came from Zelda's deck.

I kept plodding along, scanning from side to side. The circus seemed eerily empty, filled with shadows. I heard the audience cheer in the Big Top; Calvin must be in the middle of his act.

Spotting something ahead, I bent over to pick up another playing card, the six of hearts. With two dropped playing cards making a dotted line that led from Bela's recently burgled tent toward the general direction of Zelda/Aldo's trailer, I knew how to connect the dots.

As I approached the trailer, I heard raised voices, an argument in full swing. Aldo was shouting, so upset that he still sounded high-pitched and falsetto, and not in an attempt to maintain his transvestite identity. "What did you want with my magic cards anyway? It wasn't enough for you to steal my fortune-telling deck, so you had to steal my playing cards, too? And my makeup kit? You're trying to ruin me!" He had his wig in his hand, and a smear of cold cream had removed only the first few layers of eye shadow.

Fazio was still in full clown makeup, his bright red nose planted in the middle of his white-painted face, his pink hair sticking out in all directions. "You have nothing I'd even want to steal—certainly not your amateur makeup kit! You are a fake and a disgrace!"

Before they could come to blows, I interrupted, holding up the two playing cards. "Are these from the deck? I found them on the ground near Bela's tent—there's been another robbery."

Aldo grabbed the playing cards, as if he could make a good start with only two of the fifty-two. "Yes, there has—my cards and my makeup kit."

Fazio asked, "What other robbery?"

"Someone took Bela's Air Commander medal right before his trapeze act."

"Bela never goes anywhere without that gaudy thing." Aldo crossed his arms over his too-obviously padded chest, then turned to the clown. "Why would you steal the poor vamp's Air Commander medal?"

"I *didn't* steal it! And I didn't steal your damn cards, either!

Or your makeup kit. I am a completely honest, law-abiding citizen."

"Then what about my Reuben sandwich?" Aldo demanded. Fazio hesitated just long enough for the fortune-teller to pounce. "I knew it—you took my sandwich!"

"Those may be two unrelated cases," I said. "And, Fazio, you're not off my list of suspects—I know you've been keeping secrets."

The circus clown seemed to turn even whiter than his greasepaint. "You . . . know my secret?"

"Your clown license is expired, and that's enough to make me suspicious," I said, deciding not to bring up the clown-car drunk driving incident. "I can bring in the real police at any time, but for now I'll keep looking."

I stalked off among the dark trailers and tents. I hoped I could find the Air Commander medal in time to take it to the vampire trapeze artist before his act, just to give him a psychological boost. The crowd in the Big Top continued to cheer the lion tamer's show.

I paused at Annie's tent. Since the tent flaps were open, I looked in. The fat lady was inside, lying on her bed, and appeared to be asleep, covered by a mounded blanket. She looked like a mountain range under the comforters. More plates piled with cookies, brownies, ribs, and wings remained within easy reach; someone must replenish them all day long. I left her to rest.

I circled around, trying to keep an open mind, but ready to find Fazio responsible (okay, I admit, I was guilty of clown profiling). There, outside the front of his tent, I found the red ribbon and gold disk—Bela's Air Commander medal, just lying on the ground. Not only was the circus thief persistent and random, he was also clumsy. Why steal things, then drop them all over the place like a cat losing interest in a mouse?

In the Big Top, the crowd cheered and applauded as Calvin finished his show. I grabbed the medal, deciding to confront the clown later. At the moment I had to get the Air Commander medal back to the vampire trapeze artist before he started his act.

I expected to feel a tingle of magic; if the Air Commander medal were really a spell-impregnated amulet, I should have been able to sense the power even with my numb fingers. Then the "gold" disk rotated as I dangled the ribbon, revealing *Made in China* stamped on the back; I suspected the disk itself was nothing more than coated tin.

But Bela somehow had it in his head that he needed this thing for his bat transformation, so I might as well be of service.

I raced to the Big Top at the best speed I could manage—joints and muscles tend to stiffen up postmortem, so it's a good thing I keep myself in shape. So many spectators were milling at the main tent opening—mummies, werewolves, ghouls, vampires, a very tall ogre—that I couldn't get inside, so I ran around to the side by Oscar Kowalski's office trailer. I pushed my way through a smaller stage entrance, holding up the medal. "Wait—I have to get this to Bela before he starts!"

But the ringmaster had already announced the performance, and the crowd drowned out my voice. Spotlights shone on Bela, high up on his trapeze platform, and the audience gave suitable gasps as the light swung down to illuminate the hundred sharpened stakes.

For all his prima donna behavior, Bela was a true showman. Even without the not-so-magic medal around his neck, he showed no sign of nervousness as he grabbed the trapeze and swung out over the yawning gap. As Bela began his act, Kowalski withdrew to the side of the tent, where he saw me holding the red-ribboned amulet. "I found it," I said, "but too late."

The ringmaster gave a snort. "He doesn't need the thing. It's all in his head, and I can't let him make excuses. The show must go on."

Above, Bela did a beautiful somersault loop, then caught the trapeze bar again.

"His ego needs to be taken down a notch anyway. He demanded a big pay raise. Does he think the circus is actually making any money? We're holding on by a spiderweb here."

I lowered my voice. "I know about the bankruptcies, Mr. Kowalski."

The ringmaster frowned. "So then you know I can't pay Bela any more, but I can't have him leave, either. If he refused to do the show tonight, and I had to refund all these tickets . . ." He gestured to the audience. "I might as well bury myself six feet under without a book to read."

Bela swung back and forth on the trapeze, increasing his momentum and height as he set up for the climax of the show.

Kowalski looked up. "The fumble is all part of the act, you know. He better not chicken out tonight."

At the apex of the swing, Bela flipped himself into the air, spun three somersaults, then reached out to catch the returning bar, fumbled and missed—just as I had seen him do that afternoon. Bela wore a panicked look, his arms outstretched as he plummeted toward the pointy wooden stakes.

The audience gasped. A necromancer screamed in a high womanish voice. Kowalski and I waited for Bela to transform into a bat.

And waited.

He flailed and thrashed in real panic. In the last instant, Bela squeezed his eyes shut, either in a last-ditch attempt to concentrate or to avoid seeing so many sharp wooden tips. And then he slammed into them. Since he'd been falling spread-eagled, Bela managed to impale himself on a goodly number of the one hundred stakes.

Kowalski gaped. The monsters in the audience screamed; some chuckled, thinking it was part of the show. But when Bela sizzled and fumed, his body boiling and flesh sloughing away to leave only a skeleton that crumbled to dust, people began running out of the Big Top. A few stayed and applauded.

"I have to manage this crowd!" Kowalski said as he bolted away from me. "The show's over—you saw it finish. Nobody's getting refunds."

Disgusted, I held up the Air Commander medal and called after him. "I found this by Fazio's tent—and I bet he also stole Aldo's deck of fortune-telling cards."

Then I had another thought, realizing that the uproar would let Fazio know that Bela was dead—and the clown *knew* he was responsible. If the amulet truly had no magic, I didn't know whether this counted technically as murder, but at the very least he had caused a deadly accident, messing with the vampire trapeze artist's head before a dangerous act. Fazio had some explaining to do, and I had to stop him before he fled the circus.

I pulled out my cell phone and called Officer Toby McGoohan, commonly called McGoo (by me, at least), and told him to roll the squad cars, that we had a death at the circus and a possible murderer to arrest. McGoo likes to hear things like that. He's my BHF—my best human friend—and we've helped each other on many cases. I knew I could count on him now.

First, though, I had to prevent the escape of a deadly circus clown.

CHAPTER 5

I expected to find Fazio at his tent, stuffing valuables into a hobo sack so he could run far from the Quarter. That's what *I* would do, if I were a killer clown cat-burglar responsible for the death of a vampire trapeze artist.

I did find Fazio in his tent, but he wasn't packing up to leave. Instead he was wailing, outraged. "They stole my nose! The little bastards stole *my nose!*"

The clown whirled to face me, and I saw that the big red nose was indeed gone from the middle of his face. More shocking, though: The fake nose wasn't the only thing missing. Fazio's *real* nose was gone, leaving a cavernous empty sinus socket draped with a few shreds of rotted flesh. The makeup had been smudged around his eyes, and I could see the sunken hollow look, the grayish tone to his unpainted skin.

"You're a *zombie!*" I cried, demonstrating my detective abilities.

"Not just a zombie," Fazio insisted. "A clown, too. That's my true calling in life—and afterlife."

A zombie clown, I thought. Now *that's* scary.

Fazio moaned, covering the nose hole in the middle of his face. "All I ever wanted was to make people laugh." Then he looked up at me. "Why are *you* so surprised? You're undead, and you came back to keep solving cases. Why can't I still be a clown just because I'm a zombie? Maybe that's why I rose up in the first place—to make people laugh."

Actually, he wasn't making anyone laugh that I could tell, but I decided not to argue with him.

He touched his cheeks. "Put on enough greasepaint and a wig, no one can tell the difference. I still do my job." A wave of anger passed through him again. "And those little goblin bastards stole my nose! I thought we were done with them for good! Last time they were here, the twins stole everything that wasn't superglued down." He let out a huff. "In fact, we *tried* supergluing everything down . . . which did prevent the thefts, but kept us from using the items at all. Bad idea. And then they stole the tube of superglue."

"Which way did they go?" I heard sirens wailing in the distance. McGoo responded quickly, especially when he knew he'd have a nice arrest on his record without having to do the footwork.

The clown sniffled again—which came out as a loud hooting sound without his nose—and pointed out the tent. "They grabbed the nose off my face and ran that way. Somebody must be hiding them."

"What would they do with a clown nose?" I asked. "Can you sell it on an auction site somewhere?"

"They don't *do* anything with what they steal—they just steal it. It's an illness. That's why you find so many things just lying around on the ground."

I bolted out of Fazio's tent, hoping to intercept the kleptomaniac goblins. The circus midway was full of attendees streaming toward the exits, chattering about Bela's spectacular (and, most agreed, *entertaining*) death. Some unnaturals still insisted it was part of the show and were trying to figure out how the trick was done.

Then I spotted another playing card lying on the ground and a necklace a few steps beyond that, then a baseball cap, and an eye patch. This was like a scavenger hunt. All of the bread crumbs were heading toward the fat lady's tent.

I heard a scuffle and a squeal, and I put on a burst of speed; zombies can move quickly in emergencies, or when they're especially hungry. "Over here!" I yelled, hoping someone else would come running. I already knew Fazio was sounding the alarm among his circus friends, who were already alarmed after the death of the vampire trapeze artist (or maybe just because of the approaching police sirens).

The flaps of the fat lady's tent were down, but I yanked them open. I saw Annie struggling with her enormous dress, pulling down the fabric folds to cover her body—and the dress itself, or something inside it, was fighting back.

"Quickly, my dears, quickly!" When she saw me, a look of horror crossed her face (I often get that reaction). She did not look like a sweet granny now; her whole face was much skinnier, as if someone had deflated her. Annie still had many chins, but they hung like wattles around her neck.

As she struggled and thrashed with her recalcitrant dress, the fabric tore, and a goblin's smooth, ugly head poked out. The second young goblin also squirmed and broke free, ripping the dress to shreds as they both escaped from their unorthodox hiding place. Inside the tentlike flower-print fabric, they left behind a rather scrawny-looking Annie in a one-piece bathing suit. The goblins hissed and snapped, annoyed to be exposed.

Goblins are like small, gray-skinned elves . . . if those elves happened to be born from a mother saturated with toxic waste and poisonous thoughts. Their huge mouths were filled with needle-like teeth, and their glowing eyes could have been used as a plumber's utility light. As the goblin twins tried to scramble away, Annie wrapped her arms around them and pulled the creatures close to her in a motherly embrace.

There was hardly anything to Annie now. With all her loose skin, she looked as if she was wasting away, despite the numerous plates of ribs, cookies, etc., she consumed every day. Then I realized that if she had been hiding the kleptomaniac creatures, they might have eaten much of the food.

The fat lady's eyes were wide, her expression desperate. "You can't take my boys!" She yanked the goblins closer, practically smothering them. "I was trying to protect them, and they helped me when I needed it most! They're so sweet." She held out her hand, and one of the goblins tried to bite it. Annie giggled.

More shouts came from outside the tent. Fazio, the now-noseless clown, staggered in, accompanied by Aldo, who'd thrown on his wig while he ran, as well as the werewolf lion tamer, who still held his bullwhip, ready to use it.

The vampire ringmaster barged in right behind them, distraught. "The police are coming. What the—" He stopped when he saw the goblins. "What the hell are those two doing here? With all the arrest warrants—"

As the kleptomaniac goblin twins tried to bolt, Calvin cracked his bullwhip, and they skittered back into Annie's protective embrace.

"I won't turn them out into the cold," she said with a sniffle. "They're just misunderstood. They stole things, but they didn't mean anything bad by it."

"Nothing bad?" Kowalski cried. "They stole Bela's Air Commander medal. Without it, he didn't think he could turn into a bat—and now he's dead!"

Annie was disturbed by this. "But he started out dead."

"I mean he's really dead now!"

"Well, I'm sure they're very sorry," Annie insisted.

"The medallion was fake." I held it up so everyone could see the words *Made in China* stamped on the back. "No intrinsic magic."

Annie sounded defensive. "There—no harm done."

The clown and the fortune-teller looked at the strangely emaciated form of the fat lady. Aldo said, "What happened to you? You used to be so . . . so . . ."

"Fat," she answered.

"I was about to say *substantial*." Then Aldo remembered his priorities. "And what happened to my fortune-telling cards?"

"I lost weight, thanks to your magic cards." She sniffed, sounding glum. "When Harriet left the circus, I wanted to be in better shape to mother you all. It's quite a job! I wanted to be healthy, go on a diet, so I signed up for a guaranteed Gypsy weight-loss routine. Mean Cuisine. I lost four hundred pounds— and now I can't stop!"

Aldo scratched his wig, which was already askew. "What did my fortune-telling deck have to do with it?"

"I needed your cards, ones with real magic, and that's why I took your deck six months ago." She sniffed and made an excuse. "Well, you did leave them lying around a lot." When the fortune-teller glared at her, she turned away. "I just had to have two specific cards, the fat lady and the skeleton. I superglued the cards together, read the spell from the Gypsy diet book, and *this* fat lady started to look more like a skeleton. Worked like a charm!"

"Uh, it *was* a charm," I pointed out.

"But because of the superglue, I couldn't separate the cards again. Impossible to break the spell. And I realized I was going to lose my livelihood! Being a fat lady is all I am . . . and believe me, there was a lot of me." She pulled at the excessive folds of her torn dress. "Everybody loved me when I was a fat lady. Everyone wanted to hug me, lose themselves in my expansive . . . everything. I needed another fortune-telling deck, a fresh skeleton card and a fat lady card, so I could break the magic."

"So you stole my other deck, too!" Aldo said.

"The goblin boys did." Annie sounded ashamed. "You were much more careful after losing the first one, and I wasn't exactly nimble enough to slip into your trailer unnoticed. The boys came back to the circus, looking for shelter and hoping to hide from the police, and I just asked them to do me that one favor. Unfortunately, once they got started . . ."

Officer McGoohan and four uniformed cops charged into the tent, all trying to fit through the open flap at once, as if they were performing their own circus clown act. Fortunately, because it was designed for a fat lady, the tent opening was double-wide.

McGoo's a rough, tough cop who gets himself in trouble more often than the criminals do, but he and I have gotten each other *out* of trouble enough times, too. "Shamble, tell me what's going on here."

I rattled off a quick summary. "Fat lady hiding kleptomaniac goblins in her dress, a vampire trapeze artist accidentally murdered because he couldn't change into a bat, deck of magic fortune-telling cards stolen—among other things."

McGoo nodded. "Oh, another one of those cases."

The goblins tried to bolt as the policemen rounded them up, and Calvin used his whip with great enthusiasm as well as precision. Even after the goblin thieves were handcuffed, they snapped with their needle-like teeth, trying to bite the hands that arrested them. Fortunately, among his other useful defensive items, McGoo kept a roll of duct tape on his belt, with which he secured the criminal goblins' mouths.

"Oh, my poor dears," Annie wailed. "They just need some love and understanding."

"They need a little time behind bars," I said. "Or at least doing community service." All in all, I doubted the stolen items added up to more than a misdemeanor.

"There are other arrest warrants for those two." McGoo was shaking his head. "And the fat lady was aiding and abetting."

"For petty theft," Kowalski said, troubled. "Bela might disagree, but he never liked to accept blame for anything. He did sign a waiver acknowledging the inherent risk in performing death-defying feats."

Kowalski stood next to Annie. "The circus is like family, and Annie is part of it. We're not pressing charges against her, and we'll return all the stolen items to their rightful owners."

"Except for my magic deck," Aldo grumbled.

"I can track down another one," I said. "Part of my services."

"And my Reuben sandwich."

"Can't help you there. . . ."

Without asking permission, the clown and the fortune-teller worked together—a victory in itself—to open the trunks in the back of Annie's tent, moving aside the plates piled with cookies and gnawed rib bones. Fazio lifted out a bright red ball. "Here's my nose!"

Digging deeper, they also found what was left of the deck of magic fortune-telling cards. Aldo was dismayed as he counted through them to find the skeleton and fat lady cards torn in half, by which Annie had apparently broken the weight-loss spell; other cards were missing as well, probably strewn on the ground somewhere along the midway.

The former fat lady wept, still clutching at straws. "Maybe if everything's returned, there won't be any charges filed?"

"Suit yourselves." McGoo shook his head as the cops wrestled the still-squirming goblins out of the tent. "Those boys have already gotten themselves into enough trouble, more than just robbing circus folk. They'll probably serve a year in juvie, maybe get out early for good behavior. Or maybe not."

"Yes, they are quite a handful," the fat lady said. "Even I have to admit that." Looking longingly after the wayward goblins, Annie drew a deep shuddering breath, then turned to Oscar Kowalski. "I don't suppose the circus has any use for a *skinny* lady? At least until I fill out a little bit? The spell is broken, and I'm gaining weight again . . . and it'll be even faster when the twins don't eat most of my food."

The ringmaster thought long and hard. "I could use someone who understands the circus—and business. I'm no good at handling the day-to-day paperwork, the administration, managing the employees. I'm a showman, not an accountant." He propped himself up, snatched off his top hat. "I never was much good at the business side of things. You'd think a vampire circus would *want* to be in the red."

Annie finally brightened. "I can help. I can be like a mother to everyone. And if I manage the money, it'll be like giving everybody an allowance!"

Fazio had reapplied his nose, although his makeup remained smeared. He looked at the remaining platters of food. "Annie, you wouldn't happen to have a banana-cream pie I could smash into someone's face? Just for the gag?"

"Sorry, dear, I only have cookies."

The zombie clown threw cookies at Calvin, but nobody laughed. Rather, the werewolf lion tamer caught them and munched politely.

Aldo came up to me, smiling. "Thank you for everything, Mr. Chambeaux. You did track down the cards, and the thieves. And if you can find a replacement deck . . ." He held out his abbreviated deck of magic cards, shuffled them, and extended the pile to me. "Pick a card, any card."

I did, looked at it myself, then slid it back into the deck. "No, thanks."

Aldo frowned. "Don't you want to know your future?"

"I'm a detective," I said. "I'd rather figure it out for myself."